"I am obsessed with what H.M ...
vivid prose, the captivating m ...
of nature that is Hessa. Utterly ...
I loved getting lost in. I can't wait for the next book."
Claire Legrand, *New York Times*-bestselling author of *Furyborn*

"H.M. Long takes us on another epic, fast-paced adventure in
Temple of No God. As exciting and gripping as its predecessor,
this standalone in the same world starts with a bang and doesn't
let up, full of intrigue, betrayal, and action sequences that don't
disappoint. Hessa is a heroine to be reckoned with."
Genevieve Gornichec, author of *The Witch's Heart*

"Once again, H.M. Long pulls us effortlessly into a landscape of
warring gods, tribes and impulses. What a joy to return to Hessa's
side as, having battled herself and won, she draws her axes again
– this time to build a better world. Sure, there's a fantastic fight
scene for everyone and the pace never falters, but where this book
really shines is in its emotionally nuanced depiction of character.
Temple of No God is a worthy sequel to Long's impressive debut,
and I can't wait to see what she does next."
Lucy Holland, author of *Sistersong*

"Long certainly made her entrance known with *Hall of Smoke*,
but with *Temple of No God*, she solidifies herself as one of the
great new voices in epic fantasy. *Temple of No God* is a story about
adventure, war, and godly strife, but at its heart, it is also a poetic
yet action-packed exploration of grief, longing, and obligation.
Bold characters, shocking twists, and heart-pounding action will
keep you turning pages long after lights out."
M. J. Kuhn, author of *Among Thieves*

"This book is a bonfire on a bleak winter night. Exciting and dangerous, brilliantly plotted and paced, this is the perfect followup to *Hall of Smoke*. Come for the axe-smash battles, the crumbling empire, the dangerous cults, and the perfect puppy companion, and then stay for all of that stuff, because it rules."
Joshua Johnson, author of *The Forever Sea*

"While knowledge and responsibility weigh on Hessa in a manner reminiscent of many warrior-legends of popular European mythology and heroic fantasy, *Temple of No God* does not succumb to the dreary moroseness of the aftermath of conquest. Instead, we get to witness Hessa relish her role as victor while contending with her status as a vanquisher. I was particularly struck by Long's needlepoint focus on the gloomy pressures of militaristic endeavor, and appreciated the bright flickers of Hessa's magical forays into spiritual realms. Fantasy readers who like their heroes battle-hardened yet thoughtful and tender – not in spite of war but because of it – will enjoy *Temple of No God*."
Suyi Davies Okungbowa, author of *Son of the Storm*

"A darkly realised world full of rich lore and characters that leap off the page."
Rob Hayes, author of The War Eternal trilogy, the Mortal Techniques series and more

TEMPLE
OF NO
GOD

Also by H.M. Long and available from Titan Books

Hall of Smoke

TEMPLE OF NO GOD

H. M. LONG

TITAN BOOKS

Temple of No God
Print edition ISBN: 9781789095562
E-book edition ISBN: 9781789095579

Published by Titan Books
A division of Titan Publishing Group Ltd
144 Southwark Street, London SE1 0UP
www.titanbooks.com

First edition: January 2022
10 9 8 7 6 5 4 3 2 1

A CIP catalogue record for this title is available from the British Library.

Printed and bound in the United States.

For Marco and Eric, who convinced me to try again.

ALGATT, EANGEN, AND THE NORTHERN TERRITORIES OF THE ARPA EMPIRE

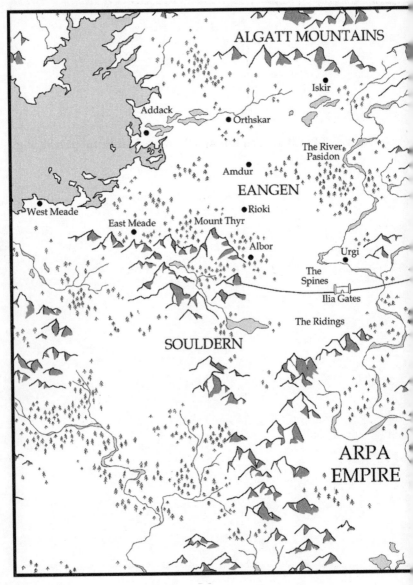

ALGATT MOUNTAINS

Iskir

Addack

Orthskar

The River Pasidon

Amdur

EANGEN

West Meade

East Meade

Rioki

Mount Thyr

Albor

Urgi

The Spines

Ilia Gates

The Ridings

SOULDERN

ARPA EMPIRE

ONE

Howls drifted towards the sleeping settlement. They merged, harmonized, and thrummed through moss-laden trees, a sound as ancient as the fallen goddess who had taught it to humanity; as old as the line of priests who had served her, of which I was the last.

I raked in a breath and added my own higher, discordant note. The howls rose to meet mine, increasing in pitch and fervor until the whole valley rang, from forest-laden crags to the unwalled village and its lush farmland, silver in the moonlight.

To my right, my war chief Briel, with her knot of braids and broad shoulders, lifted her horn to her lips and blew. The call ended in a twisting crack, silencing the raiders and giving way to the screams of villagers. A baby shrieked. Dogs barked. A handful of lights flickered as villagers tumbled from their homes.

I marked my breaths, steady and even. Though my heart beat hard in my chest, there was no need for fear, no anxiety or prayers. It was our reputation, not our axes, that would bring us wealth tonight.

The village below knew who we were—the Eangen, the barbarians, the heathens from the North. We'd finally come to the Arpa Empire, and we brought recompense for centuries of fear and taxation and spilled Northern blood.

And there were no legions, nor armies nor emperor to stop us.

I started forward, leading a wall of fifty warriors out of the trees, in a row of round, painted shields either side of me.

"Survive tonight and you'll be back at your hearths in a fortnight,"

Briel called down the line. Her horn hung at her hip now, its bronze brim glistening against the ochre of her padded tunic. She bore a spear and a shield painted with foxes, the former resting atop the latter's rim. "Now off with you."

The first of our warriors bellowed and broke out of the line—one of my cousins, Sillo. He closed the fifty paces to the village in a reckless dash, shield braced at his shoulder, sword flung out behind him. More men and women followed, yelling and laughing and chanting as they burst over the muddy streets and boardwalks of the hapless village like children at play.

Briel cast me a look, her eyes etched with grim good humor and more than a little resignation. "Are you coming?"

"I'll keep watch."

Briel held my gaze for a moment more, assessing me, reading the weariness around my eyes, then set off after our horde.

I took up position in a muddy pasture at the edge of the village to watch the raid unfold. Firelight swept the streets as raiders hauled villagers from their homes and into a corral of shields and axes in the center of the village. Arpa villagers ran, axes pursued, and somewhere in the cacophony of noise I heard a man singing.

My eyes found the singer as he emerged from the nearest house with a torch. He was one of mine—as much as his tribe, the Iskiri, could be called mine. A lupine creature with a kohl-streaked face and long, muscular arms, he sang in a rumbling, chanting timbre.

"Iskiri!" I called, pointing to the roof of the house he'd been in. "Give us some light."

For a moment I thought he would not obey, considering me with his head cocked to one side. Then he gave an elaborate bow, grinned to show teeth scored by ritual carving, and tossed the torch. It landed with a *whump* on mossy thatch, not so different from the rooves of our own homes, two weeks and one ancient border away.

The thatch began to smoke and smolder. Flames bit, and the foggy darkness retreated in a hollow, roaring sigh.

His task complete, the raider threw out his arms and took up his song again, this time much louder. Wind gusted over his bare head, carrying the fire from roof to roof as he prowled into the village proper.

I watched sparks and flaming curls of straw drift like a veil between me and his retreating form.

Memories toyed with me. They were always there, wound in the smell of smoke and the clash of steel, but tonight, our last night, I did not push them away. They flared and extinguished like the falling sparks; glimpses of a day when it was my people who had feared raiders in the woods, with their horns and torches and falling axes.

But we, unlike these Arpa villagers, had fought back. Victory had been true victory, our survival earned, and peace hard-won.

This village was no conquest. What was victory if there was no one to resist? What was a victory over peasants, whose gods were dead and whose rulers had abandoned them?

That thought made my stomach sour and the screams in the smoke took on a cutting edge.

A shadow hurtled towards me.

My shield moved instinctively, out in one quick blow. The rim cracked off bone and I raised my axe for a second blow, muscles moving in sequences I'd known since childhood.

I froze mid-strike. A stunned Arpa woman moaned in the mud at my feet, a bundle clutched to her chest. A baby's fragile wails merged with the pounding, roaring, and shouting of the raid as the woman's— the girl's—dazed eyes found mine.

Her pupils were uncoordinated, stuttering and dragging apart. Closing her eyes again, she clutched the child and began to babble in her own language.

"The Mother, the Mourner, hear me, hear—"

I backed off. We were alone in our quarter of the night, two women and one infant. On our left, the flames swelled. With each passing second the light increased, her prayers became more fervent, and my blood thundered louder in my ears.

3

She expected me to kill her, harm her, or at the very least drag her back into the burning village. But as the seconds flicked past, all I could do was stare.

I felt her fear, deep in my guts, watery and hot and crippling. A child's terror at horns in the night, or a young woman's in a smoldering Hall of Smoke.

I had been her, once, and the memory left me feeling tired. So very tired.

"Go," I said in her language.

The Arpa's eyes flew open. Her lips still twitched in frantic prayer, but her rhythm faltered.

"Run," I insisted, the word coming out as a growl.

The girl found her feet. Her infant's wails grew as she took two tottering steps sideways, her eyes flickering between my face and my axe. Then she staggered into the fog with a ripple of skirts and patter of bare feet.

The night quietened in her wake. On the far side of the village, a horn blast signaled our victory—again that hollow, disgraced word.

My eyes still fixed on the spot where the girl had vanished, I relaxed my shield arm and swung my axe at my side, trying to loosen the tension in my shoulders.

Then, in place of the girl, the tepid night divulged someone else.

Firelight ran along the curved blades of a poleaxe—a long, bearded axe-head and a hooking sickle blade—held by a fog-shrouded figure. I became aware of my breaths deepening and my vision narrowing. The man was alone and his posture was not that of a vengeful farmer, nor was his clothing. His shoulders were spread beneath a robe of earthen, darkened yellow, and his stance was calm. He knew how to carry himself, and he was not afraid of me.

I understood my situation very clearly. I was alone and my back was exposed. The village was close, but my chances of reaching its cover—burning cover—before intercept weren't good.

Still, I crouched, letting my compact, muscular frame slip into a familiar stance; weight low, feet rooted, shield raised, and the haft of my axe pressed into the rim.

The newcomer advanced, straight-backed and deliberate.

I slipped a half-step backwards, then another. The wind shifted and smoke gusted into my face, raking through my nose and lungs.

One step. Two. The stranger followed, the wind plucking at his robes and carrying a fine, pale ash towards me. But that ash didn't come from the burning village. It came from the stranger's skin.

My second, unnatural Sight awoke.

Magic. It gusted off him like chaff from a threshing floor, both glistening and blanched. No sooner had it left him then it gained a life of its own, eddying and fluttering in a cautious swirl around me.

I froze, watching the tide of magic merge with the smoke and fog. Though it came within arm's reach, it did not dare touch me. No magic could. But this was not an assault—I realized that at the same time as the sounds of the village muffled. This was a shroud, concealing and shielding. Concealing a second attacker.

A cold blade hooked around my neck.

I stilled. There was no time to berate myself. My world simply crystalized, centering on my exposed throat, the presence at my back, and the certainty of death. My reflections of a few minutes before—that faux nostalgia and mourning of a proper challenge—echoed now, sick and senseless.

But there was more power here than these strangers' ashen magic. I inhaled, letting my own strength, golden and warm and tasting of honey, awaken.

"No words," an Arpa voice said from behind me in my ear. His weapon, whatever was hooked about my throat, had to be small—a sickle? The voice again was male, languorous and calm, and his Northman was thickly accented. "Do not speak."

His free hand pressed into the small of my back and a spike of panic shot up my spine, but I contained it. Keeping quiet, I allowed him to guide me out into the fog and away from the village.

The first man, the one with the poleaxe, preceded us. I watched ash swirl off his robes as I sifted through everything I knew of the Arpa, their gods, and their magic. This tasted nothing like those. This presence, this unnatural power, tasted of wrongness. An absence. A lack.

"Drop your weapons," my second captor said in my ear.

My fingers clenched on my axe and shield, but the blade of his sickle was close and sharp. Never mind my assailant's actions; one wrong move and I'd slit my own throat.

My fingers released. My axe and shield hit the cropped grass with hollow, fateful thuds.

"And the knife."

I pulled a long knife from its sheath across my upper thigh and dropped that too. Then my captor prodded me back into movement over cropped grasses and swaths of mud.

"Stop here," the voice commanded.

I complied. My heart slammed against my ribs in great, jarring beats. I blinked rapidly and willed myself to focus, willed my thoughts to stay coherent. I could survive this—I had overcome such odds before, and I would again. But who were these men, and where had their magic come from?

Power like this had three distinct sources. First, the most common, was the passive force that sustained all life, in earth and blood and air. Second was the benevolence of a God or the interference of a Miri— powerful beings once worshiped as deities. And the third source? The High Halls, the Realm of the Dead, and those who had once been gods.

The Arpa had no gods anymore. The Miri they'd worshiped had been annihilated, along with their magic. The only flicker of power in this entire province should have been me and my priests.

The first man stopped walking and faced me, poleaxe braced on the earth beside his leather-shod feet. The burning village glowed through the fog, but the diffused, dancing light wasn't enough for me to make out his face. All I could see was the line of a straight Arpa nose and the fall of shoulder-length, light hair.

"I am Siris," the first attacker stated. "You are Hessa, of the Eangen, of the priesthood of Thvynder."

The blade at my throat bit in. Though I hadn't noticed myself waver, the second attacker put his hand on my back again, stilling me like a shy child. Blood began to trickle down my neck, sticking stray black hair to my skin and seeping into the collar of my tunic.

"Yes, I am," I returned in the voice I had learned from one of my long-dead mentors. It was low, bold, and steady, and as I spoke the words, their truth strengthened me. I took and released a steadying breath and transitioned into the Arpa language, forcing my tongue around their clustered vowels and stark consonants. "And you would do well to bow."

"Your god has no power here," Siris replied, slipping into Arpa as well. It flowed from his tongue, liquid and smooth. "We bow to no god but our own."

"Your gods are dead. I watched them die, a long time ago."

Silence fell, interrupted only by the muted roar of the fires. I could no longer hear shouting from the village. No screams. No orders.

My eyes flicked to the houses. Pale dust still saturated the fog, but the layers of shadows and light parted. There, for an instant, I saw Briel. My war chief stood, unmoving, on a path between hovels. Silhouetted as she was by the flames, I couldn't tell where she was looking, but my heart leapt. Perhaps she'd sighted me.

Then her face tilted up to the sky in a dazed, senseless kind of rapture. As I watched, she dropped her weapons, continuing to stare up at a shroud of smoke-laden fog as the flames leapt higher over her head.

"What have you done?" I asked, fear for her and my people burning in my stomach.

Siris stepped closer, and I caught my first glimpse of his face. Unlike most Arpa, he wore a finely trimmed beard. His cheekbones were flat and his eyes languorous, almost sleepy beneath a widow's peak.

"Did you truly see our gods die?" he asked in a conversational tone. "Each and every one?"

My breath was too loud in my ears.

The man went on, gesturing back to the village: "Your people are alive. They are simply distracted, unaware of your absence, or the smoke, or the flames. They're also unaware that my priests have surrounded the village, and that they will remain blind until they suffocate, or burn, or their throats are slit. They see only what we desire them to. We are Laru, Hessa, priests and heralds of a new and powerful deity. And it is long past time we met."

With these last words, he laid his weapon down upon the soft grass—far out of reach of my booted feet—and closed the remaining distance between us.

My grip tightened on an axe that wasn't there and my whole body shuddered with the effort of holding still—of keeping my magic contained beneath my skin.

Before I lashed out, before I took control, I needed to know what Siris wanted—and what he thought he could do.

Close enough now that I could smell the damp and sweat of his clothes, the stranger met my gaze. His lips pulled into a thin, distracted smile. Then he raised his hands and laid warm, sweat-slick fingers over my eyes, like slats on a window.

Only the sickle around my throat kept me in place. His fingers pressed in and spread out, caressing the sides of my face as he finished whatever he was doing.

Siris retreated, scrutinizing me.

I blinked back at him and, as the moment stretched on, calm settled into my bones. Nothing had happened. Impervious to whatever curse he'd tried to lay, my senses eased like muscles in warm water, plucking at things that my natural facilities could not see—more threads of power, more whispers of Arpa sorcery. I felt them like I felt a drop of blood trickling down my collarbone, heard them like I heard the distant crackle of the burning village, and tasted them like sweat on my lips.

The sorcery came from these two men—priests, "Laru," I understood now—but they were not alone. My own power, visible to the Sighted alone, spread into the fog like windblown snowflakes in a golden, midwinter dawn. It condensed into a dozen threads, threads that led to more enemy priests in the village.

I turned my attention back to Siris, and I knew my eyes were edged with the same gold. "Did you expect the High Priestess of Thvynder to be without protection?"

For a moment Siris stared into my eyes, gilded and flashing in the darkness. Disdain was thrust aside by understanding and then sudden, visceral fear.

"Kill her," he shouted, stumbling back. "Now! Now!"

I shoved back into the second priest, slipping my fingers between the sickle and my throat. At the same time power exploded with my body at its axis, slamming into the priests and knocking them to the ground. Fog and flame cavorted into a dozen eddies, leaving me and the toppling men on a patch of open ground.

I caught the sickle's blade. It sliced into my fingers to the bone, instantly making my hand hot and slick. I'd expected the pain, but still cried out. I hurled the weapon aside with a hollow clatter and sprinted back towards my discarded shield and axe.

Siris moved at the same time, already back on his feet. He seized his poleaxe from the ground and swept it into my path in a low, artful pass.

I dove for my weapons. He came after me, his footsteps little more than a rustle of grass and a sigh in the fog.

Heedless of my bleeding hand, I snatched up my shield as another blow fell upon me. The axe blade of his weapon struck my shield and I hinged it out, directing the blow into the night and darting inside his guard. In the same move, I hacked at his knees.

He tripped backwards. My blow missed by a fraction, slicing through the dark yellow of his robe. I followed up immediately, punching my shield out and smashing his arm as he hit the ground. The blow was clumsy, my grip slick, but he dropped the poleaxe.

I shifted, kicking his weapon out of reach and standing over him with axe at the ready. Around us, the fog roiled. Ash surged towards me, thickening and billowing like the underbelly of a summer storm. But it still didn't touch me.

Out of the corner of my eye, I saw the priest who'd held the small sickle climb back to his feet. Weaponless, he stared from his comrade to me in horrified panic.

I feinted towards him, quick and sharp. He bolted into the fog.

Good. My weariness from earlier in the night swelled back, redoubling into a jaded, cool determination as blood dripped down the back of my shield. I returned my attention to Siris.

The priest retreated across the muddy earth in a dazed, pawing crawl. This close to me, his pale magic flickered around his fingertips, like a candle in a draft.

"Who gave you your power?" I asked him. I battled to keep hold of my shield with my bleeding hand. I needed to bind it soon, before I lost too much blood or the pain became unbearable.

"My god did," he bit back, forcing out each word with a bubble of crimson. I had burst his right eyebrow and the corner of his lips—blood dribbled into his eyes and through his short beard too.

"Does your 'god' have a name?"

Instead of replying, he tried to stand, and I allowed him to—though I stayed between him and his fallen weapon. His foot slipped, but he found his balance and straightened halfway, shoulders hunched and head bent in pain and frustration.

"Whatever creature you serve and call a god," I told him, "they are nothing. Harm me or my people again, and I will annihilate you. I will murder your 'god' before your eyes and drink their blood like wine. Do you understand me?"

I had no intention of drinking any blood, but I had grown adept at abusing the Arpa's fear of barbarians over the past months. Their notions about Northerners had proved a useful weapon, whether or not they were founded in fact.

Siris glared at me. It was a childish expression, his teeth bared in hatred and his shattered jaw twitching with pain. He strained, trying to exert the power I'd smothered.

I flicked my axe at the fog. The last of his dust vanished with the gesture and we were left in a pre-dawn haze of moisture, smoke, and the threads of my own, dominant magic.

Sounds came through the fog again—Eangen battle-howls and the startled screams of Siris's priests. Two of the golden threads, which I could still see trailing off into the gloom, vanished.

I eased back up to my heels. "Flee. Go back to your god and tell them how you failed."

He heard me, but didn't move. With every second that his sorcery did not obey, Siris's trembling spread and his hatred increased.

"The Empire will unite. Under *my* god. With *my* power." He spat the words, glaring at me with such abhorrence that my heart stuttered— half in unexpected uncertainty, half in a forgotten kind of elation.

It was that elation that grew, iron-scented and fierce. My knees loosened. "Your gods are dead, Arpa."

Frustration snapped his lips into a snarl. "My god is not. My god is vast, powerful. And he will come for you and your people."

Cold trickled down my spine. I braced for another attack; the vengeful, desperate spasms of a wounded animal. But it never came. Siris, still covering his jaw with a trembling hand, stumbled off into the fog.

I watched him go, blood trickling down the fingers of one hand while I kept my axe firmly clenched in the other. Grasses shivered under the droplets and a white flower bowed, stained with crimson and threads of amber ichor: the blood of a mortal, threaded with the stolen magic of the High Halls.

I glanced down at the bloody flower for a silent, uninterrupted moment. The Laru's threats were aggrandized, but he wasn't entirely wrong.

My power should have been alone here, tonight. Yet it wasn't. Magic from an unknown source had returned to the Arpa Empire, the Empire that had jeopardized my people for centuries and knew me by name. With that power, leaders would rise, followers would flock, and unity of

11

one form or another would come. The Arpa Empire might truly threaten our borders again, and this time we would no longer be the forest tribes in the North, disorganized and unworthy of the Empire's attentions.

We would be a threat to be eradicated.

I curled my fingers in on themselves, letting the pain wash over me in blanching, burning waves, and set my jaw.

As Siris had said, I was Hessa, High Priestess of the Eangen. And if the Empire threatened my people?

I would destroy it.

TWO

Five months later, water closed over my head. Cold slammed into my lungs and I stifled a gasp, lips clamped, throat contracting and chest bucking.

I curled my knees into my chest and willed myself still. Blood thundered behind my eyes, but gradually began to slow. My muscles eased, my eyelids fluttered, and my awareness expanded.

I opened my eyes in slow, languorous blinks. The water was clear, brimming with sunlight from one side of the lake to the other. It diffused through the ice overhead, brighter here, darker there where the wind had piled snow into drifts. It shone the brightest through the hole I hacked in the ice every morning.

I pried my limbs from their fetal curl and let dense muscle pull me down towards the gloom. The cold was a distant thing now, a burn and a pressure so all-encompassing it became part of me, like the flesh of my tunic-clad body, the strands of long black hair eddying around my face, and the tips of my fingers, latticed with both ritual scars and the harsh, clean slashes of a sickle's blade.

I let the cold anchor me there, suspended in the lake; one gasp between life and death, one mistake between the smothering depths and the bitter sweetness of the Waking World.

I returned to the surface when I could bear it no longer, draining my lungs as I went. As I emerged, the winter wind buffeted me, low and swift and swirling across the frozen lake. I squinted into it, grasping the lip of the ice and willing my lungs not to seize.

The ice-locked lake spread around me, silent and sleeping. Beyond its shore of snow-heavy cedars, wind-swept pine, and stark, leafless oak and ash, smoke rose in steady gray wisps. The hearthfires of Albor. Home.

Between me and the shore, there was a girl. I noticed her belatedly, sitting in a drift of snow like it was a throne, the tips of her white hair tangling in the fur of her cap and her kaftan's silver clasp. Her skin was tawny, like most Eangen, but her hair set her apart—as white as the snow she perched in.

She watched me with a disapproving scowl, reminding me so strongly of her father that my breath snagged in recollected fear. But the feeling fled and I hauled myself up onto the ice, picked up the axe I'd wedged there, and straightened, dripping.

"My mother will be very unhappy," the girl said, standing too, and brushing off the snow from her long, heavy kaftan and wool trousers. The way she carried herself had changed in the last season, and it was not simply due to her brother's departure for the far north, her broadening hips, or the men who had begun to eye her when they thought I wasn't looking. She was more cautious, and held an understanding of her place in the world in her cold blue eyes—the eyes of her dead father, the Son of Winter, and of the goddess whose name remained etched in this land and my scars, long after her death.

Eang. The Brave. The Watchful. The Vengeful. The Swift.

Responsibility resettled on my shoulders like a yoke. Mourning the lost peace of the underwater world, I pried my numb feet from the ice before they could freeze there and shoved them into fur-lined boots. Then I set aside my axe, grabbed my pack, and freed a spare tunic.

"Why is that?" I asked.

Thray glanced down the lake as I exchanged my sodden—and now ice-rimmed—garment for the dry undertunic and a sumac-red overtunic, trimmed with geometric patterns in yellow-gold. For a moment, the wind raked across my muscled belly from a sky of raw and unadulterated blue. The sun had just topped the trees to the east, glancing down at me and the girl and the lake locked in ice, but it gave no heat.

"You should not go under the ice alone," the girl informed me, as I pulled on my cloak and gathered my things.

It's the only place I can be alone, I thought. I pinched the end of her nose. "I'll deliver the warnings."

She screwed up her face and stepped back, tugging her nose indignantly from my grasp. "Don't— Hessa!"

I grinned and handed the girl my pack and axe, using my newly freed hands to close my cloak. My senses were sharp and clear and my skin flushed, but I didn't want to linger on the lake. "Come, I need to get back to the hall."

Thray fell into step behind me, scowling and scolding all the way. My black hair was frozen before we reached the short path to the village, grating against my cheeks as we wove through the cedars and tangles of sleeping vines.

I half listened to the girl, focusing on my steps—my feet now aflame with renewing heat—until we passed through the village outskirts and ring wall, and approached the doors of the great, central hall.

The houses around us were low, constructed of weathered wood and thatch and mushroomed with snow. Few residents were in the streets at this time of day, and those I saw were fur-wrapped and red-cheeked.

Everyone was accustomed to my daily pilgrimage to the lake and didn't bother me, but this morning something had changed. They watched me, eyes lingering on my face as if I could answer some question I wasn't aware of.

I slowed, glancing at Thray. The girl looked back at me and lifted one shoulder.

"Has something happened?" I asked the nearest woman.

"There're travelers in the hall," she returned, arms full of a little boy, who stared at me through huge, dark eyes beneath an oversized fur cap. "I didn't see them, but I heard."

"What travelers? Algatt?"

"I don't know, High Priestess." She shook her head and I left her, redoubling my pace while Thray ran to catch up.

The hall rose above us. Its wood was weathered and gray, though it was less than a decade old, and its angles as steep as the bulk of Mount Thyr. The mountain's snow-laden peak loomed over the town, jagged and glistening in the winter sun. Its slopes were sheer until, some distance down, they transitioned from rock and ice into the skirt of forested foothills in which Albor sat, all laden with snow.

As to the hall, it too was formidable, even austere in some opinions. But I found that austerity fitting. This hall had been constructed on the charred remains of the old one, the Hall of Smoke, where I'd spent my childhood. Its steep, double-tiered roof and spreading wings symbolized the strength and solidity of the new age, and its only adornments— other than snow and icicles—were the ends of its exposed beams, each carved with beasts: a bear, a fox, a lynx, and so on.

And, of course, there were the hall's doors, great oak bastions intricately carved with runes and coils and depictions of plants and animals, together proclaiming the name of the building: the Morning Hall, seat of the Vynder priesthood and their High Priestess.

Holding my pack under one arm, Thray hauled one side of the door open and I stepped through, catching my breath as heat curled around me. A central fire blazed within a rectangle of knee-high stones, and the vaulted chamber was full of the scents of smoked cedar beams, burned sage, fresh bread, and the two dozen Vynder priests who called this home.

Today the hall was packed with forty men and women in wool and fur and scowling faces. Children craned to look down from the hall's deep, encircling balcony that housed multiple Vynder families, and a stranger stood by the fire.

His back was to me and he wore an ambiguous, heavy winter cloak, but there was no disguising his foreignness. He clutched a silver helmet with hinged cheek plates under one arm, his cloak falling from one shoulder over glistening, plated armor. His hair was blond, cropped short, and I caught sight of a distinct, straight nose as he turned his eyes upon me.

16

Thray, who had just closed the door at my back, halted. I pulled my axe from her arms—a calm movement—and murmured, "You stay out of sight."

Her face was pale as she slipped into the shelter of the crowd, and I faced the newcomer.

The man's eyes flicked from me to my axe, his expression a mask of forced passivity. He took in every bit of me, from my frozen braid to the missing top of my right ear and the freckles that layered my nose and cheeks.

Another man, Nisien, appeared at my side and bent to my ear. He wore his head shaved and beard short, unlike the other men in the room, who wore their hair long and painstakingly tended. His Soulderni skin was a shade darker than mine and his frame taller, but he was clad in our layered tunics, trousers, and legwraps—the style of Eangen, his adopted home.

Nisien didn't comment on my sodden state. The familiarity of his voice warmed me as he explained, "A messenger. Come all the way from Apharnum. Estavius and I escorted him up from the border."

I studied the faces in the crowd, noting our friend Estavius near the front. The only Arpa welcome in the North, his handsome face was angled towards the fire and he clasped a cup of warm mead in hands the color of sun-bleached bone.

The messenger was Estavius's countryman, but he made no move to interact. I did not blame him. The Empire had once called Miri like him gods, and if he did not want to involve himself any further, so be it.

"So he's Arpa," I said to Nisien, looking back to the messenger. "Did they come because of the raids? Or the Laru?"

Nisien shrugged. "His message was for you. But I assume it's the raids."

"Does he speak Northman?"

"Well enough, yes."

I nodded and started towards the newcomer, unclasping my cloak with one hand as I went. The other still cradled my axe, hooked loosely at the top of the haft.

Nisien followed at my shoulder, wordless.

The messenger watched as I took up position next to the flames. I set my axe down on a nearby bench and pulled my cloak free, letting the heat of the fire rush over my flushed, damp skin as I sat. He took in my disheveled state, suspicion cycling into a resigned discontent as he understood who and what I was.

"I am Hessa. What do you want?" I asked.

The hall was silent except for the pop and hiss of the fire, the brush of heavy clothes and the squeak of a floorboard.

"I come in the name of Bresius, Emperor of Arpa," the messenger began. His Northman wasn't perfect and his accent was thick, overaccentuating consonants and rolling what should have been soft, shushing 'r's.

"Emperor?" I returned, neither scornful nor kind. "Last time I stepped into Arpa territory, someone called Cassius was on the throne and his arm was rather short. How much of an 'empire' does this Bresius rule?"

"Cassius is besieged in Apharnum by Bresius's forces, and will not live out the summer." The emissary's eyes flicked across my body to my braid, now dripping on the floor.

His weapons were nowhere to be seen, but I straightened. Part of me wanted to demand the messenger wait until I'd put myself together before having this conversation, but I wanted this man out of my hall, away from my people, as quickly as possible. We all had reason to hate and fear the legionaries, who'd fallen into increasing lawlessness since the death of their gods.

"Cassius will soon be deposed by Bresius," the messenger clarified, a spark of irritation in his eyes. "Bresius has reunited Apharni and the Lake Provinces, the Southern Territories, and, of course, Souldern. He has only to reclaim Nivarium, which is under the control of his cousin Eolus, and the capital itself, in Cassius's hands."

His mention of Souldern surprised me, but I did not show it. Nisien eased closer. Souldern was his homeland and that of many others in the room, lost over the last decade to the same decay and conflict that had taken the rest of the Arpa Empire and its territories. Since then more and more of his people had fled north, over the former Arpa border to Eangen and the shelter of our living, breathing god.

If this Bresius had retaken Souldern, it had happened recently enough that we hadn't heard. It was a shock, and it was dangerous. As I'd feared when I'd faced the Laru during our raids last year, the Arpa Empire was back to our doorstep, and with it the threat of unified, if godless, legions.

Thray's mother Sixnit approached, presenting me with a cup of hot honey wine. I gave her a meaningful look but she did not leave, sitting her round hips on a stool and watching the proceedings with casual hostility.

"You're telling me that there are three contenders for the throne," I clarified. "Cassius, Bresius, and Eolus. And your lord, Bresius, has yet to take the capital or Nivarium?"

"In due course."

"Then he is no emperor," I pointed out. "None of them are. I understand that your emperors must ascend to properly claim the title—and you've no gods left to grant him that Ascension. So he is not emperor, and what can he have to say to me?"

The messenger's jaw tightened, but he nodded and drew a preparatory breath. "Last summer your people began raiding Nivarium, and in that you proved yourselves a threat to the Empire. But you also showed yourself against the Cult of Laru, who hold Nivarium in their sway. You encountered the Laru's head priest, Siris."

A few murmurs drifted around the hall and I narrowed my gaze. If this Bresius was an enemy of the Laru, that changed matters.

"Yes, I met him." I set my warm cup down on the rocks that lined the fire and rung out my braid. More droplets of cold water pattered onto the floorboards beside my boots. "And defeated him."

The messenger nodded. "We know. As I said, Bresius has yet to regain Nivarium. It is technically ruled by the third contender, Eolus, for whom the Laru labor. So, Bresius has a proposal for you, Hessa of the Eangen. When the snow melts, return to Nivarium with his blessing. Distract Eolus. Raid and scourge the land as you please, as my lord's mercenaries, and he will pay you royally for the privilege."

A second ripple passed through the hall, this one incredulous and hostile. I kept my gaze on the speaker, ignoring the tumult.

"The Eangen will not fight for the Arpa," Briel, Vynder priestess and my war chief, cut through the murmur. "If we raid, we go in our own name, for our own benefit. We would never trust you."

"Bresius could have his throat slit tomorrow," Nisien pointed out, still hovering at my shoulder. "Your rulers never last long."

"Not since we killed your gods," a gentler voice added. Thray had pushed through the crowd to give the Arpa a blatant, cold glare.

I looked up sharply but the girl's mother had already intervened, leaving her stool to drag her daughter out of sight.

"Your Bresius will need to offer more than money and weak promises," Nisien said.

I glanced at my friend, then off to where Thray had vanished into the crowd. This proposal from Bresius was not overly compelling, but in it I saw something beyond talk of riches and hired swords.

An opportunity. An opportunity to insert myself into the chaos south of the border, to have a hand in what the Empire became, and, if I could, gut it from the inside out. I could help forge a new Empire under a ruler I approved of. Or obliterate it.

But that would mean leaving home, Thray, Sixnit, and the Hall. It would mean involving myself in foreign games of power and bloodying my axe in someone else's name. I wanted none of that.

What I wanted, however, hadn't mattered in a long time.

Just for a moment, I closed my eyes and drew a breath deep into my belly. When I released it and opened my eyes again, I was composed.

The envoy continued, his focus traveling through the crowd. "You will be paid in gold and silver and whatever else you people desire." I didn't miss the disdain in that. He did not think much of us, this hall, or anything we might hold dear. "Also, Bresius requires a personal guard of eight Vynder priests to escort him into the capital, Apharnum, which he will take by the end of summer. Then Cassius will be executed, and you will ensure the Laru do not interfere with Bresius's Ascension."

The room rippled with whispers.

I couldn't keep the surprise from my face. "What?"

"You and your Vynder have shown yourselves more than capable of managing the Laru threat," the Arpa said to me, his tone edged with nearly genuine deference. Nearly. "You are a Curse Breaker, the Nivari say. You have the blessing of a powerful god. You, Bresius believes, can withstand the Laru and see him crowned."

I paused. The title of Curse Breaker summed up my gifts well—I could extinguish unnatural power. I broke my enemies, so long as they wielded magic themselves. But against human foes and mortal blades, it had little value.

"Bresius would have you by his side," the messenger continued, "ensuring his Ascension. Just eight priests capable of combating the Laru, including yourself. You would meet him at the Apharni border, south of Nivarium, by the last moon of summer."

I exchanged a look with Nisien, and saw my own incredulity reflected in his eyes. Still, though I knew the deal was not a good one, I was tempted. Since I'd met Siris last summer, my anxiety over the state of the Arpa had grown. Now I was being handed the opportunity to slip into the heart of the Empire, and I couldn't let it pass by.

Yet, as Briel and Nisien had said, the Eangen would never fight for an Arpa. Not for mere wealth, in any case.

"It's not enough," I said, letting a little grudgingness seep through. "My people won't rally."

The Arpa man watched me for a long, long moment, then reached to a satchel beside the hearthstones and pulled out a scroll. He held it out, and Nisien stepped forward to take the object.

"Very well," the envoy said with gravity. "I've a second offer. Raid as you please in Nivarium, take whatever you wish, but you'll receive no extra payment. Save Souldern."

Halfway through unrolling the scroll, Nisien froze. The rest of the company disintegrated into murmuring knots, but everyone still watched me. They always watched me. We had no queens, no kings for them to look to—only a god and a high priesthood that, through fault and trial and choice and will, had come to me.

"Souldern?" I repeated. "Bresius would give up the province? Freely?"

"With concessions for trade," the messenger said with a tempering nod, "but yes. The terms are there."

Nisien looked down at me. Concern settled in the creases around his eyes, the usual patterns of age exacerbated by a decade of near constant travel at Estavius's side. But under it all was an incendiary, soul-deep hope. His homeland hadn't been free of Arpa rule in centuries.

The Arpa emissary watched us, pale face full of firelight. Memories came with the sight: a white lake and a massing army of his people, gray-eyed and inhuman, at the closing of the last age.

My composure waned and I reached for my cup of wine.

"I'm willing to consider this and bring it to council," I said. "You can remain here until we've finished our deliberations."

The envoy's eyes flicked around the hall, between my people's hostile, cold expressions, but he nodded slowly.

"Nisien will take care of you." I gestured Nisien forward, my lips brushing the brim of the cup. Steam prickled my nose and honey wine, scented with pine, warmed my throat as my friend led the foreigner away.

I thought of the ice then, of the stillness and pressure of the water, of the cold stripping away all thought of clan and future and daily life. For a heartbeat I suspended myself there again, bare feet towards the gloom, hair floating up towards the winter sky.

Then I drained my cup, left it on the stones around the fire, and slipped away through the crowd.

THREE

I stopped at the edge of a snow-locked mountain meadow. Snow swept past me, gathering against the bulk of an old, weathered shrine. It was simply constructed, little more than a collection of four posts and a tiled roof, now buried by the downfall. Its peak cast a sliver of shadow across the meadow under the noonday sun, visible every so often through a break in the clouds.

I shrugged my pack and shield into the snow with a *whump*. The wind gusted, tugging at the fur edging my cap and clacking the bare branches of poplar and oak and ash above my head. White-blanketed evergreens swayed. There was little else to hear; the birds were silent, and though I'd seen lattices of animal tracks on my climb through the forest, there were no creatures in sight.

I adjusted my footing with a muffled clack of snowshoes and pushed my cap back from my forehead.

Eang. Eang.

My former goddess rose through my mind, but I didn't speak. My past lurked beneath these trees—Eangi ritual, desperate prayers, and the last time I'd seen my first husband, Eidr, alive.

I brushed at my nose, sniffed, and eased my weight into my heels. Eang, Goddess of War and deity for whom the Eangen were named, was dead. But something of her power remained here, at her shrine, in her holy ground. And, if one knew how to open it, her doorway into another world.

I reached for my golden Sight. It welled, revealing a crack in the world not a pace ahead of me. It glowed, as amber-gold as my power itself, and slim and subtle as a fracture in a clay pot.

As it sensed my magic, the crack began to widen. Light, warm and undulating, spilled out into the meadow, shafting across the snow and trees like a slice of autumn sunset.

I drew in one more lungful of the icy, Waking World. Across the meadow the shrine crusted over with latent magic, gold running through the cracks and seams of the old wood and lacing out under the snow, off into the trees until everything shimmered and cracked. Then, holding the breath deep in my belly, I picked up my pack and shield and stepped through the door to the High Halls.

The landscape remained the same, the forest and the meadow, but the very fabric of the world twisted. The sun faded and a bitter midwinter night broke over me. Above my head, the sky separated into four quadrants—the perpetual lavender twilight of the western Realm of Death, the clean dark of the midnight north, a star-cast east and, to the south, the looming peak of Mount Thyr, backed by the first rays of a sudden, new dawn.

With every beat of my heart, the cold tripled. I put out a hand to steady myself, but placement of the trees had changed. The pine I'd intended to grab was gone. I staggered and my pack swung out, pulling me off-balance.

I bit back a startled curse and half toppled, half sat in the snow. For a moment I floundered gracelessly, trying to get back up, then my tired body realized how comfortable I was. I let out a huff, pressed my lips into a line, and let my head fall back into the drift.

An owl hooted. Squinting up, I saw six of the creatures roosting above, silhouetted against a midnight sky as crisp and sharp as a blade and studded with stars. Each bird was different, yet the same—a variety of white and grays and browns obscured in the darkness. But each had the same eyes, round and bright as harvest moons.

These were not true owls, but messenger constructs once made by Eang—feathers and bones bound by the breath of a lost deity.

I struggled out of my pack. I knew these owls and I'd passed through this door a hundred times, but my heart still fluttered and my lungs struggled to process the colder, clearer air.

"Fetch Gadr and Imnir," I said to the birds, clearing my throat. "And Thvynder's Watchman."

The nearest owl, a gray male with black-tufted ears, ruffled his feathers.

"Go," I repeated around a mouth full of mittens. I pulled them off with my teeth and leaned forward to untie my snowshoes, artful contraptions of cord and hide and bowed wood; a gift from one of the men I sought today.

Free of the snowshoes, I gave the birds a moment to comply while I put my mittens back on and got to my feet, dislodging the snow from a nearby spruce as I grabbed at it. Needles stabbed through the knitted wool and the snow fell in clumps, marring the pristine surface around me.

The owls still hadn't moved, watching me with dour expressions.

"Gadr, Imnir, and the Watchman," I repeated to the birds, hardening my voice. "Off with you."

Two of the birds took flight, leaving their fellows to glower. The black-tufted male ruffled his wings even further and tipped his beak down in a strigine scowl. Then he took wing. The last three, a slate-gray female, a brown, moon-faced male, and a second, smaller white male, promptly closed their eyes and pretended to sleep.

I let them be. The cold pried into my bones by now, despite my months of bathing in the ice. Time and distance were unpredictable in the High Halls, easy to manipulate if one had the skill, but it would still be several hours before my guests arrived. I needed to get warm.

I set my shield against a tree and unlashed a woodsman's axe from my pack. I cleared a patch of ground and built a fire, irritating the remaining owls by hacking branches off dead trees and striking flint and tinder. But once the fire burned, sending the snow and dark and cold into retreat, the birds fluttered closer to the warmth.

By the time dawn turned the eastern quadrant of the sky from midnight blue to deep purple, then violet and a crescendo of pale pinks and oranges, the owls perched on the closest branches and basked in the heat of the flames.

I watched them with something close to fondness, stoking the fire around a pot of morning grains and nuts. I'd made tea, too, of pine needles from the nearby trees, and as I sipped, the power of the High Halls, inherent in everything around me, seeped into my blood. It strengthened me, hazing my eyes with gold as I looked up at the owls.

"See, I may not be Eang," I said to the owls, "but I'm not a terrible mistress, am I?"

"Do they often reply?"

A man emerged from the trees, his blond beard crusted with ice and his equally blond hair escaping from a fur-lined wool cloak and hat. The cloak was fastened to his broad shoulders with the silver pin I'd given him at our wedding, eight years ago, and his eyes hazed with the same power as mine. A power kept secret by us alone, High Priestess and High Priest of Thvynder.

I smiled. The expression was genuine, but it was an ally's smile rather than a lover's. Still, my heart clutched at my ribs at the sight of him, every line of his face reminding me of struggles and duties I would rather forget.

"Imnir," I greeted him, setting my cooling cup of tea aside.

"Hessa." My husband came to a stop before me. He gave a squinting, half-smile in return, but didn't reach for me.

I made room by the fire. He sat, holding his hands towards the flames as I studied him. It had been months since I'd last seen him, and the high lines of his Algatt cheeks, the paleness of his Algatt skin and hair, and the twitch of his Algatt lips struck me as eerily foreign.

"What is it?" Imnir asked. "Is everything all right, or is there something wrong with my face?"

I gave a small laugh but continued to watch him with a distant curiosity, waiting for my heart to pry itself off my ribs. "It's your face. I haven't seen it in a while."

"Hmm." My husband sat back to study me in turn. The ice in his moustache and beard formed perfect strings of pearls, framing lips slightly indented at the bottom left—the result of a scar whose cause I'd never learned. He was not handsome, his nose a touch too round and his eyes too far apart beneath straight brows, but I could imagine he'd been so in his younger years—before violence had stolen his first wife and children, and etched those green eyes with grim, guarded lines.

And he was Algatt. My people and his had been enemies for centuries – the peace our marriage secured could not erase that. He had killed my kin, as I'd killed his.

"I'd prefer to only tell the story once," I added absently, pulling my gaze away. "When the rest arrive."

Imnir nodded slowly, his gaze dropping to my hands. "Those healed well."

The scars I'd gained from the Laru's sickle glistened white in the firelight. Last time we'd seen one another, right here in this quiet corner of the High Halls, I'd just returned from the raids. My hand had been a stiff mess of flaking scabs and I'd been perturbed, wrestling with the first real threat I'd encountered since the Upheaval – since the Arpa gods had died, and Thvynder had risen to power.

"Do you have a spoon?"

I blinked. "What?"

"That's hot." He nodded to the pot. "And I'm starving. Unless you were planning on eating it in front of me, which is cruel but not unexpected."

"I planned on sharing," I admitted with a small smile. "Go ahead. There's tea too."

"What kind of tea?"

I nodded to the needles in the pot, still resting to the side of the flames. "Ours."

He eyed the needles, then my cup. "Is it wise to drink it so often?"

I shrugged. Our power was a consistent thing, with no need for replenishment, but I could not imagine visiting the Halls without taking a little more of its magic into my bones. It was our right, after all, whether or not he feared the long-term repercussions.

"I'm quite well, husband," I assured him.

27

He inclined his head, giving in, and I edged the pot of morning grains from the fire. We sat with it between us and I leaned over to dig a spoon from my pack. I picked up my tea again, but he shook his head when I offered it to him.

"I didn't expect you to be the first to arrive," I said, settling the rejected cup onto my knee.

He shrugged and dipped the wooden spoon into the steaming grains. "I was near Gadr's Door."

I watched him blow on the spoonful. Gadr's Door to the High Halls, like Eang's, rested in a place once sacred to one of the Miri—the beings formerly known as gods by Eangen, Arpa, and Algatt alike. The doors could only be opened by very few; those whose gods had given them leave to, or who already possessed the magic of the Higher Realms.

The Algatt once worshiped Gadr, but unlike Eang, Gadr had bowed to Thvynder. He still lived with his people in the mountains to the north of Eangen, branding himself a vagrant, goat-herd king.

"But Gadr wasn't with you?" I asked.

"No. Ah—" Imnir bared his teeth to take a tentative bite. His breath steamed out and I watched as he winced, grumbled something inaudible, then finally chewed. "I never really know where he is."

I finished my tea, shook out the cup, and took the spoon when he offered it. I scooped my own bite, resting the utensil on the edge of the pot while it cooled.

"How have the Iskiri been?" I asked. The Eangen tribe who lived closest to Algatt territory often gave us cause for conversation.

Imnir scratched at his beard, dislodging fragments of melting ice in a fine rain. "They still dispute our claim to the lowlands," he admitted. "They've been hunting there all winter, on land that was allocated to the Algatt. Their Devoted slink about the forests, leaving talismans of Eang and howling like wolves."

I frowned at that. Imnir's and my marriage stemmed the hostilities between the Eangen and Algatt on a formal level. In the villages, age-old feuds seethed, the old stories were still sung, and former slaves and half-bloods struggled to find their place. Furthermore, not everyone had bowed to our new god. The Iskiri Devoted, a sect that had refused to acknowledge Thvynder, were among the most difficult to control. They'd proven that by trying to put a knife in my back more than once. So much so that a new phrase had begun to circulate the North—*Never turn your back on an Iskiri.*

"Has there been bloodshed?" I asked.

Imnir glanced at his feet for a moment, adjusting them in the snow. "A half-blood woman put an arrow in the thigh of an Iskiri farmer, so, yes."

My eyebrows rose. "So it's her Algatt blood she's loyal to? That's your problem then, not mine."

"Half-bloods are everyone's problem."

"Then why wasn't I told?"

"It was only last week."

"Was the woman punished?"

Imnir nodded and accepted the spoon again. He spoke dispassionately, factually, but I saw unhappiness around his eyes. "A fine was paid in reparation."

Though this had become common practice, my lips pinched. Had our peoples really come to this? Paying fines instead of defending their honor?

"And the Iskiri farmer's family?" I pressed.

Imnir swallowed another bite and passed the spoon. "They swore not to seek vengeance but it did not go well. The half-blood will need to watch her back."

"After eight years, I really hoped this would have stopped."

"The Iskiri are erratic and violent. Peace hasn't changed that." Imnir followed my line of thought. "Perhaps if you were more visible, it would help. You should come north. Live with me. Otherwise, what is this for?"

He emphasized his question by gesturing between the two of us.

I bristled. "You could just as easily come south."

"That hardly fixes the Iskiri problem. Besides, Sixnit would poison me," he returned. "Or I'd find a Soulderni sword in my gut."

I snorted and took another bite of food. Besides being Thray's mother, Sixnit was my best friend. "Six and Nisien would not harm you. Well, Nisien would not."

"No?" His eyebrows rose, still clung with damp. "I've seen the way that horseman looks at me."

"You accused him of sleeping with me. And you made me cry, in the beginning. Nisien's my friend, and he had good reason to mistrust you."

"Whether or not you were sleeping with him was a valid question. And you never cry."

"No one who knows me and Nis would say that. I do cry. There's no shame in tears. It keeps me from becoming a stone-heart like you."

The ghost of a frown touched his lips, but I couldn't tell which topic had caused it. "How can I know any of that if we're a world apart?"

That question made my belly ache in a strange, hollow way, and my throat constricted. But beneath that was uncertainty. Imnir hadn't wanted us to be together for years, and I'd abandoned all hope of a proper marriage and family. So why was he bringing this up, now? What had changed?

I reached out to take his hand. It was a light touch, but it took a great deal of effort on my part.

He looked down at our hands for a moment, then ran a thumb over the back of my fingers. His skin was cold, red, and pinched. "It would help if we had children."

I jerked my hand back. "You're the one—" I spluttered, scarlet with embarrassment and rage. "You're the one that refused. You decided my belly was empty before we ever really tried."

"I know." His admission was as much of a shock as his suggestion. He looked at me sideways and pointed to me, somehow indicating every bit of my body at once. "But maybe I was…wrong. It's been a long winter. And you…"

I waited for him to go on. When he didn't, I prompted in a deadly tone, "And I?"

"We're getting older." He spoke of both of us, but his eyes flicked to my stomach.

I thought my cheeks might rupture, red with fury. Yes, Eangen weren't known to live long, for one reason or another. Yes, most women had borne their children by my age, and the midwives' wisdom was to avoid later pregnancy at all costs. Enough young women died in childbirth; the older women, and their babies, perished far more easily.

But he was the one who had discouraged having children, had declared me barren within a year of our marriage. He was the one who pushed me away in the dark of the night, when I'd found the will to reach for him. He was the reason I'd swallowed my desire to have a daughter, a son, and given Thray and her half-brother Vistic all my rootless parental love.

I recast his words into a challenge, swallowed my anger and raised my chin.

"I'm thirty," I replied, voice deadly flat. "I'm not gray yet. If you want children, come to Albor and find my bed."

Imnir looked trapped between exasperation and uncertainty.

He was saved from replying as two figures materialized from the forest. One brimmed with unnatural power—golden to my eyes—millennia of influence, and a lifetime of my ire. Without my Sight, however, he could easily pass as human. His head was shaved, his beard braided and knotted with horsehair. He wore Algatt clothing—an angular brown tunic that came to a point between his knees, over trousers wrapped in ornately woven legwraps. He was Gadr, a Miri, and former god of the Algatt people.

I'd met the second being when I was eighteen, when he was only a traveler called Omaskat. I had aged since then, but he had not, maintaining the appearance of a straight-backed thirty with sun-lightened, dark blond hair. His tunic, visible beneath the fall of a dark cloak trimmed with fine braid, looked black in the night, but as he entered the firelight it swelled back to its customary sea-blue, embroidered about a keyhole neckline and belted at the waist.

Omaskat, the Watchman of Thvynder, face of a faceless God and the being chiefly responsible for bringing stability to the North—despite my youthful interventions. He inclined his head. "Hessa, Imnir."

Gadr sunk down without a word, grunting with approval at our pot of grain and holding his hand for the spoon. Neither he nor Omaskat commented on the fact that I was holding that spoon like a knife, and Imnir was leaning away from me.

"That's my food," I snapped. Gadr still retained much of his former power, but he was no immediate threat to me. If anything, we stood as equals in our new world, discredited Miri "god" and gifted priestess. "I have important news."

Gadr pursed his lips, leaned forward, and stuck two hooked fingers into the pot. Incensed, I barely stopped myself from slapping his hand away. Equality or no, it was foolish to test Gadr's limits.

I snatched the pot away instead. Gadr grinned and Omaskat watched it all without comment. He sat at the fire and extended his hands to the warmth—habitual, more than necessary.

Above our heads, the remaining owls rustled. One cracked her eye and peered at Gadr for a long moment, then noticed me watching her and shut it again.

"What news?" Omaskat asked. His eyes flicked to my empty pot of tea on the edge of the fire, amber and thick with pine needles, but didn't comment.

I told the three men about the Arpa messenger and all that we'd said, quickly and simply. Even Gadr did not interrupt, sucking porridge from his fingers and watching me with calculating eyes.

"The Arpa messenger is still in Albor?" Omaskat clarified when I finished.

Imnir wrinkled his nose and fed a stick into the fire. "And he's still in one piece?"

I nodded, glancing from my husband to the Watchman. "Yes, he's there, and he's fine. Waiting the results of this council."

There was a moment of quiet, each to their thoughts, before Gadr spoke up.

"The Algatt will go," he said simply. Glancing at Imnir he added, "Two thousand shields, I suppose? We will be ready by spring."

I tamped down a surge of selfish displeasure. Even though the messenger had come to the Eangen, I'd known the Algatt would need to be involved. Gadr himself had rebuked me after last season's raids, raging that I had not warned or involved his people in the venture.

But raiding in Nivarium, as I'd discovered, was not simply a matter of beating our shields at fleeing farmers. The Laru were there, priests with real—if unexplained—power, and I could not be everywhere. I suspected that we would need Gadr if we decided to answer Bresius's call.

Still, that did not mean I was at ease with the thought of plunging the Algatt back into their pillaging ways. What if, once their swords were wet with Arpa blood, they decided to turn them back on the Eangen?

Imnir's voice drifted through the back of my mind. *It would help if we had children.*

Beside me, my husband shook his head, cracked another stick, and flicked half into the fire. "Bresius would never let us keep Souldern, it's too valuable. The iron mines alone are worth going to war over."

"We'll make him give a blood-oath," I returned without looking at my husband. I focused on Omaskat instead. It was his opinion, as the Face of Thvynder, that truly mattered. "What does the God say?"

Omaskat made a contemplative sound but didn't reply immediately. I wished, not for the first time, that he was easier to read. His thoughts were fleeting and veiled—a hint of contemplation, a brush of revelation, a simmering, cautious conclusion. "It is… an opportunity, at the least. One we need to explore."

"Ah, come now," Gadr prodded. He leaned forward, shoving his bearded face into Imnir's line of sight. "You remember the raids, old man. You remember the way your blood sang. You remember winters without hunger, with lofts full of grain and mead and meat. We should do it."

"With *Eangen* grain and mead and meat?" Tension rippled down my arms and my fingers clenched into the cold fabric of my trousers. "My world died in those raids. Albor burned in those raids."

Gadr shrugged. "It was the way, and your people were equally to blame. Eang was Goddess of War, not victory."

I leaned forward, oblivious to the heat of the flames on my face. "You weren't so cold when the Arpa butchered *your* people. Or have you forgotten it? Little girls hung from trees by their own braids? Their eyes gouged out?"

Imnir's eyes remained fixed on the fire, but I saw him grow still. He did not need any reminder of the Arpa's slaughter of his people. He'd lost his first family to them, as I'd lost mine to the Algatt.

Gadr's expression faltered into a snarl. "Of course I remember. All the more reason to bring our swords to the Arpa now. Times have changed. There has been peace, yes, but my people are restless. Your people are restless, too, especially your Iskiri and their Eang-worshipers. Give them another enemy to fight, Priestess. Give all of us one."

Imnir spoke, his words saturated with an incendiary sort of calm: "I'll go, gladly. I agree with Gadr—it will be good for the North to have a common enemy. And Hessa, you're right when you say this is an opportunity we can't pass by. Bresius will bring us to the heart of the Empire. Let's stick a knife in it."

Gadr gesticulated at my husband. "See? The priest understands."

"The decision to go south is not so simple," Omaskat tempered. "Particularly this stipulation of Bresius's, that you are to escort him to the capital and see him ascended. I think this is far more than playing bodyguard."

Gadr went quiet, but his silence was a strained one. He squinted off into the forest and subtly caught Omaskat's eye, as if to shush him.

"What?" I demanded of the Algatt's former god. "What do you know?"

"Very little," Gadr said in a broad, all-encompassing way. "Or so they tell me."

Imnir and I both looked at Omaskat. The Watchman gave a wan smile, then cleared his throat.

"There is power in Apharnum that the Arpa emperors harness, and use to ascend," Omaskat admitted. "Beneath the old Temple of Lathian. Though now that Lathian is dead, it is a temple of no god, and that power is inaccessible."

"Where does the power come from now, if the temple has no god?" Imnir asked.

"It's a remnant, the place where the blood of one of the Four Pillars, Eiohe, once spilled. Consider it… something like the White Lake," Omaskat explained. Thvynder had passed millennia asleep in a sacred lake in the Algatt Mountains, after the Miri banished their god-siblings. "Power remains where Eiohe's blood fell, and that is the power Lathian once used to 'ascend' his emperors. It's also the power he would have taken for himself, if he'd made it back to Apharnum in his physical form, and one of his priests gave him the blood to drink—the Miri cannot touch it themselves, or so the story goes."

I glanced at Gadr. "You tried, didn't you?"

"I did not." He sniffed. "But there are tales. Old Arpa gods annihilated in the attempt. It's not worth the risk. A certain level of… awareness, remains in the blood, and it recalls that it was the Miri spilled it. Even if I found a priest to collect the blood for me, there would be a high price to drinking it, I'm sure."

"In any case," Omaskat resumed his explanation, "that is the power that would have made Lathian unstoppable. A force to reckon with Thvynder themselves."

Goosebumps rippled up my arms.

Omaskat went on, "As to the Ascension itself, it is… an unnatural ordination, one that imbues a human host with long life and the power to control the Arpa people. But here is my true concern; the blood is said to lie behind a door to the Arpa's High Halls. That realm has fallen to corruption since the fall of the Empire, and the ability to open the doors lost to the Arpa. I would not be surprised if Bresius, after seeing your power against the Laru, believes you can open that door and gain him access to the blood again. *That* is why he wants you by his side for the Ascension. The Laru are secondary."

Imnir and I exchanged a glance.

"Could I open it?" I asked, gesturing at Imnir to include him. "Could we?"

Omaskat nodded. "Of course. You've the blessing of Thvynder." Pointing to the remnants of my tea, he added, "And you've enough of the High Halls in your blood that you're practically part of the scenery. So, yes, this is an opportunity. But a dangerous one, one with possibilities we cannot yet predict."

I looked at Imnir again. Despite all the words that had passed over the fire tonight, it was a natural movement; I sought his thoughts like I might my war chief's or Nisien's, and that instinct caught me off guard.

I was even more surprised when he looked at me too. A moment passed between us, the understanding of two humans among the inhuman, and I felt a little calmer.

"And if Bresius did ascend?" I asked, turning my gaze back to Omaskat. "Somehow? What will he become?"

"An Ascended Emperor of a new and united Arpa Empire," Omaskat returned grimly. "Nearly immortal, immensely influential... For better, or for worse."

"Is there any way Laru priests could open the rift and use the blood?" Imnir asked.

Omaskat shook his head. "No. Only you two, myself, and the Miri will have passage anymore. Perhaps some fell creatures could still get through, but very few."

"There's no chance the Laru god is a Miri?" I wanted to know. I thought of Estavius, waiting with the messenger in my hall. "One who didn't obey Lathian's call, during the Upheaval?"

Omaskat shook his head. "No. Maybe a half-blood? I'll know more soon."

Imnir spoke up again. "Well, if Thvynder agrees to the proposal, Hessa and I can lead the Vynder guard together."

"Or not," Gadr interjected. "Why don't we raid on our own and leave Bresius and these Laru dogs to kill each other? Then we can play the vultures. If the Laru can't get at that bloody puddle anyway, there's no need to bother."

"Because the Laru do have real power of some kind. A strange kind." Reluctance still churned inside of me, still sapped the strength from my limbs. But as I looked at Omaskat, the truth of my words gave me strength. "Even if we don't understand where it's from, it's there. And in a land with no gods, whoever they support as emperor will eventually take control, one way or another, with or without Ascension. Then the North will be under threat again—perhaps not the same level of threat as we would if the Empire had an Ascended Emperor, but a threat all the same."

"Agreed," Omaskat said, his tone one of finality. "There's much I need to learn about these Laru and the Ascension, but we need to move now."

Gadr stood up. "Fine, then. The Algatt will raid, and I expect that Vynder guard for Bresius to be half ours, Imnir."

Imnir nodded but didn't speak, nor did I. With a grunt, Gadr brushed the snow off his trousers and strode into the night.

Omaskat let out a long, even breath. "I should go too. I'll send an owl, Hessa, once I've spoken to Thvynder."

At the mention, I glanced toward the sleeping owls. Sometime during the conversation they'd slipped away, and the lattice of branches above us was barren.

"How soon?" I asked the Watchman. "If that Arpa messenger stays too long, someone will put a spear through his eye."

"Tomorrow." Omaskat now stood, shaking snow from his clothing and folding his cloak more firmly around himself. "I may also seek the advice of Fate, but… Well, we all know how misleading she can be."

We did. Fate, sister-god to Thvynder, had woven herself into the fabric of time during the conflict in which Thvynder was bound beneath the White Lake and Eiohe's blood was shed in the south. She occasionally granted visions to those who sought her corner of the High Halls. But though the visions were always truthful, she often presented them in a way that bewildered and manipulated the seeker.

"Either way, I'll have your answer by tomorrow," Omaskat affirmed. "Also, Hessa, Vistic says hello."

Vistic was Thray's half-brother, and at the mention of him, a smile warmed my cheeks. "Then tell him I love him."

"No eleven-year-old boy wants to hear that," Imnir chided, but there was humor in his eyes. He wasn't close with Vistic, despite having spent more time with him than I in recent years, but he liked the boy well enough.

"All the more reason to tell him, preferably in front of a large audience," I said.

Omaskat took this all with a nod. "I will. Goodbye, Hessa. Imnir."

We murmured our farewells and the Watchman of Thvynder slipped off into the night as Gadr had. In the ensuing quiet, Imnir sidled back toward me and looked at the pot questioningly.

Some of my warmth faded, our earlier conversation returning to me. I frowned at him, but gave a slight nod of concession. He took some porridge, the clink of the spoon filling the space between us for a few moments. Then he passed the food back to me and brushed off his hands.

I sat back, eating in slow, deliberate mouthfuls and not looking at my husband. As I ate, I shook sodden pine needles from the teapot and returned the pot and cup to my pack.

To the south, a summer sun began to spill over the mountaintop. It broke across the sky—the violet west, the sleeping east—in great, golden beams, though our fire still rested in the mountain's icy shadow.

Imnir shifted to face me, knees drawn to his chest and arms draped around them. Between his knees, his fingers laced together—graceful fingers for a man, though as scarred and calloused as my own. He had not been a priest of Gadr in the days before the Upheaval; he had served Frir, sister of Eang. We both wore the scars of the blood sacrifices they'd demanded.

"Our people, fighting together against the Arpa," he said, green Algatt gaze resting into my dark brown Eangen. "There will be conflict between our people along the way. It's inevitable."

I couldn't push my thoughts back any longer. "Do you truly think it would be different, if we'd had a child? If we'd made a home together?"

The easy lines of Imnir's body tightened and his fingers, still laced over his knees, whitened slightly. "I think so."

"Some of my people say that I was cursed by Frir, for killing her sister," I said. I took up the last bite of grains and raised it to my mouth, adding more quietly, "And that's why we've no children."

"Frir doesn't have that kind of power anymore," Imnir said, almost absently. "She still shepherds the dead, but she's a shadow of what she once was. She has no more worshipers, no more blood sacrifice fueling her. She's under Thvynder's thumb."

I cleaned my spoon off in the snow. I knew the stories of Frir's former days, the good and the bad. There were tales of mourners bartering with the goddess for the lives of their dead lovers, stories of children returned to the arms of their parents. They were, every one of them, stories of inevitable death—of souls pulled from the living bones of Frir's hapless enemies, or loved ones returned to life as murderous monsters.

Imnir took the empty grain pot from me. He scoured it with snow and set it aside. "If you want to share my tent in Nivarium, I won't stop you."

"Nor I you," I added, packing both items away in my pack and knotting it closed. My words sounded more like a challenge than I'd intended. "Though I don't intend to get with child in Arpa."

"We'll practice then," he quipped, cocking a flirtatious eyebrow.

The expression and tone were so foreign to the hard lines of his face that I covered my eyes with the back of one hand. "Gods below, don't be coy. You're terrible at it."

"Ah." He shrugged nonchalantly, but I didn't miss a slight flush on his cheeks. "I'll never do it again, then."

"Thank you."

Imnir stood and offered me a hand. I took it and let him help me to my feet. His fingers were cool in mine, and his touch a strange mixture of unfamiliarity and belonging, obligation and distant, hollow want.

The last was the hardest to bear, because it was not his hand that I wanted in mine, or his touch that would fill that void. And I knew that he felt the same way about me. But here we were, with none but each other.

"I should go." I squeezed his fingers before I picked up my pack. I slung it on and grabbed my axe and shield and snowshoes, standing quietly by as he nudged the last of my fire apart with a stick and kicked snow over the coals.

The heat died in a sizzle and drifts of smoke. Cold surged in, eager and prying into my bones.

Imnir tucked his hands under his cloak and nodded north. "Sure you don't want to come with me?"

I looked towards the rift, that slim crack of amber light that would take me back to the Waking World and Albor. With the sight of it, the full weight of the night's discussion fell on me, uncertain and full of the promise that, no matter what, the world I returned to was not what it had been yesterday.

I regrouped and considered Imnir. "Again, you could come with me too."

He stepped backwards into the trees with a resigned nod. "Another time, then."

Above his head, beyond snow-laden branches and bows, the south's rising sun shone more brightly into the divided sky. The half-light shadowed Imnir's face and, just for a moment, I could imagine he was someone else. The husband I'd bid farewell to, here in the High Halls, after his death. Or the one I might have taken, if Imnir and obligation hadn't been in my way.

"Keep well, wife," he added.

"Husband," I murmured.

He stepped off into the trees and I passed through the rift, out of that crisp, otherworldly night. The sun struck my face and the snow swelled higher, rooting me back in the daylight and uniform sky of the Waking World.

By the time an owl swept into the Morning Hall that night, I'd shuttered my heart to thoughts of husbands and children, choosing instead to dwell on more pressing matters—the Arpa, Laru, and the potential mobilization of the Eangen army.

Thvynder's verdict did not surprise me. I watched an owl flutter into the rafters and heard Omaskat's voice, audible to my ears alone, declare that Thvynder had agreed to Bresius's proposal.

That same night, a pair of axes appeared at the foot of my bed; ancient and familiar, to equip me for the coming fight. Galger and Gammler, the legendary weapons of Eang; weapons I hadn't seen since the day the Goddess of War fell.

I sat with them in the darkness, watching distant firelight from the main hearth slip across their blades. The hafts of the axes were nearly the length of my arm and their bearded blades edged with fine, glistening steel. They were heavily decorated, runes and images of owls nearly lost in the twining of endless patterns, from the tip of their sweeping beards to the harsh, armor-piercing points at their backs. The hafts were embellished, too, wrapped with fortifying coils of steel, embossed with runes and ancient magics, both blessing and preserving the weapons.

Come spring, I would take these up, and the Eangen and the Algatt would return to the Arpa Empire as mercenaries and raiders. Together with Imnir and six of our priests and priestesses, I would follow Bresius to the Empire's very heart and either establish or destroy it in the temple of the Arpa's former God of Gods, Lathian.

The Temple of No God.

FOUR

My nerves hummed as we left the budding forests of southern Eangen and climbed to the old Arpa perimeter, at the foot of the Spines. These ancient towers of rock and moss, ferns, and fetid ponds stretched high into the sky, as tall as the trees that interspersed them, but little remained of the border's deep ditches and wooden watchtowers. Only one tower still stood; we'd torn the rest down, using the wood to rebuild our towns after the Upheaval.

The ditches were eroded and overgrown, their deadly host of staves dismantled, but I saw a new bridge pieced together from pungent pine. Three Arpa legionaries waited for us on the other side; silver-armored, a single banner snapping.

Somewhere back down the lines of four thousand Eangen and Algatt shields, Briel raised a horn and blew. Other horns picked up the call, riding the wind until the whole of the Spines rang. The rumble of footsteps and hooves, the grind of leather and mail and the chink of weapons diminished, until I could hear the crack of the legionaries' pennant. It was red, emblazoned with the head of a boar. The Ilia Guard.

Estavius, the picture of an Arpa legionary in his heavy cloak and glistening plate armor, dismounted on the Eangen side of the bridge and approached alone. I dismounted, too, landing softly among the grasses and wildflowers as a dog trotted up, deftly avoiding hooves and buffeting my thigh. Nui, offspring of Ayo, the old, gray hound that had once followed Omaskat and now resided with Vistic at the White Lake.

The hum of my nerves calmed as I scratched the thick, bristling fur along her spine.

Nearby, Imnir readied to dismount. My husband hadn't spoken more than a handful of words since we joined forces yesterday for the march south. This wasn't abnormal—our relationship was a practical thing, and we often got along better without words—but I noticed now that he looked haggard. As I followed his gaze towards the three legionaries and the cobbled Arpa road cutting off into the Spines, I understood why.

Living as far north as he did, I doubt that he'd seen a proper Arpa since the day legionaries had murdered his family—Estavius excepted. His eyes, usually blithe and shuttered, held a deep, smoldering animosity now.

I didn't blame him.

Estavius crossed the bridge to speak to the other Arpa and I moved closer to Imnir.

"Should I be meeting Bresius alone?" I asked my husband. Nui started to break away, but I brought her to heel with a snap of my fingers.

"No." Imnir dropped down beside us, earning a sharp look and a flick of the ears from Nui. The angled fringe of his hair fell over his eyes as he stretched his neck and shook his head, dislodging tension like water. "He should see us united."

We passed through the Spines quietly, with myself, Nisien, Estavius, and Imnir at the head of the train. After an hour in the cool rocks and damp, we emerged onto a strip of open ground where the Soulderni Ridings began.

But first, the Ilia Gates barred our path. A fortress of stone, it seemed untouched by the decade since its last official habitation. Walls higher than the Morning Hall spread to either side of it, cutting off north from south.

The Ilia Gates were formidable, indomitable, and glistening in the sunlight. It was a glimpse of what the Empire had once been—and what it might be again, unless I found a way to stop it.

Nisien joined me as, behind us, four thousand Eangen, Algatt, and Soulderni warriors spread out to wait. Nui, oblivious to the tension of the moment, leapt into the sea of hip-high grass and saplings between us and the gate and commenced trying to eat a hapless moth.

"I thought you were leaving that dog in Eangen," Nisien commented.

"Thray wanted me to take her."

His eyes softened, but there was a grimness to them. He hadn't spent much time with Thray in recent years—her approach to womanhood had left him somewhat at a loss—but he still cared for her, and he knew my absence would be difficult for the girl. And for me.

Thray hadn't just wanted me to take the hound. She'd begged me to.

"*She'll protect you and watch over you, when you're sleeping and busy,*" the girl had insisted on the morning I left, her eyes still puffy from a sleepless night. And though I knew Nui would likely be more trouble than she was worth, I'd agreed. Not only to soothe the girl and her fears for my safe return, but for myself. Nui was a reminder of Thray and home, and all that I'd left behind. All that I fought for.

I hated to leave Thray. I hated to leave Sixnit and Albor and the warmth of the hall. But that wouldn't stop me from doing it.

Watching the dog snap at another moth, I crooked a melancholy smile.

"Then I'm glad you'll have the mutt to watch your back," Nisien said, and bumped his shoulder against mine, "when I'm not there to do it."

More sadness crept into my face. I didn't bother hiding it, though I checked to ensure Imnir's attention was elsewhere. "You better come back to me after this."

My friend grinned, a boyish expression that reminded me of the night we'd met, in the music and firelight of his homeland. "I will, little Eangen."

Ten minutes later, we stepped into the cool of the Ilia Gate's central courtyard with Imnir and Estavius—the rest of the company remained in the rippling grasses at the foot of the Spines. Estavius led the way, passing through stone archways and cloisters and into a square of daylight. We were lightly armed—I left my new axes attached to my saddle, choosing instead to carry only my thick knife, hung horizontal across the thigh, while Nisien and Estavius wore round-pommeled Arpa swords and Imnir an axe through a loop at his hip.

With his helmet held smartly beneath one arm, Estavius stepped into the courtyard. We halted behind him, still contained by the shadows of the nearest cloister. I stood between Nisien and Imnir, and not just because the two men bore little affection for one another. Imnir's jaw was lifted and his focus was across the courtyard, where our Arpa escort joined six waiting men. The muscles in his throat flexed.

Estavius stopped in the middle of the yard. I expected him to bow, to salute, or give some other sign of respect to the welcome party. These men, one of whom was certainly Bresius, did not know who or what he was—a Miri and a former god—and I'd thought he intended to keep it that way.

But he did not bow. Instead, he gave a casual tilt of the chin.

"Castor." Estavius spoke in Arpa, his voice as cool as the stone around us. "Yours is a face I never thought to see again."

The centermost legionary bowed, a good-natured swoop of the arm accompanied by a dry smile. His eyes were blue, wide-set in a face that had aged well since I last saw him on the shores of the White Lake, ten years ago. His signature Arpa nose looked as though it had been broken at least once since, but the crook provided much-needed contrast to the prettiness of his eyes and the fall of his tight, light brown ringlets.

I lowered my chin, fully aware that my breathing had slowed and my hand twitched towards the hilt of my knife. Sure, it had been a decade since this man had helped a mad Arpa priest drug and torment me, but the sight of him made old instincts burn.

"I hardly expected to see your face again either, Estavius," Castor replied. I saw something else flicker through his eyes—surprise? Unease? Estavius, after all, would be considered a traitor for making his home in the North.

I studied the other Arpa, looking for cues as to which one was Bresius, but from the attitudes of all the Arpa present, this was a meeting of peers.

Bresius hadn't come. I frowned.

"Please," Castor went on, pulling my attention back to him. "Introduce your companions."

I stepped out into the menial warmth of the sun and asked, "Have I changed that much?"

Castor's smile cracked. There was no real recognition in his eyes but he nodded to me and, as he did, I noticed an irregularity in the fall of his hair. A horrific scar roped through it, ending on his left cheekbone. "Greetings, Hessa, High Priestess of Thvynder."

Shock fluttered through me. I'd seen enough wounds to know that scar had not been caused by a common injury. Whatever Castor had suffered in the years since our last meeting, it was a miracle he was alive—and no surprise, then, that he might have misplaced a few memories.

The thought left me oddly disappointed, as if his ignorance stole the power from my own memories of leers and threats and restraining hands.

Nisien saw the wound too. Catching my eye, he stepped past me and offered Castor a bow.

Again, Castor's eyes showed no recognition, but he sensed now that he should know us. His lips twitched in frustration.

"Old friend, allow me to present Hessa, High Priestess of the Eangen," Estavius began, stepping aside and gesturing to me, then to Nisien. "And Nisien of the Soulderni, a Guardian of the North. Also Imnir, High Priest of the Algatt, husband to Hessa."

Imnir, still in the shadows, didn't move.

Castor's expression was blank during this, nodding to each of us. "I am Bresius's liaison, given my experience in the North," he explained, despite the fact that he obviously remembered little of that experience. "The emperor could not make the journey and sends his regrets. I've been assigned to bring you to him, High Priest and High Priestess."

Castor's reappearance had already put me on edge, but this turned me entirely. Bresius had sent a lackey to watch over us?

Imnir spoke up first. "That was not the agreement."

Castor shrugged. "I'll be your guide, and you will be glad of my company, I assure you. We can keep to the mountains for most of the journey, but traversing southern Nivarium will be dangerous. It is my task to ensure the treaty is upheld and the terms fulfilled—to make sure you're where you need to be, so we all can get this over with and go home in one piece."

I felt Imnir's eyes on me, but I focused on Nisien instead. It was Nisien and I who knew Castor. The Soulderni returned my glance, but his opinion was obscure.

"Bresius seems content to work with you, Hessa, but I myself am curious to know," Castor said, noting our silent communication. "What are the limits of your power? This Vynder magic? It is not like Eangi Fire, I've heard tell. No more boiling the blood of your enemies?"

I watched him for a pointed, quiet moment. "With it, I slew the Goddess of War and broke the Laru's thrall."

Castor grinned, a broad, genuine flick of the lips. "That I know. But is it useful against common men?"

I felt Imnir shift in the shadows, easing his posture as if preparing for a fight.

"I am a Curse Breaker," I said, using the Arpa phrase as Estavius had recommended. "No unnatural power can be used upon me, but I can use it upon others with… similar blessings."

"Miri?" Castor prompted. "And Laru, humans infused with divine power?"

"And creatures, ill-begotten. Demons. Monsters."

"But you cannot affect life-magic? Or blood-magic, I've heard it's called in the North."

"It seems he's 'heard' a lot of things," Nisien murmured, low enough that only I could hear him.

"Of course not," I returned, hiding a smile at Nisien's words but also perplexed by Castor's question. Blood-magic created life. It could not be manipulated or utilized, except by a true God or an immensely powerful Miri, like Eang had once been. Castor's question either revealed a gross over-estimation of my abilities, or his own lack of comprehension regarding the magics of our world.

"So a common man with a sword?" the Arpa prompted.

"I will dispatch with a sword," I returned.

"I see. And your husband?" The legionary moved on to Imnir, switching into Northman. "What do you lend to the cause?"

"I See," Imnir replied, emphasizing the second word. "And I Hear."

"How basic. See and hear what?"

"The dead."

Imnir's pronouncement filled the courtyard, and I swore I caught a whiff of the salty, twilit sea that was Frir's Realm of Death. Though he rarely used his gifts, I knew they were powerful and dark, and far more potent than he'd admitted. He'd carried them over from his previous service to Frir, and amplified them with the magic of the High Halls.

"So you are a…" Castor searched for the word in Northman and came up blank. He looked to Estavius and said something in Arpa that I didn't catch.

"Necromancer," Estavius translated.

"Of a sort," Imnir returned.

Castor nodded slowly. "But your skills are not offensive?"

"I will be able to see and sense the Laru," my husband countered, his expression calm. "My axe will do the rest."

Imnir was lying, though there were few in this world who would have known it. My husband had been a Priest of Death. He didn't need any weapons to kill.

"Fair enough." Castor nodded. "And I assume the rest of your Vynder have similar capabilities?"

I nodded. They were considerably lesser and more varied, but Castor didn't need to know that yet. His presence, and condition, still unnerved me.

Castor pulled something small from his pocket, then crossed the courtyard to hand it to Estavius, who passed it to Imnir. It was a small bottle, filled to the cork with a viscous liquid that looked black through the gray glass.

"This is Bresius's blood. Bind him to his word," Castor prompted. "Your service, for Souldern and peace. I will offer my own blood, too, in pledge that I saw Bresius take this from his own veins, and that I bore it here without tampering."

"Did Bresius ask for any pledge in return?" Imnir asked, lifting the bottle high and examining it in the light of the sun. Blood-oaths were a common practice across the known world, but for the Eangen and Algatt they were a remnant of a former age, when blood was used to bind and break in the names of Eang and Gadr and Frir.

"No." The legionary shook his head. "Take that as a pledge of his goodwill. Besides, should you betray him, you'll be hilt-deep in the Empire. You'll hardly escape."

He delivered his words placidly, but the threat of them curled around my ribs. I was confident we could fight our way back north if necessary, but that didn't mean I relished the risk. No, I understood it, accepted it, and thought it manageable, but did not relish it.

The urge to stop all of this, to bolt out of the courtyard and turn back our armies welled up, but I kicked it back down. I wanted to do this. I would do this—for the security of the North, the ones I loved, and for Souldern.

I said, "Then fetch me fire."

A minute later, two other legionaries brought in a brazier. Heat wafted into my face as Imnir and I took our places to either side of it, he with the blood and I with a length of cloth I'd brought for the occasion.

We went through the motions with practiced gravitas. This was blood-magic, the most pervasive in our world, wrought with the innate life-force of all living things, and was to be treated with the appropriate respect.

I held out the cloth, pushing aside all other thoughts and distractions. Imnir slowly poured the blood out onto the fabric— stinking and putrefied, despite the strength of its seal—and restated the terms of the agreement. Castor affirmed them in Bresius's stead, before cutting his own hand and adding droplets to the soiled cloth.

I dropped the fabric onto the coals. It began to burn, releasing the sickly-sweet, heady iron of fouled blood into the air. I longed to cover my mouth and nose but held back, watching through the tendrils of black smoke as Imnir stoppered the empty bottle and Castor half closed his eyes against the smoke. He seemed undeterred by the stench.

"Very well, then," Castor said when the smoke had cleared. "The Ilia Gates are open to you. Bring your armies through, Hessa. We will travel with them until we've broken through the Nivari border. Then they can go their own way, pillaging as they please, and you and your guard will accompany me south. We will rendezvous with Bresius at the border of the Apharni Province, on the delta of the Nivari River by the last full moon of summer."

On the sweeping hills of the Soulderni Ridings, south of the Ilia Gates, we camped for the night. The air was thick with anticipation, voices were loud and laughter reckless. The sky was clear, so few erected tents, and the camp was a sea of cookfires and tangles of songs and storytelling.

I laid my bedroll with my Vynder guard, but we shared a fire with Nisien and Estavius. I was grateful for this. It was my duty to be with my people on this first night out of Eangen, but come morning, my friends would be gone.

The Vynder settled in around the fire, passing bowls of stewed meat and barley cakes. Half the company was Eangen, half Algatt, as Gadr had insisted. They'd all trained together but the distinction between tribes was still visible—Eangen on one side of the fire, Algatt on the other.

To my right sat Sillo. He was a Vynder who, through a twist of fate, was both my cousin and my stepbrother—though I rarely thought of him as the latter. A little over twenty, he was nearly the height of a Soulderni, with broad shoulders and agile, lanky musculature beneath padded tunic and loose trousers. His black beard was knotted at a narrow chin and his face was handsome in a wild, unkempt sort of way. But despite his masculinity, his deep-set eyes and cast of freckles would forever remind me of his sister, Yske—lost in the same raid that had taken my first husband.

Next to him sat Lida and Ifling. They were sisters from Addack, the northern coast of Eangen, and though their faces looked alike their forms could not have been more different. Lida was lean as a hungry wolf, with large eyes, no waist to speak of, and a trail of tattoos down one side of her jaw. Ifling was all feminine curves, her round-cheeked smiles enough to sneak through the guard of the cruelest enemy. Both of them wore long tunics, just past the knee and split up the sides to reveal fitted trousers, and their dark brown hair was woven into crowns. Above each ear, they wore decorative spikes of narwhal tusk tucked into their braids like short, slim horns: carved, sharp, and perfectly deadly.

Then there were the Algatt. Next to Imnir, directly across the fire from me, sat Hete. She was the oldest in the group at fifty. Her gray braid was as thick as my wrist and fell down the length of her spine. Her hard-edged face softened only when she looked at Mynin, the young man at her side. They weren't related, but she'd adopted him after the Upheaval. He was in his early twenties, his straight, dark blond hair kept in a tuft at the base of his skull. He wore a short sword on one thigh and his cheeks were scarred from a childhood sickness, but his eyes were kind and warm.

Last was Silgi. She was a little older than I and had dark hair for an Algatt; a deep, brooding auburn that bespoke an unnamed Eangen somewhere in her ancestry. But her skin was pale, freckled, and she wore signature Algatt paints of blue and yellow smudged into her hairline.

Each of them wielded the magic of the High Halls, though only Imnir and I knew to call it that. They all had the Sight—the ability to sense and see unnatural things and hidden magic—and they would be more resilient to the Laru's influence than common warriors. At least, I hoped they would. And each one of them had different abilities.

Silgi had an affinity for herbs and healing, and a touch of foresight that made her deadly in a fight. Mynin and Ifling had both found themselves with an ability that the others called Shadow Walking—meaning that they moved swiftly and without being seen. Hete maintained she'd gotten nothing out of drinking "that putrid concoction," but despite her gray hair, it was becoming clear that she was not aging as fast as she should have been, nor was she plagued by the aches and pains that troubled her peers—and, after a long day, me. Lida could predict a storm down to the moment of its arrival and Sillo had inherited an ironic combination of the brute strength most attributed to Miri like Gadr, and a singing voice that had once, he claimed, calmed a raging she-bear.

As I looked around at the company, I couldn't help a swell of pride. Other than Briel, my war chief, these were the best of the Vynder. I was glad to have them at my side. But when my eyes strayed to Nisien and Estavius, that elation waned.

As the night drew on, I found myself wandering toward the edge of camp with the two men. I surveyed the spread of fires and milling raiders, then looked past them to the snaking belly of the Pasidon River in the light of moon and stars. Nui loped beside me.

Morning would come quickly, full of preparations and organization. There wouldn't be time for goodbyes, so I'd best do it now. A practical farewell, I told myself, no tears or melancholy words.

But when Nisien tugged me into a rough embrace, my resolve shuddered. I held him fiercely in return, burying my cheek in his chest and squeezing until he winced. I didn't care if anyone saw. I might be High Priestess, but I loved as fiercely as anyone else.

"I can't breathe," Nisien protested.

I let him go, but reached up to tug on his beard. "Don't you dare shave this and turn Arpa while you're away."

He batted my hand away. "I'll grow it back before I see you again."

I looked at Estavius, who offered me a small, reticent smile. "I'll look after him."

"I know." I took Estavius's forearm in a firm grip and squeezed. I added, "What do you think of Castor? Honestly?"

Estavius hesitated, then let out a short breath. "I do not know. I thought he must have died at the White Lake, but he did not. Be cautious with him, Hessa."

"Does he know you're a Miri?" Nisien asked. "If he survived the battle…"

"He might know and just not remember," I pointed out. "That scar was no common wound."

"Well, if he knows, or remembers, he'll tell Bresius." Nisien scowled. "What will *he* do?"

"Consider me a threat, fear we are going to betray him, any number of things," Estavius returned. "I hope he will just assume that I'm back in the Empire to reassert myself as a deity, and I may have to play into that. Hessa, let me know if Castor acts suspiciously, but keep your focus on your own task. Leave this to us."

I nodded—he was right, and there was no point in worrying myself. Still, I asked, "Don't you already have enough on your shoulders?"

Nisien shrugged. "Only running errands for Thvynder."

Estavius frowned at him. "Errands?"

"Important errands. Including investigating the other would-be emperors," Nisien said to me, "Cassius and Eolus."

Estavius gave a small, exasperated sound.

"I'm not supposed to talk about it, though," Nisien explained.

"Investigating Cassius, who is holed up in Apharnum?" I clarified, staring between the two of them. "How will you investigate a man inside a besieged city?"

"Eolus is first on the list," Nisien amended, picking at his short nails and ignoring a second, quelling look from Estavius. "He was in Apharnum, too, but no one's seen him in some time, so the assumption is that he fled north."

"He's allied with the Laru," I reminded them. "You'll be careful."

"No, we'll be wildly reckless," Nisien tossed back at me, but his eyes were soft. "We'll be fine. We've spent a decade hunting demons and fell beasts, I'm not sure how you could possibly worry about us anymore."

"I know how easy it is to lose people I love," I retorted, taken by a moment of self-pity. "All I'll have once you're gone is Sillo and Nui."

"Briel," Nisien reminded me.

"Only until we're over the mountains," I corrected. "Then the Vynder guard will go south with Castor and she'll stay with the raiders."

"You still have Imnir," Estavius said, but gave an apologetic wince when Nisien scoffed and I frowned towards the river.

The men followed my gaze after a quiet moment, watching the dark water wend past. The wind tugged at our hair and clothes and the sounds of the camp drifted to us—still all song and boisterous shouts, even this late into the night.

After a few minutes of staring at the water, I regained my composure.

"There's so much at stake," I finally said. "And we've so little understanding of it all. I don't even know what I'll do. Will I crown a new emperor, or slit his throat?"

"We'll be there, at the end," Estavius replied. "Whatever the end may be."

I smiled at them. I wasn't completely free of melancholy, but I had a hold on myself now. "Then I'll see you at the end, my friends."

Nisien reached out to pull me gruffly into his side again. He ground his beard into my hair until I laughed and smacked him away, and Estavius watched us with a half-smile. His pale eyes were sadder than I expected and, if I'd been less distracted by swatting Nisien, I might have wondered why.

"At the end," he vowed.

FIVE

Fog wafted across my face. It condensed on my clothes and weapons, tickled my nose and glistened off the wildflowers beneath my boots.

Far ahead, through an occasional tear in the miasma, I glimpsed our destination—a Nivari border fort of stockade walls and four watchtowers, built on a rocky rise in the center of a marshy pass between the mountains of Nivarium and Souldern. Reeds swayed against a backdrop of slate-gray mountainsides, brushed with muted greens and reds in the evening light.

Half-completed ditches and piles of earth covered the area before the fort. Castor had informed us that this outpost, along with a dozen others like it on the Nivari-Soulderni border, had been built during a hard, cold winter. The fortifications were incomplete, and only two hundred legionaries were garrisoned within.

It should be an easy fight—take the fort, sweep through the pass, and cross into Nivarium by sunrise. But this was our first conflict of the season, and my blood thrummed in my veins.

My shoulder brushed Sillo's as I crouched, bracing my round shield on the ground and scanning the murk ahead. His eyes smudged with black, Sillo flashed me a determined smile. He was ready.

In the grass ahead of us, down a land bridge through the marshes, I made out paths from dozens of feet: Imnir and his Algatt scouts, sent off twenty minutes ago.

I listened for sounds of the Algatt being discovered, but I heard only the lap of water and the shuffle of the army at my back; four thousand shields and axes, ready to break the Nivari border like a river through a dam.

An Algatt horn broke through the violet dusk, long, deep, and winding into a sharp crack. My ears pricked and I held my breath. A short blast followed the first, then a longer one. The retreat.

I dug in my heel and sunk lower, lifting my shield. I braced Gammler against the rim while Galger remained strapped in a brace across my back, her engravings glinting over my shoulder.

The presence of the axes consoled me more than I cared to admit, and it wasn't just because the sight of them made the Eangen's eyes glitter with pride, or the Algatt glower. With these blades in my hands, my old and new lives merged; the weapons of the fallen Eang and the power of the undying, faceless Thvynder.

Nui slipped past my legs. I resisted the urge to snatch after her and maintained position, watching the hound bound out of sight.

Sillo glanced over. "You should have left her in Eangen."

"I should have left you in Eangen," I retorted, and gave him a feral, if practiced, grin. "Now hush. Nui can take care of herself."

The Algatt horn sounded again, so close I jumped. At the same time a bell began to clang, deep and rippling through the fog. The fort was coming to arms.

Briel cast me a prompting look and hefted her shield. Her movement brought the rest of the warriors into a line, shields locking.

Footsteps thundered up ahead and the fog began to shift. Someone screamed, far off in the marsh, and Nui flashed through the reeds with a bark that made me wince.

Sillo cut me an *I-told-you-so* look.

The Algatt burst into sight in a thundering, bloody horde.

All sound faded. I was a girl again, shield locked with my fellow Eangi, facing Algatt raiders in the wilds of the Eangen north.

But this time, our wall divided before them. I glimpsed Imnir's face, laughing and streaked with sweat as the Algatt flowed through the shield wall and took up the back lines, gasping for breath.

More footfalls came, seconds behind them. The shield wall snapped closed and Sillo began to hum a low, steady note.

I exhaled, emptying my lungs and settling into my bones. Then I dragged in a new breath and began a full-throated cry. Down the line, more voices joined in. Each had their note, discordant and eerie, simultaneously drifting and driving through the mist.

I transitioned my cry into a cracking howl as Arpa legionaries stumbled into sight. The foremost Arpa slipped in panic, crashing to the ground in a mess of shield and spear while his comrades skidded behind him.

Just as the Eangen war cry began to fade, the Algatt one rose. Undulating and punctuated with yips, it surrounded us; both beside us and in the marshes, right beside the Arpa. The hair on the back of my neck rose.

Legionaries shouted. Arrows burst from the reeds. They hammered the Arpa like rain, dropping men even as they frantically began to form up, lifting shields and converging under the shouts of a commander.

I broke the line. For an instant I stood alone beyond the wall, only my lynx-painted shield between me and the staggering, shouting Arpa. Then Sillo was there, beating his shield and bellowing like an angry bear. Briel raised her horn and blew. Four thousand warriors flooded forward.

The first line slammed into the Arpa. I bounced back, drove in a heel and threw up my shield just as a spear darted for my face. Briel and Sillo closed their shields before mine and I moved low, hacking Gammler across the ankles of the offending Arpa, hooking one and sending its owner down in a crash of armor and weapons.

The gap he'd left instantly closed. A sword stabbed out, missing me by a breath. Briel knocked the weapon down with her own sword and shoved her shield through the gap, slamming her body into it like a lever.

Wood strained, Arpa shouted and bodies jostled into my back.

Then the Arpa shield wall fractured. Briel slipped into the gap, shield-first, and I hurled myself after her, fallen arrows cracking beneath my feet.

The world took on a blunt, fractured quality. Gammler's pointed heel punctured armor. The blade arced. Men fell and the smell of mud, blood, metal, and bodies pressed in on me, thick and sickly and profoundly familiar.

And a dormant part of me awoke. She snaked through my veins and burst through my skull, blood-hot and sharp as iron. There was no fear in her, no hesitation, no hunger or anger. She simply moved, hacking and blocking and bracing her way through the melee as night thickened, the fog turned cold, and her eyes stung with sweat.

The Arpa retreated towards the fort, fighting every step of the way. We followed, fog swirling and parting with the movement of our bodies. An Eangen next to me slipped; I slammed Gammler into her opponent's face and pulled her upright. I cracked the axe free and turned. Sillo took a blow from a shield rim and I dropped his attacker with a slash across the knees.

The Arpa broke, thundering through the fort's main gate as archers assembled on the walls.

Briel's horn blasted. I looked back to see my war chief standing on a rock, out of bow-shot and girded by reeds. She tucked one hand into her horn's mouth, changing the cry into a distinct, fluttering signal.

I threw up my shield at the same time as a thousand others in a unified clatter of wood and hide and iron. Arpa arrows thudded into wood and flesh, but Briel had already adjusted her signal.

Shields locked into a roof, we surged towards the wall.

I slammed into the fortifications with my shield flat over my head, pressing myself against rows of hastily hewn trunks as arrows whisked and thrummed down behind me. Bits of peeling bark snagged on my clothes and the scent of mud and pine filled my nose.

Sillo hit the wood next to me, two arrows protruding from his shield. With a hack of his axe he broke them off and snapped the barrier back up.

He met my gaze with a prompting grin. "Ready, cousin?"

Briel's signal changed a third time. Our archers, hidden back in the fog, loosed a volley of high, flaming arrows. They tore through the fog in hollow ripples of sound and light and, through a crack between Sillo's and my shields, I watched them vanish over the ramparts.

"Now!" I bellowed, dropping my own shield and taking Gammler in two hands.

Sillo crouched, flattening his shield into a platform at the same time as, all down the walls, dozens of others did the same. More flaming Eangen and Algatt arrows soared over us as the Arpa bellowed, my raiders roared, and I leapt.

I only stood on Sillo's shield for a moment before he thrust up. I jumped again, hooking Gammler's head between the pointed tips of the stockade wall. Then I was climbing up the haft, hauling myself over the wall and jumping onto the platform on the other side.

I nearly toppled right off. The platform was narrower than I expected, dropping within a pace into the belly of the fort—a belly full of massing legionaries, blurs of tunic-clad servants, a scattering of torches and flaming Eangen arrows.

I noted all this within a heartbeat. More Eangen and Algatt followed me over the wall, tumbling and leaping into place via axes and anchors.

The Arpa archers already occupying the walls turned, abandoning bows for short swords under the command of a captain with a plumed helmet.

I knocked the nearest archer off the wall with a punch of Gammler's heel and turned on the next. He swung his nocked arrow towards me and drew, but I was already sliding between him and the wall, kicking him after his comrade into the melee of the fort below.

My raiders and I followed them down, sliding down ladders and converging on the gate—the bulk of us forming a defensive wall with commandeered shields, while the rest threw off the gate's braces. The barrier itself was already buckling and splintering under the assault of axes and hammers from the other side.

Then, all at once, it was over. My horde burst through the gate, the Arpa's shouts turned to panic, and the glint of fine Arpa plate armor was overwhelmed by a roiling mass of painted faces, muddy mail, and blood-darkened axe-heads.

I returned to myself, panting and sweating under the shadow of the ramparts. There were no more enemies beside me, no more bloody threats or flashing swords. I took a second to lean against the wall and watched my warriors drag the remaining legionaries into a clutch in the center of the fort.

I shook the tension from my shoulders. Beneath my sweating skin and fatigued muscles, my heart hammered far too fast and my lungs burned for breath. There were too many bodies in the fort, underfoot and blank-eyed, too much blood and shouting.

Briel slowed as she passed me, jogging through the gate. "I saw Nui go into the marshes," she called. She saw the expression on my face and added with narrowed eyes, "Go. Get some air. I've got this."

I peeled myself off the wall. "Sillo's right. I should have left that dog at home."

Briel shrugged and went on her way, shouting for the fort's commander to be brought to her.

I ducked through the battered gates as the fort's bell rang out. This time it was no urgent, clear peel from the western watchtower—this was a jarring cacophony of clatters and clangs, my raiders beating its waist with their weapons. The sound harried me as I returned to a night of drifting fog and dwindling conflict. Many warriors were still out here, setting up a perimeter, tracking down remaining legionaries and assisting the wounded. I glanced around for Imnir, but didn't see him. Instead, I saw Sillo hauling a young woman to her feet, and an Algatt fishing a spear from the marsh.

At the edge of the reeds, I stopped and whistled. Nui didn't appear, but someone had organized the lighting of torches. Light bloomed throughout the fog and reeds, golden orbs pushing back the mist and throwing the bodies into stark relief.

One such body lay on the ground nearby, half in the water. Gaps between his armor welled with blood and his breaths came in shallow, panicked wheezes. His lower body was contorted—spine twisted, legs limp—in a way that told me, should he survive, he would never walk again.

Not entirely conscious of what I was doing, I put Gammler's blade to his throat. I meant to let it sink into the tender flesh beneath his jaw—not so much a mercy, but a practicality. If he wasn't fit to run, carrying word—and fear—of our victory to his people, we had no use for him.

Still, my arm wouldn't move. The Arpa gasped up at me, eyes bulging white against a face so smeared with mud and blood that I couldn't discern his age. But his fear, that was young—boyish and bewildered.

What did his age matter? Nothing mattered, not when this man's supposed gods were dead. If Arpa souls were anything like Eangen, his would lie trapped in the bloody muck of this marsh until the end of time, unless someone released him and guided him to the Arpa's afterlife—which I wasn't even sure existed anymore.

That thought truly chilled me. Killing was something I'd long hardened myself to, but I'd always done so with the knowledge that death was not the end of existence. Frir and her servants came for the souls of all Northerners.

But this Arpa? What would happen to him?

"Should I do it, or will you leave him for one of your Iskiri to torment?"

Imnir watched me from deeper in the marsh, every line of his body written with exhaustion. He dragged his blood-clotted fringe from his forehead and approached, accompanied by a splash of water and the rustle of parting reeds.

I hesitated, then stepped back from the dying man and waved for Imnir to go ahead. My concession surprised him. He paused over the Arpa, but when I still didn't intervene, he set the tip of a sword at the man's throat and flicked.

Slowly, life seeped from the Arpa's veins. I watched his face for another moment, observed the pain and confusion turn to a kind of startled relief.

"Are you hurt?" Imnir asked, sounding more perplexed than concerned. However the battle around him had played out, whatever had transpired in the minutes since I'd seen him laughing and sprinting through our shield wall, it had left him sour.

"No," I said, letting my chin sink into a slow shake. "I was thinking of the dead. You served Frir. Do you know what happens to Arpa souls?"

Imnir rubbed at his beard with the back of one hand, still holding the sword. "I never asked. I didn't care. I still don't."

My lips pressed together, simultaneously embarrassed and annoyed. "You and I are priests of the only real God in this world," I pointed out. "If we don't care, if we don't ask, no one will. We and the Miri are the only ones who *can* release them."

"The Arpa aren't our responsibility." Imnir pointed his sword out into the fog, sweat-soaked, bloody hair in his eyes. "I know some of my people are dead out there, and I'll go tend them now. Will you see to the Eangen, or must I do that for you too?"

A sharp retort leapt onto my tongue, but I held it back. Imnir was often gruff, but this was more than that.

I glanced behind him, back in the direction that he'd come. "Did something happen?"

The question made him catch himself. His expression was still stormy, but he directed its force away from me, looking out across the battlefield towards the fort. Sniffing, he raked his hair out of his eyes and gave me a flat smile. "I hate being muddy. And I'm sick of death."

With that he strode off into the fog, stomping mud off his boots and taking a torch from an Algatt woman.

I let him go, wrinkling my nose and calming my angry heart. Imnir might be in a foul mood, but his sentiment was one I could sympathize with. He'd apologize eventually, and for now, I needed to think of the Eangen dead.

I whistled for Nui one last time and started to follow Imnir, but my eyes caught on the Arpa corpse. I could feel his soul now, I realized. Upon his death it had settled in the earth beneath my feet, still dazed, still relieved. But I knew it would not last long. Soon, he would cry out for release. And no one would heed him.

I focused on the world around me once more. Eangen, Soulderni, and Algatt moved across the battlefield, tending to the wounded and stripping bodies of armor and weapons. I forced a last thought of the dead legionary from my mind and made for a dead Eangen woman, crumpled on the moist earth against a backdrop of brooding, night-draped mountain.

I'd known my people would die in this venture, but that didn't make this easier, or my anger at myself any softer. I should have been with this woman as she passed on. Not looking for a dog—and certainly not with that legionary.

I fumbled Gammler back into the brace across my back, set my shield aside and dropped into a crouch. The woman's close-set eyes were cracked, as if she had perished in the middle of closing them. One of her hands was buried in the bloody bowl of her stomach while the other still reached for a spear.

Beneath the earth, I felt her soul settling, as quiet and stunned as the legionary's. I reached out to close the eyelids of her corpse, already piecing together the final rites in my mind.

"Sister, sister…" I began.

Golden Sight flashed over my eyes, unexpected and bright. Another hand came into focus, already resting on the woman's cheek in consolation. It was small, a child's, but so pale that it could never have seen the light of day.

I scrambled back with a strangled cry. He couldn't have been over three or four years old, but the child's eyes were far, far too intelligent for his age.

For a stuttering heartbeat, my mind scrambled to rationalize a child's presence on the battlefield—for this was no vision. He surveyed me wordlessly, his hair Algatt pale. His skin was ghostly, but he was flesh and blood and present—until I eased my hold of my Sight. Then he vanished.

It was his eyes that truly unnerved me, though, cedar-green and rimmed with the tell-tale amber traces of the High Halls. This child was not alive, nor was he a resident of this world. His tiny, booted feet did not even bend the grass.

"Son of Frir." I bowed my head.

"Go on, give her the rites." The voice came not from the child, but from a woman. I stood as she emerged from the marsh in the same direction Imnir had come, clad in a long robe of dark linen. The V of its neckline fell nearly to her navel, revealing a spire of tattoos up the center of her chest. I recognized those tattoos—they were the same that covered Imnir's forearms. A woven belt wrapped about her waist, hung with a pouch and a knife with a bleached bone handle.

Her hair was thick and black, cascading over one shoulder in a series of knots and loose braid. Her eyes were large and deep-set, nearly necrotic, but creased with lines of kindness, and the whole of her frame radiated the amber-gold of the High Halls.

This was Frir, the Shrouded Lady, the Shepherd of Souls; former Goddess of Death.

Sister of Eang.

SIX

I leveled my chin at the sister of the goddess I'd betrayed and murdered.

The child, one of her servants—those who died before birth, adopted to the breast of the Shrouded Lady and given enough life in death to age a handful of years—looked between the two of us in silence.

Frir was here, in person? I'd only a second to wonder if she was the reason Imnir had lingered in the marsh before my Sight flashed gold again. I searched the night for other unnatural guests and a dozen more children flickered into view, moving among the dead and casting eerie glances towards the woman they called Mother.

Frir stopped across from me. She rested her fingers lightly on the child's head, and he drew away from the deceased. He nuzzled into the Miri's skirts and continued to survey me from behind a fold.

Even now, my instincts screamed to fall to my knees before Frir and grovel. But Thvynder's unseen hand was like a stake in my spine. This was no goddess. Frir was like Gadr and Estavius, dangerous and deserving of respect, but not worship. The same magic flowed in both our veins.

I crouched, overly conscious of Frir's scrutiny, to dip my finger in the dead woman's cooling blood. I used it to draw a rune on her forehead and offered a soft prayer to Thvynder.

Towards the end of my prayer, Frir stooped and picked up the child. He leaned into her breasts in a perfect image of mother and son, thumb stuck in his mouth and tiny fingers fanned out across his pale cheeks.

Something in my heart twisted, old and aching and lonely—and unnerved. Whose child had this been, lost before he took his first breath?

My words faded and I stood back, conceding the body to Frir. She beckoned in its direction and, before my gold-hazed eyes, the Eangen woman's soul slipped from the earth. Her departure from the corpse and the earth beneath it was a duplication, her living aspect departing her dying one, though neither was ethereal. She was wholly herself, if pale, and, if I did not look at her straight on, imperceptible.

A bark drifted to me through the marsh. Nui, finally returned. I suppressed a flare of irritation, keeping my focus on Frir and the boy.

"I can still smell her on you," Frir said. Her voice was hushed and effortlessly soothing, but I didn't miss the edge beneath it.

I stepped away, distancing myself as much as I could without being too obvious. "What?"

"My sister." Frir shifted the child. The dead Eangen woman stood next to her now, dazed and quiet, blinking down at her own body with a shaking hand over her mouth. "Gods below… you even look like her. With those."

My shoulders clenched, newly conscious of Galger and Gammler framing my face.

Frir's eyes remained on me, but I couldn't read her expression. "You smell of my sister and you lie with my priest. How much you have cheated me of, little Eangi."

Her use of my former title chilled me almost as much as the possessiveness in her words, and they far less than her tone. It was level and deadly, economic in its threat.

And I felt it in my bones. I stiffened and stared at the Miri as I felt a sudden, unnatural pull. It was a sensation like falling asleep, of floating halfway between my physical body and a second, disconnected existence—but this was more aggressive, more insidious, and dreadfully cold.

Frir was pulling my soul towards her, her lips twitching in a subtle sneer. All the while, she held my gaze, as if daring me to resist.

I responded with a snap of golden magic. Her hold eased, a rope beginning to fray before breaking altogether. My soul surged back into my bones and I staggered in shock and horror.

Why had Frir done that? She bowed to Thvynder, but attacked his High Priestess? I could understand her anger over the death of Eang, but her behavior was rash and reckless. And what right did she have to be jealous of my relationship with Imnir?

"It was worth a try," Frir murmured, as if that justified her attack. Without a hint of remorse, she reached out to take the hand of the newly deceased woman. The dead took it with detachment. "Now come, my loves. The High Halls await."

My throat tightened. I could confront her, demand an explanation and ask why she'd been in the marsh with my husband, why she was so possessive of him. But I was too shocked and angry, and besides, her expression brooked no questions.

I had one last glimpse of the little boy, staring back at me over the Shrouded Lady's shoulder, then the three of them were gone. My golden Sight faded, the world regained its normal hues. Eangen and Algatt voices swelled, hurrying between tasks and gathering casualties.

I stifled a gasp as Nui barreled into my legs in chaotic greeting. Relieved and unsettled, I crouched, clutching her to my chest and letting the musty, wet stink of dog and marsh anchor me.

"Stupid dog," I murmured, kissing the top of her head.

"What was that?" Castor approached, filling the space the Shrouded Lady had left with a different brand of uncertainty.

"You saw her?" I asked. I stayed crouching beside Nui, who tucked her ears back as the man approached.

"I saw you talking to someone I couldn't see," my old enemy returned, stopping a few paces away and resting one hand on the round, wooden pommel of his Arpa sword. He was clean and untouched by battle, having stayed back with the supplies. "Was it the dead woman? Can you see souls like your husband?"

I stood up, more than a little relieved to look at him instead of the corpse at my feet. Nui remained at my side, tail thumping against my thigh.

"I can see many things," I said evasively. "But yes, I saw the woman's spirit."

"Mm." His eyes were curious, but he didn't press.

"What of the Arpa souls?" I asked. "Who will tend them?"

Castor shrugged, unsheathing his sword an fraction and driving it home again in thought—or abstract warning. "There are cults that claim to be able to release the souls of our dead, but I don't know if that is true. Much has fallen aside in the last decade, Priestess. The Arpa suffer without their gods."

I detected something real in his voice then, raw and human. I watched him carefully, but didn't interrupt.

"Once a new emperor is on the throne, he will restore order," Castor concluded. His eyes lingered on the butchered Eangen, then he wrinkled his nose. "Until then, it's not my concern. I'll leave you to your dead. Will your war chief let me question the prisoners? Presuming they haven't killed them all yet."

I nodded. "Tell her I sent you."

He moved off without another word. Beckoning Nui, I soberly made my way to the next body, and the next. But even when dawn came, when we left the blazing remains of the fort behind, the mist cleared, and the sun shone upon us, I couldn't forget a pair of innocent eyes, watching me over the shoulder of the dethroned Goddess of Death. And I could not forget the feeling of my own soul, prying itself from my bones.

I trudged east at the head of the lines with Briel as the broad, marshy pass narrowed between the mountains and ascended. The incline wasn't steep and my pack was with my horse at the rear of the train, but I was tired and troubled by the night's events.

I surveyed the rocky, scrub-strewn Arpa road ahead of us and hoped we'd reach the top before the warm morning sun baked us into its smooth, time-worn cobbles. But the markers that lined its way seemed irrationally far apart, accentuating our weary progress.

"Priestess." Castor arrived with a clatter of hooves. "I need to speak with you."

I joined him on the scrubby shoulder of the road as Briel and the others continued. Castor watched them, obviously agitated by their progress.

"What is it?" I asked. "What's wrong?"

"I interrogated the fort's commander before his demise," he replied, eyes flicking along the road and back to me. "Ride with me, we need to reach the top first. Tell your men—people—to wait."

I bristled. "Why?"

He offered me an arm. "I'm your ally, Priestess. Trust me. You need to see this before anyone else."

Trust was certainly not something I ever intended to give him, but I accepted his arm. He shifted his foot out of the stirrup and I used it to leap up onto the horse's flanks, leaving the wooden back of his saddle between us. The horse shuffled unhappily, but began to move at a click of Castor's tongue.

"Hold up the lines," I called back to Briel as we broke into a trot. She and everyone else in sight stared at the two of us. "I'll signal when you can proceed."

Briel's horn sang out as Castor and I passed the forward scouts and separated from the rocky crags that girded the road. Exposed to the cool mountain breeze and the blinding morning sun, I threw up an arm and squinted.

Castor reined in the horse on a broad, flat lookout of sunbaked stone and stubborn alpine grass. Before us lay the Arpa province of Nivarium.

Mountains stretched to the north and south in a string of rocky heights, swaths of forest, and glistening lakes. The mountains gradually rippled down into a high plateau, which ended a few days' ride east in a long cliff. This in turn dropped off into the Nivari lowlands, where lush farmland, endless marshes, and low, forested islands stretched to the distant eastern sea.

It was a breathtaking sight, familiar from last year's foray, but this time something was different.

Nivarium was dying. Stark stretches of tree-clad mountainside stood out orange and gray against shocks of desperate, rare green. The marshy lowlands, which should have been a rippling sea of green reeds, elevated fields, and sprawling villages, were now scarred with great ribbons of death—gray, lifeless vegetation, flattened by the wind. Many of the visible villages sent no hearthsmoke into the sky, and wildfires had turned stretches of once verdant forest to ominous scars of black. Part of the plateau to the south had even collapsed, forming a great, crumbling half-moon of rock.

We stood at a turning point in the landscape; to the north, the desolation eased, yielding stretches of true, healthy green forest and marsh and field. Smoke from inhabited villages smudged the horizon and, when the wind turned, I caught the scent of summer, of life and promise. But the further south I looked, the more severe the damage was. The wind from that direction smelled like char and emptiness, and it felt like the hot breath of some great beast on my cheeks.

I slipped down from the horse and walked to the edge of the lookout, where the Arpa road meandered into a switchback down to the plateau.

"Has there been a drought?" I asked Castor, though my instincts told me this was no natural phenomenon.

He dismounted after me, taking the reins in one distracted hand.

"No." He drew up and surveyed the vista. "The commander said this began last autumn, before the snow fell. Crops failed. Forests died. Not everywhere—he said it's better in the north, so there's still plenty pillaging to be had. But the further south we go, the more we will see of this. The Laru claim it's punishment from their god for not resisting the barbarian invaders. The land is dying."

"The land, but not the people?" I asked, my gaze still trapped by the desolation.

Castor nodded slowly. "Not the people, nor animals. At least not directly, though hunger will be a challenge this winter. Just the vegetation seems to be affected."

I was quiet for a long moment. "How could the Laru god do this? The priest I met was powerful, but this is— This is something else entirely."

"I don't know. You're the priestess. I'm a soldier."

My breath came out in a hiss. "Your emperor brought my people here to raid, Castor. I can't send them into *that*, not when we've no idea what the Laru are doing or how they're doing it."

Castor's grimness retreated and his eyebrows rose. "I've no answers for you."

I thought of the army behind us, four thousand souls who'd given themselves to this cause. Who trusted me to lead them.

"I can't leave my people alone in a land like this," I said. "Not until I know what the Laru are doing."

"I showed you this so that you could prepare your people, not for you to abandon your oath on the Nivari border," Castor said, his voice hardening. "The Laru are punishing the Nivari, as they claimed. Besides, isn't that creature Gadr accompanying your people? And more of your Vynder? Surely they're competent enough to protect themselves, if need be."

He wasn't wrong; Gadr was irritating but powerful, and my Vynder could be trusted. But that did not lift the weight of responsibility from my shoulders. I was still their High Priestess.

I stared at the gray marshes of the lowlands. I was on an open ridgeline, armed and free, but I felt snared. Finding Nivarium like this was like happening across an unexpected corpse in the brush, ominous and repulsive. My eyes dragged south, marking the increase in the devastation, and my anxiety redoubled.

"We'll travel with the horde down to the plateau," I reminded Castor after a quiet stretch. "I'll learn what I can, and if I'm satisfied, we can separate and go on our way as planned."

Castor considered this, then nodded. "I suppose there's time for that. Perhaps you can even stop whatever it is?"

I expected some jibe or snide edge to his suggestion, but there wasn't one. He was genuinely asking, calculation in his blue eyes. His deference unsettled me as much as when I'd seen him back at the Ilia Gates and realized he remembered none of the strife between us.

Again, it left me feeling deflated, and unsure where I stood. Could I resent someone for crimes they didn't recall committing? Could I push past what he used to be and open myself up to the possibility that he was someone else, now?

"I know Bresius would approve if you did," the Arpa continued. "He hardly wants to inherit spoiled land, and you are the Curse Breaker."

"I'll see," I tempered. Then I added, as if testing the words, "Thank you for showing me this first."

His calculation retreated into fine lines about his eyes as he gave a half-smile and ducked his chin. "Of course, High Priestess."

SEVEN

That evening we swept over a village, letting the villagers flee through cursed forests and dead fields. They'd carry word of barbarian invaders throughout the Nivari highlands, laying the foundation for our summer of raids and stirring up the fear we wanted to precede us.

But as I stood outside the low walls and surveyed a devasted forest to the east, that outcome felt more and more uncertain.

We camped around the empty village as the following day dawned, keeping our tents and cookfires to the north and west side, where green trees still spread their lofty bows and fields clung to life. Vynder stood watch and there was a forced good humor about the camp, though I saw the glances my people cast to the death in the south and east. I heard mutters of dissent, and saw the unease in the faces of our scouts as they came and went.

"I don't want to send them into this," I murmured to Briel as we stood together, later that day. The field before us was spoiled, rows of sprouted barley gray and rattling in the breeze.

Briel finished drinking from a flask and passed it to me, wiping droplets of water from her lips. "We'll head north, not south. It doesn't look so bad up there."

"Still," I said between distracted sips. "I hate the thought of leaving you."

Briel took her flask back and fixed the cap, then tapped me on the arm with it in mock rebuke. "What, Gadr and I aren't good enough to look after your flock?"

I tried to smile, but couldn't quite manage it. "That's not it."

"Well," Briel nodded over my shoulder, towards Imnir, Castor, and Gadr heading in our direction, "then go investigate, Hess."

I descended a rocky slope with the three men in tow. Nui bounded ahead into a desolate swath of orange pines as my boots skidded through deadfall and loose rock.

I slowed, finding my balance without touching the affected wood.

Every tree here was dead. Every needle still on the branch had turned ochre, and the layer of new deadfall around my boots was thick. No other life pried its way up from beneath this blanket, no saplings or mushrooms or moss or ferns. No lichen crept up the trunks of the trees, just scant patches that flaked off along with the bark and desiccated trails of old sap.

I saw no spark of magic, no ashen dust or amber glint. If magic had done this, it was long gone. The only spark of life here was the moths.

They flickered aimlessly through the trees, their wings full of sunlight. I saw scores of them scattered throughout the woods— fluttering, alighting, resting on tree trunks with white and gray wings folded. One fluttered past my face. I gently blew it away.

The crack of a stick made me jump. Gadr had broken a branch off the nearest tree and was peering at the graying wood inside, sniffing.

"No insects, no rot." He threw the branch down and squinted up at the canopy and the moths. "No life at all, except those."

Beyond him, Nui jumped up, snapping at one moth after another. I hastily interceded, bringing the dog to heel and holding her head against my thigh. She whined.

"We don't eat mysterious moths in cursed forests," I chided.

She whined again, and I proceeded to ignore her.

"I've never seen anything like this," my husband said. He stood on a relatively clean section of rock above us, keeping his boots from the spoiled needles of the forest floor. He'd taken the time to wash this morning, and his blond fringe fluttered across his eyes, light and clean.

Castor wandered through the trees nearby, one ear turned toward our conversation.

Gadr blew out his cheeks. "Bah, I can't say I have, either. But it's obvious what's happened."

I looked at him, perplexed. "It is?"

"Life-magic." Gadr pointed to the exposed, gray inner wood where he'd broken the branch off the tree. "It runs through everything, even death—insects, rot. But that's gone here. It's left this section of the forest entirely."

The back of my neck prickled. "That's possible?"

"Obviously it is." Castor absently brushed a wayward moth from his tunic, his tone imperious. "The evidence is right before us. Larun, it seems, can affect life-magic."

Ah, there was the old Castor.

"Larun?" I asked. "Is that the god's name?"

He nodded, watching the moth flutter away. "Yes, that's what the Nivari are calling them."

I flicked my gaze to Imnir and found him already watching me. He knew what I was about to ask him. "Would Frir know anything about this?"

Imnir shook his head. "She would have warned me if she did."

A sly grin tipped onto Gadr's face. He looked Imnir over, head to toe. "Yes, she would, wouldn't she? What was it you did again, to make that hag like you so? It certainly wasn't your looks that got her."

Discomforted by Gadr's implication, I crossed my arms over my chest. Imnir didn't look at the Miri, but a hint of color crept up his neck. I couldn't tell whether it was from anger or embarrassment.

As much as I wanted to know more about Frir and my husband and whatever Gadr meant, now wasn't the time. "I meant you could ask Frir now."

"I can do that," Imnir said. "But she's probably back North. I'll have to send an owl, and the reply may take some time."

"Fine," Gadr said, waving another errant moth away from his face. It lost balance in the disrupted currents of air and plunged towards my trousers.

Unnerved, I brushed it off. It toppled to earth, where it struggled on its back among the pine needles and twigs. "Gadr, if Larun is doing this, where could his power come from?"

"Power comes from many places." Gadr shrugged, philosophical. "Many beings left the High Halls. They rut and breed and pass on their abilities. Some is natural. Some comes from ritual. And some power can be... acquired. Or stolen."

The Miri gave me a pointed look, which Castor noted with curiosity. I kept my expression a stoic mask. Only Imnir, Nisien, the Miri, and Thvynder knew that I'd taken my magic from the High Halls. Even my Vynder priests and priestesses didn't know their power came from the honey and water that I harvested there, and not a direct, divine hand.

"So you don't know," I summarized.

Gadr shrugged. "No."

"Well then," I looked between the men, "all we know is that someone, likely the Laru's god, purged the life-magic from sections of Nivarium. Is this going to hurt my people?"

We fell silent, each to their thoughts, leaving only the creak of dead timber and the soft rustle of parched needles falling through the sunlight. One brushed at my cheek as it fell, and I swiped at my face with a disgruntled hand. The longer my boots rested on this dead land, the more I was inclined to think it wouldn't outright harm us, but that didn't mean I felt at ease.

"I don't see how it would," Gadr concluded, kicking at the deadfall. "Whatever happened here is done, and look—I see no bones, no sign that any creatures were caught in this, let alone humans. I say it's fine. I'll keep any eye out for anything abnormal while you go south."

He spoke calmly, and I was inclined to trust him. But I didn't like this, the not knowing, the threat to my people that I couldn't understand. It didn't follow the laws I knew, and that left me feeling a frustrated shade of helpless.

Imnir spoke from the rock shelf above, his boot still well back from the blanket of dead needles. "What are we going to do now?"

"Well, we've got a few more days before we separate from the horde. I'll keep looking for answers." I started climbing back up the hill, passing Imnir. He caught my eye, and the spark of suspicion in his gaze made me smile. "I need to capture a Laru priest."

EIGHT

I crashed into a doorway and hit the floor of the Arpa home with a thud. Galger clattered away. My arm hit the leg of a table as I rolled under it, scrambling to pull my limbs in after me.

A flash of plate armor. Half a dozen shadows following me through the doorway, interrupting the daylight in flashes, and shouts in Arpa. A sword hit the table with a crack.

I was already out the other side, snatching up my fallen axe and twisting its haft with both hands to deflect a deft cut. I followed the movement with a thrust of my own, driving the tip of Galger's blade into the neck of the nearest legionary. He staggered and I ducked right, avoiding a flashing spearhead and casting a desperate glance around the house.

It was long and nearly windowless. Wooden walls hung with herbs, clothing, and family talismans penned me in. But there was another door at the far end, past a clutch of terrified Arpa villagers in their night clothes.

I leapt a fallen stool and barreled out the door. The legionaries gave chase, shouts and pounding boots harrying me into a hazy pink dawn.

Chickens scattered. I darted left, skidding in the mud around another house and back into the main street of the village with my heart hammering in my ears.

The chaos of battle swallowed me, Eangen, and Algatt, and Soulderni running and fighting and ducking. I avoided a knot of combatants and paused for the barest second in the mouth of an alleyway, trying and failing to catch my breath.

Only minutes ago, my small raiding party had broken over the village. It had been serene in the half-light of dawn, surrounded by a palisade wall, lush, living farmland, and sweet-smelling fruit trees that rustled in the breeze. There'd been no sign that this village, unlike the last we'd taken, would harbor a detachment of legionaries.

No sooner had we scaled the wall then a hundred Arpa soldiers emerged from the houses, barring the gates and trapping us in the town. There was no time for fury, regret, or berating scouts—we fought for our lives.

Raiders and legionaries burst across the mouth of the alleyway I stood in, and two enemies caught sight of me. Instantly, they charged. I blocked a blow and cut a legionary's knees out from under him, snapping the axe back to puncture another man's thigh.

They dropped, and I backed up. The main battle careened on down the street, but I'd won another second of reprieve. I dragged stinging sweat from my eyes—the morning was already hot and moist—and searched rapidly for Sillo, Briel, or any other Vynder in my vicinity.

I heard Briel's horn, high and demanding. Gathering my strength, I started toward her, weaving deeper into the warren of pathways.

A wall of legionaries closed in front of me. My heart slammed into my chest and I tried to divert, but there were more coming up the next path, stepping over a dead Algatt woman.

I braced, putting my back to the wall of the nearest house and facing down four long spears. The world shrank to my rattling breath, Galger, the glint of the Arpas' pale eyes beneath their helmets. Tactics flicked through my head, but four spears, no room to move—this was bad. Very bad.

One of the legionaries toppled, revealing Imnir. He met my startled gaze before he slashed at a second legionary and threw the man down.

My muscles reawakened. I knocked a spear out of the way and darted toward my husband, slashing a legionary's throat as I went. Imnir dispatched the last and threw an arm around my back, shielding me as we sprinted out of the alley and back onto the main path.

"Thank you," I panted.

The sound of Briel's war horn drowned out his reply, followed immediately by a second blast—an Algatt horn. Gadr, with reinforcements. By unspoken agreement Imnir and I made for the sounds, running shoulder to shoulder through the streets.

We hit the village's main square just as Gadr and a swarm of howling Algatt plowed into sight. The Miri fought like a hero of old, dispatching legionaries with the ferocity and force known only to the former gods and long-dead Eangi. He wielded a commandeered spear in a blur of weapon and muscle, and the raiders surged in response.

Eangen and Algatt merged, back-to-back, shield to shield. I saw the blending happen in fragments, between cuts and blocks and stolen glances. The Algatt Vynder called Hete saved an Eangen man with a thrust of her shield. An Algatt boy tossed an Eangen one a fallen weapon. Sillo and two Algatt faced off against six legionaries.

We'd fought in concert a dozen times before, on a smaller scale. But today, when our lives were threatened and our lines scattered, we fought together.

Imnir and I joined them, and a handful of minutes after we entered the village, it was over. Villagers and the remaining legionaries escaped through side gates like rats from a burning house.

I broke away from Imnir, stepping over a fallen legionary and rejoining my Eangen Vynder. They'd mustered to Sillo, who stood beside a half-Eangen girl I'd never seen before.

"Is everyone all right?" I called. "Where's Ifling?"

"Here." Lida answered me. I just glimpsed her round-cheeked sister, bloodied and sitting on the ground, before amber flashed through the corner of my vision.

A young man in a robe the color of yarrow and ochre darted out of a house and sprinted for one of the village gates, helpfully thrown open by a bellowing Arpa legionary. The plumes on the legionary's helmet declared him to be a captain, and ensured that as soon as he shouted, he took a red-fletched Soulderni arrow to the throat.

The man in yellow skittered around the captain as he fell, shoving aside a hapless woman and bolting to freedom in a swirl of ashen gray magic.

Other fleeing villagers surged away from him, repelled by an unseen force.

It took me an instant to respond, adrenaline and exhaustion turning my wits to mud, then I gave chase.

"A Laru!" I shouted to Sillo. "With me, now, now! The rest of you, make sure there are no more and warn Imnir!"

Hard-packed earth. Bodies. The gates. I darted around screaming villagers and out into the farmland east of town. Fresh, warm wind struck my face, drying my sweat and conjuring more in the same, thick breath.

The Laru, robes flapping around his churning legs, fled across a field of tufting barley. He caught sight of me barreling towards him and let out a panicked shout. He tried to speed up, but his foot caught on a furrow and he lurched forward.

I spurred myself harder, faster, trying to catch up. Sillo reached my side somewhere in the middle of the field, followed by a second, smaller form. The half-Eangen girl again, with the sheaf of blonde braids bound in a broad leather wrap.

The stumbling Laru caught himself on one hand and changed direction, plunging into a patch of green forest.

Branches lashed me as I followed. Summer woodland rushed into my senses, verdant green, rich deadfall, and clouds of insects. I squinted against the latter, Galger held in two hands and Gammler still in place at my left shoulder.

Sillo passed me, longer legs eating up the ground between him and the Laru. An instant later, he snatched the other man by the robes and threw him into a tree.

"There," Sillo shouted, locking one big hand around our captive's throat and grabbing one of his flailing wrists with the other. He glanced at me as I came to a panting stop a few paces away. "All yours, cousin—"

Laru magic rushed into Sillo's face like a whirlwind, invading his mouth and nose with terrifying force. I cried a warning and lunged just as Sillo reared back, clawing his face and throat as if the magic was a physical thing.

The Laru squirmed free and bolted.

"Sillo, fight it!" I shouted, grabbing at his arm as he collapsed. My cousin sat down hard—he didn't seem to have heard me, or have the presence of mind to utilize his own magic. This was the problem with inhabiting a world where we were the only ones with real power—training and theory were one thing, but being murdered by an inhuman force was entirely another.

The Laru vanished through the trees. I glanced after him in frustration and broke Sillo's thrall with a flick of will. Ashy magic shattered, drifting down to the roots and deadfall.

I waited only long enough for my cousin to start clawing back to his feet, then I took off after our prey.

I thundered across rock and loam and roots. The Laru was a blur of yellow robes and pale hair ahead of me, bursting into full sunlight as the trees ended in a shoulder of gray rock, smoothed by weather and spattered with moss and lichen. The edge of the plateau.

Footsteps approached from behind. I risked a glance back and sighted the girl who'd followed us from the village. She sprinted up behind me with a spear in hand, ducking branches and leaping off a boulder. In seconds, her longer, younger legs had outpaced me.

"Fall back!" I shouted after her. The rock grew steeper, the path between forest and empty sky narrowing. Gods below, had I ever been as fast as her? No, likely not. "Girl!"

She either hadn't heard or ignored me. She charged after the Laru with the steady, leaping gait of a mountain goat. But though she was fast, she was no Vynder. If she caught the Laru it would not go well.

Sillo drew up to my side, disheveled and breathing heavily, but intact.

"Who is that girl?" I asked.

"Uspa," he panted. "She likes me."

The name struck me as familiar, but it wasn't important then. "She's going to get herself killed."

"You might be surprised."

We both cut off as, up ahead, Uspa tackled the Laru. They went down on the open rock in a tumble of limbs and curses and a burst of ashen magic. Power wrapped around the girl's throat like a noose as the Laru rolled free, leaving her arched and scrabbling—right on the edge of the cliff.

Sillo barreled into the enemy priest. I lunged for Uspa, breaking the Laru's hold and dragging her back from the precipice.

I spun back on the young men, sweat-sodden hair stuck across my face. "Sillo, don't kill him!"

My cousin grunted in response, trying to pin the other man to the ground. The Laru's booted foot connected with Sillo's chest and the bigger man reeled, giving just enough space for the Arpa to squirm away.

I stuck out the end of Galger's haft. The Laru tripped in the midst of his lunge for freedom, hitting the stone with an audible crack.

Sudden, unexpected quiet washed over us, backed by the sound of the wind and a distant, irreverent songbird. It sang three descending notes, sweet and melancholy.

The Laru wheezed, coughed, and rolled over with a sobbing moan. Ashen magic shuddered around him, but now that I had a moment to examine it, it was clear that he hadn't half the power of the Laru I'd encountered last year.

I turned Galger about and rested the blunt head of its haft against the soft flesh above his hip bone, blade arcing around his side. At the same time, I extinguished his magic. The remaining dust vanished.

"Don't kill me," he rasped in Arpa. Blond hair stuck to his face with sweat and his cheeks were scarlet with exertion. "Please, please!"

"What's your name?" I asked. Nearby, Sillo helped the half-blood to her feet, murmuring to her. From the way his hands lingered, they were obviously acquainted. Well acquainted.

I frowned, but returned my gaze to the prisoner. He still did not move, but his throat worked until his name emerged like a question: "Odacer?"

"Well, Odacer." My voice hardened as memories of what we'd left at the village, the bodies and the blood, combined with thoughts of the moth-ridden, lifeless forests. I leaned down to look him in the eye. "You're going to tell me about your god."

NINE

I suspended Odacer between two living trees at the edge of our hasty camp. The arms of his robes fanned out, reminiscent of wings as he shuddered and quaked between them.

Castor sidled up. Again he'd spent the battle with the supplies, because, as he'd said, "We can't have the Nivari learning that you're allied with other Arpa, much less Bresius."

He was right, but as I took in his clean clothing and unhurried posture, my jaw tightened. He was a legionary, just like those who'd trapped us today. I wanted to hold him accountable for our dead, for what his fellow soldiers had done.

But no. Castor, for all our history and his Arpa blood, was my ally. I had a task to complete, and the yellow-robed young man was a far better focus for my ire.

I took stance a pace away and slipped Galger to rest in her rings on my back-brace. The motion had taken me weeks to perfect, and the weight of the weapon now settled beside her fellow with ease, framing my head as they used to frame Eang's.

As flawed as my former goddess had been, I pulled at the memory of her now—her deadly gaze, her intensity, and the blood of a thousand battles on her lips. It was a mask I'd often worn since I'd taken the mantle of High Priestess, but the coolness, the weariness of my voice was my own.

"I will not toy with you," I told the Laru.

He stared at me, round cheeks pressed up by his gag. The terror in his face affirmed the conclusion I'd drawn on our walk back up from the lowlands: Odacer was a coward. He'd hidden during the attack, when his power might have turned the tide, and he'd fled without trying to help a single soul.

"I will not kill you." I spoke low, letting my accent soften the hard consonants of his language. "But if you do not answer my questions, I will kill your magic. Every drop of it. And I will keep you for myself."

I didn't elaborate, letting the Laru's imagination and the rumors about me and my people provide whatever details he feared the most. Odacer's nostrils flared, his robe-clad ribs and defenseless stomach shuddering with every breath.

"But if you comply," I added, "I'll let you run. Understood?"

He didn't dare to nod, but his eyes held mine. He'd heard me.

Satisfied, I asked Castor in Northman, "My Arpa is acceptable?"

Castor nodded slowly, somehow noncommittal. He eased himself down on a nearby fallen trunk and crossed his ankles before himself. The day had grown even warmer and his tight curls were sweaty, despite avoiding the fight. "Your point was quite clear."

I looked back at the captive and gestured to Lida. She stood to one side with Ifling, who'd recovered since the battle and looked as tired and grim as I felt. Lida came forward and ungagged the priest, who gasped and spat. His lips were clumsy though, and spittle trailed down his clean-shaven chin.

"Will you answer my questions?" I asked him.

He nodded, legs trembling.

"Why were there legionaries in your village?"

The priest gulped, blinking fast and shuddering against his restraints. "Their captain was born here. They stopped on the way up to reinforce Fort Arrius but you… you burned it down. So they stayed."

If he was willing to give me information this easily, either he was as desperate to save himself as I'd hoped, or he was intentionally misleading me. I pressed him with more questions, hedging out the extent of his supposed knowledge—it wasn't much—and gleaning what information I could about the nearby towns and movement of Arpa troops. What he did know he delivered hastily, though as time went on his fear transitioned into wearier, hoarser compliance.

When it seemed that the man was at the end of his will, I broached the topic I truly wanted to discuss.

"Is there a temple in your village?" I hadn't seen one, but if this priest lived here I assumed there should at least be a shrine. "A temple to Larun, with other priests?"

The man's throat visibly constricted. "N-no."

I watched him for a moment, deciding whether or not I believed him. "If I find evidence of more priests when I search that village, I'll kill you and question them instead."

"There's no more," he rattled out. "I swear. I'm… I'm alone here."

"Who is your 'god'?"

Odacer's shaking stilled at that. "Larun," he said, his breaths deepening with reverence and, perhaps, a spark of renewed courage.

Castor watched us, bemused.

"What kind of 'god' are they?" I asked. "A god like Lathian was?"

"Yes."

"Does he look like a man? Does he have a physical form?"

The Laru blinked rapidly again, looking both panicked and confused.

Castor shifted forward, pressing his palms into the tree trunk and adding a word in Arpa that I didn't know.

The priest's eyes cleared. "Yes."

"He's an Arpa?" I gestured at Castor. "He looks like you? With the noses?"

Castor looked half-offended. "Noses?"

I glanced at his nose, a classic, straight-cut Arpa feature, and shrugged.

Odacer lifted his chin. "He is one of us."

"He doesn't change into anything else?"

"No."

It wasn't uncommon for Miri and those like them to have alternate forms that they could take, usually to travel quickly or masquerade as something other than themselves. Gadr was bound to his physical body, but Estavius became wind, the Northern Miri Esach became a storm, and Ogam, Thray's father, had been able to inhabit anything in between.

I continued this line of questioning for some time, but Odacer's answers became more and more obscure. Soon, I realized the young Arpa man simply didn't have the details I needed—he was repeating tenets and doctrines with little understanding as to what they meant.

"You've never actually seen Larun yourself," I finally observed.

"I do not need to." There was a new edge to Odacer's voice. "I have his power. As the Priests of Lathian once had that of the God of Gods."

I licked my lips, reminded distantly of a young Eangi girl, mindlessly defending a goddess who was no goddess. "I see."

Quiet settled over us, and the sounds of the broader camp swelled in—voices, movement, the shuffle of hooves. The cries of the wounded had died down, but I could hear urgent conversation and the hiss of hot iron in water.

"What is your power?" I began again. "What is its extent? Does it differ between priests?"

Tension ran across his limbs in a rapid shudder. Questions of Eolus's troops and of the nature of his god were one thing, but even this lesser priest realized how vital the information I wanted was.

"We turn minds," he said, pushing the words out in a way that might have been threatening, if he hadn't been suspended by his wrists with his magic stifled. "Force people to see and feel what they do not... Or not see and feel what they do. I did not actually strangle the girl"—at this, he snorted in contempt, gaining a little more courage—"she only thought I did."

I recalled the cords of magic around Uspa's throat, back at the plateau's edge.

"And Larun?" I asked. "What can he do?"

Odacer spoke with the utmost reverence. "He kills, and he gives life."

That was both chilling and too broad. "What do you mean by that?"

"Surely you saw the forests." An undertone crept into the Laru's voice, something snide and assured. He met my eyes fully.

I let my head tip to one side, watching him in silence until he looked down. But I was worried. Why would Larun use his power to strip Nivarium to this extent? If what we'd heard was true, half the province was nearly crippled. Surely that went beyond simple punishment of the Nivari people.

"I did," I answered. "Did you see him do this? To the land?"

Odacer shook his head, eyes still downcast. "No. But it's his doing."

"Why did he do it?"

"Recompense."

"That's all?"

He nodded.

I chewed on this for a moment and glanced at Castor, checking his expression for any insight. He only shrugged.

"You can't do it, though?" I asked Odacer. "Kill the land? Can your high priests?"

"I cannot. Others of my order might."

I didn't like that. More questions, more possibilities.

"So your god has the power to kill the land itself, and also give life?" I clarified. "How does he do that?"

Head still bowed, Odacer gritted out, "Perhaps you should ask him."

Castor lifted his eyebrows. "That is an idea," he said to me in Northman. "I'm sure he'd love to meet you."

The thought made my stomach watery, but I kept my focus on the Laru and laced my arms over my chest, letting the muscles of my upper arms stand out, emphasizing the image of the Barbarian Queen the Arpa thought me to be. At the same time, I let my magic swell, rushing across his skin like invisible ash on the wind.

He shivered.

"Where does his magic come from?" I asked. "How did he become a 'god'?"

The priest was fidgeting now, anxiety swelling back to its former, trembling level. "He was always a god."

"When did he appear? Take his first followers?"

"Three years ago."

"And when did the land start to die?"

"Autumn, last year. It started in the south and came north."

So, it started just after we'd left, as the fort's commander had told Castor. After I'd met Siris and shown the Laru that I was a true threat. I was still in the midst of my contemplations when Castor stood and came to stand at my shoulder.

"Give him a few hours in the heat," he murmured to me in Northman, conspiratorial and calm. "Let him ponder his fate a little longer, see if he remembers anything useful."

I cast my gaze from Odacer to the sun, angling through the trees to the west. Perhaps a few hours of sweat and rampant imagination would be more effective than threats, and I wouldn't turn down an opportunity to wash the sweat and blood from my skin.

"When the sun is high, I'll come back." I pointed to Ifling and Lida. "These two will remain with you. When I return, I expect you to answer all my questions. If you do not, you'll begin to learn what it means to belong to the Eangen. Understood?"

There was no waver to my voice, no emotion or hesitation of any kind. I sounded more like Eang than I ever had before, and my own skin crawled.

I left. Barely a few steps on, Uspa straightened from where she'd been resting against a tree. She had recovered from her sprint and the Laru's attack, her face cleaned of sweat and shoulders straight.

"High Priestess? We need you."

TEN

A corpse lay at the center of a knot of Algatt. He was Algatt, too, and young—perhaps sixteen. My throat cinched as I passed through his people and knelt. I'd never met this boy in life, but recognized several Algatt leaders among the crowd, their faces pale and angry and hollow. He was well-known, then.

More of his mountain clansmen gathered around us, interspersed with silent Eangen. They watched as I laid a hand on the boy's chest, still beneath a tunic soaked with sweat, blood, and dirt. No heartbeat, no breath. Just cooling fluids, muscle, and the arch of lifeless ribs. It was his thigh that had taken the killing blow, uselessly bound with a bandage so soaked with blood it was nearly black.

A young woman knelt on the other side of the body. She was older than the dead boy, but I saw the similarities in their features. Siblings, perhaps. Or cousins. Her gray eyes, glassy with shock and tears, fell upon me like millstones. "Do the rights. Get it over with, please."

I held her gaze for a breath, the weight of it threatening to pull me down into a well of memory. I knew that look. I'd worn it myself, many times before.

I thrust the thought from my mind, turning my power outward—towards Thvynder—and my thoughts downward, to the corpse beneath my hand.

"Thvynder, Thvynder."

I felt the presence of Frir's servant before I saw him. I raised my eyes to find the same small boy I'd seen at the fort crouched beside the sister, directly across from me.

Tension scuttled up the back of my neck as the boy offered a small, sad smile.

The Algatt onlookers could not see the boy, but they saw my reaction. A whisper snaked between them. The sister reached out to take the corpse's hand, her face creasing with renewed anguish when his fingers didn't respond to her touch.

Doubly conscious that most of my watchers were Algatt, I pressed my hand harder into the dead young man's chest. Warmth still leaked out of him, fleeing as his face bleached beneath an angled Algatt fringe, now matted with dirt and sweat.

I spoke the words and dipped my finger in the boy's blood. I drew the rune on his forehead, forming each line with care. Then I sat back and prayed, quietly and quickly. Frir's servant sat back, too, and we both watched as the boy's soul eased from the earth where he'd died.

As with the woman at the fort, the soul was no ethereal thing. It was a reflection, a division of flesh and blood and spirit—one body made for the Waking World, and the other for the High Halls. Both existed here, in this moment, simultaneously.

The man sat up, eyes round, hands reaching for his kinswoman at his side. But before he touched her, he saw the blood on my hands, and Frir's servant. His grief and shock locked into a stunned mask.

"No," he croaked. "I saw the legionary. His sword— No!"

Pity turned in my chest.

"This one is here for you." I indicated Frir's servant, conscious of the watching raiders, listening but not seeing. "To take you to your rest."

Frir's servant reached for the dead boy's hand, and I thought I saw something in his too-intelligent eyes that I recognized. Then both he and the deceased's soul vanished. Amber washed over my vision, clean and rife with a scent of honey and sea salt.

I stood up slowly, offering the sister a nod of respect and regret, and then I backed off. The Algatt surged in, ready to see to the body, and I turned towards Sillo's friend, Uspa.

She still stood behind the crowd, near Imnir, who'd just drawn up. But she wasn't looking at me. She was looking at my husband, her expression written with concern. He, in turn, stared at the body through the press of onlookers, his skin pale and his fringe falling into his face in sweaty clumps.

Uspa's hand lifted, reaching out to cup his upper arm in an intimate, over-familiar gesture.

"Imnir?" I moved towards him, my voice sharper than I'd intended. Uspa's hand dropped and I spared her a short, hard glance. The girl backed off, giving us space. "Are you hurt? Did you know the boy who died?"

Imnir nodded, but the furrow between his brows told me there was more. "I did."

"How?"

Uspa hesitated an instant longer, then took her leave. Now wasn't the time to analyze her familiarity with Imnir; I was glad to see her go.

"A cousin, distantly," Imnir replied. "But we were kin."

I longed to ask more, to decipher the look on his face. His tone didn't match his eyes, all aching and unrest and even a shadow of fear. This was not grief for a distant cousin. A reminder, then? An echo of the past he'd rather forget?

A rise of voices pulled my attention back to the Algatt mourners. They parted, letting the sister of the deceased shoulder out of the crowd and flee into the forest.

Neither of us moved after her. We'd both felt her grief before, and she didn't look like a woman who wanted to be comforted.

She disappeared and the silence between us stretched until Imnir regained something of his control.

He cleared his throat. "Frir's servants always unnerve me."

Before I could reply, shouts erupted from the woods. Raiders started moving in the direction of the Laru prisoner at the same time as I heard a terrified, male scream.

We reached Odacer just as the grieving Algatt woman drove a knife into his neck. It was not a clean cut, bursting out through flesh and sinew in a cascade of blood and the cacophony of the Laru's hysterical, gurgling sobs.

Ifling and Lida hauled the Algatt woman back. She tried to slash again, her face splattered with blood, but Ifling managed to pin her wrists behind her back. The knife fell to the forest floor with a *thump* that seemed far too soft for the carnage it had caused.

I stopped in my tracks. Shock, rage, frustration, understanding— it all collided in my chest as Imnir brushed past me and took the murderous young woman's face between his hands. She stilled and Ifling let her go.

"It was him," she shook out. "He was the one that killed my brother, my little brother, Imnir. I'm sorry, I'm sorry. But it was him, I couldn't—"

Imnir spoke to the young woman, steady and calm, even though his own eyes were still red. She trembled and babbled but didn't shake him off, and when he let her face go, her hands hung limp at her sides.

She fell into his chest. I flinched, expecting Imnir to push her away. But he embraced her, tight and firm, as if his arms could ward her against all the grief in the world. I watched the exchange, stunned at such a show of compassion from my reserved husband. His arms had never held me that way.

I shouldn't have cared. I didn't care. I told myself that, over and over. But watching the two of them, I was suddenly and painfully aware of the gap between us, and my isolation. Yes, Briel was still in the camp, but soon I'd go south with Castor and she would head east. Sillo would travel with me, but I was both his elder and leader. I couldn't be weak, not with him.

"He killed him," the young woman repeated into Imnir's shoulder, and the meaning of her words finally wheedled through my distraction.

I furrowed my brows. Odacer hadn't killed her brother. When that soul had looked at me, struck with grief and confusion, he'd spoken of a legionary and his sword.

"Lida," I called, and the Vynder woman came towards me, looking pale and drawn.

"High Priestess, I'm—" She started to apologize, brushing strands of thick brown hair back from her face.

I shook my head to silence her. "No, I know you would have stopped it if you could. Did Odacer bewitch her?"

"What? Why?"

"She thinks he killed her brother. He didn't."

Lida blinked, her expression becoming more dismayed. "You mean, did he trick her into killing him?"

"Suicide by raider?" I suggested.

"No. No, High Priestess. Not that I saw. And I would have seen anything like that, I promise you."

Still unsettled, I watched Castor go to Odacer, slung limply between the trees, and begin to cut him down.

The battle had been chaotic, the girl stricken, and the Laru a clear and easy outlet for the girl's pain. Perhaps she'd just been mistaken.

"Never mind," I said to Lida, and nodded to the corpse. "Burn his body."

The next morning, I sat alone at the mouth of my tent, staring sightlessly in the direction of the place the Laru had died. His soul was still there, muffled and weak, far enough away that I should have been able to forget about him. But I couldn't.

He joined a host of other burdens in my head. My body ached, I missed home, and the prospect of leaving the army loomed over me. Already, Briel had brought me word that individual groups of Eangen and Algatt were mobilizing, despite the Laru danger, and within two days the great barbarian army would be dispersed across northern Nivarium to fulfill their half of Bresius's contract.

I, too, would have to fulfill my obligations and go south with Castor and the Vynder guard. But until Castor arrived to pester me, I absently cracked twigs into tiny sections and piled them before my folded legs.

Nearby, Nui nosed about summer-warm earth and drying deadfall.

"Thvynder," I murmured. "What do you think of all this?"

There was no answer. The twig I'd been dismembering was now scattered in fragments, so I rested one forearm on my knee and reached for another.

Nui vanished off into the bushes, and I began the dissection process again.

"Thvynder," I repeated, letting gold flash over my vision. "I beg council."

Still, no reply. I wrinkled my nose, cracked the twig in half, and shifted up onto my knees. Thvynder's silence wasn't a surprise. I was outside of their territory, and even a god as vast as mine couldn't see and hear everything.

But I had other methods of communication.

I began to draw runes, scratching them with my stylus of a stick. Beckoning. Messenger. Owl.

Lastly, I scrawled an uncommon rune. Geda. It was the name of one of Eang's sisters, a goddess who had betrayed her and been stripped of her breath. That breath had been formed into the owls that were Eang's messengers, while the rest of Geda was ushered into Death by Frir.

Satisfied, I ducked back into my tent. I ignored my mail, but grabbed Gammler before returning to the dappled sun, careful to step around the runes.

"Nui!" I called. When the dog didn't reappear, I whistled between my teeth.

The hound's head appeared through a fall of ferns. Several nearby raiders looked up from their own tents too.

"Come," I urged the hound. "I'm going to wash."

One of Nui's ears dropped in canine consideration. Then she shook her head at some insect and sat down to scratch at her neck.

"Nui, come."

The dog continued to scratch.

"Well, you can find me if you change your mind," I muttered, then strode away.

A few minutes later, I piled my clothes on a rock beside the creek outside of camp. I wasn't alone; other men and women were here, washing and talking and enjoying the water as the hottest part of the day settled in beyond the treetops. I dug my nails into my scalp and submerged my head, letting the cool water uproot sweat and dirt and gods knew what else. I came up spluttering and shook out my hair, squinting as a man stripped on the opposite bank and waded in.

"Priestess." He offered me a wry, tired smile and vanished under the water. When he resurfaced a few moments later, hair plastered into his eyes and beard shedding water in droves, he found me still watching him, and he grinned again, wider this time.

"I know you," I accused.

"You do," he affirmed, drifting down to sit in the slowly moving water. Around us, the rest of the bathers scrubbed and chatted. No one cast us more than a passing glance. "We fought together. A raiding season, say, thirteen years ago?"

Thirteen years ago, when I'd been an Eangi. That was the year I'd married my first husband, Eidr. The connection threatened to pull my mind down sober roads, but I focused on the cool of the water on my scalp and the swell of summer heat through the canopy.

"What's your name?" I asked.

"You don't remember it?" There was a playful edge to his voice that made my eyes sharpen. Few men had tried their luck with the High Priestess, particularly since I married Imnir, but Iskiri were not known for being overly cautious people. And this man was certainly Iskiri; his incisors were etched with singular runes, and his accent had their high, tapping 'T's.

The Iskiri who had joined the raids this summer had pledged themselves to me, but that did not mean they were entirely loyal. Their Devoted still called for my blood, as payment for the death of Eang. They were not to be trusted. But the previous day had been long and difficult, the sun was warm, and the refracted light made the muscles of his shoulders and arms glisten. His eyes, a dusky mixture of gray and brown, dark-lashed, were fixed upon me. And he, I knew, was the kind of handsome that rarely looked my way.

So why was he looking at me now?

I wasn't sure I cared, though that was reckless. I was full of the strange man's gaze, the memory of Imnir comforting the grieving Algatt woman, and how he had never once done so for me.

"Should I remember?" I asked.

"Mrandr," he relented. "My name is Mrandr. And I saved your husband's life."

Again, Eidr. If this man's intention had been to edge his way into my graces—or my tent—he was doing a poor job of it.

"When?" I asked, despite myself.

"The Algatt had come down at Orthskar, then scattered." The man drifted closer, and I tensed. "We Iskiri were harrying a group of them back upriver. Drove them right into you Eangi."

I found myself nodding slowly. I remembered that day. "We'd just found the trail of a second raiding party."

Mrandr nodded back. "Which came back as soon as they heard the horns."

I fell silent, turning the memory over. Eidr and I had been promised at that point, bound to marry in the autumn, but we didn't often fight together. I'd been with a man called Vist, Sixnit's late husband and Vistic's father.

We'd held our own at the mouth of a narrow cleft. I recalled the burst of heat in my mouth—Eangi Fire, Eang's gift to her chosen priests and priestesses. I remembered turning the bones of an Algatt warrior to dust with a scream. I recalled Vist's face when the battle ended, how he'd bundled me under his arm in a rough embrace and kissed my bloody hair. Friendship. Warmth. Trust.

For a fleeting second, I remembered what it was like to be an Eangi. Always together. Never alone.

"Eidr—that was his name, right?" Mrandr was speaking again, pulling me back to the moment. "He would have taken an axe to the back of the head if I hadn't stopped it. Felt good, saving an Eangi, especially during my first raiding season."

I eyed him. "How old were you?"

"Twelve."

I couldn't help laughing. "Now I know why Eidr never told me."

Mrandr grinned. If he hadn't been handsome before, that expression did the trick.

My body, however, was still naked and beginning to cool, despite the sunlight filtering down around us. I stood and pulled my hair into a twist over one shoulder, squeezing it out in a spatter of droplets on stone.

His eyes followed me, lingering here and there before settling on my face.

"Well, Mrandr," I said. "It seems I owe you a debt."

His expression abruptly clouded. "That wasn't why I told you."

I wasn't convinced. "Oh, it's not?"

The young man gave in. "I want to come to Apharnum."

"Apharnum?" I tugged my tunic over my head and freed my hair from the collar. "Why would you want to do that?"

"I've never been there before. I'm… adventurous."

"It's the heart of the Empire," I reminded him, gathering the rest of my clothes under an arm and picking up my axe. "A world away from home. And Bresius is only expecting eight members of the guard."

"I hear your husband is bringing a retainer," Mrandr countered, mirroring me on the opposite shore, wringing out his black hair and tugging on his trousers. "The half-Algatt girl?"

"Which girl?"

"Uspa."

The name hit me like a slap in the face, but other bathers were watching us now, and I didn't dare show it. Imnir was bringing the girl with him to Apharnum? Why? And how dare he do so without talking to me first?

I picked up Gammler and leveled it at Mrandr. "And you think I'll bring you, because you tell me a story about my dead husband? Your kinsfolk have tried to kill me three times. Why should I trust you?"

Anger snapped across his handsome features. "I am not my kinsfolk. I'd follow you willingly, Hessa—I saw what you were, back then, and I see who you are now. I am offering my honest service. I'll carry your gear, see to your horse. Watch your back. At least let me earn your trust, and do what my traitorous 'kinsfolk' would not."

There was sincerity behind his ire, so much that I believed him. But I hardly trusted my instincts now, not faced with reminders of Eidr's death and the sudden possibility of my second's disloyalty.

"I don't even know you." I lowered Gammler, too angry and disconcerted to put another sentence together. Snatching up my boots, I turned away from the river and stalked back to the camp.

ELEVEN

I t was only as I entered my tent, face still burning with indignation, that I remembered the runes I'd written earlier that day. I scanned the trees, searching for any sign of an owl.

Either they were hiding in the shadows, hoping I wouldn't spot them, or they hadn't arrived yet. Nui was also absent, and the solitude of my tent felt more like a curse than a reprieve. Still, away from prying eyes, I found some of my self-control. I sat on my bedroll, brushed pine needles and dirt off my bare feet and put my trousers and shoes on. I raked my fingers through my hair and braided it, shaking more droplets out onto the forest floor.

By the time I'd tied the braid off, I knew what I had to do.

I found Imnir. He was with Castor and his Vynder—Hete, Mynin, and Silgi. Castor was speaking, but as soon as I drew into sight he fell silent and cast Imnir a warning look.

My husband turned. I saw his hand dip to the long knife at his thigh, but he stopped himself. Nodding to the right, he stepped away from the group and off into the trees.

I followed.

"I need to speak with you after," Castor called, indelicately. "All of you. Your Vynder too. We're leaving at first light."

I ignored him, shouldering around a spruce and facing down my husband.

"What?" he demanded, one thumb tucked into his belt—still suspiciously close to his knife. Neither of us needed weapons to harm one another though, and we both knew it.

"The girl, Uspa." I tried to speak calmly, but my heart hammered. "You're bringing her to Apharnum?"

Imnir held perfectly still, as if one wrong move could set me off. "I… yes?"

I brought my voice down to a level, warning tone. "If… I understand if you want a lover. But have the courtesy to—"

"A lover?" Imnir laughed, sharp and jagged. "Hessa, if I don't bring her with me, your people will murder her in her sleep."

I held my tongue, eyeing him.

"She's not my lover. She's the one who shot an Eangen farmer," Imnir said. "More specifically, she shot one of six sons and daughters, four of whom are here and out for blood. So I made her my retainer, to protect her. She's young enough to be my daughter, Hessa. Surely you don't think so little of me."

I saw the hurt in his eyes, but it wasn't enough to disarm me. "Why didn't you tell me?"

"Because I only made the decision early this morning," he returned, dropping his voice. "She found a black eye and a limp overnight, and she won't tell anyone who did it. I've known her since she was a child, Hessa. She was at our wedding."

Our wedding? I recalled a hall packed with Eangen and Algatt, a young girl pouring wine and that name—Uspa. That's why it had sounded familiar.

The last of my anger ebbed, leaving a strange melancholy in its wake. It wasn't exactly pity for the girl—she'd risked peace in the North by attacking farmers, not to mention that making an enemy of the Iskiri was a special level of stupid. My unhappiness stemmed from the indignance in Imnir's eyes. I didn't want him to look at me like that.

That caught me off guard. This realization wasn't precisely new, but it was old, forgotten, dredged up from the days when we'd first been married. When I'd met his eyes down the long table of our wedding feast in the torchlight; when we were younger and still treasured the hope that we might be something, together. Something that would change the North forever.

"I understand." I drew a steadying breath, trying to shake the memory off. "But it will look odd if you bring her. People will assume she's… They'll make the same assumption I did. Why not send her back north? The first group will go in a few weeks."

"She'll be in just as much danger passing back through Eangen. I have to keep her with me." Imnir drew closer, eyeing me in a way that made me feel exposed. But, softening his voice, he added, "I promise there's nothing untoward between me and the girl, Hessa. The fact that you'd assume I would… I've never betrayed you or our oath."

I flushed, discomforted as much by his sincerity as the topic. The edge of my anger was gone but it left me embarrassed, and his honesty opened a door to feelings I didn't have the strength to handle right now.

"Nor I you," I admitted.

Something like peace fell between us, and my tense muscles began to relax.

"Well," I edged past the moment before it could become something more, "you can't bring a young woman with you. No one will believe she's just an aide, and that will jeopardize all you and I stand for. I'll take her. She can be my retainer, and I'll pick someone for you."

Imnir considered, then slowly nodded. "You'll protect her?" There was a genuine question to his voice, and it irked me.

"Of course I will," I promised. I would—that was my duty as High Priestess, whether or not Uspa was a murderous half-blood with terrible judgement. "Besides, you'll be right there with us."

"Then we've a compromise," Imnir decided, and started back towards Castor and the Algatt Vynder.

I fell in beside him, ignoring the curious gazes of the Algatt priestesses and priests as we reappeared.

"Priestess," Castor's voice called when he caught sight of us. "Gather the rest of the Vynder? We need to prepare for tomorrow."

That night, after Castor's plans for our morning departure had been laid out and my pack readied, I made my way to Briel's fire. She caught sight of my fraying braid and produced a comb, which she plied into my hair as her son, little older than the boy who'd died yesterday, filled our wooden plates with flat cakes and roasted meat.

More Eangen chatted over food at their fires. I set my meal aside to cool and closed my eyes, letting Briel's fingers pull the lingering tension from my body.

Finally, when my hair was braided, she sat at my side and we ate together. We didn't speak—ours was not a friendship of empty conversation, and all the necessities of my leaving had already been discussed. So we ate in silence while, around us, my Vynder and Eangen warriors spent their last night together.

It was not long before Briel's son began to sing, leaning against a nearby tree. His voice already had a man's deep timbre, edged with a boy's free lightness.

He was hardly old enough to remember before the Upheaval, but he sang a war song from those days, a bold declaration of bravery and vengeance and victory. It had only ever been sung during conflict with the Algatt, and every older ear around the fire knew that. Perhaps the boy did, too, and didn't care. There were no Algatt around our fire tonight.

The song approached a section of call and response. For a moment I wondered if anyone would join in. Perhaps, I thought, I should intercede before they did and take up a different melody, one less divisive.

Mrandr started singing the next line before I could part my lips. He eased down across the fire and settled his shoulders back, stomach puffing. Briel's son responded, and then everyone began to sing.

I relented last. My voice slipped into the final verse, low for a woman's and always a little raspy about the edges. Mrandr met my eyes over the fire and unfurled his handsome grin again, before throwing his chin back and howling in a way that, inescapably, reminded me of Eidr. But this time, the reminder was grim and determined, instead of raw.

Every single Eangen howled with him. They yipped and churred, laughed and bayed, and my heart swelled so huge I thought it might burst from my chest. The sound was heady and full, thrumming through my body like blood—blood and memory and generations of discord.

It was the sound of home. The sound of Eangen, of pine and deep winters and sweet mead, of waterfalls glistening on Mount Thyr and a summer meadow with Sixnit and Thray, Vistic and Nisien. My family. My people. My identity.

The sound of a land so very, very far away.

Silence fell. The swell of my heart transitioned to a distant ache and my eyes fell on Mrandr again, though he wasn't looking at me. He was taking a cup from another man, similar enough in features to be his brother.

I'd told Imnir I would choose a retainer for him. Mrandr had offered his service to me. Wouldn't it be fitting, then, to force the two men upon one another? A small smile crept onto my lips. Such a pairing would advance our cause, too, having the Algatt High Priest aided by an Iskiri warrior.

As if to affirm my decision, an owl hooted.

More than a few people jumped. I stood, conscious of all eyes converging on myself and a gray owl with black-tufted ears, perched on the pole of the nearest tent. My blood still humming with the song, I reached out an arm.

The owl fluttered to my hand. I glanced around at my people, a hundred faces in varying shades of firelight and shadow, and smiled. It wasn't a joyful smile, but one of comradery and solidarity.

"Don't let me interrupt you," I chided, then to Mrandr said, "Can you be ready to leave by first light?"

The man paused with his cup halfway to his lips, stunned eyes darting between me and the owl. "Yes, yes, High Priestess. Of course."

"Good," I said, and returned to my tent.

It took a few moments for the next song to begin, and by then I was seated with the owl squinting down at me from a tree. I recognized this one as the grumpiest of Eang's parliament, but tonight he seemed subdued.

The voices of my people wove through the trees in a softer, more melodic song as I met the owl's gaze. "I need you to bear a message to Thvynder."

By first light, I'd dismantled my tent, rolled and bound it to the bottom of my pack with my bedroll, and made for the creek. Nui trailed behind me, surprisingly docile. She kept close to my heel, resting her chin on my knee when I crouched by the water.

I fondled her ears. "You've been a good dog," I assured her, and for an instant I battled the urge to send her back north with the wounded. But the animal's return to Eangen would only make Thray fear for me more.

"Good morning, Priestess." Mrandr parted from the forest, still thick with twilight. He dropped his pack and crouched across from me. He plunged a flask beneath the surface of the water, looking sleepy, but offered me a squinting smile. "I'm glad you changed your mind."

I leaned around Nui's head to splash my face with water, then sat back on my haunches. Next to me, Nui sunk into a similar position, watching Mrandr and the forest behind him with a twitching nose.

"I didn't entirely change my mind. You'll be serving as an aide to my husband," I admitted. "You understand how… it would look."

He seemed taken aback, but quickly regained control of himself. "And the girl?"

"She'll be my ward," I said with a wan smile, straightening. "She seems brave, but I'll likely spend more time keeping her alive than the other way around. I'd still appreciate your loyalty."

I saw a flash of disappointment in Mrandr's face. I couldn't decide whether to be flattered or annoyed. I meant what I'd said to Imnir—I'd always remained loyal to him and our oath, for the sake of the North, and I would continue to do so. If this Iskiri truly believed otherwise, perhaps I'd do better to leave him behind.

With visible effort, he nodded. "I understand. It will be an honor to prove myself to you."

Satisfied, I led us to the edge of camp. He walked behind me, Nui still trotting at my heel, and I tried not to think too deeply about his frustration, or the way it dredged up an incendiary satisfaction in my heart. There was guilt there, too, and a voice that whispered, *Never turn your back on an Iskiri*.

I glanced over my shoulder. Mrandr stared fixedly at the ground ahead of his feet, but as he felt my gaze he looked up. There was no murderous intent there, no anger, just dissatisfaction.

"I'm grateful for your offer," I said. "And I do hope that you prove yourself. My relationship with your kin has been difficult."

He nodded grimly. "I know. I'll do my best."

We stepped out of the trees into an overcast dawn. The empty Arpa village lay in a violet haze, gates yawning and crops rustling in the breeze like a murky sea. Beyond it, the ridge of trees I'd chased the Laru through cut across the edge of the plateau, but it didn't completely obscure the marsh and forest and dikes of the lowlands. They stretched all the way to the horizon, where a sliver of sun peaked out between the sea and a low-hanging blanket of cloud.

In the hush of dawn, in this pocket of living world, I could almost pretend that those lowlands were not scarred by ribbons of Laru death.

Imnir stood ready with Hete, Mynin, and Silgi, just beyond the tree line. A quiet crowd of early risers lingered around them, sleepy-eyed and squinting, ready to say farewell.

"You should say your goodbyes now," I told Mrandr.

He nodded and we separated. I took the hands of my Vynder in parting, save for Briel, who appeared to be berating Sillo. I kept my farewells simple and few, letting my bearing and the calmness of my expression set the tone for this departure.

The High Priestess and High Priest were leaving. The weight of that showed in some of the onlookers' eyes, though others laughed and jested. We might never return, and in our absence? My raiders forged off into a land scarred by and subjected to the Laru, with only Gadr and lesser Vynder to protect them.

I thought about making a speech, but words felt redundant. Goodbyes complete, I scratched Nui's boar-bristle spine and looked for Mrandr. I found him in the trees with a knot of young warriors, their faces obscured by the shadows. My eyes snagged on the line of his shoulder and muscles of his back, which narrowed down to a series of simple belts and choice weapons—an axe, a long knife, and a hatchet.

"There're the horses."

Imnir's voice pulled me back to the moment, to Nui's fur beneath my fingers and the ache of my muscles, stiff from another night on the ground.

Uspa approached, leading a line of horses. My own bay mount, called Serka, was among them, and Uspa led her by the bridle ahead of the group. There was a look of determination about her, but as she came closer I saw half of her face was covered in bruises the color of a stormy sky.

Imnir had warned me, but I hadn't been expecting this. The girl limped, and by the way she angled her torso and let her belts ride low on her hips, her stomach or ribs were bruised as well.

My eyes flicked to Imnir. He gave me a look that said, *I told you it was bad.*

Uspa didn't notice the exchange, handing over Serka's reins with a respectful duck of her head. One eye was swollen nearly closed, but she faced me straight on and made no move to conceal it. Her knuckles, I noticed, were unmarked. Whatever had happened, she'd either been caught unawares or hadn't fought back.

"I'm honored to serve you, High Priestess," the girl said, blinking her one good eye. "This will heal fast, I promise. It won't slow me down, and I won't burden you."

Her assurances were ardent enough that I felt a pang of pity, but that didn't excuse her lack of judgement. She'd made an enemy of the Iskiri *and* chased down a Laru priest against my orders.

It was best, I thought, to bring her recklessness to a halt right now.

"Yes, it will slow you down," I informed her. "And you will be a burden if you don't acknowledge your own limits and obey orders. To start with, you need to tell me who did this to you."

She looked as if I'd struck her already bruised face. "I— High Priestess, I understand."

"And?" I prompted. "Who did this to you?"

Her stricken expression cracked with barely controlled anger. "I don't need you to fight my battles."

I looked at her for a long, hard moment, then raised my eyes to Imnir. He stood some distance away beside his horse, watching us.

Uspa regained her composure. "I'm sorry. It was a stupid fight, and I don't want anyone else involved."

I scrutinized her for one more minute, calculated to make her squirm—which she did—then relented. "I can respect that, as long as it won't happen again."

"It won't."

Mrandr appeared out of the trees. He noticed our exchange and changed his course, diverting to introduce himself to Imnir.

"Thank you for not…" Uspa licked her lips, not looking at me or Mrandr or anywhere but her boots. "I know how it must have seemed, when Imnir… I should have come to you and explained."

"He should have explained," I countered. "Uspa, I think you may be brave, and maybe even a good asset. But yesterday I told you to fall back, and you disobeyed. That isn't bravery. That's selfishness, and it's going to get you and others killed. Understood?"

I saw the muscles of her throat flex. "Yes, Priestess."

"You brought a horse for yourself?"

"Yes, Priestess."

"Good. Then say your goodbyes and mount up."

She ducked her head and moved off, leaving me with Serka's reins. The horse tossed her head with a clink of tack, nipping at Nui. The dog skittered away.

Briel filled the space Uspa had left, offering me a crooked grin. "You're mean, Hess."

"She's going to get herself killed," I said, observing again Uspa's limp as she approached a pair of warriors at the edge of the trees. One obviously had mixed blood like she did, while the other was wholly Algatt—white-blonde and blue-eyed. None of them embraced. Not close family, then, or maybe even friends. They smiled pleasantly and one clapped her on the shoulder. Acquaintances, at best.

Empathy. It lit again in a corner of my chest, and I tamped it down.

Briel cast an eye between the two of us. "I heard her story from Sillo."

"Sillo?"

"He has his eye on her, and she doesn't seem put out by his attention either. You might be playing midwife by the end of this trip."

"I will not," I snapped, perturbed by the idea on more than one level. "Sillo wouldn't be that stupid."

"Then what's wrong with your face?" Briel peered at me more closely. "You're moping, aren't you?"

I leveled my chin at her, eyes flinty and brows cocked. "And if I am?"

She made a show of grudgingly opening her arms. "Fine."

I pushed aside thoughts of Uspa, laughed softly, and seized Briel in an embrace. She sputtered and squirmed and I planted a kiss on her cheek, which she wiped on her shoulder as she disentangled.

"That was unnecessary," she reprimanded, but she was grinning, and so was I. "Listen. Since I won't be there, all you've got to watch your back now are a mutt and a half-grown, half-Gatti warmonger. Promise me you won't do stupid things like run off alone in forests and pick fights with Laru?"

I started *tsk*ing a response when Sillo interjected, "I'm not a mutt."

He sidled up to us, ruffling Nui's ears. I eyed him, thinking about what Briel had said about him and Uspa before he added, "Castor's here."

Sure enough, the Arpa had emerged from the forest. He wore a fine Arpa tunic, blue lined with white, and fitted trousers for riding. He accepted a horse, already arrayed with his gear, and mounted up.

The rest of the guard took this as their signal. Ifling and Lida parted from their friends with embraces and kisses and tossed insults, Sillo jogged off to claim his horse, and I looked at Briel one last time. But I saw more than her—I saw all the onlookers, Eangen and Algatt alike, and my guilt at leaving them returned in full, throat-cinching force.

"Protect them," I charged Briel as I mounted up. I noticed Uspa doing the same some distance off, swinging astride a gray gelding under Imnir's proprietary eye.

"I will," Briel promised, slapping my thigh. "Me and good old Gadr."

I glanced along the trees. "Who isn't here," I noted.

She shrugged. "Did you expect him to wake up early just to say goodbye to you? Remember what I said. Don't be stupid."

"I won't." I smiled down at her one last time. I was suddenly and ardently reminded of saying farewell to Thray and Sixnit, and Nisien and Estavius, and my heart contorted in my chest. "Farewell, my friend."

"Farewell, Hessa."

TWELVE

The first day of travel passed in relative silence. My thoughts were full of home, Thray, and Larun as Castor led us south across the plateau on an Arpa road, which cut through the varied landscape with the same stolid indifference it always did. Whether the land was living or dead it carried on, slashing through cursed forest and lush meadows.

The plateau itself was not quite flat, intruded upon by the mountains and foothills from the west. We topped rises and guided the horses down serpentine stretches of road, descending into cool valleys cut by meltwater. There we splashed through shallow rivers and looked up long, meandering waterfalls, before we ascended back into the sunlight.

"It will be harder to conceal ourselves in the lowlands," Castor told me as we stopped at the bottom of one ravine to fill our flasks and water the horses. Sillo had stretched himself out on a flat boulder nearby, enjoying the cool shade, while up on the far side of the valley Uspa and Hete kept watch—Uspa's shield and spear marking her out from the older woman's vulpine silhouette. A few trees stretched up beyond them, green-leafed and welcome. "The curse is worse there, and there's less cover. So we stay on the plateau as long as possible."

Three days after leaving the army, we came upon the great landslide I'd seen from the pass. Signs of civilization peppered the road as we rode closer, decorating the largest stretch of living land we'd seen yet. But the farmhouses and hamlets were still abandoned, fields infested with weeds and fences falling into disrepair.

The destruction here was of a different sort.

We surveyed the devastation from the top of a ridge. Crumbling houses of wood and stone, once arrayed on narrow streets, now clung to the clamshell brim of what had been a picturesque river valley. Arpa roads converged here from north and south through long-abandoned fields—marked by overgrown paths and ditches—but now their fine cobbles buckled and ruptured. They ended in collapsed bridges, which stretched like stunted fingers into the valley. Below, piles of debris—stones, carved pillars, shattered domed rooves—turned a rushing river into a glinting black lake and a series of rapids, descending into the lowlands.

"I've heard of this… But I had no idea it was so bad," Castor said from the back of his quiet white mare. His cloak, short to the thigh, flapped around him, and he gathered it into his sides in an oddly reticent posture. "This was a city called Mircea, named after its patron goddess. After the goddess's death, it began to collapse into the valley. But many people stayed, unwilling to believe their goddess was gone and would not save them. I heard stories about the city falling into the valley in a single day, but I never…"

He trailed off, gesturing vaguely at the scene before us. Beneath me, Serka shook out her mane in the wind.

"Is there anything valuable left in the city?" This question came from Mrandr, astride his own mount a few paces behind my own.

"Possibly," Castor said, noting Mrandr as if he hadn't really seen him before. "There was a palace and temple on the opposite side."

We all followed his pointing finger to a more or less intact, separately walled and elevated portion of the city. It lay on the far side of the rift, graced by several towers and domed rooves, and punctuated by yawning windows.

"That is one reason why we will investigate before we move on." Castor glanced at Mrandr again and smiled. Mrandr's return smile was cautious at first, but warmed into a greedy crook.

"No reason to waste a visit," the Arpa said to the rest of us. "Besides, the road I intend to take off the plateau leaves the palace quarter, so we'll need to go through it. But I warn you, even a ruin as godless as this will have had its pillagers… and unexpected residents, both natural and unnatural. Priestess, I believe you and I should scout the city and the temple tonight, before anyone goes in."

Imnir sat back in his saddle with a creak of leather, but didn't protest.

I eyed Castor, struck by the notion of us scouting alone. We always scouted in pairs, so his request was in line, but Imnir would have been an equal choice. Why me?

Well, whatever his reasoning, I would go. I wanted to explore that city, and it would be an excellent opportunity to reacquaint myself with my old enemy.

"Fine," I agreed.

"We'll wait until after dark," Castor added. "We'll round the valley to the north, keeping shelter behind that line of trees, and camp at the valley's head. Then tomorrow we'll take the road into the lowlands."

"If the road is still there," Imnir commented, surveying the city skeptically from beneath his wind-lashed hair. "What if it isn't?"

Castor shook out his cloak and picked up his reins again, loose upon his lap. "Then we leave the horses and climb down, or ride another two days to the next easy descent. But there's a fort in that area which I'd rather avoid."

My hand drifted to Serka's neck, and I absently scratched her warm coat. I had no desire to leave her, or climb down into an unstable valley. But my mind was full of other matters—namely a foreign temple and the fact that tonight Castor wanted to lead me into it alone.

We traveled another hour. Abandoned farmhouses came and went, their gardens turned savage, plastered stone walls crumbling and fences buckling, before we sheltered behind a mangy old orchard, rows of tangled trees heavy with unripe fruit. Bees and insects hummed in the leaves of the trees and the high grasses between them were replete with pink yarrow and white bursts of blossoming wild carrot.

I sat vigilant in my saddle, watching the eerie, hushed landscape pass. The presence of life here should have been a relief, but the lack of human occupation perturbed me. There wasn't so much as a bent stem of grass to mark someone's passing, or an upright bucket by the many streams that trailed down into the valley. This place was alive in a land of death, yet no Nivari risked living here?

Closer to the foot of the mountains, the orchards ended and the road turned onto an enormous bridge. This feat of engineering spanned the broad mouth of the river valley, stretching from one solid shoulder of bedrock to another. It was backed by a pass heading west into the mountains, dark and damp and obscure. Cold wind gusted down the pass, cooling the sweat on my cheeks and rustling the fringe of Serka's mane.

The bridge was broad and more or less intact, though it was strewn with rubble and looked as if a giant had bitten away great chunks of its western side.

I watched Imnir ride out to its center, backed by gray, wet rock and the descending rush of the river. Hete rode with him to scout the perimeter of the city, some twenty minutes' walk away, and they returned with word that the settlement looked as uninhabited as Castor had promised.

The sun tucked itself over the mountains to the west. Shadows of the peaks stretched across the plateau, drawing themselves across the desolate city like subtle, creeping claws, and the heat of the day fled. Some of the party left to hunt, and I checked over my gear while Uspa set up my tent—which was now our tent. Nui lay on the newly shaded earth nearby, panting amid trampled wildflowers and rustling grasses, and the horses were set to graze.

Mrandr approached me once he had finished setting up Imnir's tent. His dark hair was hedged with sweat, but as he neared he offered me a broad smile.

"High Priestess," he said.

In the tent, I heard Uspa setting up our bedrolls go quiet. She was listening.

"Mrandr," I replied. "Is my husband treating you well?"

He gave a noncommittal grunt, sweaty bits of hair flopping out around his face. "He ignores me."

"Probably for the best. What do you want?"

Mrandr crossed his arms over his chest, hips forward, the dense musculature of his arms obviously, and intentionally, displayed. My lips twitched, almost a smirk, but I managed to hold myself back.

"I'm no expert," he said, dropping his voice a fraction. "But it strikes me that a temple and a palace likely had a good bit of valuables. And what do you do with valuables when you've no time to flee with them?"

"Hide them," I concluded, not precisely enthusiastic at his line of thought.

My expression must have changed, because Mrandr cleared his throat. "Is… ah, is the Arpa really going to give us enough time to look around tomorrow?"

I raised my brows at him. "I thought you wanted to come with me for the adventure, Iskiri."

He looked chagrined. "Well, not *just* that. If I come back with enough gold that I never have to plow my own fields again, I wouldn't be disappointed."

"What are you suggesting, then? You want me to convince Castor to hold here for a few days so you can ransack the city?"

Mrandr shrugged. The hint of a smile crept into the corner of his mouth. "Just convince him to let me come with you tonight, to scout. Better yet, you and I can go, now, get the lay of the land."

Inside the tent, there was a pointed *whump* of a bedroll being shaken out. Uspa's sentiments weren't articulate, but I agreed.

I cleared my throat pointedly and looked at Castor, surveying the lowlands beyond the edge of the camp. As eager as Mrandr seemed, I couldn't help concluding that there was some reason Castor wanted him and I to scout. And I'd rather find out why than add a flirtatious, gold-hungry Iskiri to the mix.

"No," I said with finality. "You'll have time to treasure hunt tomorrow."

Mrandr's face clouded and he unlaced his arms. "What? Why?"

Uspa, inside the tent, had gone quiet again. I wondered if she'd report this entire conversation to Imnir.

"Because that city is crumbling off the mountainside, you're not a Vynder, and I granted you a boon by bringing you south at all," I replied. "If you live through this summer, you'll go home rich, one way or another. I promise."

For an instant I thought he might protest, then he sighed and cracked a smile. "Of course, High Priestess."

I smiled back—it was hard not to, however much I disapproved of his greed—and he left. I watched him go, the wind tugging at loose strands of my hair and reminding me that I had a day's worth of sweat on my face.

"Uspa," I called, crouching down by the open tent flap. "I'm going to wash, do you want to come?"

I paused in my crouch. Just as I'd come into sight, Uspa had set down her spear and dropped from a crouch to a kneel. Now she fussed, laying the spear beside her bedroll.

"Yes, Priestess," she said, smoothing the nervousness from around her eyes. "Of course, Priestess."

I let Castor lead the way across the bridge, eyeing both his tunic-clad shoulders and our surroundings as we picked a path through the rubble bridge and descended the other side in the clean light of a half-moon. Nui followed me, nose questing and ears pricked forward.

There were more trees here, wind-harried saplings and hip-high shrubs covered with small orange flowers. The latter gave off a subtle scent, sweet and vaguely like the marsh lilies that appeared at home in the spring. I filled my lungs with it, permitting myself that one moment of relaxation. Then I let all my senses, and Sight, seep into the land.

There was cool evening wind, constant and sweeping south down the spine of the mountains to flatten the loose fabric of my trousers against my thighs. I sensed the looming peaks at our backs, slumbering, watching, and felt the scrubby gravel beneath my boots. I heard the crunch of it, the churr and whine of insects among the sweet-scented shrubs, and the yip of a fox in the crumbling city.

The settlement was still surrounded by a wall here, more or less intact but choked with vines and deadly-looking red berries. We passed several gates, all without doors and curtained with more vines and brave saplings, the latter plunging their roots around cobblestone and the rubble of toppled outbuildings.

At the widest gate, Castor beckoned me and drew his sword. He wore no armor tonight, and the lack of it made him look oddly small— lithe and quick and accessible, instead of aloof and commanding.

I followed, hefting Galger over my right shoulder and letting its weight sink into my hands.

Castor stepped over a fallen beam and glanced around. Nui nudged ahead of me, head down, and I ducked around a curtain of ivy to stand at the Arpa's side.

A street opened before us, cluttered with rubble and enterprising foliage. Nui ranged out, sniffing and stalking, but though she was alert, her hackles weren't raised.

I took a deep breath through my nose. No rot on the air, besides the rich, pleasant sweetness of deadfall and wood. No putrefaction, just musty, damp rock and moss, young growth and earth. This city had been empty for long enough to forget its human inhabitants.

And forget it had. Slowly, wild animals disturbed by our entrance began to return to their nocturnal business, fluttering, scuttling, and creeping through the shadows of the buildings. A fox yipped again and a night bird trilled three descending, melancholy notes. An owl's medallion eyes caught the moonlight, under the eaves of the nearest house, and my heart skipped a beat. But this creature had no gold haze about her; she wasn't one of mine, bearing a response from Thvynder.

Castor nodded ahead up the street. "Care to see the temple first?"

"We've barely scouted," I returned.

"There's no one here, your husband said as much," Castor insisted, pointing to the dog. "And she looks content."

Nui, traitorous creature that she was, wagged her tail at his attention.

"The Algatt didn't come inside," I countered. "I'm not going deeper into this city until I know it's not a trap."

"We'll make a winding path to the temple, then." He indicated the elevated, second tier of the city, which I could just make out over the rooves of the decrepit houses. A domed roof glistened in the moonlight, and goosebumps prickled up my arms. "Follow me."

We didn't creep, though I took each step with care. Moonlight played tricks with the shadows and I stumbled more than once, but Castor seemed to have no trouble navigating his way through. Nui, too, moved freely, leaping over debris and investigating every corner, her tail lashing behind her.

We turned down countless side streets, all the while meandering our way closer to that elevated portion of the city. Long porticos of carved pillars lined the way, disheveled in their grandeur, and overgrown wells graced intersections and squares. Ancient trees, hemmed by paving stones, rose stolidly into the night sky. The rustling of their leaves sounded like summer rain, soothing and mundane.

My shoulders began to loosen. More and more, I was inclined to believe Castor's assessment—there was no one here. Everything, from beams to ornate wooden furniture spilling from the upper storey of one house, lay where it had fallen.

But there was one thing about this place that was, most certainly, unnatural.

"There are no dead."

Castor cocked his head. "What? The bodies? I assume they've been cleared away or… eaten, I suppose."

"No, the souls." I gestured to the houses all around, the rubble and the debris. "You said half the city fell into the ravine in one day."

"Then their souls are at the bottom of the ravine."

I frowned at him. "Not all of them, surely."

"The souls of my people are not something I want to think about." He led me down another street, and Nui bounded to catch up. "We've spoken about this before. If the dead are gone, they're gone, and that I'm grateful for."

"They can't be gone unless they're released."

"Then Larun is releasing them," Castor snapped.

I stopped walking. "You seem very sure Larun's doing this," I said.

Castor glared into an empty alley. "He is. I *am* sure of it. But Bresius denies just how much of a threat Larun is." He gestured broadly, indicating the broader world—and, I knew, the swaths of dead land. "But this creature is growing very, very powerful. And the people of Nivarium, the Empire, will follow power."

"If Larun is releasing the Arpa souls, does he have passage into your Realm of the Dead?" I asked, though I didn't truly expect him to have an answer. "He would have to."

Castor began to shake his head, then seemed taken by a stray thought. He discarded the impulse and started walking again.

"Clearly," he muttered, "someone does."

His tone dissuaded further questioning, but that wasn't why I let the conversation drop. We had reached the bottom of a grand staircase, leading up into the second tier of the city. Its retaining walls had burst in several places, letting cascades of earth down into the city below, but the staircase itself was intact, drawing my eyes up to the secondary wall and the waiting, domed roof of the temple.

"I'm ready," I told Castor, taking the bottom step. I'd dig up the topic of the Arpa dead next time I had a Laru priest in my possession. "Let's go."

Another gate, another wall, another vine-choked courtyard. This one was octagonal, a common Arpa shape, with five parts of the octagon comprised of wall and gate, and the remaining three of large archways. Two led off to other sections of the compound, including the palace— that arch marked by its two, pointed towers. Those passages were thick with darkness, but the one in the center, the highest, held a doorway.

The door was intact, painted a startling jade hue and studded with tarnished fittings. It was huge and set in a frame of richly carved limestone, an arm's length wide and so intricate that I couldn't help but stare.

Statues of gods clustered in upon one another, each captured in the midst of some action—a reaching hand, a graceful fall, a darting sword.

Their details were obscured by blushes of dark moss and moon shadow, but Castor's eyes roamed over each, up and up towards the top of the arch.

"Who are they?" I asked, stepping in closer.

"Liana, Goddess of Bounty." Castor pointed to one at my chest height, a middle-aged woman with an apron full of grain and a half-moon headdress of interwoven wheat and sunlight. "Hylias, of the Dawn." This was a bull of a man with the sun bursting out of his mouth. "Orien… see his flute. A god of music. Ah, and the Three, clustered there. The old woman, the mother, and the sister."

I pushed onto the tips of my toes to see the last one, my fingers pressed into the wall for balance. The Three had a section of the doorframe all to themselves, standing shoulder to shoulder with their hands intertwined, ornate headdresses framing their faces. One was a little girl, her headdress an arch of flowers. The second was a pregnant woman, her head bowed demurely and the tines of her headdress long, like spears. The last was an old woman, keen-eyed and wise, crowned with a full moon whose detail had been lost to time. She held a curved sword in one hand, grasping a hilt with an odd shape, like bone.

"The Mother," I repeated, eyeing the pregnant woman in the middle. The sight was a quiet reminder of Imnir's offer, months ago in the snows of the High Halls, and with that my heart twinged unhelpfully. "Is she also called the Mourner? I heard an Arpa woman pray to someone like that, once. The Mother, the Mourner."

"Yes. They're very common," Castor said. "The Three were a goddess—singular—of the cycle of life, birth to death, and of women in general."

I let my eyes linger on the faces of the goddess for another moment, my mind momentarily wandering back to thoughts of the Arpa dead, Frir and Imnir. Then I dropped back down and indicated the door of the temple. "Shall we?"

It took both of us to force the door open. Sunken into its hinges, the barrier's moss-ridden bottom grated across the ground, making Nui skitter back and silencing the cries and rustles of every animal within hearing.

Moonlight cut across the newly revealed floor, and my breath caught.

Beneath smears of moss and decomposing leaves, a mosaic glistened up at me in shades of jade and teal, punctuated by obsidian black.

Castor and I crept inside. My Vynder senses roamed into the shadows, as did Nui and her echoing, clicking claws. As my eyes adjusted, a pattern emerged beneath a decade of dust and grime on the floor—flowers and tumbles of water, ivy and waves, reeds and lilies, all tangled together and curling off into the shadows.

"Mircea was a goddess of rivers and waterfalls," Castor explained. He kept his voice low, but it still echoed, quiet and distant. This chamber was large. Very large. "Sister of the Goddess Among the Reeds, in the lowlands, Alathea."

I pried my eyes up and stepped further into the chamber, conscious of every step I took on the intricate floor.

"This was her central temple?" I asked, though it was more of a statement. I felt power here, in the air and the stones and even the moss. I pulled it into myself, sifting through and feeling for where it congregated. "Her holy ground?"

Castor nodded, as I walked on. He stayed where he was for a moment, watching me, then followed with quiet, measured steps.

I found the rift in the very center of the chamber. Just as Eang's shrine in the mountain meadow had held a door to the High Halls, so did Mircea's. It was still here, intact and whispering power from one world to the next—a single golden line, so pale it was nearly white, and slim like a crack in a pot.

The door sang to me, tasting of honey as it always did. But here, it also tasted of sweet water and cool, melting snow.

The magic in my body reacted in a sudden, aching impulse. The smell of the Arpa High Halls was like the scent of baking bread to an empty stomach—it seized me, turning my insides like a physical force and dragging me closer.

It promised satiety. It promised strength.

It promised power.

THIRTEEN

I held back, forcing my breath to stay even. I'd never felt a pull like this before, not at Eang's door nor Gadr's. But this rift, I reminded myself, did not go to the Eangen High Halls. It went to the Arpa's higher realm, a realm corrupted by the loss of its rulers, and I'd no idea what dangers lurked there.

"What is it?" Castor asked. His blue eyes were fixed on mine, taking in every change in my expression.

Of course, he wasn't Sighted; he couldn't see what I saw. The bleached golden crack in the air was invisible to him. But I saw his hunger. He might not be able to see the door, but I suspected he felt its pull.

I slipped Galger back into her sheath and drew a steadying breath, forcing that unnatural want back behind my ribs.

"A door to the High Halls… Or, the Arpa High Halls, in any case." I circled the rift, taking it in from all sides. Nui's claws still clacked off in the darkness, and I took her ease as confirmation that this place was safe. Relatively speaking.

"The Penumbra." Castor cleared his throat, following my gaze without knowing quite where to focus. "What is it like? You looked at it as if…"

"It's just a golden line." I spoke more tersely than I'd intended. The last thing I wanted was Castor taking too much of an interest in the High Halls—Penumbra—and accidentally discovering its magic. "Nothing more."

"Can you open it?" Castor's voice was tighter than before. "Can we go through?"

The scent of the door washed around me again, pungent and distracting and promising power. "No."

"But you *could*," he pressed. He stood close enough to the door for its light to fall on his face, brushing his Arpa nose with white-gold, his curls casting shadows across his wide eyes. He could have been one of the carvings outside the door then, the ideal Arpa.

"I could," I returned, tempering myself. "But I've no idea what's on the other side and no need to go there. Your gods are dead. Creatures, things they'd once bound, may rule your Halls now. And what if Larun *does* have passage? What if we walk right into his hands?"

"Then you can manage him. Or did someone else slay Eang?" Castor pushed. "What better place is there to learn about him?"

I put another pointed pace between us and tucked one hand through my belt, by my long knife. The conversation we'd had in the street, the expression on his face when we'd spoken of access to the High Halls, fell into place.

"You knew this was here," I accused. "The rift."

Castor watched me for a measured moment, then gave a half-shrug. "I know where all the holy grounds for the Old Gods are, but no one can utilize them anymore. They just… call. I know you felt it."

"And you want to go through?" I returned. I was glad that the darkness hid my face. Castor couldn't know about the magic of the High Halls, could he? Was it just the rift's hunger that pulled him, or something more?

"The Blood of Eiohe is behind one of these doors, in the old Temple of Lathian." Castor indicated the general direction of the rift. "Many, many priests have tried to pass through since the fall of the gods, but none have succeeded. In order for you to keep your word and see Bresius ascended, you'll have to bring him through it. So I need to know you can." I didn't reply immediately, and Castor scrutinized me. "You're not surprised? You knew the blood was behind a rift?"

"Yes, I knew," I returned. "There is always a rift in a god's holy ground, and there has to be a reason no one has been able to ascend in a decade."

"Did you know Bresius would want you to take him through?"

I shrugged. "It crossed my mind. Yes, I can do it. I can open the rift and bring Bresius through. But I will not do it tonight. It's too dangerous. There's... something wrong, here."

"The Penumbra cries out." Suspicion still glinted in Castor's eyes, but as he said those words, his tone became distracted. "The whole of the Empire is out of balance, the Living World and the Higher. It wants us to go through. It wants us to make things right."

"Make things right in the Penumbra?"

"Yes."

The rift's pull increased, setting my teeth on edge and making the magic in my blood turn. Yes, I was sure there was something off about the Arpa's Higher Realms.

"I order you to take me through tonight." Castor abruptly closed the distance between us, leveling his shoulders and looking down at me from his greater height. "I am Bresius's voice, my word is his word, and you're bound to his contract. Take me through the door."

As the echo of his voice faded, I realized the click and scuffle of Nui's explorations had stopped. I saw that she watched us from near the door, her canine silhouette turned towards us.

Castor noticed this, too, and seemed to take hold of himself. "Listen to me. All I need to do is claim something from the other side—a talisman, something to show Bresius that you passed the test."

"I don't care," I returned, my expression flat. "You do not belong in the High Halls, Castor, not until you're dead."

"The Penumbra," he corrected, his muscles visibly tensing and his fingers flexing at his sides as he strove not to clench his hands. "And why wouldn't I belong there? Why shouldn't I go there, if you can?"

"I'm a priestess."

"You're a human being," he returned with a cold, tart edge to his words that chilled me. "As mortal as the rest of us."

"How kind of you to remind me."

A low growl began to roll through the chamber, and the both of us looked to Nui at the door. I could tell from the angle of her shadow that she was not looking at us. She was not growling at us, either.

She was growling at something outside.

Castor and I went still. Nui's warning growl intensified, turning into a sharp bark as a shadow filled the doorway.

Nui was thrown into darkness. Castor drew his sword. I pulled both Galger and Gammler in two, deft tugs.

The door ground further open. More light cut into the chamber, running across walls of pillars and alcoves and hidden statues of Arpa gods, frozen in the midst of their revelries. But the light also revealed the silhouette in the doorway; thick hair, a feline, muscular back, and lean, powerful haunches.

And then it roared.

Castor and I stood frozen, side by side, as the beast's bone-rattling roar battered us. It filled the chamber to bursting, echoing and compounding and turning my guts to water. It drowned Nui's terrified, yipping howl, but her shadow bolted across the chamber toward us.

Then the bulk of the beast was through the doorway. The slice of moonlight cleared, leaving the shadow of the great cat to slink deeper into the temple.

Its roar faded to a low, menacing rumble. My eyes flicked between the danger and the door.

I summed up our chances of escape. Not good.

"The gate," Castor snapped, his voice low and tense as a bowstring. "Take us through."

My heart had stuck somewhere in the back of my throat, but now that the beast's roar had faded my head was clear. My impulses snapped, tugging me towards the golden crack and the relative safety of the Penumbra. Its promise swelled again. Power. Sweet honey and seeping, soul-transforming magic.

But that was the very reason I could not—could *never* take Castor there.

Nui fell into guard before us, head extended low and yellow teeth just visible in the gloom. She growled at the nearly invisible form of the lion as it prowled between us and the door, occasionally cutting through the shaft of moonlight with a flick of its long tail.

I had never seen a beast so large. That fact welled up unhelpfully in the back of my mind, supplying comparisons to the various wolves and bears I'd faced during the course of my life. Even the Eangen demi-god bear Aegr would just rival this creature.

My Sight, let slip in my shock, reasserted itself. I glimpsed the lion's eyes, flashing as it paced back across the shaft of moonlight. Gold. Pale, white, glistening gold.

"It's from the Penumbra," I whispered.

"It's going to eat us," Castor replied, his usual aloofness now riddled with genuine horror. "We need to run."

"No. We're between it and the rift." I dropped Galger back into her brace and grabbed Castor's forearm with my newly freed hand. I tugged him left, taking each step with measured care.

For an instant he resisted, the iron muscle of his forearm trying to pull out of my grasp, but my grip was strong. He fought for only a second before following me, his pale face fixed on the prowling lion and his sword extended. Nui retreated behind us, a warning growl still reverberating through her chest.

After a dozen paces, something soft brushed my back. I gritted my teeth, stifling a cry, and released Castor's arm to touch a moth-eaten hanging and a cool, stone wall. Still keeping one eye on the lion and one hand on Gammler, I reached out and found the smooth lines of a doorframe, short and filled with a barrier of wood and peeling paint.

There was a latch, little more than an iron strip and cradle. It was rusted shut. I could smash the door, maybe—my hand roamed, feeling more iron fittings across its surface, holding the wood together. But the sound would certainly draw the beast's ire.

Wordlessly, Castor backed into the door's alcove. I stepped out a pace, grabbing Nui by the scruff of her boar-bristle neck and tugging her in with us. She snarled and snapped at me, but I crouched and barred an arm around her chest.

"Hush," I soothed, burying my cheek in her ear. I felt her tremble against my ribs, but at the contact my own pounding heart began to slow. She relaxed, too, if only a fraction.

A voice in the back of my mind screamed to run. It took all my willpower to silence her, trusting my Sight and my instincts as the lion continued to prowl in and out of the slice of moonlight.

It took an interminable period of time for the great cat to slink further into the chamber. I could smell it now, over the damp-and-earth stink of Nui's fur. It stank like dens and forests and musk and hot, carrion breath. The closer it crept to the center of the temple, the stronger the scent became, until I swore that I could feel its breath gust across my face.

Then the rift to the Arpa Penumbra swelled with light, recognizing one of its denizens. It began to grow, to stretch and yawn, crackling up towards the ceiling and down into the intricate tiles of the floor. The lion's huge face came into relief, full-moon eyes reflecting a light only it and I could see.

It stopped before the rift and turned its head, slowly, to look at me. Our eyes locked and I felt my mouth dry, my heart sputter, and my tongue turn to lead.

There was uncanny intelligence in its gaze. Then its tail flicked, the door between realms yawned, and the lion ducked its great head through.

Air rushed through the temple, sweet and wild and thick. I flinched involuntarily towards it and felt Castor do the same. The barrier of Nui's back stopped me, her rough fur tickling my cheeks as she shied back into my body. Castor took two full steps out before he managed to regain control of himself.

The lion vanished. The rift rippled and shrank back to what it had been when Castor and I entered: demure, waiting. Calling.

That was when I felt Castor's sword tuck under my chin. The flat of the blade was cold against my jawbone, and it did not waver.

"Take. Me. Through."

"You want to follow a man-eating lioness into another world?" I asked, holding perfectly still and praying Nui wouldn't jar me into the blade. Anger began to seethe in my stomach, but I kept my voice level.

"I obey my lord," he said.

"Bresius has no idea what he's asking of you. Or me."

"Take me through. If that beast can go through, surely I can."

"It's from the Penumbra, Castor. I'm going to stand up now."

His blade did not move and I felt the shadow of him behind me, his greater height lording over my crouching frame. I felt a spark of fear then, old and young. I pushed it aside and eased back, readying to stand. Nui broke free at the same time, claws clattering on the mosaic floor.

His sword followed me, its flat bumping my jaw.

"You're looking a lot like my enemy right now," I gritted out.

"We're alone here, you and I. I can tell them the beast took you." His voice was calm, easing into the power he'd claimed over me. "Your husband can still crown the emperor. I don't need you."

"And I don't need you," I returned with equal calm. In the darkness, my hand had fallen to the knife at my thigh. I loosened it and shifted my grip on Gammler. "I'll lead the guard to the Delta alone, tell Bresius you got yourself killed, and there will be no one to question us."

"He'll never believe that."

"It doesn't matter. He hired a barbarian queen. I'll give him one."

"I'm the one with the blade at your throat."

In one quick movement I spun, hooking Gammler around his leg and jerking. At the same time I drove his sword back with my knife, granting myself just enough space to dodge.

Castor hit the wall. I backed off, putting a few paces between us before I stopped. From this angle, my back to the main door, the dispersion of moonlight and the glow of the rift were enough to watch him stagger to his feet.

He still had his sword, but he didn't raise it. Instead he hovered, shoulders hunched with rage and threat, before he came to a decision.

He sheathed his weapon. I shoved my knife back through my belt, but only to switch Gammler into a two-handed grip.

"Do you know how I survived the White Lake?"

Of all the things I'd expected him to say, this wasn't it. This also wasn't the time to share. What if there was something else in the city? What if the beast came back?

Castor went on, regardless. "We ran. A dozen of us. We fled as our gods died, on the day that Thvynder rose, and the mountains—they took us. We couldn't get far, not as injured as we were. We hid in a village for weeks. Wolves killed two men in their sleep. Three died from their wounds. Then… something else came."

It was his tone more than his words that made me let him continue. It was level, but there was a quiver behind it, a taut bowstring of bitter memory. "It stalked us. A wraith. A demon. We kept watch, but it always took someone, eventually. My brothers. One by one."

Goosebumps crept up my arms and some quarter of my heart twisted. The pain in his voice—it was human, it was raw, and I knew it well.

So many monsters had shaken their bindings or slipped out of the High Halls back then, things that should have never returned to the Waking World. The being he spoke of could have been any one of them.

"It gave me this, but it never took me." He pointed to the terrible scar in his hair, his words hard-edged and forceful, echoing around the chamber. "I walked from the mountains to the wall with the only one of my brothers that remained. I survived the Eangen winter. I survived beatings from my own people, rogue legionaries who would have taken the clothes off our backs and left us to freeze. We made it to the wall, and we made it back home."

I didn't speak, watching the door and the rift out of the corner of my eye.

"When Bresius eventually came to power, he called for me." Castor lowered his voice again. "He'd heard what I'd survived. He saw what that creature and the winter had made me into, and he justly made me his right hand. He charged me with fetching you and ensuring you can do what he needs you to do. I will not fail."

"This isn't the time," I said, as curious about his past as I was. All I could think of was how badly I needed to get out of here, back to my people, before that lion decided to wander back. "You say you know of other doors? I'll prove my abilities at one of them, not here, not with that beast waiting on the other side. Or coming back at any second."

Castor paused, his lips curling as he prepared for another attempt to convince me.

The rift shifted again. Light swelled into the chamber and I backed up. "I'm done, Castor. Run like the gods below or get eaten."

I jogged off across the chamber. I whistled for Nui, sparing a glance for the Arpa only when I reached the slice of moonlight. Behind him the rift's light fluctuated, stretching and growing as something approached its other side.

For an instant Castor remained, staring at the place where the rift called to him, unseen to his mortal eyes. Then he sheathed his sword, turned away in grudging, frustrated concession, and ran to join me.

FOURTEEN

INTERLUDE

A year after my marriage to Imnir, I stood on the shores of a white lake, girded by mountains. The afternoon was cool and overcast, one of those days in late spring where the earth smells of summer and the breeze of winter. Brave seedlings unfurled from the rocky earth and snow still clung to the south-facing slopes, shedding seasonal waterfalls. They formed into a lattice of shallow creeks, like fingers creeping across the valley floor. But not one of them flowed into the lake, nor ran anywhere near it. They arched around it instead, bowed and twisting, repelled by unseen forces.

This lake was set apart. Sacred.

Other.

I squinted at the surface of the milky water. It was here, three years ago, that I murdered my own goddess as the Miri who had called themselves the Old Gods clashed with the New. It was here, on the shore where I stood, that Algatt warriors and Arpa legionaries had fought and died, and their blood had turned the water pink.

An entire age of our history had ended at this lake. My life as a priestess of Eang had ended here, too, with her blood on my face and her axes in my hands. And a new god, a true god, one that had slept beneath the surface of this lake for millennia, had burst forth.

The breeze freshened, rustling the skirt of my ceremonial gown—a pale, fireweed green, embroidered with flowers and wings and intricate runework—and I glanced up. Slate-gray rain clouds moved in from the south-east, overshadowing an ancient, low forest on the southern side of the valley. Smoke rose from a settlement, hidden beneath the swaying tops of the evergreens, and a few talismans dangled from branches on the edge of the tree line to warn travelers away.

A man left the forest and strode across the open ground toward me, splashing through a shallow creek as he went. The angular fringe of his hair blew into his eyes on the cooling breeze and the sleeves of his tunic were pushed back, revealing forearms laced with decades of ritual scarification and strips of tight, geometric tattoos, from wrist to elbow—the mark of the disbanded priesthood of Frir, just as the lattice of scars on my fingertips marked me out as a former Eangi, priestess of Eang.

I tucked a tiny, stray black braid into its knot at the back of my head and watched him come, wordless. But though I remained outwardly calm, adjusting the three-pronged comb that held my braids in place, my stomach gave an uncertain tug at the sight of him.

He stopped at my shoulder and we stood together for an instant, surveying the milky surface of the lake where our new god had once slept.

"I didn't know you'd arrived," I said mildly.

"Only an hour ago," Imnir told me. He stood close enough to acknowledge the bond between us, but not close enough to be considered intimate. "I came through the Halls."

"Do you have what we need?"

Imnir nodded back towards the trees. "It's all there. And the acolytes are ready to begin."

"Are we?" I asked, casting him a look between solidarity and grim good humor.

A small smile creased his face. He gave a half-shrug as he unhooked a drinking horn from his belt. "I am."

I accepted the vessel and crouched down on the lakeshore. Imnir watched me through the wind-tossed fringe of his hair, tucking his hands through his belt like a loitering shepherd.

"Thvynder, Thvynder," I murmured, pressing the mouth of the horn beneath the surface until my hands, too, were submerged. Water poured into the cavity, so thick with minerals that it was opaque.

I held it there until the horn filled to the brim, then stood up. I transferred the now heavy vessel to one hand and brushed the other dry on my skirts, prompting Imnir with a glance.

We headed for the woods. No one greeted us as we passed through the tree line, but the talismans clacked in the cool wind—figurines of hounds, a young boy, and sticks smoothed with careful hands and carved with runes. More runes, deft and simple, were etched into the trunks of the trees. They lay high up in the branches of the gnarled pines, dripping long streams of sap. Wards of protection, warning, and sanctification.

We joined a path. Some of our more aesthetically inclined acolytes had set a line of standing stones beside it, hip-high rectangles of sun-bleached gray rock painted with blue and yellow and topped with offerings. It was an Algatt tradition, as the clattering strings of talismans was Eangen. Our old ways of worship, traditional and ingrained, adapted to a new God and new cultus.

We did not speak as we walked. But I pondered a confession, turning the words over in my mind and weighing whether or not it was true, if the time was right, or if the shock I'd elicit from Imnir was worth the risk.

Firelight swelled through the trees and I caught the sound of a woman singing, her voice sweet and light. She turned an old Eangen song into a wordless melody, twisting the higher notes and cutting them off in a way that echoed through the trees. A drum joined in, low and steady, and wind whisked through the canopy with renewed intensity. I could smell rain now, heady and heavy, and the shadows of the forest thickened.

We emerged into the small settlement just as rain began to fall in a cool, steady patter. Here, eight huge pillars rose into the treetops at the end of a broad central path: the remnants of an ancient temple. These had been commandeered as the supports of a new structure, a high hall whose doors had yet to be hung in freshly hewn frames. This allowed our one hundred acolytes—men and women from both Eangen and Algatt clans—to pass freely to and from its torchlit shelter, while tents of hide and canvas spread off into the trees. These served as living spaces, connected by well-worn pathways and interspersed with firepits, all covered in preparation for the coming storm.

Imnir and I walked through the camp, and at the sight of us more acolytes hastened into the hall, calling to one another and sheltering their heads from the rain. I covered the brimming mouth of the horn with one hand and we picked up our pace, but the rain was still light enough to simply speckle our clothes with dark droplets and back the song with a gentle rhythm.

Before we entered the hall, I glanced at Imnir.

"I missed my bleeding this month," I said, then preceded him into the firelit shelter.

He made no sound, and I couldn't resist a quick, almost coy glance over my shoulder.

Imnir had stopped just outside the hall's entrance, hands slack at his side and rain flattening hair into his eyes. He stared at me blankly, uncomprehendingly, as the sound of the singer and the drum grew louder to combat the rain.

"You're pregnant?" he clarified.

"There's a good chance. We've been here for six months... my time hasn't come in six weeks."

My coyness fell away as his expression grew blank, and my heart gave an indignant turn. I hadn't expected him to be joyous—no, our relationship and circumstances were too complex for that—but there wasn't so much as a flicker of solidarity in his eyes.

"Imnir?" I prompted.

The rain soaked the shoulders of his tunic, then he shook his head sharply. "I have a family," he snapped, and shouldered past me into the hall.

"Had a family." I grabbed his wrist. Lake water overflowed from the horn, trickling down the back of my other hand and soaking into the cuff of my sleeve. I fought to keep emotion from my voice, but it was there, like a beast beneath a dark sea. "So did I. But Eidr is dead, and we're bound to one another, you and I."

He pried my fingers away and opened a pace between us.

"You're not pregnant," he said, throwing the words at me like weapons. "That's one curse you can't break."

I stood, listless with shock, staring at him. It wasn't fair, wasn't true. Or was it?

He stormed his way through the acolytes toward the central fire as the music continued, light and sweet. They—young men and women, Algatt and Eangen in their ceremonial gowns and tunics—scattered from his path, the new beams of the hall stretching above their heads.

Curse. The word turned over in my mind, sickly and vicious. That was what the Algatt said of me, here in the mountains. Imnir and I had been married a year, and I'd yet to conceive. I'd been married before, but borne no children then either.

So they said I was cursed. Cursed by Death, because my body could not create life.

They were wrong. I was the Curse Breaker. But I'd seen enough of the world in my twenty-two years to know that matters were not always that simple.

I felt eyes upon me. Imnir had situated himself at the far end of the hall by the ancient stone altar, and now one hundred acolytes turned to me in question and expectation. They saw me there on display, framed in the doorway, backed by the rainy forest; my small, muscular frame sheathed in a priestess's gown, the ceremonial knife at my hip, the missing top of my right ear revealed by the braids in my hair. They saw the gilded horn in my hands, brimming with lake water. And they saw the pain in my clean, unpainted eyes.

I slammed that pain away and raised my chin in solemn defiance. I pulled the cool of the rain and the storm-laden air into my lungs and tugged at the threads of my amber power to settle myself.

Perhaps I was with child. Perhaps I was not, and my bleeding would come tomorrow. But the turmoil that came along with that thought—that knot of hope and fear and grievous uncertainty—could not rule me now.

I raised the horn in both hands and proceeded through the hall. The singer and the drum fell silent, leaving my footsteps loud in the quiet as I took my station next to Imnir. I raised my chin again, trying not to think of the flatness of my stomach beneath my breasts, visible to every eye in the room.

I began to pray.

"Thvynder, Thvynder," I said, my voice rising above a distant rumble of thunder and the patter of rain on the roof. "Headwaters of Life, Weaver of the Stars; Pillar of the Four; Eternal, Undying. Today these acolytes pledge themselves to you."

I'd planned to say more, to fill the rafters of the hall with flowing words and proclamations, but I felt too dire for that now. I nodded to two acolytes at the side of the hall, and they hefted a large iron bowl off a fire. It steamed and hissed as they set it on the altar before Imnir and I.

My husband's contribution to the ceremony lay within, a mixture of herbs and honey gathered from the High Halls. The honey rippled and flowed like water in the firelight, as amber as the magic in my veins.

I hoped that Imnir saw the defiance in my eyes, the refusal to let what had transpired between us affect this ceremony.

Whether or not he did, he looked up over the heads of the acolytes and began to sing. His words came slowly, weighty and clearly delivered. It was more of a chant than a song, a repetition that every acolyte knew. They joined in, backing their words with harmonies and the steady rhythm of drums.

Surrounded by their voices, I poured the lake water into the bowl. It sizzled and steamed, saturating the air with the pungent scent of the hot herbs and honey.

Imnir spoke then, letting the acolytes carry on the chant as he made the kind of speech I couldn't bring myself to. He spoke of the future, of the unity of the Eangen and the Algatt, of the power of our God and of the ways these acolytes would serve them, in all the towns and villages of the North. He spoke of the old ways, of the false gods we had once worshiped—Eang, Gadr, Frir, Esach, and many more. He spoke of how those gods had fallen or submitted and how, now, by Thvynder's blessing, we would share in their power.

One by one, the acolytes came to the basin before me and dipped a cup under the surface of the water. The drums continued but the voices faded, leaving space for the rain, the shush of clothing, and soft footsteps. I could smell the storm now, too, even above the scent of the mixture; petrichor and earth and damp pine needles, sweet and aching of childhood.

Sillo presented himself before the basin and dipped his cup. He was one of the last, young and gangly and disheveled, even on this sacred day.

"Cousin," he murmured. He made an effort to look serious, but I saw affection in his eyes, and a wild kind of excitement. He and the other acolytes knew little about this mixture or how it would affect them, but they knew that, come tomorrow morning, they would be changed. And many, like Sillo, craved that change.

Others looked more sober. The woman who came after Sillo was one of the oldest, an Algatt with gray-blonde hair and permanently downturned lips. Hete. She met my gaze with a nod and took her portion, her calloused hands holding her cup with absolute steadiness.

Finally, the basin was empty. I watched our acolytes situate themselves around the hall, sitting in clusters and holding their cups with reverence. Silence fell, without a ripple of clothing or the beat of a drum.

Outside, thunder rolled. Rain splattered on the growing mud outside the doorways and Sillo murmured something to his companions that made them laugh softly.

As Imnir and I stood next to one another and the last acolyte settled in, they lifted their cups. High Priest and Priestess, we watched as they drank the mixture down and settled their shoulders, coughed, or closed their eyes.

It did not take long for them to quieten. They stilled, leaning against the walls and pillars of the hall, and against one another. Eyes closed, breathing deepened.

Thunder rolled even closer now, but the acolytes were no longer here. Yes, their bodies remained here in the safety of the hall as the rain came down and Imnir and I watched over them, but their souls had passed out of this world, through the veil, and into the High Halls where Omaskat, Watchman of Thvynder, waited for them.

Our task was complete. Now all that remained was a long, vigilant night, guarding our new priests and priestesses against the dark. Our Vynder priesthood.

Imnir moved off without a word. Stepping over a sleeper, he went to the banks of chopped wood on the left side of the hall and filled his arms, then set about stocking the fire basins around the chamber.

I rounded the altar, too, wandering through the ranks and ensuring that each was breathing, each was safe. I Saw the magic in them now; amber clinging to their lips and fingers, and the sides of their empty cups. They would awaken thinking the magic had been gifted to them directly by Thvynder's hand—they would have no idea that it, instead, was granted by the honey and herbs of the High Halls that Imnir had gathered. And until they, perhaps, rose to the rank of High Priest or Priestess, they would never know.

It was a secret that no one in this world, other than Imnir, the loyal Miri, and myself could ever know. It was a secret that could unhinge the balance of the world, a balance we'd fought so hard to establish. It was a secret that had turned Miri into gods—and me into a woman who killed them. It was a secret that Eang had once kept from me, and now I, like her, kept from all.

I picked up a cup, slipped from a young woman's hand, and set it upright at her side. A lock of hair had tangled in her eyelashes and I gently removed it, tucking it behind her ear as her spirit wandered the Higher Realms.

The gesture was maternal, and as soon as I recognized that, I straightened from my crouch and looked for Imnir. I saw him just as he passed out of the door and into the rain.

I was left alone in a sea of sleeping Vynder. I could cry now, if I chose. I could sink to my knees and beg Thvynder to ensure I *was* with child.

But that was weak. I told myself so, even as my eyes burned and my lips twitched in scorn—scorn of myself and my weakness and how easily this subject broke me. Perhaps I should reconcile myself to a future without a family. Imnir seemed to have done so, in his own, twisted way.

I returned to the head of the hall and sat beside the basin, where I could see every sleeping Vynder. I rested a hand on my stomach, and passed the night.

My bleeding came the next day. I sat alone in my tent with an aching belly, looking at the blood on my fingers and vowing, with all the determination and defiance in my bones, that this next moon would be the one. I would not give up yet. I would not leave my husband's side. He might not love me, but he was still human. I would make him want me.

But the next day, Imnir left without a word. He and most of the Algatt Vynder departed, filtering off into the mountains to their new posts. Only some twenty priests and priestesses, from both Algatt and Eangen tribes, would remain permanently at the temple by the lake. Most of the Eangen prepared to leave, too, and I, after days of indecision, went with them. Perhaps, I thought, all Imnir needed was time.

Months turned into years, and though Imnir and I occasionally met in the High Halls and the Waking World, our meetings were cool. Three years became four, five, seven. I locked hope and longing away, leaving only the practicality of action and belief.

The divide between us grew, and I learned to ignore the emptiness inside me where a family might have been. I had other purposes to fulfill, and a life to live.

But sometimes, when I saw Imnir from a distance, I wondered.

FIFTEEN

Castor and I returned to camp, trudging across the dark landscape with only Nui and the churr of insects to break the silence. The wind had cooled significantly, whistling through the mountain crags from the north, and I wished I'd brought my cloak.

A figure waited on the bridge over the ravine. I assumed either Mynin or Silgi, as they'd been paired for second watch. But as we approached, Imnir straightened from where he'd been leaning against the crumbling rail.

"Will you tell him?" Castor slowed, speaking to me quietly. What had happened in the temple still hung between us, unspoken and smoldering. I could still feel his sword at my throat, and feel the pull of the corrupted Penumbra in my blood. "Will he keep his head, or need I fear an axe in my back tonight?"

"He'll keep his head," I replied, not answering his first question. "All the same, I'd get back to camp and be good, if I were you."

He cast me a resentful glance, but picked up his pace. He passed Imnir, giving the other man a short nod before he continued across the bridge.

I approached my husband.

"Waiting up for me?" I asked, unsure what to make of his appearance. My anxiety was still high from the night's events, the wind nipped at me, and now that Castor was gone, my weariness made itself known. All I wanted was the quiet of my tent, not a confrontation with my Algatt husband.

Imnir brushed Nui's questing nose off his trousers and picked up my cloak, folded over the rail where he'd been leaning. "I was. Here."

His thoughtfulness surprised me. Softening a little, I took the cloak and slung it around my shoulders, Galger's and Gammler's heads and hafts still protruding to either side.

"Thank you," I said, genuinely.

He nodded, noting Castor as the other man vanished into the dark. He started walking, and I fell in beside him as we made for camp.

"How did it go?" he asked.

"Castor tried to force me to take him through a rift into the Arpa High Halls—the Penumbra, he calls it—in the temple." Anger edged into my voice, but for Imnir's sake I pushed it back. I'd been truthful when I told Castor that Imnir wasn't the type to fly into a custodial rage, but I also didn't want to make the situation out to be worse than it was. "He might have lost his memories but he's still the same bastard he used to be."

"Force? He threatened you?" Imnir halted halfway across the bridge. To our left the waterfall maintained its steady path out of the mountain heights and down into the valley, burbles joining the rush of cold wind.

I hesitated, stopping a pace ahead of him and turning. Nui sensed the sudden rise of tension and pushed her nose into my thigh.

"Yes, but I managed him," I said, scratching the hound and scrutinizing Imnir in the moonlight. Was it a trick of the shadows, or did I see indignation pass over his face? And worry, there around his lips? "He may ask you, next time."

"Next time, what?" Imnir asked, still examining me, distracted.

"Next time we're near a Penumbra rift. He wants in, to prove we can do it, he says. But they have a pull, Imnir, one that the rifts in the North don't have."

"The 'Penumbra' isn't what it used to be." Imnir started walking again, and I fell in at his shoulder. "Do we need to be rid of Castor, Hessa? I don't like this. I don't like him, or that you two have a history."

Despite the cold, his closeness and his... care, warmed me. He'd waited up for my return, and brought my cloak, and otherwise shown concern that he hadn't in years. I'd no idea where it had come from, or why it manifested tonight, but I'd be lying if I claimed not to appreciate it.

Still, I wasn't sure what to do with it and too tired to decide, so I kept the topic in more familiar waters.

"A history Castor can't remember." I frowned and tugged my cloak more tightly around myself. It didn't sit properly, not over the axes, and wind seeped in the gaps. "It's… I still don't know what to think of that. He can't remember the way he was, or helping the priest poison me."

"That doesn't change the fact that it happened," Imnir stated. "Like you said, he's still a bastard."

I nodded. Tonight had proven that. "I know."

"Do we really need him?" he pressed as we reached the far side of the bridge and started towards the camp, overgrown fields rustling to either side. "If you don't want to do it, I'll gladly push him into the ravine. Just a little… shove." He flicked his finger towards the precipice. "No more Arpa nursemaid."

I grinned at him. "Well, he does have his uses. We'd struggle to find our way to Bresius on our own. And there will be trouble if we show up without him. We could lie, of course, but I'm not sure it's worth it. We didn't trust him to begin with—nothing's truly changed."

Imnir made a sound that implied he disagreed, but relented. "What of the city itself? Anything we should know for tomorrow?"

I told him of the lion as we neared the outskirts of the camp, tents silhouetted against the light of low-burning fires. Silgi and Mynin sat by one, watching our approach. My eyes burned with fatigue by now, and though there was a rare ease to Imnir's and my conversation, I still itched for the quiet of my tent. There, away from his watching eyes, I could sort out my thoughts of him and Castor and the Penumbra.

"We'll have to pass through the palace complex to reach the road," Imnir realized, slowing a little to give us a few more moments of privacy. "What if that beast is still around?"

"Hopefully it's nocturnal," I said with forced lightness. I bumped my shoulder into his in farewell and stepped towards Uspa's and my tent. "We'll be cautious. But there will be no time for treasure hunting."

"Your Iskiri will be displeased," Imnir observed.

"My Iskiri?" I repeated, tugging my cloak more tightly around myself and stifling a yawn. "He's your aide."

Imnir's flat-lipped frown broke as he picked up the yawn. Flapping a hand at me and turning towards his tent, he said, "Fine. I'll see you in the morning, wife."

"Husband."

As I'd pointed out to Imnir, after Castor's and my encounter with the lion, there was no question of searching the city the next day. I'd kept our Arpa guide's threats from the rest of the group, but both Imnir and I kept a firm eye on him as we broke camp, mounted up, and rode out across the bridge.

We returned to the courtyard in the full light of day, wary and ready to run. Tensions were high as Nui, Sillo, and I ranged ahead on foot, picking a vigilant path past the yawning jade door, across the octagonal courtyard, and into the shade of one of the archways.

The archway led to a tunnel, wide enough for two horses to pass abreast and tall enough that bannermen wouldn't need to lower their standards.

Sillo wrinkled his nose. "I swear I can smell the beast."

I spared him a glance, my focus lingering on the end of the tunnel and the placement of my feet. There was a stink in the air, musky and feral, but it was dull enough that I didn't think the animal had passed recently.

We neared the end of the tunnel, squinting as daylight cut through the opening. There was another courtyard here, this one long, rectangular, and graced by a single oak tree. Its large paving stones bucked and jutted up against one another, every seam exploding with weeds and roots, while vines twined up pillars to either side.

Nui nosed around a human form. My heart skipped a beat before I realized the person was unmoving, vine-draped, and moss-clad. A statue, one of dozens.

The nearest, a naked young woman currently being inspected by Nui, held a bowl up with two hands toward the overgrown tile rooves and the clear blue sky.

Sillo picked his way towards the statue while I whistled sharply back down the tunnel. The clatter of hooves signaled the rest of the party was on its approach, and I went to join my cousin.

He stood before the young woman, examining her nudity with a critical eye.

"This is unrealistic," he declared, pointing to her breasts, heavy and full over a muscled stomach and broad, smooth hips. "Very misleading. I've yet to see an Arpa woman with these proportions."

"Sillo!" I smacked him across the back of the head, but I was laughing. Nui, delighted by the conflict, barked and leapt up to brace her paws on my cousin's chest.

"What? Get off, you mongrel." He pushed her away. "Down! Hess, I've eyes, you know. I observe things."

"Like Uspa?" I prodded.

He cleared his throat and looked away from the statue. "Yes?"

"Well, observe things that might kill us, please," I chided, prodding my cousin on ahead. "Move along."

Sillo threw his hands up and complied as the rest of the party came into sight. I was still grinning when I met Imnir's eyes, next to Castor at the head of the train, and he raised his brows curiously.

I raised mine back, earning an uncertain smile from my husband, then I prodded Sillo in the back again. "Hurry up."

We jogged ahead, Nui bounding up to the fore. Wind rustled through the leaves of the tree, the horses' hooves clacked, and my braid slipped off my shoulder, swinging like a pendulum as I ran to the far end of the courtyard.

We checked each side passage, each branching opening. We saw nothing larger than a rabbit in the whole complex and, finally, came out into the palace itself. It looked much like the temple but grander and broader, with a great lording gateway. Its doors were shattered, however, scattered with years of debris.

Mrandr wasn't the only one to stare at the shattered doors of that palace. Even my mind swept through its halls, wondering what riches might have been hidden or forgotten or lost in the city's evacuation.

But though Mrandr's face darkened and he cast Imnir and I a frustrated glance, no one openly protested.

Past the palace doors lay a gate in the wall. Only blue sky showed over the ramparts, accessed by a broad staircase.

Castor immediately looped his horse's reins on a ring in the wall and jogged up the stairs. I moved after him, followed by Uspa, Imnir, Mrandr, and Sillo.

The world opened before us. I'd looked out over the lowlands a thousand times in the last two weeks, but this view took my breath away. The river emptied below us, lacing out like the branches of a tree, bright and blinding in the sunlight. I watched the wind pass over seas of living reeds, casting intermittent shadows across the expanse to the north. There they gathered into a stormfront, slate-gray, brooding, and hedged with wisps of white.

My eyes fell to the road at the foot of the wall. It wove a serpentine path down, steep, pockmarked by landslides.

Castor looked from the storm to the road, then at Imnir and I. "That storm is two hours away, at most. We can make the descent if we leave now."

No one fought the decision. We returned quickly to the courtyard and converged on the gate, heaving until Sillo, Ifling, and Imnir could slip through and push from the other side. The rest of us hauled, earning our freedom with sweat and burning muscles as the storm crept south.

Nui darted down the road first, nose sniffing and tail wagging. I took Serka's reins and stood to the side, letting the others pass while

I watched the city at our backs. Vines swayed in the yawning palace doors. A distant statue bowed to scoop water from a fetid fountain.

Pallid golden eyes watched me from the shadows beyond the palace doorway. They did not blink or waver, did not catch the light, but my Sight registered them as if they reflected the noonday sun.

I froze. Serka raised her head, nostrils flaring.

"Hessa?" Imnir drew up beside me, following my gaze with a hand on the hilt of his sword.

"Don't tell the others." I didn't dare take my eyes from the lion. "Just bow, husband."

It took Imnir a second to register what I was seeing, then his eyes widened behind his windblown fringe. We both bowed, low and respectful, towards that glowing, golden gaze.

The lion blinked once, and vanished into the belly of the palace.

Our descent was slow and painstaking, and just as the road leveled out into the lowlands, turning south down a shoulder of the endless marshes, the skies opened. Instantly sodden, we mounted up and cantered through another battered gate, into the courtyard of what had once been a gatehouse and watchtower.

The rumble of thunder and the sweet smell of rain on moss and stone harried us into shelter. We swept the ruins and, deeming them safe, we saw to the horses and hunkered down to wait out the storm.

The storm settled in too. I stripped off my outer tunic and sat in the doorway of the watchtower in my undertunic and trousers with Nui. The others kept watch, made a small fire in a forgotten hearth, and cleared space for sleeping. We were all tired and frayed, and conversation was light.

I brushed out Nui's thick fur with a horse brush and flicked clumps of hair into the rain. She stank of damp and worse, but she rested her head in my lap, and the task was calming.

My mind drifted to the lion, the temple, and the rift to the Penumbra. I thought of Castor, now somewhere higher in the tower, keeping watch with the still-brooding Mrandr as his partner. I thought of the end of our road, the Temple of Lathian, the Blood of Eiohe, and its door to another world.

Imnir sunk down against the doorframe across from me and glanced out at the rain. It splattered on the moss-lined stones of the courtyard and thunder rolled out across the marsh, the reeds waving, beyond a line of willow and birch.

"Can I sit with you?" he asked, though he was already settled in.

I looked up from my brushing. "Sure?"

Imnir stretched out his legs, intruding upon Nui's space. She shifted, flopping one huge forepaw onto his lap, and I leaned forward to continue brushing.

Imnir listened to the rain, occasionally glancing into the tower as the rest of our party went about their business. I left him to his thoughts, eyeing him for a time before I asked, "Has something changed?"

Imnir watched me tug a clot of Nui's hair from the brush and toss it into the rain beside the door. "Nothing's changed. Must you do that right now?"

"Yes, I must, look at her." I set aside the brush and picked up Nui's head, turning it so that Imnir could see her tired, sleepy eyes. She pouted at him, then rolled onto her back, offering us her stomach to scratch. "She loves it. And yes, something has changed. You brought me my cloak."

Imnir ground his back into the doorframe to get more comfortable. "It was cold."

I gave him a pointed look. "Imnir. You know what I'm saying."

"I don't trust Castor," he said, as if that explained everything. He reached to scratch Nui's belly, speaking low. "Do you?"

I reminded myself that Imnir did not share Castor's and my history, like Nisien and Estavius did. "Not at all."

"What happened between the two of you?" my husband pressed. "When you traveled together, before the White Lake?"

"He..." I sorted through possible explanations, and chose the simplest. "Well, you know the core of it already. He hated me. I hated him. He helped a priest of Lathian drug me near to death. But beyond that, he

147

was just another Arpa legionary who thought—thinks—Northerners are less than the shit on his shoes. I thought he'd leveled out, but after last night…" I shrugged, letting the motion finish my sentence for me.

Imnir mulled over this for a quiet, rain-pattering moment. "Why would he choose to work with us even though he can't remember what happened when he was in the North? What does he want?"

"Acknowledgement," I decided. "Power. Bresius trusts him and he seemed very concerned about how 'rightful' that is."

"He's the son of a leader?"

"A senator, I think," I said, using the Arpa word, since Eangen didn't have an equivalent. "But I don't think his father has any power anymore. Estavius told me most of the senators were either murdered or had to flee. Maybe he's not even alive." That thought gave me pause. "I don't know if he has any family left, actually."

"You don't pity him, do you?"

"Of course not," I replied. "But someone with no family to protect is dangerous. All they have left is their own ambition."

Imnir met my gaze. The look was so direct, so clear and challenging, that my mind momentarily blanked. My attention filled with the green of his eyes and their rim of sun-bleached lashes.

Imnir was that someone. He had no family. At least I had Sixnit, Thray, Vistic, and Nisien to temper me and keep my head above the water. But Imnir did not have anyone he held so closely. Maybe Uspa, but I wasn't sure how much of that bond was obligation and how much was genuine affection.

"I'd say someone with something to lose is far more dangerous," Imnir countered. "He'd go to the ends of the earth to protect what he loves. Or to get it back. But someone who has no one? What do his ambitions matter? What is there to strive for? Why keep living?"

His words put me on edge. He meant them. Felt them. And along with that came the implication that I did not fill that void.

I could almost see the divide between us widening again, one that a cloak on a cold night and a flicker of concern couldn't mend. Perhaps

I should have reached out, should have tried to stop that gap from growing any larger. But his kindness was weighed against years of apathy and hurt. I'd tried to give us a family, to make something of our situation. He'd pushed me away.

And beneath that lay a deeper, more profound fear, one I couldn't quite look in the eyes. What if the gap between us closed, and we failed a second time? What if we could never have a family, never make peace, and that failure broke us forever?

Nui felt the change and sat up, shaking herself out in a flurry of dust and hair.

The moment shattered. Both Imnir and I stood, coughing and cursing as Nui leapt out into the rain and began to roll around on the stones, destroying my work with a fresh coating of damp and mud.

"That dog is sleeping with the horses tonight," Hete called from her bedroll within sight of the door, mending a tear in her spare tunic.

"Fine by me." I squinted out at Nui. But Imnir's words hung in the air, and when I looked back, I saw him watching me.

I wondered from how deep had his assertions come, and what he had meant by them. I remembered his offer, in the High Halls last winter. Children. Family. Was that what he thought of, what he was asking for as he stared at me now?

Whatever it was, I'd no desire to face it. I broke his gaze and stepped out into the rain after Nui. Rain splattered onto my shoulders and head and began to run through my hair, cold and tempering.

When I looked back again, Imnir was gone, but I felt no relief. And that night, as I lay out my bedroll next to Uspa and combed the tangles from my dry hair, all I could think of was the way Imnir had held my gaze—full, open. And challenging.

SIXTEEN

The next morning, the screech of an owl jerked me awake. A familiar shape landed in the rafters over my head and shook himself out with a muffled ripple of feathers and a fine rain of moisture. He fixed his golden eyes on me.

A vision overwhelmed my senses before I'd had a chance to rake the hair from my eyes. I tasted rich, earthy forest air, and heard the wind through the canopy of a stolid, evergreen wood. My feet were bare, toes pressing into the pleasant damp of dew-laden moss.

Omaskat was not here, but I saw Vistic among the trees. We were in the woods near the White Lake, on a cool morning. Or rather, he was.

Just a year older than Thray, the boy had their mother's mouth and hooded eyes, along with his father's black curls. He wore a tunic of Eangen green, familiar because I'd watched Sixnit spend a winter embroidering its hem and keyhole neckline with bands of runes and intertwined geometric patterns. There was a cloak around his shoulders, too, short and gray and patterned with herringbone, and held at his shoulder by a fine, circular pin.

When he looked at me, his eyes were as gold as the owl's. And though he spoke with a voice on the cusp of manhood, I heard Omaskat's presence mingling with his words. And that mingling? That was Thvynder.

"If the god called Larun can curse the land as he has, we must assume his priests can too. Be careful, Hessa. Larun's power must have grown substantially since your last encounter, if he can wreak such havoc."

Once, I'd found it disconcerting to hear a boy I'd cradled speak like this, but now I simply accepted it. Still, my heart ached a little at the sight of him, the scent of home in my lungs, and the feel of its wind against my cheeks.

"Where does Larun's power come from?" I asked.

Vistic shook his head. "We are searching for that answer, but it is not of the High Halls. Not purely, anyway. Perhaps blood-magic, of a kind—sourced more from ritual than inborn power."

"I see." I took a second for my thoughts to settle. "What about my mission? Am I to kill Bresius? Give the power to someone else?"

"That will be decided soon," Vistic replied. "Estavius will bring you the answer. Stay the course, and stay alert."

No more detail, no more explanation. As he finished speaking, something about Vistic changed. I couldn't pinpoint it—not even with my Sight. But I understood that he stood before me as Vistic now, and not the God.

He smiled. "Auntie."

"Vistic." I smiled back, warmth flooding through me. I heard the owl give a half-hoot of irritation, and I knew we didn't have long. Even the power of Thvynder could not connect us forever, so far away.

Vistic knew it, too, and the edges of the vision began to blur. The sensation of the moss around my feet faded away and the sunlight through the canopy grew dim.

"Come back safely, auntie," Vistic called, all boy now, no God, no impending man.

A pang of loss surged up in my throat. I took in his face one last time, the path and the forest and the fading breeze, and said, "I will."

I began the day thoroughly homesick. By the time I'd washed my face and eaten, I'd reconciled myself to my task again, but the unrest of my conversation with Imnir the night before had returned. I had no idea what to do with him, and no desire to bring those topics up again, so

I cinched my axes and belt into place and stepped out into the clean, misty dawn determined to forget last night had occurred.

Except Imnir waited for me in the center of the courtyard. Uspa had readied Serka—it was, admittedly, nice to have an aide—but my horse's reins were in one of Imnir's hands, while the reins of his own horse were in the other.

Imnir's expression warned me I wasn't going to like what he said next.

"It's our day to scout ahead."

"No, it's not," I replied warily, fixing my pack to Serka's saddle and taking the reins. "It's Uspa and Mrandr's."

"No," Imnir said, swinging up into his own saddle. I saw Uspa behind the bulk of her own horse, head down as she cinched the girth. "She's not riding out with an Iskiri. Let alone that Iskiri."

"Did you decide that, or did she?"

"We both did," he returned.

Mrandr was currently exchanging a joke with Ifling, who grinned a little too widely and raised her chin a little too high at his attention.

Maybe Uspa wasn't as reckless as I'd thought.

I relented, and Imnir and I rode into the dawn at a walk, keeping off the road and passing through the thin stretch of forest that girded it. Nui roamed ahead. The air was cool and heady with moisture, filled with morning birdsong and scented with mud, vegetation, and bursts of yellow marsh flowers. Across the road, willow, birch, and ash were still in the breezeless morning, backed by mist-diffused dawn light.

Time passed. I thought of Thray and Vistic, of home and Sixnit and the Morning Hall. Eventually, Nui tired and came to trot beside Serka as the sun rose and the mist began to thin. Twisting in the saddle, I caught sight of the rest of the party following us, small in the distance.

Imnir still hadn't spoken. I glanced at him as I turned back to the path ahead and directed Serka around a boulder. He was comfortable in the saddle, tattooed and scarred forearms resting easy, his hair wound into a fresh topknot and his fringe fluttering into his clear, pensive eyes.

Some dusty impulse wormed its way into my stomach. He wasn't an unattractive man, particularly with the dawn light in his eyelashes. I wished I could capture this image of him, to hold away from the mire of our history and keep it for myself.

But it wouldn't last. It never did.

By mid-morning, the sun had burned off the mist and the heat had come. Nui fell behind and sweat made my tunic cling to my back and my black hair burn on my scalp. In a long, open stretch of sunlight between two copses, I pinned the reins under one thigh and dug a fine cloth I'd picked up at the last raid out of my pack, pale blue and fraying at the edges. I wrapped it around my head like a kerchief and tied it off, settling the length of my braids over one shoulder.

"You look like my grandmother," Imnir observed.

I gave him a wan look. "Complimentary, as always."

His eyes traveled across my face, and it sent a rush of uncertainty through me.

"You're confusing me, Imnir," I said, looking back ahead up the road. "You suggest trying again to have children, but you won't come to Albor to make it happen. You show me a little kindness, but deny it. You talk about men with nothing to lose like you're one of them, but when I tried to make something of us, you pushed me away."

At the last he jumped in. "That was a long time ago."

"Yes, it was," I acknowledged. "So why change now?"

Quiet fell, filled with the horses' hooves and the wind in the reeds. "Last winter when I suggested... I don't know. I woke up one morning and realized I was still alive, Hessa, and it made me wonder if I shouldn't... try harder, with you."

"But you wouldn't come to Albor," I said, intentionally cool.

"You wouldn't come to Algatt," he returned. "I made the suggestion. Meet me in the middle."

"Me leaving Albor to come live with you is not meeting in the middle."

"Hessa," he twisted in the saddle to look at me, incredulous, "you're not making this easier."

I remembered standing with him in the doorway of the temple at the White Lake, telling him I might be pregnant. I heard again the anger in his voice.

I already have a family.

My throat clotted, my mind closed down. Some part of me knew he was right, that I wasn't making this easy. But neither was he.

I cleared my throat, leaning forward and patting Serka's neck to cover my emotion. "The horses need to rest soon."

My husband paused, perhaps deciding whether or not to push, then he relented. "Let's pass these trees."

A few minutes later, the shade of silvery birch leaves closed over our heads. Relieved, I tugged my kerchief back from my forehead and peered ahead, searching for the next tree line and whatever lay beyond it.

A moth fluttered past my cheek. I blew it away and wove Serka through a patch of saplings, sprung up where their huge, ancient forebearer had toppled in a storm. The downed tree was half-decomposed, the curling white and gray of its bark peeled away from its insect-riddled wood. The great arc of its roots stood up against the backdrop of the marsh, tangles stripped clean by the rain. No moss grew on them, and no grasses or vines cluttered the edge of the hollow the roots had left in the earth.

I was rounding the hollow when I saw the bones.

It was filled with them. Some were white. Some were taut with shrunken, desiccated meat and sinews. There was the arch of a ribcage. There, a hoof, and puffs of fur. Peeling antlers. And skulls. So many skulls.

Deer. Rabbits. Beaver. Martin. Birds of all sizes. My eyes flicked between them, identifying each one until I realized that two of them stared back at me through empty, human eye sockets.

"Imnir!" My voice emerged higher than I'd intended, my nerves tight. This place was too quiet, too peaceful, too far removed from the horror of what lay in that hollow.

We dismounted in unison. I took the reins of his horse without a word and led both beasts several paces away, binding their reins to a branch before I returned.

The realization that neither of the horses had shied caught up with me only as I returned to the side of the pit. There was no smell of death, no reek of putrefaction. Just the rich mud of the marsh, the breezeless heat, and the churr of insects in the reeds.

Dread curled in my stomach as Imnir crouched beside the pit. He'd picked up one of the human skulls, the one with the least flesh, and tilted its face towards the light.

I covered my mouth with the back of one hand. The neck was still attached, enough for me to see that its throat had been cut. I'd seen death worse than this, I told myself, but my stomach refused to settle.

Back in the pit, I saw a patch of fur that was an entirely undamaged—if desiccated—rabbit. Its throat had been slit too.

"This isn't a bone pit," Imnir murmured, voicing my own inevitable thoughts. "These were sacrificed. And all around the same time too."

"You can tell when they died?"

Imnir nodded, brushing a thumb across the head's taut, dry cheek. He set it back down in the pit and wiped his hands on his trousers as he straightened, looking at me with an uncharacteristically worried expression. "It was a few months ago."

A moth fluttered into my face. Imnir swatted it away and I retreated a step, my dread compounding into a terrible suspicion.

We both watched the moth flutter away into the trees. Trees that, three paces from where we stood, were girded by deadfall, and too much unfiltered light.

I pulled Gammler from its brace and forced my feet forward.

A line became visible in the forest floor. On one side, grasses waved and wildflowers bloomed. On the other, all life had been stripped away.

Imnir came to walk with me, shoulder to shoulder on the edge of that line of death. There was no resentment between us then, no division. I was as grateful for his presence as I was for the axe in my hands—my husband, broad-shouldered and calm, once priest of the Goddess of Death.

White bark curled from tree trunks in rustling, lifeless scrolls. What few leaves remained on the trees were shriveled and ochre-orange, while the ground beneath our feet crackled with deadfall.

Only the moths dared to venture here. They fluttered between the barren branches as they had in the dead pines on the mountainside, gray and white wings full of sunlight, blending into the birches they landed on.

I looked around for Nui, but she still hadn't caught up.

"A pit full of sacrifices and… this." Imnir tasted the last word as he said it, his eyes sweeping the scene. "Did the Laru kill those animals and people? Or someone else?"

"I see no remnant of magic," I added, scuffing one toe over the line of death as my thoughts converged. "Imnir… The Miri never asked for human sacrifice, not in any situation like this. But when we spilled our blood, it fed Eang. Our life-magic gave her extra strength. I know it was the same for Frir."

Imnir nodded, the scars on his arms white in the sunlight between his tattoos.

"Could the Laru's god gain strength from blood sacrifice? Even though he's not a Miri?"

He pushed the back of one hand over his sweaty forehead, careful not to touch his face with the inside of his fingers—fingers that had just held a severed human head. "I don't know, Hessa."

The way he said my name, all solidarity and burden, softened something inside me.

"Finding them together…" I indicated the pit of sacrifices, then the dead region. "Would the sacrifice give enough power to kill this section of land?"

"But why?" Frustration edged into Imnir's voice. "What's the point? If his power requires that much death, why use it here? For this? There's no village, no temples, nothing abnormal. This isn't the place to make a statement."

I felt another suspicion coalescing in the back of my mind. The horses were still calm, unaffected by their surroundings, so I rested Gammler's head on the ground beside my feet.

"What if... What if the dead land is part of the sacrifice itself?"

Imnir looked at me sharply. "Why would you say that?"

"The Laru's power, the power of their god... what if it doesn't come from the Higher Realms or the Miri at all? It's like nothing I've ever seen before, and surely we would sense if it was like ours." As I reasoned aloud, my words came faster. I indicated the dead half of the forest. "Vistic suggested the magic could come more from ritual than inborn ability so... could this be where his magic comes from? He's not just pulling life-magic from blood sacrifice, but from Nivarium itself?"

Imnir became very quiet. Distantly I heard a bark from Nui and a whistle, two sharp calls from Sillo that indicated the others were approaching. But Imnir and I had a few more moments of privacy.

"I'd say it's impossible," he finally said. "But this age is not the last. The rules have changed, and I think we should open ourselves up to the possibility that... the possibility that you're right. Without the Miri to govern the Empire, any kind of monsters could have risen to power, and who knows what secrets they've learned. What they can do."

"Larun must not have access to the Penumbra," I mused aloud, grim and resigned. "Otherwise, he'd have no need to harvest like this. It seems like a great deal of effort for a temporary magic."

"Temporary?" Imnir repeated.

I gave a small shrug. "The magic of every Laru I've encountered weakens over the course of a fight. Siris, Odacer."

Imnir's expression shadowed. The back of his hand brushed mine; intentionally or not, I couldn't tell. He glanced back through the trees again, to where Sillo and the others were now in sight, and murmured, "We keep this suspicion from Castor for now, agreed? That this might be how Larun is harvesting magic? And the others, we shouldn't tell them either, not until we know for sure."

I made a small sound of affirmation and thanks.

His hand touched mine again—intentionally now, a slow brush of knuckles that somehow calmed and tensed me all at once. Then he strode off towards the company and I stood alone on the border between green, rustling life and gray, moth-ridden death.

I brushed the back of my hand on my tunic, half-heartedly dislodging the sensation of Imnir's touch, and followed him.

It wasn't until the dead forest was an hour behind us that I began to feel calm once more. Imnir and I had agreed that we should separate, keeping one of us with the main group at all times. Hete replaced me scouting by Imnir's side and I fell in beside Uspa, quiet and vigilant.

Mid-afternoon, Imnir and Hete returned. They rode at a canter, and the gravity of Imnir's expression made me instantly rein Serka in.

"More bones?" I asked.

"No, but there's legionaries guarding the road ahead, at the next village," Imnir said, directing his words to me and Castor at once. "There're fortifications too; watchtowers, a wall, and a gate. Is there another way?"

Castor, who had remained particularly aloof since our confrontation in the temple, sat back in his saddle. "The locals may have another path, away from the road. We could spread out to search."

"And if we don't find any?" Sillo asked.

Castor shrugged. "You're barbarians—burn the village and slip through in the chaos. But for now, let's try to find another path. Hide the horses in the trees. We'll search on foot."

Imnir volunteered to stay with the horses and gear in a copse, Silgi with him. Ifling and Lida immediately paired off, binding their legwraps high and stringing their leather shoes around their necks before jogging off down a muddy shoreline. Hete tugged Mynin away, the younger man obediently falling into step, while Sillo eyed Uspa suggestively. I caught the wisp of a smile at the corner of her mouth, but it was Mrandr who spoke first.

"You," he called to Uspa, "we've not been paired yet."

Uspa paled a little, but her voice was light as she said, "No need to start today."

"Better to go with a Vynder," Sillo said, his tone surprisingly diplomatic. He ruined it with his next sentence, however. "Besides, she prefers my company, Iskiri."

A challenge was etched into Mrandr's raised brows and *is-that-so* expression.

"I prefer my own company, actually," Uspa interjected, picking up her spear from where she'd leaned it against a tree. "And dogs. I enjoy dogs. Nui, will you be my partner?"

The dog, currently panting in the grass nearby, looked up and wagged her tail in affirmation.

"Nui's staying with the horses, and Uspa can come with me." I cut both Sillo and Mrandr off before meeting the girl's eyes. I'd given her little attention since she became my aide, and now seemed an opportune time to change that. "Unless you'd like to replace Silgi and stay with the horses?"

Uspa nodded, surprising me with her passion. "Yes, High Priestess. I'd be honored to go with you."

"Good. Then Sillo and Mrandr can get to know each other." I didn't spare either of the young men a look as I said this, instead adjusting Galger's and Gammler's straps across my chest. I nodded towards the marsh. "Nui, stay. Uspa, follow me."

SEVENTEEN

Despite my best intentions, there was little conversation as Uspa and I picked our way from one grassy, muddy hillock to another in search of a path. The girl focused on her steps, occasionally using her spear as a staff in a way that made me cringe, and swatted mosquitoes away from her ears. I did the same, scanning our surroundings while I tried to remember how to make polite conversation.

It was Uspa who finally said, "Do you not want me around Sillo?"

I paused, grasping a sapling to pull myself up onto a dry area. I could just see over the waving heads of the reeds from this vantage, so took our bearings as I pieced together my reply. The marsh here was healthy, though in the distance I could see swaths of gray and black death.

"You can do as you please, as long as it doesn't interfere with our goal," I answered. "But you should know Sillo could have married a dozen girls by now, and refuses to choose."

She gave a nervous laugh. "I wasn't thinking of... I see."

I clasped her wrist, helping her up the muddy incline. I'd been married and widowed by her age, but that didn't seem helpful to point out. "Whatever you *were* thinking of, I've no intention of stopping you from spending time with Sillo."

"I understand." Uspa fell in behind me as we crept down the shallow ridge. "What happened back at the horses... I know Mrandr from back home, see."

I spared her a glance over my shoulder. "Oh? How?"

She shrugged. "We crossed paths a few times. He has a reputation."

"What do you mean?"

"There's a girl he's supposed to marry, back up north," Uspa admitted, looking uncomfortable. "But everyone knows he shares his brother's wife and has at least one child by her."

I was unsure of how to reply. My own father had married my mother's sister after her husband died—thus forging Sillo's and my strange, cousin-sibling status—but while having more than one spouse wasn't unheard of where there'd been an unexpected death and children needed to be provided for, sharing spouses otherwise wasn't acceptable.

"Was that the wife's choice?" I asked.

Uspa didn't say anything for a moment. "I don't know. I've never met her. Anyway, I don't like Mrandr, and I don't want to be around him."

All of a sudden, I didn't much either, and it left me feeling oddly disappointed.

"Well, if we're talking about men," I said, coming to a decision. "Tell me about your relationship with my husband."

"What do you want to know?"

"How did you meet?"

Uspa took a second to formulate her tale while I took another look over the heads of the reeds. I could see few trails of smoke in the distance, perhaps marking out the village, and checked for any irregularity in the marsh that would mark a proper path.

"I was six," Uspa began. "My mother died in the Upheaval, and what was left of her family didn't want me. One of her cousins took me to Imnir's village and offered me to whoever would feed me. Imnir was the one who took me in, as a ward. There were a few others, a boy, an old woman, a man, Biran. We kept Imnir's house, but he was never home—too many bad memories there, I suppose. He had a memorial to his old family out back, his wife and son and daughter."

"He only had a daughter."

"No, there was a baby boy," Uspa said, her tone a mix of fact and resignation. This was a tragedy we were accustomed to. "Died in the womb. He tried to cut the baby out and save him but… well, that's how Imnir knew. That he had a son."

The sensations of the world retreated and for a few steps, the agony of that situation saturated my every thought, every feeling.

"They're buried at the house?" I asked, searching for something practical to grab hold of.

Uspa hesitated. "Yes."

"What?" I pressed, unsettled by her reluctance.

"They're buried at the house," Uspa said, though she wouldn't look at me.

I stopped walking, perplexed at why this would make her so uncomfortable. "Uspa. What is it?"

She reluctantly slowed and turned towards me, still not meeting my gaze. "Nothing, High Priestess."

My curiosity only grew. "Tell me. Now."

Uspa wavered for a moment. "The bodies are gone. They washed out in a storm and… I couldn't find the bones. So they *were* buried at the house, but now… You cannot tell him, High Priestess. It will kill him."

Unease crept up my spine. "Imnir doesn't know?"

"No," Uspa snapped. Hearing the sharpness in her voice, she quickly paddled backward. "I mean… No, High Priestess. I looked for them… But I couldn't find anything to put back in the graves." She choked a little on that, and I imagined her pawing around in the mud and rock of a rainy mountainside, searching for bones. The thought made me shiver.

"I filled the graves back in, and never told him," Uspa continued. "He was rarely there, anyway… He only came every few months, to give us food or tools."

I gestured for her to start walking again and she gratefully moved ahead. I stayed quiet as I walked behind her, heading toward what looked like a steady hedge of reeds that might mark a path. My mind was full of the image of Imnir trying to save his infant son, or him returning to the house where his daughter must have taken her first steps, where he'd held his wife on cold winter nights.

Not only was the house empty, but so were their graves. And he didn't even know.

No wonder he'd rarely visited home. But the fact that he'd allowed others into that place, into the crux of his pain, struck me.

"The old woman who lived with us, she taught me to use a bow and a spear," Uspa continued. "She said I'd need to know, being a half-blood, that I'd need to always take care of myself and not be a burden. 'There's grace in this world for kin. There's familial obligation and protection,' she'd tell me, 'but nothing for a half-blood that can't earn their keep.'"

I thought about consoling her, assuring her that she wasn't a burden—but it wasn't true, so I kept my mouth shut.

She had continued speaking: "The boy married and left. Biran died, but he never really liked me, so that wasn't all bad. Then the old woman died too." Her voice grew harder now, guarding the pain of that loss. "I was alone. Imnir arranged for me to join hunters, on the edge of the mountains, and that was a good place for me. Other half-bloods there. And I saw Imnir more often."

The last of my suspicions about Imnir and Uspa's relationship fell away. Imnir had offered kindness to Uspa in a world that saw her as a scar, the unwanted result of the violence and suffering that once divided the North.

It was a kindness that I couldn't help but esteem. And, perhaps, despite Uspa's mistakes, I could learn to extend her the same mercy.

"Those two raiders you said goodbye to, when we left the horde," I asked, remembering how formal their farewell had been. "Were they some of the hunters? Your friends?"

"Yes." There was a lightness in her voice.

"Do you miss them?"

"Yes." The lightness faded. "But Imnir told me to come, so I came. He's… he's the closest thing I have to family, High Priestess. I put myself in a bad situation back at home, I know that. So please don't mistake what our relationship means, to him or to me."

"I don't," I said firmly, then added, "at least, not anymore. Thank you for being honest with me."

"Of course," she said, then added in a murmur, "thank you for not murdering me."

I stopped and looked back at her, cracking a startled grin. "Oh? Were you afraid I would?"

"Yes," Uspa admitted, grinning back and swatting at insects. "You're terrifying."

I started walking again, not casting her a second glance. "Good."

Uspa laughed, and this time when silence fell between us again, it was easy.

We reached an open stretch of water, a great lake within the marsh, and stopped to replot our course. Tucked behind a line of reeds, knee-deep in the water, I peered across the surface of the lake as a swarm of mosquitoes and gnats condensed around us.

"This is impossible," I muttered. "There's no other path. We'd do better to scout the village."

Uspa pressed forward, craning to see. "What about—"

I grabbed her by the belt and jerked her back into the reeds with a splash of limbs. She managed not to cry out but shot me a half-accusatory, half-mortified look as she staggered to find her footing. The cloud of insects around us whirred and scattered.

"Down!" I insisted.

There, out on the open water, a shallow boat passed by. Two Arpa men and a teenage boy in short, belted robes were aboard, along with a young woman in simple skirts hiked up to her knees. They were dark-skinned for Arpa, their lean bodies sunbaked and covered with wiry muscle. The two men stood staggered, one to each side with long poles in their hands, while the young woman shook out nets in the belly of the craft and the boy stared out at the marsh.

His gaze swept towards us. Uspa and I went absolutely still. I felt the water tugging at my thighs, my boots sinking deeper into the muck, but I dared not straighten. Nor could I flinch when insects took the opportunity to land on every bit of my exposed skin, my face and throat and the backs of my hands, and started to bite in droves.

Uspa pressed her lips into a tight line, her head shuddering towards her shoulder as she struggled not to swat the gnats away.

The boy's eyes passed over us. For a moment I thought his gaze lingered, felt him look right at the stand of reeds we huddled behind. But a breeze rustled the stalks between us in a serendipitous wave, and he was blocked from sight.

The wind also swept the insects away, and Uspa and I raked clean air into our lungs. Then the breeze died, the tufted heads of the grass drooped again, and the boat was gone. The insects reconverged and I barely stifled an exasperated growl.

Uspa's reaction was more violent. She instantly flailed and spluttered, toppling onto a hillock of dead plants nearby and clawing at her face and neck.

"Can we—" Uspa cut herself off, but I saw the frustration in her eyes.

"Yes, let's go." I swatted at the cloud and offered her a hand, which she clasped. "We're done here."

"I can't breathe." There was a whining undertone to her voice, or perhaps that was just her trying not to swallow any more insects. She grimaced, slipping as she tried to stand up. Her hand, still clasping my wrist, was slick with mud, splattered insects, and bright specks of her own blood. "Are we going back to Imnir? I mean, Priestess—"

The girl looked so disheveled that I had to smile. "No."

On her feet again, Uspa's expression relaxed slightly, but she still looked uncertain. "Then where are we going?"

"I'm done searching. You and I are going to follow that raft."

At the edge of the village, we crouched. Both Uspa and I had streaked mud on our exposed skin by now—a happy accident that both soothed our insect bites and deterred the clouds from delivering more. It cracked and flaked as I crouched in the ankle-deep water and watched the settlement through white-flowering bushes.

The village was built on one of the many rocky peninsulas that latticed the lowlands. The road, also taking advantage of the dry ground, stretched past houses of wood, mud, and woven reeds. They were subtle things, their clay-and-reed colors blending in with the marsh and rock amid weeping, fluttering veils of willow trees and silver birch. An elevated wooden watchtower guarded the road north, and I could make out part of a wall spanning the roadway and stretching well into the marsh on either side. If there was another wall to the south, I couldn't see it. North, after all, was where the barbarians came from.

Armor glinted atop the tower, and I crouched lower.

As to the shoreline where Uspa and I skulked, docks stretched out into a lake. A dozen boats bobbed at moorings or were pulled up on shore, interspersed with nets laid out in the sun. Women and children were disentangling and mending the nets while others stretched out racks of fish to dry.

A knot of men relaxed in the shade, watching them. Though they wore no armor, they had the look of soldiers, and the women gave them a large berth.

So, this town was well-guarded and somewhat fortified, as Imnir had warned. I'd expected that, but I still felt a twinge of unease. I didn't relish the idea of burning and hacking our way through the village—there were too many possibilities, and too much risk.

I took a few minutes to scan the shoreline, count the soldiers, and weigh the fortifications, then glanced up at the sky, noting the direction of the sun and the angle of the road.

"I'm done," I murmured to Uspa. "We should go."

"Wait." She leaned down on all fours now, peering towards the unarmored legionaries. No, past the legionaries. "Do you see that? In the center of the village?"

Peering between the houses, I saw stools and clay pots and barrels, a few stray chickens, and an old woman bouncing a baby on her knee. Then, in the center of the settlement, my eyes snagged on something else.

A tree. I'd seen it before, but now when I touched my Sight, I glimpsed a haze of gold.

The tree was a willow, and beyond its waving veil, I saw that it was split up the side to create a great, yawning hole—large enough to shelter in. Flowers were laid all around the tree's base, shorn and bunched and stuck into vases of everything from silver to clay. There was a bronze statue there, too, right in the mouth of the tree's gaping split, but I couldn't see its features from this distance.

The golden haze, however, I could make out. It clung to the bark of the tree, faded and ghostly, but present.

"I've seen one of those before," Uspa murmured. She was no Vynder—her human eyes would only see the tree, the statue, and the flowers. But she was a child of the North, and her next words were true: "It's a binding tree."

Binding trees were tools of the old world, places where Miri, fell creatures, or demons who could not be killed were bound by magic and rune and the strength of their binder.

"The tree is… broken?" she realized. "But the flowers… and the statue."

"Yes." I pushed myself back from the bushes and started off, already retracing our way to the rest of our company while turning over this new development. "Whatever was in there is free. And it's being worshiped."

EIGHTEEN

The night came, humid and close. I swam with my head—and the heads of Galger and Gammler—just above the water, ignoring the brush and tangle of plants against my legs as I neared the docks.

The shallow lake slept beneath an overcast sky and a haze of swarming insects, but the settlement was still awake. Torchlight swelled around the binding tree and the music of flutes and drums drifted towards me, light and sweet and heady. Smudgefires sat in stone basins here and there throughout the village and near the guard posts, casting minimal light and shedding drafts of dusky, herb-scented smoke to ward away the insects.

Every so often, the music paused for a chanting line of prayer. The prayer, drifting towards me, made my skin crawl even more than the touch of tepid lakewater and the shadows of watchmen on shore.

My hands found the side of a low boat, tied to a dock, and I waited.

Sillo, Hete, and Uspa converged upon me, one by one. Sillo, the tallest, carried his bundled tunic on one bare shoulder, while Uspa swam as low in the water as she could to avoid the insects. We'd all smeared our faces with mud early on but hers was almost entirely washed clean from the eyes down, and her hair floated around her in pale blonde clots.

As soon as they neared, I slipped down between the docks and toward a patch of well-worn, muddy shoreline. Waterplants stuck to my legs and belly as I switched into a crawl, found land, and darted into a stand of scrub.

The others joined me. Sillo came last, clad only in his sodden trousers as he laid down the bundled tunic he'd been carrying. He dried his hands on the fabric, then unfolded it to reveal pouches of oil-sodden tinder, fire starters, and his weapons.

The wind shifted, and I caught the scent of the smudgefires again—low and dense, like bitter tea. The insects buzzing around us abated.

"Start your fire, make sure it's caught, then get back into the lake. Meet at the horses and wait for the gate to open," I reiterated the plan as, deep in the village, the music and chanting continued in steady repetition. Whatever ritual they were performing, I sensed it was a common one—there was little urgency to the prayers. A daily dedication? A familiar, seasonal rite?

I could only hope that whatever they worshiped hadn't chosen tonight to pay a visit.

"Understood," Uspa replied, taking up the fire starters. Mud trickled from beneath her eyes and down her water-washed cheeks, just visible in the ambient light of veiled stars and distant fires.

Hete raked her sodden gray hair from her face and tied it in a practical knot. She nudged Uspa and, marking where the village watchmen were with one deft glance, slipped off into the night.

Uspa gave me a tight smile of farewell, then darted after her. Sillo's eyes lingered on the girl momentarily before he pulled his dry tunic over his head and rebound his hair.

Music still tumbled from the village, but activity seemed to be limited to the center. The remainder was motionless, save the smudgefires and a woman leading two children into a house. The door closed behind them with a soft creak and candlelight swelled beyond open shutters, warm and universally familiar.

Sillo nudged me and nodded towards the docks. Two watchmen—legionaries, from the shape of their silhouettes—were heading our way.

We separated from the bushes and darted to a three-sided hovel. From its shelter we stepped into the lee of a house, then into a dark alcove between it and a woodshed that stank of chicken droppings.

More stalking through the shadows, more moments tucked into corners, then we found a clear view of the village center. I was fiercely aware of the flames Hete and Uspa were setting, of how fast they might grow, and of how little time we had to see what we needed to and get to the gate. But I kept my breathing calm as we eased into sight of the binding tree.

The villagers were gathered around the tree and a priestess, who knelt before the tree's yawning opening. She was middle-aged, thin and small-eyed, with hair the color of wheat and a robe of nondescript brown. She was the one beating the drum, the instrument resting on one arm and thigh as she set a steady rhythm with a carved tipper. Smoke drifted past her, foreshadowing the blaze to come.

"I don't see anyone," Sillo murmured. He didn't need to specify just what kind of "anyone" he meant. Whatever the villagers were worshiping, whatever had once been imprisoned in that tree, they would be our biggest threat. If they were nearby.

But there was no sign of any creature, beast or otherwise. Only some two hundred villagers with sleepy toddlers in their laps, listening to the priestess chant. Even the shadow of magic I'd seen around the tree earlier was unchanged, as dull and old as it had been in the full light of day.

This close, the offerings at its feet glistened all the more, though— not just the bronze statue and silver vases, but jewelry, glass articles, and statuettes of semi-precious stone, arranged around the roots of the huge tree. It was a modest hoard, but a hoard nonetheless.

I couldn't help but smile at the thought of Mrandr's anger when he learned we'd passed this by. But a second thought sobered me; the villagers and their legionary guards must have real faith in their protector to leave such riches in plain sight.

"Whatever was in that tree isn't here now," I said, leaning my back momentarily against the nearest wall. "But I doubt they're far off. We need to go. Now."

We set off, low and rapid and a little reckless, to the north side of the village.

The following events came swiftly. Sillo and I tucked ourselves into a patch of bushes near the wall, within sight of the gate. Uncontained fire—Uspa and Hete's doing—became visible among the houses, and the scent of woodsmoke overwhelmed the subtler, herbal scent of the smudges on the humid night breeze. Villagers began to shout, to scream, and I sighted what I thought might be Uspa and Hete slipping back into the lake.

Sweat made my tunic cling to my spine, and it wasn't just from the latent heat. I heard the Arpa legionaries bellow, saw armored figures appear in the murk with torches and buckets in hand. They came from houses and tents, and, as we'd hoped, from the watchtower. Not all of them left their posts—legionaries were disciplined, not prone to rashness—but it was the change we needed.

Sillo and I slunk towards the watchtower steps. It was an open-sided structure, with only a simple roof and half-walls against weather. It stood beside the gate—a double-doored barrier of split logs bound with iron pegs and heavy rope. This was secured on our side by a heavy bar and, next to it, the spears and shields of absent legionaries were propped in a neat row.

I took up a shield and looked at Sillo, though both our faces were obscured in the darkness. "I'll take the tower, you get the bar on my signal."

He nodded, slipping into the blackness beneath the tower to wait.

I hit the top of the watchtower stairs shield-first, toppling a legionary who'd stuck his head out to see who was coming. Galger fell. Two more legionaries drew their swords and charged.

There was a smudgefire in a brazier near the door. I kicked it, spraying glowing coals and clusters of ashen herbs into my assailants' faces. I jerked Galger free in the same movement and slammed my shield into a blinded, howling legionary. He staggered into the side of the tower and I pinned him against the half-wall. I heard his sword drop and kicked its hilt, sending it spinning across the floor through coals and ash. The last standing legionary instinctively shied from the clattering blade and I lodged Galger into the unprotected back of his thigh. He went down with a shriek, which redoubled as he rolled into coals.

Flames bloomed everywhere in the village now, filling the air with a constant, deadening roar. The only sounds to reach me over it were screams and shouts—more than enough to obscure the cry of the legionaries.

Fingers clawed into my arm. The soldier I'd pinned against the wall found grip and jerked me off-balance. My hip hit the floor, but I still had hold of the shield. It became a roof as the legionary threw his weight into me, kicking and striking as he worked himself free. Hot coals seared into my clothing and bare knuckles as I shifted my weight, trying to stand.

His fallen comrade, bleeding from the thigh and retching in panic, shoved him a sword. He stooped to snatch it and turn on me, blade extended.

I was already inside his guard, knocking his blade aside and driving Galger's haft into his face. I flipped the weapon, slashing the head of the axe into my opponent's wrist. The sword fell again. Galger's haft struck his gut, and I shoved him out the door.

He toppled down the first stretch of stairs, off into empty air, and crashed into the earth below.

I was left with one dead legionary and the one with a bleeding thigh. Keeping one eye on him, I leaned out over the half-wall. "Sillo!"

A grunt and a thud were my only reply. The bar coming free.

I left the bleeding legionary and thundered back down the stairs. I was just in time to grab one side of the gate while Sillo heaved the other wide, wincing at the sight of my singed knuckles.

Thundering hoofbeats reached our ears. In moments Imnir, Castor, and the others had hurtled through, Nui streaking behind them.

I laughed breathlessly as Sillo and I unfolded from the shadows. The last three horses slowed to a trot as I slipped Galger back into her brace and darted for Serka. I leapt up into the saddle in the way Nisien had taught me long ago, on the grassy sea of the Soulderni Ridings, and glanced over to ensure Sillo had done the same.

Imnir milled beside me as the others headed on up the road, past the blazing village. Only a handful of figures scattered from their hooves and Nui's streaking, snarling form—all focus was on the fire, just as we'd intended.

I took a second to grin at Imnir and rake stray hair from my eyes, then we were off. We galloped through wafts of smoke and drifting heat. Off the road, villagers and soldiers darted between the buildings, black silhouettes against livid flames, while elders huddled with children and livestock—panicking chickens, milling goats, and a scattering of lowing cows.

Buckets of water arced through the air, voices clamored and cried and wailed, but over it all I heard something else.

Chanting. On the far side of the village, where the road stretched off into unadulterated night, I drew in Serka's reins. The animal pranced anxiously as the Arpa priestess I'd seen by the binding tree came to the edge of the road, just close enough that I could make out her words—a prayer, recited over and over again. Her short-cropped hair was a ring of gold around her head against the blaze and she was alone, every other soul occupied with saving the village or watching it burn.

I sensed something beyond the sound, off beyond the burning houses. It was soft, faint, but out of place—an echo of something that once was.

"We need to go," Imnir called to me. "Now."

"Where's Uspa?" Sillo's alarm cut between us, accompanied by a clatter of hooves. The others were some distance up the road but he'd circled back. "Hess! Hete said she was right behind her but she's not here! Her horse is, but not her."

Imnir eased back in the saddle with a deadly kind of control. His eyes, amber-green in the firelight, met mine in something between accusation and request.

"Go," I called to Sillo, waving him on up the road. "Do *not* follow us."

I never heard Sillo's protest. Imnir had already spurred back towards the village, and I drove Serka after him. I tucked low in the saddle, hefting Gammler from her brace with two firm jerks.

We thundered past the chanting priestess, giving her a wide berth. Imnir flitted from firelight and silhouette to smoke and shadow ahead of me, avoiding Arpa in a rapid search. Preoccupied with their burning homes, most of them barely looked at us, barely noticed we were not legionaries.

I ducked around flaming wafts of thatch, navigated twisting paths and smoking gardens. We hit the shoreline and rounded the settlement, never faltering in our pace or our search.

"She must have passed us!" I shouted to Imnir. "Gone around us, after the horses!"

"Or she's dragged off, wounded in the streets," he bellowed back, fear tainting his voice in a way I'd never heard before. He drove his mount up the village's broad central path as I reined in.

I held there for two panting, wheezing breaths. Serka shuddered and danced beneath me, unnerved by the chaos and the flames. I had to go after Imnir—there was no way I'd let anyone go back into that village alone, let alone the man I'd pledged myself to—but the flames, the smell of the smoke and burning flesh, momentarily choked me.

Someone lunged out of the marsh. I'd barely registered movement before nails dug into my tunic and jerked me from the saddle.

Serka bolted. I hit the ground with a crack and rolled—an instinctual burst of self-preservation that took me away from Serka's hooves and right into the mud of the shoreline.

I tried to climb to my feet, slipped in mud, and fell again. My attacker lunged again, a tall, wiry frame darting at me with shocking speed. I still had Gammler, somehow. I swung it just as a hand closed over my mouth, nails digging into my scalp, my ear, my throat. My back hit the end of a dock, hard enough to bruise.

I felt my axe meet flesh but the nails dug in more, prying and tearing, crushing my head into the wood. My vision blurred and hot, sweaty flesh ground into my lips. I screamed—in terror? Frustration? Rage? There were no feelings then, no reason, no division between impulse and action.

I bit the hand crushing me.

There was no blood, but I tasted magic. It tasted like the same irregularity I'd noticed earlier, during the priestess's chanting; little more than an echo, something dank and forgotten. And yet terribly, vengefully alive.

I hurled my power into the creature's chest. It howled and reared back.

My right heel found a rock and I pushed off. We flipped. I slammed my assailant down and leapt, smashing my knees into its upper arms— too long, too strong, and ending in accipitrine nails. They scrabbled at my thighs, my hips and belt. My tunic tore. Pain burst over my lower ribs, but I did not stop moving.

I smashed my palm into its chest and released amber-tainted magic with all the force of the raging fire behind me. My attacker screamed. It was a horrific, jaw-cracking howl of pure bloodlust and rage. If it ever had been human, it was no longer.

We were nearly of a height, the thing and me. Its arms were thin and its flesh the color of wet slate, sunken as it might be on a corpse or the starved. But this enemy was very much alive, its soulless eyes flashing at me in the shadows.

Though I'd only ever encountered something like it once before, I knew what it was. A demon. Descendants of an Old World Miri's ill-fated scheme to grant her children eternal life, most demons had been bound by the Miri over time in places like binding trees and sacred cairns. But this one was free, and it was no stretch to realize that it was this that the villagers worshiped.

Their gods were dead. So they'd taken a demon in their place.

My magic redoubled in a brilliant, cleansing blast. My pain retreated and the creature screamed a second time, realizing just what kind of foe it had pitted itself against. But still its claws came.

Kill. I had to kill it now, to stop it from tearing me apart. I barely had a grip on Galger, still in its brace, but I hauled it up, hands slippery with mud and my own amber-tinted ichor. The weapon dropped free, I spun it and stabbed its armor-piercing point into the creature's eye.

I heard a crack, felt resistance and then—less. I spun the weapon and smashed down with the blade this time, dragging up my amber magic in the same motion and channeling it into the being's face.

Its teeth, its skull, shattered. It screamed a gargling, agonized squeal and bucked.

An arrow slammed into the ground next to my feet. For an instant I could only stare at it, uncomprehending, deafened by the demon's shrieks.

A second arrow clipped my shoulder and, with that, my mind snapped back up to speed. I tried to haul Galger free but it was stuck, so firmly wedged in the demon's ancient skull that I could only haul uselessly.

Another arrow punched through my trousers and sliced into the water of the marsh. Galger's haft slipped from my fingers as I toppled sideways, hands dropping to the wound.

It wasn't deep, but hot blood bloomed across my fingers. The villagers were trying to shoot me, but either their aim was terrible or they were trying not to hit the demon.

It was dead, though—or, at least, as dead as demons could be with an axe in their face, which was not very dead. I felt the force of its power shrink, the echo fading as its life wrapped in upon itself; ancient, hideous magics turning to preservation, instead of attack.

In a minute, maybe less, it would be back on its feet. This was the moment when it could be bound, this short span of time when I could shove it back into the binding tree and lock it away for another millennium.

But I saw human shapes against the fire—two, four, seven. Bows drew taut.

I lunged, cracked Galger free in a rush of force and snatched Gammler from the mud as I bolted down the shoreline, half-in, half-out of the marsh.

Now that there was no chance of hitting the demon, the villagers unleashed all their full wrath upon me. Arrows sliced through the night to every side. I hurtled up to the shore and took off south, sprinting through the night as archers tracked my progress. More arrows flew—I felt them, heard them in a corner of my awareness—but my focus was on flight. An Arpa woman bolted out of my path, screaming, and I ducked between two houses.

I was out of the village.

Mrandr unfolded from the night. I shouted in shock and lost my footing on a patch of loose earth, hitting the ground hard and rolling, nearly killing myself on Gammler's blade. He said something indistinct, sprinting after me.

"Damn you, Iskiri!" I yelled with what little breath I had left, trying to get to my feet. I slipped again and fell, pain bursting through my ankle and the bleeding gash from the arrow. I lost grip on both axes.

Mrandr dropped something and loomed, a knife remaining in one hand, nothing in the other. His sword was still sheathed.

"Where's Imnir and the girl?" Mrandr asked, eyes darting around the night. I seemed to have lost my pursuers in the smoke, but that wouldn't last long.

"How should I know?" I straightened as much as I could without putting weight on my screaming ankle. I didn't think it was broken, but it hurt. A fresh roll of smoke from the village surrounded us, obscuring the settlement and the line of the Arpa road.

Never turn your back on an Iskiri. The phrase awoke unbidden, rising up in our solitude. Why was he here?

I caught a glimpse of the knife, still in his hand, and a satchel on the road behind him. It was singed and packed with goods, one of which was the bronze statue that had been in front of the binding tree.

"You came to steal the offerings?" I growled, though the answer was obvious. I managed to shove Gammler back into her brace and took Galger up again. "Never mind. We need to find the others, right now."

Mrandr opened his mouth to say something, then took a step toward me instead. Firelight slipped down the blade of the knife, still in his hand.

"Hessa!" Imnir's voice cut through the night. It came closer down the road, though I'd yet to sight him in the smoke and oscillating light. "Here! I have her! Hessa!"

Imnir had found Uspa. Still keeping an eye on Mrandr, I started toward him, heading up the road at a limp.

"Hessa?" Mrandr reached for me with his free arm. "Wait—"

Instinct made me step away from him, but my ankle wasn't strong—I nearly toppled, and his hand grabbed the front of my tunic, barely keeping me upright.

His knife moved. I was still battling to stay upright, Galger was slipping from my right hand, but my left shot out—seizing his wrist just as he sheathed the blade, safely back at his hip.

Mrandr met my eyes, his wide and accusatory. "What did you think I— I'm trying to help you walk!"

"I'll tell you if I need help." I released him, and he me. I managed a steady step sideways, adjusting Galger as I did. "Now, let's go."

Mrandr grabbed the sack of stolen goods and we took off down the road, my awareness narrowing to the Iskiri, the smoke, the amber blood trickling from the gash on my thigh. With every step, I feared my turned ankle would give out. With every step, I didn't allow it to, and I certainly didn't allow Mrandr close enough to help me again.

Imnir appeared on foot, shooting Mrandr a startled glance before he fell in on my other side. He was talking, shouting, but my thoughts skipped, back to the stink and the marsh and the clawed hand, grinding into my mouth. Mrandr unfolding from the night.

The road spread out beneath us as we jogged away, blood pounding in my ears and the shouts of villagers harrying our backs.

NINETEEN

Dawn broke over the marshes. Behind us, I imagined I could see the distant smoke of the village, but it could just have been the morning mist. It curled off the surface of the water in an unseasonably cold breeze, sending the tufting heads of the marsh grasses and bull rushes swaying.

I rode double with Sillo, watching the mist condense on my skin and clothes, a deep shiver running through my bones. Serka was alive, but burned and exhausted, and in no condition to be ridden. She trailed at the back of the train, watched over by Silgi and her ministrations. Nui had come through without a scratch, though her ears were pinned back in concern as she trotted along the side of the road.

The legionaries had left off their pursuit after Imnir and Mrandr had slaughtered three sometime before sunrise. Still, we could not risk relaxing yet. We simply bound our wounds, fought back our exhaustion, and moved on.

It wasn't only exhaustion I fought, but a profound unease. I'd already called out Mrandr's foray into thievery. We'd discussed the matter as we rode and Mrandr had grudgingly shared his haul with the rest of the Vynder, which appeased them. But that moment when he unfolded from the night? The knife in his hand? That hung between us, unspoken and festering, and he refused to look at me.

As we rode, the world began to lose more of its color. Reeds and bushes faded from greens and yellows to listless gray and red. The wind was easterly, distantly scented with the sea, but the marsh lent no fragrance; no rot, no flowers, no life save the moths. The wind kept them down but I still saw them, fluttering close to the water, clinging to the trunks of occasional dead trees or stands of dry, raspy reeds.

"Where is this god Larun?" I muttered to Sillo as we rode, my back to his chest. "We see signs of him everywhere, but where is he?"

Sillo gave a laughing grunt. "You think I'd know? It's your task to unravel the Laru. It's mine to keep you from falling out of this saddle."

I smiled and bumped my head back into his chest in rebuke.

Mid-afternoon, we came to a ridge near the end of the dead marsh. A line of reddish rock girded by gray reeds, it divided the land to either horizon, blocking off our view of anything further south. The road passed straight over it, indomitable as always. Mrandr and Ifling rode ahead, silhouetted against a sky of muted sunlight and thin, stretched cloud, like carded wool.

When they signaled the way was clear, we rode up to join them. Wetlands stretched before us, dead as far as the eye could see. My skin cooled and I leaned forward in the saddle, searching with no little desperation for any islands of life in the wasteland. There, to the east near the sea, green woke again; but everywhere else, the land was cursed. If we were right, if the Laru or their god were harvesting magic from this land, that power must truly be enormous by now.

The road followed the ridge east, and though it was exposed, we had no choice but to follow. We rode on until twilight swept over the bulk of the mountains in the west.

We found the remains of an abandoned settlement, surrounded still by silent marsh. It consisted of a large stone house, a watchtower, and a network of hovels and docks at the base of the ridge, accessed by a stone staircase to the south.

"We should shelter here," Castor called from the front in his accented Northman. He drew up beside the watchtower, squat and round and holding one arched doorway. It was a fair distance back from the rest of the little settlement, with a clean view in every direction.

"On cursed land?" Hete asked, eyeing the man.

"It's defensible," Imnir said, nudging his horse ahead of Castor's. He'd yet to apologize for leaving me behind, but then, I'd yet to apologize for letting him charge off into the village alone, so we'd left one another be. Our relationship was always easier when we didn't actually speak.

"Besides," he added, "this whole province is cursed. Silgi, you're with me. We'll take first watch on the road west. Ifling? Mrandr? Take the east."

I considered telling Mrandr to hold up so I could address what had happened back at the village—not the theft, but the knife. But the more time passed, the more I wondered if I'd misinterpreted his sudden appearance. There was nothing odd about him being armed, and I'd known about his greed for some time. Perhaps I shouldn't have been surprised at all.

The rest of the group dismounted before the tower's single door, and I pulled Uspa aside.

I sunk down onto a crumbling stone wall on one side of the courtyard, easing the weight on my sore but steadier ankle. Nearby, Nui snapped at a few languid moths among the weeds.

"What happened?" I asked. "How did you fall behind?"

Uspa's expression twitched, bracing for the explanation, and I noticed that one of her arms was covered with scratches. Brambles? Fingers?

"A legionary pulled her off her horse." Sillo unloaded an armful of saddlebags onto the wall beside me. "That's what happened."

Uspa opened her mouth to cut him off, her expression darkening, but she stopped herself. She looked between the two of us and then around, checking that no one else could hear.

"I fell off my horse," she admitted, forcing out each word. "I'm… I'm so sorry."

"Fell because someone pulled you off? The demon pulled me off Serka, there's no shame in it."

"Would that make it any better?" the girl asked and, as she spoke, her voice cooled. The change was sudden and startling, as if her embarrassment and irritation of a moment before were little more than a façade. She tugged her sleeves down. "My own clumsiness or a legionary bastard or both, it doesn't matter. I'm sorry. It won't happen again."

Night came. I dozed for a time, but within a few hours the need to relieve myself drove me out into the night with Nui on my heels. When I returned to the tower all was quiet, and I took a second to lean on the crumbled wall in the moonlight, taking in the night air while Nui sniffed at a motionless moth, clinging to the stone.

The wind kicked up. I turned around slowly, my Sight awakening to the taste of honey and summer sun on the air.

Estavius materialized between one blink of my eyes and the next. He tore off his helmet, blue eyes wild above sunburnt cheeks.

"Hessa," he panted. "I have news."

Estavius, Castor, Imnir, and I gathered out in the night, sheltered by three huge, barren trees. Estavius downed the flask of water Imnir had given him and poured a little of it on his face, wiping away a fringe of sweat as we waited to hear what he would say.

"Well?" Castor watched the other Arpa with a perplexed, wary brand of urgency. I hadn't told him how Estavius had arrived, leaving him to assume the man had come on foot. The sweat, real or not, affirmed this.

"Where's Nisien?" I couldn't help interjecting.

"Following Eolus," Estavius returned. "They're headed south on another road, near the sea."

"Eolus?" Imnir repeated. "Bresius's cousin? What is he doing this far north?"

"Last anyone heard, Eolus was in the capital, Apharnum, hiding out with a cohort of Laru and plotting against Cassius." Castor stretched his jaw. His eyes had a distant, critical light. "All threats to Bresius's claim must be eliminated..."

Estavius nodded. "Precisely. I infiltrated the camp and watched them for two days. Eolus has no idea that the Eangen and Algatt are here at Bresius's bidding. His lines of communication are too disrupted.

It seems he has been in seclusion further north, but Gadr's raiders came too close for comfort. He's moving to a fort, three days south-east of here, to wait out the barbarian tide in the company of a full legion."

"A fort and a legion are about the safest place in this province right now," I put in, catching Estavius's eye. "Hard to dig out a rabbit once he's in the warren. Are you asking us to intervene?"

Estavius nodded. "I think we must."

"Agreed," Castor said. "I cannot arrive at Bresius's camp only to tell him we had his cousin within our grasp and let him escape."

Imnir asked, "How many days until Eolus reaches the fort?"

"A week," the Miri answered, holding my gaze. There was a question in his eyes, and a rueful knowing. "But as I said, we're only three days away. We could easily intercept."

"How many legionaries are with him now?" My mind was already ranging ahead, calculating and plotting. I was sore and exhausted and the thought of pursuing Eolus was not something I relished. But where there was Eolus, there would be Laru.

"And how many priests?" I added.

"A dozen legionaries, three Laru priests, including one you know." Estavius met my gaze. "Siris."

Siris. Larun's head priest, who I'd met during the raids last year. If anyone could answer my questions, it was him.

Like it or not, there was only one way forward now.

I turned to Castor, who now stood silently in the latticework of shadows cast by the trees. A moth fluttered past him and he brushed it away.

"I think we should go," I said. "You?"

He raised his eyes to the sky and drew a deep breath. "We go after him."

"Then get some rest," Estavius said. "We'll leave at dawn."

Castor lingered for a moment, looking as though there was more he wanted to say, then left. Alone with Estavius and Imnir, I relaxed slightly.

I looked at the Miri promptly. "So? Anything else we should know about? Say, about what we'll do when we reach Apharnum?"

"Yes, though not about Apharnum, not directly." He leaned against the trunk of a tree. "We've found the trail of the Laru's god, and he may not be Arpa."

"Not Arpa?" Imnir repeated.

"We found a riverman, Nisien and I, where the Nivari River divides in the north." Rivermen were supernatural beings, like the Miri but less powerful—having been banished from the High Halls and their magic millennia ago. "He says he met two beings traveling Nivarium a number of years ago. Rivermen are not good with time, but it was around when Laru appeared. The riverman said they'd been over the wall."

"Two beings?" I asked, more perplexed than anything else. "Who were they?"

"And why would they come from Eangen?" Imnir added. "That priest we captured said they were Arpa."

"I've no clue who they were, but yes, the riverman saw two beings coming south." Estavius scratched at his throat, tugging loose the scarf that kept his armor from chafing. "As to why they'd come down from Eangen, I'd say it's the same reason you came to raid last year. Thvynder rules the North, but the Empire is lawless. There's no space for any creature with unholy ambition in Thvynder's domain."

"So who are they?" Imnir laced his arms over his chest. "Is one of them Larun, and the other something else? Or is Larun more than one person?"

"That, I still don't know," the Miri admitted. "But they are certainly connected to the Laru, if not Larun himself. Wherever they went, the land died around them."

"We think that Larun is harvesting life-magic from Nivarium," I told Estavius. "Is that possible?"

Estavius nodded grimly. "An ability like that is uncommon, but not unheard of."

"Wonderful." Imnir started to give a resigned sigh, but was caught in a yawn. He straightened, his feet turned back towards the watchtower and eyes crinkled with fatigue. "Well then, if that's settled, I'm going back to bed. I'm not hunting an emperor on a poor night's sleep."

TWENTY

Three days later, we reached a deserted roadside within earshot of the sea, though we couldn't see the shore in the pre-dawn murk. The dead marshes gave way to a swath of rustling, verdant coastal life— dune grasses, sand and tangled sprawls of shrubbery, and sparse old forest along the straight road.

The road stretched beneath a well-spaced grove of weeping birches, its stones smooth from centuries of passage. Sand and grasses clotted its smooth ruts though, and here and there a stone had become loose.

Estavius led us to one of the markers, checked the Arpa symbols upon it, and signaled a halt.

He whistled. A second, lower whistle cut through the murk in reply, and Nisien unfolded from the high grass. Nui darted toward him with a joyous bark but I got there first, throwing an arm around his neck and planting a kiss on his smooth cheek. I didn't care that Imnir and the others were watching. Being back with Nisien and Estavius again was like finding a little island of home and solace, and I couldn't stifle my happiness.

Nisien embraced me in return. He looked the ideal Arpa legionary now, hair trimmed close and beard shaved away, his plate armor hidden beneath a dark cloak. The sight tainted my joy, but if this was the image that kept him safe, I would not complain.

"What happened to you?" he asked, studying my tired face.

"I was fighting a demon and Arpa peasants tried to stick a few arrows in me," I returned, examining the embroidery on his cloak. It was fine white braid, stitched with Arpa symbols. He certainly hadn't been wearing this when he headed off south.

"Befriending the locals, as usual?" He raised his brows. "You'll be all right to fight tonight?"

I nodded distractedly, tugging at the braid on his cloak. "Your cloak is a little lavish for a wandering legionary, Nis."

"Estavius put me in it." Nisien tugged me toward the rest of the group, waiting around our Arpa friend. He said in everyone's hearing, "Eolus isn't far off. Half an hour, an hour. They were beginning to break camp when I left. Avi?"

"I'll keep watch." Estavius nodded, resting a hand on the hilt of his sword and starting to trudge back up the road. I watched him go, wondering how long he would remain in physical form once he was out of sight.

He vanished into the night, my question left unanswered.

I elbowed Nisien in the ribs and gave him a quick smile. "You're all mine now, horseman."

We tied the horses—and Nui, to keep her from spoiling our ambush—to trees in a sheltered area, far enough off the road to stay hidden, then took up position in the high grasses of the roadside, under the curling white bark and dangling bows of the birches.

Wildflowers waved over my head as I knelt, straining to hear past the scuffs of my warriors and the churr of crickets. Nisien took up position to my left, Sillo to my right. My cousin sat cross-legged while Uspa knelt beside him, producing a small pot of kohl and a fine stick with a crushed, frayed tip. Uspa dipped the tip into the pot and eyed Sillo.

"Sit still."

He obeyed, big shoulders relaxed and head bent back to give her a full view of his face. She outlined his eyes then drew three vertical lines on each of them. One was centered over the eyes, through his brows, and over his cheekbones, while two shorter ones clung only to the bottom lid on either side.

"Stop watching me, cousin," Sillo muttered between strokes, while Uspa sunk back onto her heels and scrutinized her work. "We've time. We're capturing an emperor tonight. I want to be remembered as a proper barbarian when these Arpa sing their laments."

Uspa grinned, her nose wrinkling and eyes crinkling. "Then you'd better paint mine well too. Hold still, I'm almost done."

Sillo settled and she began to draw up from the edge of his beard, too, onto his cheeks in short, deft streaks.

I wasn't concerned about time. With Estavius on watch we would have ample warning, and preparations like this were a good way to pass the time without wearing one's nerves to rags. It was a tradition and ritual, one held by our people for generations.

Rather, it was the painting itself that left me contemplative. Acts like this, painting one another's skin or braiding hair, were not done without some level of trust between the two parties. It was a gesture of friendship and comradery, but also commonly extended to someone you were attracted to—as it certainly was in the case of Sillo and Uspa.

Spouses and lovers were expected to perform such tasks for one another. Whatever his motives, Imnir had reached out to me that day we'd scouted together. Perhaps, tonight, I could reach back.

"Uspa," I said, glancing out into the night to locate Imnir. "May I borrow that when you're done?"

She nodded. A few moments later she and Sillo traded. He painted her eyes in thick, bold strokes from their inner corner, straight over her temples and into her hairline. Then he passed the pot to me.

I glanced at Nisien as I stood. "I'm assuming you won't partake?"

Nisien shook his head and I made for Imnir, lingering in the shadow of a tree with the other Algatt. They'd already undergone similar preparations, smudging traditional yellow and blue paints into their hairlines and across their cheeks. Mynin had blotted kohl under his eyes, too, in weeping streaks, but when Imnir looked at me his face was clean.

"Husband," I held up the pot, "shall we?"

He nodded, a little surprised, and we moved away from the others. We were still within sight, could still hear their low conversation, but we had enough solitude to make my heart beat a little faster as Imnir knelt before me and I dipped the brush into thick paint.

"Hessa," he started. "About last time we spoke…"

"Hush," I chided, brushing excess paint inside the lip of the pot. "Let's not talk. It never goes well. Let's just… be."

The man hesitated, then his expression softened and he nodded.

I thought of Eidr, as I laid the first stroke over his cheek, and I let my mind drift over the memories. He'd been red-haired and quick to smile, reckless and a little too loud, and I'd loved him wildly. We had done this for one another, before a dozen Eangi battles.

I found some rest, some bitter-sweet nostalgia, in the familiar task. Imnir watched me, every so often, but soon passed his gaze over my shoulder, surveying the darkened road in the direction Estavius had gone.

I was grateful for that, I told myself. We were very close, and the harmony of my thoughts might not withstand the attention of my Algatt husband.

When I lowered the brush, his gaze returned to me. Just as they had in the rain at the watchtower, my thoughts blanked. It wasn't that there was love in his gaze, but there was a kind of solidarity and appreciation. It was guarded, though, obscured by the thousand ghosts that stood between us.

"May I?"

I realized he was holding out his hands for the tools and relinquished them.

He shifted higher on his knees, tilting my chin to the side with one warm knuckle before he made his first stroke. I tried to look off into the distance as he'd done, but he filled my vision. So I stared at his shoulder as he brushed kohl around my eyes and across my jaw at both sides, narrowing my aspect to a wolfish point.

When he was done, he smiled. It was a genuine expression, half teeth and half crinkled eyes. "Lathian himself would tremble at your feet, woman."

A grin twitched onto my lips. "Thank you."

He passed the pot and stylus back to me, then we both stood, gazing up the road to where our quarry would soon appear.

"I'm curious to meet this Siris," Imnir said, before noting his handiwork again with a smirk. "But I'm more curious to see what he does when he recognizes you. You are admirable, Hessa."

Before my face could do something less dignified, I grinned a quiet, self-satisfied smile. "I think that's the kindest thing you've ever said to me."

Imnir gave a one-sided shrug. "I don't flatter falsely."

I hesitated, then said quickly, "Imnir, I don't want us to be at odds. I don't expect you to be Eidr. I never did. But I want to be your ally, and to just… let the rest go."

He glanced over my face one more time, and try hard as I might, I couldn't decipher him. "What will come out of that?"

It was my turn to shrug. "What will be will be."

His expression lightened again, traces of a smile creeping in around his eyes. "Then we'll let it be."

He moved off, leaving me alone in the grasses. I pried my gaze from him and stared off into the waning night, paint cooling in the sea breeze, and murmured a prayer to clear my head.

"Thvynder, Thvynder, the Sleeper Risen, the Faceless. God in the North. Pillar of the World."

A violet blush pierced the eastern horizon, beyond the rustling tops of the trees, and Estavius returned. His report was little more than a nod, and we all fell into place among the grasses and morning birdsong.

Within minutes, the clatter of hooves drifted through the half-light. Sillo dropped onto three points, body tense as a hound. Uspa crouched at his side, spear low and horizontal in the grass; the huntress in waiting. Nisien lifted his head, scanning over the heads of grasses and I coaxed long, slow breaths through my nose. Ifling and Lida were behind me now, quiet with Mrandr between them. I caught the Iskiri's eye. To my surprise he grinned, all signs of the tension that had come between us a few days ago gone.

I called my golden Sight, which flared out from me like mist on the wind, dispersing to leave a flush of color that only the Vynder could see. But I saw no glowing threads. No Laru in range yet.

The hooves came closer as the sky began to burn a fierce, bloody pink. Sillo tapped one fingernail against the inside of his shield, counterpoint to the rhythm of the horses. It was quiet enough not to be heard over them, but it fed my own tension.

I focused on my breath again.

One. The first hooves passed the Algatt concealed in the grass, forty paces up the road.

Two. I tightened my grip on my shield and lifted Galger's head from the earth.

Three. Three golden threads swelled in my vision.

"Three Laru," I told Sillo, affirming Estavius's earlier count. "Let me take Siris. Sillo, Nisien, and Uspa, take one. Lida, Ifling, Mrandr, the other. Imnir and the Algatt will secure Eolus. Make sure he lives, understood?"

They all nodded, and I could taste their tension. I could hear the blood pounding in their throats, see them stretching jaws and loosening their fingers on their weapons, ready to scream and charge and kill.

Was Frir already here, waiting for blood to be spilled? Did she linger beyond the drifting veil of the birches, glaring at me with her ghostly children about her skirts? Was the little boy here too?

Grasses bowed under a gust of wind. A bird sang far off, three familiar trills that tickled at the edge of my concentration.

Dawn-edged shadows fell across the grass between me and the road in the shapes of helmets and mounted men. Still, I waited, watching the golden threads thicken and shift.

There. The threads straightened. The priests were right before me.

I rose, searching out Siris's face over the tops of the grasses and the rim of my shield.

I saw him; a blond-haired man astride a bay horse, unusual among the silver plate armor, spears, and helmets of the Arpa legionaries. Two more priests rode at his sides, one hooded and the other dozing in the saddle, hooded sickles at their belts, but Siris himself carried no visible weapons. The poleaxe he'd borne at our first meeting was nowhere to be seen. A sign of overconfidence, perhaps?

My magic needed no voice, but I gave it one anyway. I hissed. Power rushed through the air like snakes, converging upon the High Priest of the Laru.

Siris reacted before the legionaries or other priests had picked me out from the swaying grass. He threw up his forearms in an X, fingers crooked on either side, and shouted something in Arpa. Ashen magic burst into the twilight in a thick, obscuring fog.

The Vynder, Uspa and Nisien and Mrandr, exploded from the grass around me. I sprinted forward into the cloud of swirling, sorcerous dust, knees and shield parting the meadow.

I let it out in a short, cracking battle cry. The Laru's magic shuddered, buffeted by the wind, but it did not disperse.

Siris was stronger than last time we met. I'd half a breath to blink in shock, then a legionary spurred his horse between us. Two more broke out of line and off the road to flank me, only to find themselves pulled from the saddle and butchered by Mrandr and Ifling.

Panic took the company. Legionaries turned, horses reared, and shouts and screams tore through the dawn.

I saw Siris's lip twitch in something between fear, madness, and exhilaration. Despite myself, despite the failure of my initial assault, I felt a similar surge.

Yes, he was stronger now, but he was still mortal. Finally, I faced an opponent I could fight on equal terms.

The head of a spear flashed overhead, a blur against the brightening sky. I threw up my shield and took a legionary's blow, feet grinding, grass tearing up at its roots. To my right, Nisien slit the fastenings of my attacker's saddle and helped its occupant to the earth with a dagger to the thigh.

Another spear connected with my shield, scraping off the rim and down towards my belly. I twisted out of danger and batted aside his next thrust with Galger. I hooked his spear, smashing the rim of my shield under the man's jaw in one quick jab.

His horse bolted, carrying the gargling man out of my path and presenting me with full view of Siris again. I shook Galger free of the spear and hurled myself into the breach.

Siris drove his heels into his horse's flanks. The animal, already prancing, fled—directly towards Uspa, up ahead.

"Bring that horse down!" I sprinted after him, dodging another spear and flying hooves. He kept to the road; I diverted off and thundered through the high grass, keeping the priest in sight and trying to round him.

The girl immediately crouched and braced her spear in the center of the road. The horse shied and reared, avoiding the glistening spearhead at the last second, but that was all I needed to catch up.

I dropped my shield and seized the priest by the robes. He hit the ground with a strangled *whump* and I drove my fist into his face as his horse bolted and Uspa rose from her crouch.

Siris's head smashed into the road. He rolled, disoriented eyes drifting back and forth across my face. I stepped back and leveled Galger's blade at his throat.

"Don't move."

Uspa drew up, pacing and circling like a she-wolf. Under her dubious protection, I allowed myself one rattling breath to stare down at my captive. Around us, the battle spread out—Northerners chasing legionaries, legionaries chasing Northerners beyond the edges of my sight.

Siris closed his eyes and laughed. It was a tired sound, rasping and clawing out of winded lungs. But there was something beneath it, something that dragged gold back across the corners of my vision. A warning.

I threw my power at him, stronger than before. It wrapped around his throat like a lash and pushed into his blood, cutting off his laugh and leaving him to writhe upon the ground. I withdrew Galger, just enough to ensure he didn't slit his throat on the blade.

Siris's cloud of ashen dust released, falling to the earth like necrotic snow. I withdrew slowly, watching him for any sign of a trick.

"Be ready to bind him on my signal," I said to Uspa, not lowering my guard.

The girl approached, setting her spear on the ground and pulling a leather cord from her belt.

Siris coughed, now lying on his side, but I caught the smile he was hiding. It was a flaccid expression as first, but strengthened into a tiny, understated curve.

I saw the knife just in time—bone-handled, short, and flashing. He jerked it from the folds of his robes and plunged the blade down—not at me or Uspa, but through his own hand. It sliced through skin and meat and tendon and jarred off the stones of the road beneath his palm. He screamed.

The wind died. A horrible shriek came in its place, joining the end of the priest's scream—trees cracking, whispering, wailing as their wood strained and their leaves crumpled in upon themselves. Around me the rustle of grass ended in a dry, grating hush.

The shriek threatened to enter my own blood and bones. My magic instinctively surged, ready to protect me. I lunged in front of Uspa, but the attack—the curse—retreated of its own accord. It swept the land around and behind us instead, snuffing out its life in one fell swoop.

Siris stood, disorientation gone, his eyes veritably bleeding Laru magic as he rose to meet me. His hand had fully healed.

My question as to whether Laru priests could harvest magic like their god was answered. The bloody pink sunrise paled into rose over a swath of roadside as dead and lifeless as the marshes.

"Uspa, back off," I murmured, putting myself directly between the priest and the girl.

She didn't move, but I couldn't spare a second for her. Siris was speaking.

"I've been blessed, Priestess," Siris said. He seemed utterly unperturbed, unthreatened. "Last time you caught us unprepared, but my god has ensured I'm ready for you now. So, shall I poison the minds of your people, have them butcher one another and then turn on you? Or will you let me take Eolus and leave?"

Eolus. I'd still yet to see Bresius's cousin—he was Imnir's task.

Dread swept over me. I risked a glance at Uspa, who stood motionless, eyes distant, the cord she'd intended to bind Siris with loose in her hand. She looked just as Briel had in the burning village, the first time I'd met Siris. She was in his thrall.

Hooves thundered. Three legionaries barreled towards us through the dead grass. I could no longer see the rest of the battle – I could barely even hear it, distant shouts of coordination and strife. Either the conflict had spread too broadly, or Siris's magic had cut us off. I'd no idea where the others were.

The world slowed. I stared at the chargers, registered that the centermost rider was no legionary at all. He wore light armor over tunic and robe, and his eyes were round with shock and fear and a wild, reckless determination.

No soldier. This must be Eolus. Escaping.

"Yes, that is my emperor, and he's getting away," Siris shouted over the rumble of hooves, seeming to read my thoughts again. "Go on. Stop him! Turn your back to me."

My indecision—and patience—snapped. I hurled every fragment of honeyed magic I had into Siris's chest, saving a fraction to lash at Uspa. I didn't wait to see if the curse broke, but I felt Siris's magic implode in a shuddering flurry of ash and dust.

I charged Eolus.

His escort saw me coming. One continued with Eolus but the other spun back, galloping right for me.

A sword came down at my head. I ducked, seized the offender's arm, and hauled.

The man stayed in the saddle for a moment, nearly pulling me under the horse's churning hooves. Then he toppled to the earth, armor and shield and spear clattering. I planted my foot on the fallen legionary's back and took his spear.

I hurled it at Eolus's other escort. The spear thudded into his side and he fell forward, tangled in his horse's reins. Suddenly dragged down by its bridle, the animal screamed in panic, lost its footing and fell on its former rider.

Eolus was alone now, staring over his shoulder in horror. He saw me, saw Siris, and then something else behind us.

More horses approached. For a moment I let myself hope that the hulking riders were Northmen, but the shapes of their armor and helmets were far too clear. Six legionaries, battered but determined, galloped towards me.

I bolted for my shield. I couldn't see Uspa. I couldn't see anyone but my attackers.

The smooth wooden grip met my fingers and I threw up my shield, just as a spear stabbed at my neck. My knuckles crashed up inside the boss and pain exploded, rocketing all the way from crushed fingers to my shoulder.

My fingers only loosened briefly, but it was enough—a second blow from the spear sent my shield snapping back into my own head.

My vision leapt. I was on my knees. Uspa screamed nearby and grass swayed into my eyes, bending and breaking as hooves churned and men dropped from the saddle with ripples of boots and clinks of armor.

I tasted blood. My right eye was full of it, dark and swimming, and my head—my thoughts stumbled and clattered.

Then I was being dragged. A hand was dug into the straps where Galger and Gammler should have been, and I was hauled through the grass into the dawn.

TWENTY-ONE

I stumbled in the sand beside an impassive, crashing sea. My captor—the faceless, helmeted legionary who held my bindings on a long rope—slowed his horse to let me find my feet again.

I'd been here before, though then I'd been drugged, Castor had been the one to hold my leash and Eang had still roamed the North. My thoughts drifted back to that time as I found my balance in the sand and started to catch my breath.

My captor spurred his mount forward again. Sand flew into my face, the rope went taut, and my head snapped back.

Blackness. The next thing I knew, I was being dragged, my already bruised body carving a trench in the soft earth before a sharp voice intervened and the rope slackened.

"Enough of that," Eolus, Bresius's cousin and contender for the Arpa throne, said drolly in Arpa. He'd recovered from his panic during the ambush, riding his black horse with the rolling hips and easy posture of an experienced horseman. He was in his early thirties, dark-haired for an Arpa, with tight curls and the southerners' signature straight nose.

I could just see him from where I lay on my side with sweat, sand, and my own hair plastered into my face. But the rope dragging me didn't tighten again, and under Eolus's gaze—all false benevolence and self-satisfaction—I staggered to my feet.

Halfway up I spat out a mouthful of sand, making the legionaries laugh and toss mocking comments among themselves. The nearest one reached down to thump me on the back as I straightened, and I staggered again.

This man—his jaw square and heavy under his helmet—had Uspa across his horse's flanks. She was limp and unmoving, dried blood caked to her cheeks with dust and horsehair.

I glared up at the offending legionary, wiping spittle and sand from my lips with the back of my bound hands. He grinned in return and slapped Uspa on the rump before nudging his mount on ahead.

I marked his face, silently moving him up my running list of men to castrate in the near future, but it was Uspa's limp body that snared me.

She was, at least, alive. I'd heard her ragged breath between the clatter of the horses' hooves. But I had no illusions as to why she was still breathing. Siris had seen me protect her. He intended to use her against me, to control me; that was all she was to them.

I tried not to wheeze, eyeing Eolus out of the corner of my watering eyes. It was nearly noon; we'd been moving for at least four hours, our path through meadow and copse and over dunes no doubt obscured by Laru magic. At this point I'd no idea how far we were from the road.

Eolus caught me watching him. As the horses began to move again, he inquired, "Can you understand me, witch?"

The rope tugged. I began to walk. "Unfortunately."

Siris amended, "She understands some, my lord."

Eolus slowed his horse, coming to amble alongside me. "Who taught you Arpa?"

"Our slaves," I replied. Tired and aching as I was, the Arpa words were all the more difficult to wrap my tongue around, and I heard one of the legionaries chuckle at my pronunciation.

"Slaves? Taken from Nivarium, last year?" Eolus said, shooting Siris an incredulous look. "You assured me your god would intervene in these matters."

"When you are in the fullness of your power, lord," Siris returned, his tone telling me that this wasn't the first time he'd said this very thing.

Eolus twisted in the saddle to contemplate me before he asked, "If you learned from slaves, why do you have an upper Apharni accent?

Your barbarian slur mars it, truly, but it is there. You did not learn from a Nivari peasant."

Accent? It took a moment for my mind to catch up with this. If there was a regional taint to my Arpa, I hadn't been aware of it. But I'd learned from Estavius, who posed as a son of a High Priest in Apharnum, and Nisien. Nis, regardless of where he'd learned his Arpa, had spent a decade at Estavius's side. It followed that their speech patterns had bled into one another.

I realized that Eolus was tracking every thought across my face. The silence stretched, and I had no good answer. I'd never been good at deception—I made allies of enemies or put them in the ground.

Neither of those were options at the moment.

"Who did you learn from?" Eolus asked again, more aggressively this time. "Halt, halt!"

Around us, the legionaries reined in. My skin crawled as every man's attention turned to me, alone in the center of their formation as the sea crashed sparse paces from my aching feet.

"A slave," I repeated, channeling all my focus into keeping my voice level. "What he once was, I cannot say."

Siris studied me. The topic had caught his attention now, too, and dread coiled in my gut.

Neither Eolus nor the Laru could learn I had willing Arpa allies. This was why Castor never let himself be seen when we encountered his people—Bresius's whole scheme might crumble. And if they learned of Estavius and Nisien? I could not only jeopardize their mission but endanger two men I cared for.

Eolus's frown was cool and disapproving. "Woman, know that I only have one use for you, and none for your companion. I will ransom you. If your people want their barbarian queen back—let alone in one piece, and unbroken—they will leave my land. And if you want your friend to live, you will not fight back. Answer my questions, endear yourself to me, and this captivity will be far more pleasant for the both of you."

I kept my expression flat. There were only six legionaries here. How far did Eolus think he would get before the others found our trail and caught up?

This situation was temporary, one way or another. A day, maybe two. All I needed to do was keep Uspa and myself alive until we could escape or be rescued.

"My lord, we need to move on," one of the legionaries interjected, glancing back the way we'd come. "We need to reach shelter before nightfall."

Eolus scrutinized me for another long moment, then inclined his head. "Very well. But consider my words, woman. Offer me something of value before we camp tonight, and perhaps I won't let my men have you. Offer me more, and perhaps I'll spare your friend too."

At these last words, white fury nearly blinded me. I couldn't stop the rage, the repulsion from snapping across my face, but Eolus didn't react. He simply gave me a tight, high-browed smile, and nudged his horse into movement again.

The straps across my back where Galger and Gammler usually hung chafed. I glared at Eolus's back through my lashes, and stalked after him.

Mid-afternoon, the lead legionary bid us halt. We'd found something of a road by then, though it was not one of the Arpa's main, paved ways. It was little more than a wagon track along the top of a ridge, which crossed an expanse of towering, rippling green reeds with the occasional open channel. Stretches of exposed mud and driftwood islands played host to creeping things, and shorebirds scattered at the clatter of hooves. Larger, unseen beasts moved in the shelter of the reeds and, above our heads, black and red birds flitted and trilled.

I felt Eolus watching me as two legionaries dismounted, passed off their reins and jogged up the road and out of sight.

Uspa stirred on the back of her horse. She moaned, and the legionary I'd already marked for death reached back to lift up her head by the hair. He examined her face and commented to one of his companions, laughing and amused. Then let her head drop again.

Uspa caught my eye. Through her pain, through the blood and dirt and horsehair on her skin, I saw fear chase confusion, then settle on something harder and hemmed with fury. She squirmed.

I held her gaze, willing her to understand the words I could not say aloud.

I see you. I'm with you. Wait.

Uspa stilled. Her eyes were wet and red-rimmed, though that might have just been from all the dust and horsehair.

"My men are off to see if your people destroyed the next village yet," Eolus said to me, oblivious to the exchange. "Did they?"

"Did they what?" I asked, glancing up the road where the scouts had gone.

"Destroy the next village."

Not this far south, I thought. But I replied, "They do as they please."

"Do you not control them? They told me you were a queen."

"Queen is a misleading term. We do not rule one another like you do."

"So you have no kings or queens or emperors?"

"We have high priests, war chiefs, and clan chiefs," I returned. Another time Eolus's questions might have irked me, but I hoped that if I had the would-be emperor's attention, the legionaries would be less inclined to torment me. And now that Uspa was awake, my anxiety doubled. If one of the legionaries provoked her, if she did something rash...

Eolus frowned, as if trying to puzzle me out from the lines about my eyes or the cut of my filthy clothes.

Siris, in turn, watched the both of us from the back of his horse. Warm wind brushed hair into his eyes and he murmured to himself—a prayer?

"Thvynder is our ruler, if you need to think in such terms," I told Eolus, still watching Siris. Unless I was mistaken, there was a new tension in the lines around his mouth, and his gaze roved the estuary as if he'd seen—or sensed—something abnormal. "They are the only one we answer to. Who I answer to."

Eolus leaned forward, pressing into his saddlehorn with both palms. "But Thvynder has no physical form."

"Not as the Miri did," I said. Siris was still watching the marsh, and the intensity of his gaze made my skin crawl. My Sight sparked, registering the swirl of Laru magic from his eyes and hands, but there was nothing else unnatural in the vicinity.

Quiet fell, and in that reed-rustling hush, I heard the bird; three notes, mournful and sweet and descending.

Siris twisted in the saddle with a creak of leather and the soldiers looked up. Uspa, however, had closed her eyes again and didn't stir.

"What is it?" I asked the priest. I'd heard that same bird a few times since I entered Nivarium, hadn't I?

Eolus watched the Laru too. Siris didn't reply immediately, scanning the reeds like a startled hare. Only after another wordless minute, in which the horses shuffled and the legionaries glanced at one another nervously, did he speak.

"An omen," the Laru summarized. "That bird does not come from this world."

"Then it's from the Penumbra," I inferred.

"Yes." The Laru still scanned the reeds. "The Penumbra. I really would like to know who you learned our language and lore from, woman."

I avoided the question, twitching with unease. If the bird was from the Penumbra, why had I heard it before?

He frowned in consideration. "Well, if that creature is here, it's because someone opened a door that should have stayed closed. Or there has been a great amount of death. They have been known to escape when the souls of the dead pass."

Cold trickled down my spine. "But you've no one to release your dead."

"Larun does," Siris said without hesitation.

One of the legionaries spoke up then, too quickly for me to catch his words. But up ahead the scouts jogged back into sight, and I was tugged into motion.

We entered a town soon after. Built on a hill beside the sea, the settlement was whole and vibrant, if wary. Heavy palisade walls surrounded it, much more solid and intentional than the ones we'd seen so far. At a call from the lead legionary, the gates swung open.

People crowded the streets as we entered. For the first time I was glad of the legionaries' presence. Hundreds of eyes bored into me, people exclaimed and pointed, cursed, and spat in Uspa's and my direction.

They knew what we were. We were Northerners, barbarians, the same ones that had forced them to cower behind their walls.

It took all my concentration not to flinch, to keep my head high as village elders met with Eolus and guided us to the town center.

The lead legionary began to speak to the assembled townsfolk, Eolus at his side, but Siris turned his attention to me. With a flick of his fingers he directed another legionary to pick up Uspa, before taking hold of my bonds himself, and leading me into a stone building in the town square.

The central building was octagonal, with a domed roof. A second octagonal vestibule clung to it at the front, and it was to this we headed. Both sections were built of pale stone, while the rest of the village was predominantly wood, wattle, and daub.

I was tugged inside the arched entrance to the vestibule. The scent of Arpa incense folded around me, and though I'd noticed no local priests, I knew this was a temple. Judging by Siris's welcome, it was a temple of Larun.

Once inside, Siris paused to take in faded murals of old, dead gods and a central offering bowl in one calloused sweep of the eyes. There was a dark wood door on the opposite side of the room, leading into the main chamber, but it remained closed for now.

"Throw her there." He directed the legionary carrying Uspa to a far corner between a mural of Alathea, Goddess of the Lowlands, and what I guessed was Mircea, perched upon a litter born by rapids and muscled, reed-woven rivermen. Both women wore the half-moon headdresses that I was coming to associate with all Arpa goddesses, each decorated according to their realms and power.

The legionary set Uspa against the wall and left as Siris tied my bindings to a lantern hook high on the wall. I could barely sit, but I was grateful to be stationary and out of the sun.

"There will be guards outside, and I've sent the priests away so that you cannot… tamper with them," Siris warned me as he headed back towards the door. "Eolus will keep his word, Priestess. Make what you can out of this situation. I'd hate to lose sleep tonight, listening to you and your young friend suffer."

With that he left, and Uspa and I were alone in the incense-laden shadows of the vestibule. I stared at the door to the main temple for a moment before my tired eyes dragged closed, slipping into as much of a resting state as Siris's words, my restraints, and the smell of the chamber would permit me.

The sound of Uspa shifting woke me. I watched the younger woman in concern, trying to gauge her state from her movements—slow and pained. Not good, then.

"I'm alive." The sound emerged from her throat in a raspy, parched croak. "Stop looking at me like that. Please."

I leaned back against the wall, hearing the ropes above my head creak. "How bad is it?"

"What?" Uspa raised her head slowly and leaned it back against the stone. Her one eye tracked me, but the other seemed a touch too slow, and was caked with blood. "My head, my back, my ankle, or my ribs?"

"Can you run?"

Uspa held my gaze proudly, but I saw her lower lip tremble. "I won't slow you down. Do we have weapons?"

"No." I rubbed dirt off my cheek on an upraised arm. I stank of sweat and horse. "But don't worry about that. Rest."

Uspa blinked at me, her slow eye squinting closed. "Yes, Priestess."

At length, she drifted back into a half-sleeping daze. I stared at the murals on the walls, studying the faded faces of deities while I tried to organize my thoughts.

Nisien and Imnir and the others would be on our trail—Estavius would ensure that. But we were in a settlement now, walled and occupied, and I wasn't sure we could rely on outright rescue.

But neither of us were in prime condition, and escape would likely mean abandoning Eolus, wasting all the blood and suffering this escapade had already cost. I would leave the would-be ruler behind if I had to, but I held out hope of a third option. Another way out.

My gaze strayed to the door of the main temple, quiet and closed.

TWENTY-TWO

I watched Siris set a clay bowl within the larger offering bowl in the center of the vestibule. He filled it with dried leaves and a pinkish salt, doused it with oil and lit it with a rain of sparks from flint and steel.

The oil flared and the leaves began to smoke. The scent of incense filled the chamber, thick and heady and stomach-bending.

Still, the door to the main temple remained closed. I eyed it surreptitiously, wondering why it was that Siris chose to make his offerings here instead of there, and hoping I knew the answer.

"Have you decided to cooperate yet?" Siris asked, lifting the bowl to the level of his lips. He puffed on it gently, wafting smoke around the room and muttering short, condensed phrases under his breath as he waited for me to reply.

"I don't see that I have a choice," I said. "But I don't think knowing where I learned your language will be enough for Eolus."

"Tell me, then," he said, lowering the bowl. "Let me be the judge."

"I allied with your people, once," I replied, truthfully. "I traveled with a man called Polinus, from the Ilia Gates to the Algatt Mountains, and I spent time with another called Telios. I knew my life could hinge on understanding their tongue—so I listened, and learned."

Siris watched me through curls of rising smoke. "Polinus, him I do not know. But Telios... that is a name my kind would not soon forget. He served Lathian."

"He was possessed by him too. But he showed me maps of the Empire, implored me to turn to your gods, and so on."

"It's plausible that you learned from him," Siris mused. "I'll offer it to Eolus, but I'd be… more inclined to intercede for you if you answer my own questions."

"Oh?"

Siris poured a little more oil into the offering bowl. It flared, the flames settling into a steady burn. Light lapped across his face, etched with very human weariness, and for the first time it occurred to me that he, too, had been on the road for days. Furthermore, the magic he'd harvested already seemed to be waning. It still eddied around him in my Sight, but it was far thinner and less potent than before.

I wondered how often it needed to be replenished. If he ran out of power, I'd have a formidable advantage.

Siris gathered up his robes and circled the smoking bowl. The flames had condensed, blue and white licking across oil-sodden foliage. The scent of it saturated the chamber now, smoke drifting out the open door into the light and chatter of the village. Siris appeared unaffected by the smoke, but it stung my eyes.

Uspa remained, to all appearances, asleep.

"Hessa." Siris mulled the name over on his tongue. "Larun is curious about you, woman. Curious to meet you. I intend to take you to him, to speak face-to-face."

I tried not to react. Estavius had said that there was a possibility Larun was more than one being, but if his High Priest spoke of him in the singular, I thought that doubtful.

"Where is he?" I asked.

"Apharnum, he tells me, with the remainder of the High Priesthood. They hold the Temple of Lathian against Cassius. You've time to prepare yourself." Siris crouched beyond the reach of my legs. Dispersing smoke and the exposed beams of the ceiling provided backdrop to his blond hair and keen eyes. "What is Thvynder like? This 'True God in the North'?"

"Thvynder is more powerful than all the Miri combined. They always keep their word. They're present, and they're fair."

"Are they content with the North?"

I shifted, stretching my restraints with a creak of rope. "I've not heard otherwise."

"So you raid because you're bored? Not to weaken or conquer?"

"Peace doesn't suit my people, but we can hardly keep killing one another."

Siris nodded, almost imperceptibly. "Then why did you travel with so few men?"

I paused, momentarily caught on this discrepancy. "What do you mean?"

"To capture Eolus you brought… what was it, eight warriors? The legionaries claim there were more, but I disagree. So why is the High Priestess of all the Eangen traveling south with so few?"

"We were hunting Eolus," I said, the words presenting themselves without thought. "He's worth a lot more gold than the goats and grain in your villages. Gadr sent word that he was on the road south, so I took my best warriors and came to take him."

Siris considered this for a moment, then shrugged. "I'll accept that."

Relief rushed through me, but I didn't dare let it show. Carefully, I said, "May I ask you something?"

"You can, but I may not answer."

"Your magic." I let hunger enter my eyes, recalling what I'd felt when I stood before the door to the Penumbra in the Temple of Mircea and letting him see it. "How do you do it?"

Siris hovered between satisfaction and the same hunger. "I can't tell you that."

"You used your blood." I nodded to the hand he'd stabbed, entirely healed now. "A sacrifice, to begin the process?"

Siris *tsk*ed. "Ask these questions of Larun himself; you'll meet him soon enough. He granted me my abilities, as your god gave you yours. Do you know where your magic comes from or how it flows?"

I did, rather intimately, but stayed silent.

"I thought not," Siris said. "The gods keep their secrets close."

He had no idea what he was speaking of, and that almost made me feel… was that pity? My thoughts drifted back to the Temple of Mircea again, to Castor's ravenous eyes when he stood near the door to the Penumbra, and I wondered if Larun felt that hunger too.

My eyes drifted to the door of the main temple, drawn there by hope and instinct. This was a temple, and a large one. On the road, Siris had said the mysterious bird came through doors that should have been shut.

There had to be a rift to the Penumbra here. That was why the door to the inner chamber remained closed, why Uspa and I were kept in the vestibule instead of the more secure inner chamber.

Fragments of my plan surged through my mind. It was dangerous, foolhardy even, but if it worked there would be no need to escape the town, scale walls, or flee on foot through the night. Perhaps we could even take Eolus with us.

We could escape through the Penumbra.

That night, Uspa slipped in and out of sleep while I stared at the door to the inner temple and prayed to Thvynder under the cover of darkness. My magic hummed as I did, eddying in a gold haze between me and that door, and I knew my suspicions were correct.

There was a door to the Penumbra here, in this temple. And where I'd access to the Higher Realms, Thvynder could hear me.

"Thvynder, Thvynder."

Hessa. Omaskat's voice was thin, impossibly distant, and without an accompanying vision. But I could hear him.

Gooseflesh rippled up my arms and I drew a deep, deep breath. I told of our situation, quickly and succinctly, and added, "I need an escape. An opportunity."

They will send the storm. Tonight.

"Thank you," I whispered.

No legionaries came for us. My answers, it seemed, had satisfied Eolus. My knees felt weak with relief, but I couldn't relax until Uspa was safe.

I had to get us out of this.

The night dragged on. The patch of sky I could see through the archway was moonless and choked with cloud. Every so often I heard the mutters and footsteps of the legionaries changing guard outside.

Deep in the night, the sky began to oscillate with distant lightning. Illumination played about the forms of our guards, just visible through the archway, glinting off their armor as they watched the sky.

At first, there was no thunder or wind. But soon thunder began to roll, distant and low. The legionaries muttered to one another—I caught little of what they said, but one was irritated, angered at the thought of being stationed in the rain.

He left. His companion remained in place, watching as lightning lit up the sky and another bout of thunder crashed over us—closer, now.

A few breaths passed. Then, in the last echoes of the clap of thunder, the legionary turned and sauntered through the archway alone. I could barely see him, but he rounded the offering bowl and crouched over Uspa, his head cocked as he watched her sleep. Then he glanced over at me, at my bindings, and grinned.

He started to say something, but never got to finish. Uspa's left foot snapped out, catching him in the jaw. He cried out and toppled back into the stand in the center of the room. The bowl rolled, hitting the ground on the opposite side with a thud that I felt through the floor.

The legionary hit the ground at my feet with a wheezing "Oof" and I moved, twisting and kicking him again. I slammed my heel into the side of his head. He stilled.

Uspa's victorious grunt turned into a moan of pain. She struggled to sit up, cursing under her breath.

I looked from her to the unconscious man to the door. The man was close enough that I could touch his belt knife with my foot, but I needed to get it in hand before his companion returned.

"Roll him closer, just a little," I urged Uspa.

The girl cursed again but wriggled forward, using her good leg to kick at the legionary a third time. The mound of man and plate barely budged, but it was all I needed to hook the toe of one boot under the knife hilt and flick it out. It hit the dirt, and I dragged it closer with my heel.

Thunder crashed outside. I managed to get the knife between my heels and raise it up to my hands, twisting in a way that made Uspa give a snorting, exhausted laugh. Despite the indignity, I had the hilt in my hands within a minute, and sliced myself free.

More lightning, more thunder. I grimaced, fierce and determined as I hauled myself upright. My muscles ached and my joints protested, but I was armed and on my feet.

Uspa, however, had closed her eyes again, fighting for breath. I crouched, tapped her face lightly, and started to cut her bonds.

"Wake up," I hissed. "You managed that kick but now you're sleeping on me? Girl! Wake up, now."

She cracked a disoriented eye and visibly fought for consciousness. "I hurt. So much worse now—"

I pressed my hand over her mouth. "Hush. Just pull yourself together and follow me."

Another bout of thunder and lightning made us both look toward the empty archway, and when the world returned to a rain-pattering hush she seemed more collected.

I helped her to her feet and pointed her towards the door to the main temple. "Quick as you can."

"What about the other guard?" Uspa whispered. She peered at me as I drew the downed legionary's sword and hefted it. "Why are we going further inside?" Her eyes flicked wide. "Are you—are you going to leave me there?"

"What? No! Just come along." I shoved my arm under her shoulders and gestured with the knife to the door to the main temple.

Uspa made a noise of bleary resignation, undergirded by fear. I waited, knife hand pressed against the wood. In the next roll of thunder, I pushed. The door opened with a soft creak and we stepped up onto the stone floor of the inner sanctuary.

Quiet wrapped around us, interrupted only by the steady thrum of rain on the high, domed roof. It was almost completely black in here, high slits beneath the roofline providing only the slightest variance in the gloom.

But I didn't need light to see the pale golden crack in the center of the floor. It was faint, the faintest I'd ever seen, but as I entered the room it sensed me. Light swelled and the rift lengthened, stretching up to match my height. The same draw that had overtaken me in the Temple of Mircea struck me in the gut.

Uspa shuddered too. "Hessa, what... What is that?"

"I need you to wait here," I hissed, tearing my eyes from the rift. "I'll be back. Wait right here and do not move, understood?"

"You are leaving me here!" She was hardly able to stand, and I saw wild, frantic tears in her eyes. "Please don't do this, High Priestess. I can keep up, I can, please, I won't be a burden—"

"I'm not leaving you!" I grabbed her shoulder to keep her from staggering into me. I remembered what she'd told me on the marshes—how she'd been raised to believe that the moment she was a burden, she would be left behind.

"I swear," I said. "I will not abandon you. There's a door to the Arpa High Halls here. That's our way out. I *will* come back."

Uspa braced herself on the wall. She still looked hurt, and panicked, and more than a little baffled. "A door? But... where are you going now?"

I passed her the knife and took the legionary's sword in my right hand, shooting one last glance between her and the rift as I stepped back into the door. "I'm going to fetch Eolus."

TWENTY-THREE

I paused before the toppled offering bowl, just out of sight of the archway, and listened to the rain for a few steadying breaths.

Footsteps merged with the patter. A shadow approached; the other guard, awkwardly sheltering a steaming cup under his cloak as he crossed the open ground. He glanced up, noting that his comrade was no longer at his post, and looked on through the darkness of the arch.

I stepped further into the shadows and edged around to the archway, brushing against the cool stone as I went. I stepped over the man's unconscious friend on the way, his head bloodied and his body unmoving.

I didn't let my eyes linger on him, pressing instead into the shadows beside the arch and drawing in a deep, quiet breath. Lightning flashed again and the guard outside called a name, ducking into the shelter of the vestibule.

His cup of hot wine hit the ground as thunder rolled, bone-cracking and gut-watering. Then his knees, his hands, and blood followed. If he'd managed to scream before my blade filled his throat, the thunder drowned it.

Darkness wrapped over us again as he died. I paused for an instant, the presence of both his and the other guard's souls tickling at my determination and apathy. Death. More death. Always death. And with it, questions I couldn't answer.

Ignoring the exhausted shaking of my hands, I hauled the second guard out of view of the archway and began to unfasten his cloak. I took his helmet, too, along with a belt and a second knife and tinderbox, then returned to the arched entrance. The wind gusted through; a clean, brisk rush of charged air that spun dust through the vestibule, snatching the lingering scent of incense and twisting it into the storm.

I stepped outside. Rain toppled from the clouds in a swelling, slapping roar, striking my upturned face and pinging off my helmet. The markings Imnir had so carefully painted upon my skin were long smudged, but I felt the rain cut through them now, dragging black lines down my chin and throat.

I needed to find Eolus. I'd no idea where my captors had elected to sleep, but I doubted that these villagers would house their intended ruler in anything but the best house in the village.

I peered out into the sodden night. Nothing but shuttered houses, darkened with sleep, and the steady rush of the rain.

There. On one side of the square, a high, two-storey building presided. It was by no means grand, but the legionaries guarding the door told me that it was the right one. Eolus would be there.

I pulled the hood of the cloak up over my helmet, hid the sword and my Eangen clothes from sight beneath, then strode out into the courtyard. I walked with purpose, making for the big house and willing myself to look, to move, like a legionary. Thunder and lightning harried me, and the rain came down hard enough to complete the disguise.

If anyone saw me as I passed through the night, they did not raise the alarm. Even the guards outside the door only saluted—until I dispatched them both with a thrust and a slash. There was no glory in that, or what happened next.

I stepped into the warmth and light of a large living space, where Eolus slept under the watch of only one guard, who observed the storm through a north-facing window. Siris and the other legionary were nowhere to be seen.

The guard died badly. He turned just as my sword cut across the back of his knees. He hit the window on the way down and collapsed, screaming, as the sword punctured his throat.

I caught Eolus as he stumbled out of bed, disoriented and half-asleep. Taking him by the hair, I kicked at his knees, driving him face-down onto the floor.

"Do not move," I ordered.

Eolus tried to form a response, gaping in shock. The guard was still choking as I seized a coil of rope from the table—the same one that had dragged me along, all day—and tied Eolus's hands behind his back. Then I gagged him, wrapped the legionary's cloak around his shoulders, and wedged a helmet on his head.

"Now move," I snapped, pulling up the hood. Lastly, I grabbed a spear from the wall for Uspa.

Grim determination strengthened every weary muscle, every frayed nerve as I prodded Bresius's cousin out into the rain. We crossed the courtyard rapidly and re-entered the incense-laden air of the vestibule.

Uspa's pale face peered at me from the door of the sanctuary. She appeared to have recovered some of her strength, but flinched at the sight of my helmet. She relaxed again as I threw the helmet on the floor near its former owner's body and passed her the spear.

I pulled Eolus's helmet off, too, and pushed him past her, into the inner sanctuary. "Hold him, we won't have much time."

Uspa complied, thrusting Eolus face-first into the wall as I advanced, dripping and out of breath, on the rift between worlds. It swelled at my approach, beckoning, welcoming, and I set my jaw.

My exhausted arm shook a little as I reached out. The rift opened with an almost audible sigh of power, and forest-scented air wafted into my face. With a flick of my magic, I willed it to stay open.

I returned to Uspa and Eolus, grabbed one of the gawking man's arms, and pulled him towards the rift. Neither could see the portal itself, but they could tell that something was about to happen.

"What is this?" Eolus rambled, his voice muffled by the gag. The shock of his awakening and the butchery of his legionaries had not gone over well. His eyes looked glassy and I half expected him to start shrieking like a child. "What are you doing? What—"

The doorway grew, widening even further and stretching up towards the crown of the temple's domed roof. Eolus quietened as the promises of that other world rushed over him. Uspa's eyes fluttered closed for an instant, then she settled her shoulders and looked to me with a startled kind of resolve.

I beckoned her. "Go through, right here. I'm behind you."

"Stop!"

Siris's voice echoed around the chamber. He and a mass of other figures—three? Four? Six? – filled the doorway. With them came a wave of ashen magic, and I knew that they were, every one of them, Laru. The temple's keepers had finally made an appearance.

"Go, Uspa!" I snapped.

The girl bolted through the rift, spear in one hand, shoving Eolus with the other. I threw myself behind, praying Siris couldn't move fast enough to follow us through.

The world bucked, shifted, and snapped into place. Uspa, Eolus, and I suddenly stood in the Penumbra's reflection of the temple, but this place looked as though a giant had torn half the building away. Rain poured in through a collapsed roof and beat down upon a hedge of encroaching forest, which spilled over the ruined walls. There were no homes here, no settlement full of life and people. There were only the temple ruins, the forest, and the storm.

Given the weather, it was impossible to see this realm's tell-tale division of skies, but the magic in my blood affirmed where we were with sickly exuberance. This was not the Waking World, but neither was it the Eangen High Halls. My blood had never hummed like this in the Halls, nor had my desires been so twisted—out towards the forest, up into the rain. It dulled my wits, tempting me to forget the open rift at my back.

Droplets passed over my lips and through my hair. The forest rustled. Vines seemed to creep towards us of their own accord and the air thickened until it grated through my lungs.

The rain. Water seeped over my lips and onto my tongue, pleasantly burning. It did not taste like proper rain—its flavor was more that of dank caves, rocky ravines, and… magic.

I spat violently. "Head down," I hissed to Uspa. "Don't drink the rainwater."

"Help me!" Eolus bellowed. He'd managed to drag down his gag and now jerked from my grasp, throwing himself back towards the rift. "Kill them, now! Now!"

Uspa and I turned as one. Siris and another Laru had lunged through the rift behind us and now they stood, frozen in shock, with the pale golden division at their backs.

The gateway flashed, sputtered, and snapped closed. Darkness swallowed us, transforming all those present into little more than shadows against a greater gloom.

We faced one another for half a breath, in the murk and rain of another world with the screaming, ranting Eolus between us. Siris stared around at the Penumbra, his eyes filled with a mixture of terror, elation, and worship. The priest with him fingered his sickle and gaped at the rainy sky.

I did not give them a chance to rally. My power hit them both in the chest and staggered them. My body came with it, rounding Eolus and bringing the Arpa sword down on Siris—left hand locked on my right wrist, every ounce of my power in the blow.

Uspa was right behind me, spear whirling. The lesser priest tried to block with his sickle, but she smashed his defending arm in one strike and thrust her spearhead through his gut in two.

Siris would not go down so easily. He dodged my attack, taking a gash to the shoulder and chest that staggered him again but did not put him down. His magic surged, snaking out into the rain in a thousand individual threads of power—threads of power that, as soon as they came into contact with the rain, began to glisten a brilliant, opalescent gold.

Siris felt the change. Whether or not he understood what was happening, he seized the opportunity. His eyes flashed and his magic rushed towards my nose, my face, my eyes.

I rebuffed the attack with a hiss of amber, horrible certainty settling in my bones. I couldn't let him live, not now, not even as a prisoner. He was High Priest of Larun; he had the answers to my questions. But once the power of the Penumbra had its way with him, I'd no idea what he would become.

My sword pierced his shoulder. His magic jerked back, rushing to obscure him, but I was already coming in for a second blow, and a third.

Siris hit the stones of the temple's overgrown floor with a jarring limpness. For a moment he blinked up into the rain, his eyes struggling to focus on my face as I loomed over him. His magic disassembled, losing its vividness and turning back to ash. It streaked his pale face, and his yellow robes turned orange with blood from the great wound in his chest.

He stared at me long after he ceased to blink. Rain struck his wide eyes, eyes fixed on the sky of another world.

Regret burned in my chest, rapidly morphing into frustration. I checked that Uspa was all right—standing over her dead Laru with her spear in a two-handed grip—then I turned on Eolus.

Bresius's cousin lost all control, the would-be emperor crumbling as he had back during the ambush. He shrieked and ranted until he choked on his own vomit and collapsed onto the ground, clutching his stomach. Rain pattered onto his lips and he spat, cursing us in Arpa.

I flipped him onto his stomach before rain could pass his lips. Uspa watched me as I did, her face blanched around her bruises, stark in the stormlight. The rain had washed all her war paint off by now and she looked like a girl again, like any village girl in the North.

But any village girl would not have white-gold magic rimming her lips and eyes. The glow was faint, but it was present. The magic of the Penumbra was already seeping into her.

And into me. My skin rippled and my honeyed magic surged under my skin, fever-hot.

"Do not let the rain get into your eyes or mouth." I repeated my earlier command with new anxiety. The words came out sharp and compassionless, but my heart was a knot in my chest. The magic of the High Halls was something I understood, but I'd no idea how the Penumbra would affect my ward, or Eolus, or me. "And wear this."

I tore off my cloak and threw it at her. She caught it awkwardly as frigid rain trickled into my already sodden clothes.

"Why?" she asked, her voice numb.

"Eating or drinking anything in these realms is a death sentence," I lied. It was the same lie Eang had once told my people, to keep us dependent and underfoot. For years I'd maintained that lie out of necessity, but speaking it to Uspa now made my stomach turn. "Keep the water off you as much as you can. You, too, Emperor. Don't die on me yet."

I toed Eolus. He was on his knees now, shuddering, but he pulled the legionary's cloak tight against the rain.

Uspa nodded, the movement nearly invisible in the shadows. "Right. Now… now what do we do?"

We couldn't go back through the rift, I knew. The remaining Laru, the legionaries and the entire town would be up in arms by now. The only good thing was, from the way Siris had reacted to finding himself here—and their need to harvest life-magic—his priesthood had never mastered the opening of Penumbra rifts.

We were safe here, but safe was not a word I held too closely.

"Strip those two of everything of value," I ordered Uspa, pointing to Siris and the other dead Laru. "And…"

My eyes snagged on Siris's slack expression, his gaze unblinking and fixed in death. My unease, already alive and coiling through my chest, redoubled.

I should have felt relief at his death. It was his face that had heralded the news of true power returning to the Arpa Empire. It was because of him I had scars from a sickle on my fingers, and that I was here with Uspa, fleeing through the Penumbra.

But instead of a closing, instead of the alleviation of a threat, I felt only a greater unease—as if with Siris's death, a curtain had been drawn away. And I saw only a greater darkness on the other side.

As if there was no longer anyone standing between Larun and me.

"High Priestess?" Uspa prompted, and I realized I'd stopped speaking.

"We can't go back the way we came," I said, looking away from my dead rival. "So we'll have to find another door."

She blinked, still trying to wrestle with the reality of where we were. "Where?"

I stared at the brooding forest, pressing in around the ruins of the temple. "I don't know. I think I'm going to have to make one."

TWENTY-FOUR

The woods around the crumbling temple were thick and deep. We trudged and hacked, prodding Eolus and searching for anything like a trail. One did eventually appear, but it was wildly overgrown. Brambles snagged at my clothes, roots threatened to trip me with every step, and sopping branches lashed my face. Still the path stretched on, promising and… guiding.

It was uncanny. That was to be expected from a realm of the gods and dead. But I began to suspect that this forest, this path, was more than that.

In the High Halls, unwelcome trespassers found themselves haunted by thick fog. That barrier sheltered the visitor from the Halls and vice versa, and it would remain until the magic of the High Halls seeped into that trespasser through water and food and long exposure.

Here in the Penumbra, I suspected that the forest was its protection. This was no sleeping wood, no wold of stolid oaks and woodmaidens' haunts. This forest was guiding us; I saw it in the rustle of the branches and the snaking of the path, drawing us on and deeper into its heart.

We had to get out. That sense wound like a tourniquet around my stomach, cinching tighter and tighter as the rain trickled into my eyes and the Penumbra's tainted magic threatened to seep into my blood.

When we finally came to a clearing, I signaled a halt. There was a pond here, shaped like a sickle moon and curling out of sight through high, lording trees of oak and ash and ghostly poplar. There was also a muddy bank, washed smooth with the rain.

I crouched over the mud and rested my sword on my knee, its blade glistening.

"What are you doing?" Uspa asked. The hood of her cloak was so deep that she seemed almost faceless. Eolus looked much the same, his bound hands all I could see of his flesh. They were stark white, resting before his hips and a little swollen from the bindings.

I cleared my throat and answered, "I'm going to try to open a door back to the Waking World."

"Can you do that?"

I hesitated. "I can try."

"You've done this before?"

"Only once," I returned, pacing across the smooth, open stretch of mud. "A long time ago. You're not letting the rain into your eyes or mouth, are you?"

"No, High Priestess."

I drew the runes first, five of them spaced far enough apart for all of us to stand within. Then, with Uspa and Eolus watching in silence, I grit my teeth and slit open one palm. I let blood trickle down my fingers, tinged with amber, and smeared it into the lines of the runes.

Then, kneeling on the earth, I pulled at my magic. It came in a flurry of honey-flavored warmth and consolation, but there was a sharpness to it here, an aggression that made the fine hairs on my neck and arms stand on end.

The runes flared. Uspa jumped and Eolus gave a lamenting curse as light filled the dripping clearing.

In the Waking World, neither of them would have been able to see that flare. Either this was the way of the Penumbra, or the magic of this place had already gifted them with Sight.

No rift opened. I tried again, replenishing the blood. I prayed, too, a cyclical whisper of Thvynder's names and titles as rain pulled blood from my fingers in a steady pink trickle. Then I braced against the earth, open-palmed and grimacing, and threw my magic into the runes. With it I sent two desires: immediate release from the High

Halls, or an existing door we might leave from.

The meadow vanished into a world of absolute black. The rain died, and with it went all sensation except for the rasp of our breaths, the pain in my hand, and the water trickling down my skin.

"Hold still," I murmured to Uspa in Northman, then repeated the same to Eolus in Arpa. "Do not move."

Dawn light spilled across us. A landscape unfolded under its pastel glow, sweeping from a stretch of black sea to the east to familiar mountains in the west. We stood on a hill in the center of it all, blinded by shades of orange and pink and gold.

This was Nivarium, lush and alive and uncursed. The forest and the path were gone, and rather than be comforted by that, my skin crawled. Was this my magic's work, or was the Penumbra welcoming us?

Green swathed unspoiled marshes and forests and great murmurations of birds lifted from the reeds, rippling across the sky like fabric in the wind. On the coast, dawn light transformed the sea into an expanse of iridescent waves, blue and lavender and crests of captured daybreak, like a raven's feathers.

The division in the skies that betrayed the Higher Realms appeared, but it was faint. If the Penumbra had once been divided as starkly as the High Halls, it was no longer. Here, the Realms merged with one another, and they all bowed to this sudden dawn.

"Hessa." Uspa's fingers touched the back of my arm. She nodded down the hill.

There, a second, smaller shoulder of hill provided a view of the south. Upon it grew a young, sapling forest around a huge, flat rock. Smoke rose from a hidden fire on the south side of the rock, while its elevated surface presented a rift of white-gold.

"There's a doorway," I murmured in Northman.

"I can see it too," Uspa admitted, uncertainty in her voice.

I put that aside. I could wrestle with what the rain had done to the girl—and Eolus—when we were safely back in our own world.

By unspoken agreement, we crouched and pulled Eolus down with us.

"What is it?" he asked, fumbling his way into a kneel. Uspa held his arm and he was still bound, not to mention dripping with rain, but he made an effort to look dignified. Lifting his chin he repeated, "What is it? Whose fire is that?"

That was a good question. I wondered if I should leave them behind and scout. But I had a feeling we'd do better to simply make a run for the rift and hope no one—creature, demon, restless dead, or otherwise—sighted us.

In Arpa, I explained to Eolus. "There's a doorway back to…" I hesitated, unsure of the Arpa word for Waking World. "Our world, on that rock. Stay quiet and we might make it through alive."

Eolus wouldn't meet my eyes, but he nodded. He had made an admirable recovery, but his fingers, bound before him, twitched. "I understand."

Uspa clearly did not believe his cooperation. She rested her spear on the earth and pulled a knife that she'd stolen from the dead Laru.

"What's gotten into him?" she asked as she grabbed the side of Eolus's cloak and efficiently cut off a strip of cloth.

Eolus recoiled, incensed. Ignoring him, Uspa wrung the cloth out and handed it to me.

"Good question. Why'd you stop shitting yourself?" I asked the would-be emperor, sheathing my sword and taking the cloth. I turned my bleeding palm up, eyeing the gash. The cloth was still damp and I hated to put that rainwater near an open wound, but the rest of me was soaked enough that the damage was likely already done. Resigned, I bandaged my hand.

"Because it occurs to me that you have just done what I needed Siris to do," Eolus said, leveling his gaze at me. He still had the gag hanging around his throat, like a soggy, shabby bandana. "He's dead, and as his lackeys haven't rescued me yet, I assume he lied about their ability to reach the Penumbra to begin with. So, you and I need not be enemies, Hessa of the Eangen. I need someone of your quality and skills by my side."

"Oh?" I asked, arching my brows. "Really?"

"Yes," Eolus insisted, shifting on his knees. "Take me back through that… passage, and I'll see you honored and well-paid for your service."

"You threatened to have me and my companion raped," I reminded him.

Eolus snorted. "Woman, you assaulted us on the road. You can hardly expect otherwise. You're fortunate you were afforded any dignities at all. But now your value is revealed, and that changes everything."

"What is he saying?" Uspa asked, watching my face.

"He's trying to form an alliance with us, like his cousin."

The girl rolled her eyes. "I think you should cut off his head and take it to—" She stopped short of saying Bresius's name, a word Eolus would surely understand. "—the cousin."

"The head would rot beyond recognition before we delivered it," I said, though not without consideration. As much as I might despise this man and all he'd done to us, a temporary alliance would at least solve the problem of him trying to escape or attract unwanted attention. I switched languages. "Follow me, stay quiet, and I'll consider your offer."

Eolus nodded firmly. "That's all I ask."

We slipped down the hill, trotting through hip-high grasses into the shelter of the saplings and the shadow of the rock. It loomed a good ten feet up but had a natural staircase of boulders, which we scrambled up.

The top of the rock was blanched and warmed by the sun, darkening where our sodden footsteps fell. The rift hovered in the center of it, and from the fixedness of Eolus's gaze, he could see it now too. Internally cursing, I led them forward. The last thing I needed was a would-be emperor with unpredictable power—or, worse yet, one who could activate rifts. I doubted that ability would come to him quickly, but I'd no desire to find out.

The rift flickered and swelled, sensing me draw near. I started to reach out, ready to take us through.

"Remind your brother that this alliance hinges upon his ability to keep his word." A familiar woman's voice drifted up from beyond the edge of the rock, with the smoke of the fire. "If he continues to circumvent me, I will abandon him. And then where will you be?"

My blood ran cold. Uspa shot me a look and Eolus froze, head swinging towards the voice.

"Can you understand that too?" he hissed. "What language is it?"

"The language of the gods," I told him, for lack of a simpler explanation. All Miri and many beasts spoke a kind of universal tongue, one that every ear could understand. Keeping my voice low, I said to Uspa, "Wait here. Do not move, do not speak. I have to see who that is."

Uspa nodded and reaffirmed her hold on Eolus's arm, lips pressed together. I slipped towards the southern edge of the rock, taking care not to let the fall of my shadow betray me.

In truth, I already knew who the woman was. But I had to see her before I could believe my ears.

Close to the edge I transitioned to a crouch, then a belly crawl over the hot stone.

A small clearing lay below the rock, sheltered by an overhang. There was a fire here, set in a well-used pit of stone, and a cave mouth was almost directly below me.

Frir stood between the fire and the cave, arms crossed and facing out in a posture that conveyed possessiveness and familiarity with her surroundings. She wore a wrapped gray dress, cut low to reveal her tattoos. Her black hair fell past her waist, bound loosely at the nape of the neck with a carved brooch, and there was a shawl around her shoulders of deep madder. Its ends were long and thick, capable of being crossed over her chest and tied at the small of her back, but at the moment they hung slack to her thighs, pinioned by laced arms.

Across from her, within the fire itself, stood the shadow of a man, his visage formed entirely of smoke. All I could make out clearly was his shape; the strong but thin frame of a man clad in a night shift.

A child sat some distance from the fire. I recognized him with as much dread as I'd recognized Frir herself; the boy I'd seen at the border fort and after the village attack. He wore a loose tunic and leggings, gray to match the Miri woman's, and embroidered with yellow and blue.

What were he and Frir doing here in the Penumbra? And why did Frir stand in such a way at the mouth of the cave, as if she somehow… belonged, to this place?

The little boy played with sticks and rocks, stacking them up like a little fortress until they fell down again.

Frir said, "Well? Speak, sleeper."

"My brother knows what he is doing," the man assured her, speaking in Arpa. "He's as close to Bresius as he ever was, and he'll do what needs to be done."

Who was this man, and who was his brother, that he would be close to Bresius? Did the would-be emperor have a traitor in his midst? Was he a spy for Frir?

I glanced back at Eolus. He was straining to listen, but from the expression of bewildered curiosity on his face, Frir was speaking low enough that he hadn't made out his cousin's name.

"Will he? It seems to me he's doing everything in his power to drag this matter out," Frir snarled. Across the open ground, I saw the little boy flinch at her tone, curling in on himself. The sister of Eang dropped her voice, forcing even me to strain to hear. "Now that Apharnum is ready to fall, your brother's place and task are all the more vital."

"Gods below, *enough*." The man jerked, shattering the illusion of dreamy submission. He suddenly invaded the Penumbra with a smoky, soulless gaze. He leered between her and the child, who looked up now with wide eyes.

He pointed at the boy, his movements slow and fraying in the smoke. "You'll get what *you* want, and I'll get what I want. That was the agreement."

Frir did not waver, lacing her arms over her chest and considering the contrary vision levelly, but the boy abandoned his play. He shrank back, shuffling against a boulder in a way that made my hands clench.

Frir stepped between the two of them. "Heed my word or feel my wrath."

The man's sneer twitched, then he vanished. The smoke dissipated and Frir was left alone with the child, who stared at the fallen goddess with a mixture of fear and longing. The latter won. He darted towards her and wrapped his arms around her legs.

She took him up into her arms and kissed his cheek. "Do not fear, my love," she murmured into his hair. "Soon we'll have nothing more to do with that man, and your father will come to us. We'll be together, I promise."

I sunk back into my heels, stunned. Whatever I had just witnessed, one thing was clear; Frir had a spy at Bresius's side and a claim in the Penumbra, where a Northern Miri had no right to be. Perhaps this was all by Thvynder's consent, but I had a dreadful suspicion it was not.

And the child in her arms, the one she held like a son? He had an absent father. There was only one man who I knew Frir loved, one man with haunted green eyes just like this child had.

That man had once called her his goddess, and he had lost his unborn son to violence and strife.

My husband.

TWENTY-FIVE

The Waking World still dripped with rain when we stumbled out into its blinding daylight. This side of the rift mirrored the Penumbra's, save that the forest around it was more mature—and dead.

We shouldered through dripping branches of orange and umber leaves until the portal was far enough behind for my skin to stop prickling with the memory of Frir. Then I headed toward a patch of clear blue sky through the trees, and we came to the edge of the wood.

I cast my eyes over the vista. The marshes had ended, now funneling their waters into a broad expanse of the Nivari River. It laced its way south through gray and brown hills—once farmland and lush pasture, and now stripped of life. The Laru had harvested this land almost entirely, leaving only patches of vital, living forest, meadow, and fields.

"I'm pretending that it's autumn." Uspa's voice held a forced lightness. She squinted at a moth, fluttering past her face, and wrinkled her nose. "Though the smell's wrong. And these. Why are they always here?"

Eolus couldn't understand her words, but he made the connection between her questioning tone and the moths.

"It's an effect of the Laru magic. They appear after their magic is wrought… something of an overflow, as I understand it." His tone only slightly snide. He turned to me. "So, now that you've gotten me out of there alive, I ask you again. Will you join me?"

I took a second to reply, reflecting on the moths and scanning the horizon for any sign of my people. But the dead land held its secrets close. There were no campfires to catch my eye, and though there were multiple

Arpa settlements in sight—splotches of houses, circular rings of walls, and fields—only two, beyond the reach of the curse, seemed inhabited.

"I'm still considering," I told him. "I need to find my people first."

"You don't require them. I've seen what you can do alone. We should go directly back to the town. I'll explain to my guards that you and I have come to an accord. You'll not be harmed, I swear—it's the Laru who will feel my displeasure."

I ignored him, pointedly snapped a stick off the nearest tree, and drew three runes in the earth. I pushed magic into them, but made no show of it—in truth, I was terrified that the Penumbra's rain might have tainted my power. So I sent a simple flick of warm, honey-flavored power from my fingers into the earth, observing the feel of it.

It was clean. The edge that I had felt in the Penumbra was gone, purged perhaps by months and years of the High Halls' influence.

I could not say the same for Uspa. Her eyes snagged on my magic and followed it from my hands to the earth. She gave a barely contained start and looked away, quick enough not to notice that I was watching her.

She had the Sight now. Eolus likely would, too, but at the moment he was scowling at the horizon with his arms laced over his chest, and didn't notice what I'd done.

"Make yourselves comfortable," I instructed, first in Eangen then Arpa, forcing my tone not to betray just how unsettled I was. "I've summoned an owl, but we may have to wait some time. Uspa, come here."

Eolus sat down and Uspa approached me, her steps slow.

"High Priestess?" the girl asked, constructing each word around a calm, contained façade.

"How are you feeling?" I asked.

Uspa hovered, letting the butt of her spear rest in the sodden deadfall. She looked disheveled, and I was struck by the sudden thought that I should comb and re-braid her hair.

"I feel fine," she said, sounding a little uncertain. "Better than I did in the temple. Everything hurts less, and my wounds aren't as bad as I thought."

"What do you mean?"

She touched at her bruised eye, the one that had dragged and struggled to focus. It was focused now, and beneath the caked blood, the bruising had paled considerably. "This doesn't hurt, not really. Nothing does."

I bent a little to examine her eye more closely. Perhaps Uspa hadn't been as injured as I thought—that was a good thing, wasn't it? There wasn't necessarily anything unnatural about her wellness.

But that, combined with her new Sight, did not bode well.

"That's all you feel?" I clarified, nudging her towards admitting she had seen my magic. "Better?"

Uspa nodded.

"Good," I said at length. Impulsively, I reached out and squeezed her upper arm. "I'm glad you're with me."

For a second I thought she was upset or uncomfortable, but then I saw the relief in her eyes. It was deep, cavernous, and haunted. "Thank you for not leaving me behind."

That struck me hard enough to make my hand falter, slipping off her sleeve. Had the girl truly thought I'd abandon her? Had I been that callous toward her?

I was too exhausted, too burdened, and too unsettled by recent events to discuss the matter further. I simply nodded and turned away.

Uspa cleared a spot to sit on a fallen tree and I set myself to watch for the owl I'd summoned. I didn't expect it to take long, not when I'd been missing for two days. If I knew Thvynder and Estavius, the owls would have been dispatched to search within hours of my disappearance. All we needed to do was wait.

After some time, a stick cracked. I turned to see Eolus hobbling off into the woods.

"Where are you going, Emperor?" I called.

"I need to… relieve myself." Eolus glanced back at me and held up his bound hands. "Don't worry, I'm not running off. Though I'll need a moment, unless you'd like to free me."

"Relieve yourself right there," I instructed, returning to my vigil.

Eolus glanced between Uspa and I. The girl watched us converse in Arpa with a wary eye.

"That's barbaric," Eolus declared. "I'm not a dog."

I batted aside the sudden reminder of Nui and her absence. "You expected something else from me? Piss here, Emperor, or I'll tie you to a tree."

"Right here, then?" Eolus's expression darkened. Holding my gaze like a challenge, he pulled up his tunic and unbound the trousers beneath. He clearly expected me to flush or look away. He met my eyes for one last, increasingly uncertain moment, then let out a frustrated hiss. He turned his back, releasing his stream onto the dead foliage of the forest floor.

Uspa looked over at me, lips drawn down the ponderous, high-browed frown of a village gossip.

"Well, then," she observed. "He's not very polite, is he?"

An owl came within the hour. A churring screech preceded it, pulling me to my feet before it arrived.

The bird, a small, slate-gray male, made to light on a branch but flapped away at the last moment, shunning the cursed wood. He landed on my outstretched hand instead.

Eolus scrambled to his feet and stared as I looked into the creature's eyes. The owl settled himself, ducking his head twice and letting out a second mournful, dejected screech.

"Find Estavius," I said and pointed south, toward a living section of forest I'd decided we could reach by nightfall. "Tell him to meet us there."

The bird shuffled on its feet, cool skin and sharp talons moving carefully on my fingers, and took off, winging away over the forest to the east.

It was midnight before the wind came. I was on watch, my newly bandaged hand resting on my lap as firelight played off the curtain of rare, healthy willow branches around us. Uspa was asleep with her head on one arm, facing away from the fire. Eolus sat against a tree stump on the other side, his bound hands hooked across his stomach and his chin drooping onto his chest.

I looked up as the wind lifted, tangling stray hair into my eyelashes. It condensed in the shadows, rippling the willow veil, and Estavius stepped into sight. His smile was warm, hedged with a resigned kind of relief. He was glad to have found us, but when his eyes swept Uspa's sleeping form and my wounds, he realized all was not well.

"Hessa." He bowed a little, his eyes flicking to Eolus. "Nisien and the rest are a few hours behind. They'll be here by dawn. How do you fare? I see you've claimed our quarry."

I gestured for him to sit at my side, and he did. A weight lifted as he settled into place, cloaked shoulder brushing mine; fear, responsibility, and vigilance eased from my exhausted shoulders and onto his.

"I'm glad you're here," I said. My eyes burned, and I blinked hard.

He nodded. "If you need to sleep now, I'll watch over you. Otherwise, I'm very curious to know how you captured Eolus, escaped, and came two days' ride from the coast in one stormy night."

"I'll gladly tell you. But I'm afraid I've news that… It may bode ill for all of us."

I told him all that had transpired since the ambush at the road. I told him all I'd learned of the Laru and of the temple in the town, of the rift and our brief passage through the Penumbra. Lowering my voice, I eyed Uspa and Eolus and told him of the Penumbra's rain, and of the pale gold that I'd seen around my companions' eyes and wounds. I told him of Imnir's and my now-proven theory about the Laru harvesting life-magic from the land, and that Siris himself was dead. And lastly, I told him of Frir.

There was only one thing I held back, for the moment. Imnir and his son. I couldn't articulate precisely why I chose not to share this with my friend, but I'd seen Imnir's face when he spoke of Frir. Her attentions haunted him—and now that I knew she toted his dead son as her own child, I understood why. I needed to speak with him about this before I brought anyone else in.

Estavius sat quietly when I'd finished. Exhaustion washed over me afresh and I leaned my head back against the willow's hefty trunk, closing my eyes.

"I was once part of the Arpa pantheon," Estavius began, choosing his words. "You know that. You also know I was allied with Oulden of Souldern, before his death. I always had a foot in Eang's Hall, though I was usually unwelcome, for obvious reasons. Frir was the opposite."

I cracked open one eye and tilted my head to peer at him. "What?"

"Long ago, when Frir took up the mantle of Goddess of Death, she did so for all the peoples," Estavius said. "You must understand, this was before the Arpa Empire truly rose, before Lathian slipped into the ears of the first emperors. Frir served the people that *became* the Arpa, and even once the Empire was established, the people—particularly here in Nivarium—remembered her. Have you heard of the Three Faces of Death? The Elder, the Mother, and the Girl?"

I thought of the carvings I'd seen on the door of the Temple of Mircea. "Yes. Castor told me she was a goddess of women, the pattern of life and birth and death."

"That was Frir," Estavius said with a nod. "In a way. After the Empire was established and Frir's influence waned, the idea of her— her imagery, her function—was adopted and changed by another goddess, Lysta. Lysta, of course, died during the Upheaval. And after what you've just told me, I suspect that Frir, in her absence, has begun to wander the Penumbra again. Have you encountered many Arpa dead?"

I pondered that for a moment. "No. Someone's been tending to them. Castor suggested it was Larun, but if he had access to the Penumbra, he would have no need to harvest life-magic from the land."

Estavius sat forward, looping his arms around his knees. "Then Frir is back in the Penumbra."

"Back. Why wasn't I told of her history here?"

Estavius shrugged. "One human woman cannot know everything about the history of the world."

That was fair, but it still irked me. I was High Priestess, and had grown used to having insight into the mysteries of the Miri and the divine. Frir's involvement and her connection to Imnir left me feeling terribly vulnerable.

Beside the fire, Uspa slept on and Eolus's head drooped lower.

"Next winter, stay in Albor and teach me, then," I asserted. "Our storytellers need new material anyway, after a decade of peace."

Estavius grinned, but it didn't quite reach his eyes. "Tired of hearing tales of your own exploits?"

I snorted. "I'm tired of hearing of *yours*, slayer of monsters and binder of demons. What is Frir doing in the Penumbra now? Trying to gain influence?"

"I don't know. You will not tell Bresius of the spy, will you? Or Castor?"

I shook my head. "No. We'll take care of it quietly. Even if she does have a foot in the Empire, Frir is of the North, and this is a Northerner's matter."

He nodded in agreement. "Good. Perhaps Imnir will have some insight. He was Frir's priest, and all the Miri speak of her fondness for him."

Far more fondness than anyone seemed to realize. I sat back into the tree, my hair snagging in the bark and reminding me how unkempt I must look. "Why? Why is she so fond of him?"

Estavius considered this. "He was her High Priest, young, very faithful. She kept him close. That's all I know."

I accepted this. "I see. Well, I will ask him once he arrives."

"Do. Frir's power is dampened, she's bowed to Thvynder, but she is reclusive and unruly. And Thvynder does not yet reign over this land." Estavius cast a nod out to the Nivari night. "It may be that all she wants is to tend the dead and make a home with this child. Esach and Gadr and I would certainly have discouraged her from doing that in the North, if we'd known. The souls of the dead do not *belong* to her. She cannot keep them like pets."

The thought of the green-eyed boy, Imnir's son, pained me. She had him, and she wanted my husband too. Perhaps that was all—perhaps it was not. But I already had far too much to think about.

"Will you do something about it?" I prodded. "About Frir keeping the child?"

"I'll bring the matter to Thvynder as soon as I can, but you should sleep now." Estavius sat forward and unhooked his cloak from about his throat. He passed it to me. "Here, please. Rest."

I took the heavy garment. It was still warm, and smelled of a summer wind in the way that cursed Nivarium never could.

"Will you travel with us for a time?" I asked, as I arranged the cloak on the dry ground. "Now that we've captured Eolus, will you go after Cassius, in Apharnum?"

Estavius searched the fire for his answer. "Yes. But we won't travel together, at least not for more than a day or two. I can't risk Castor discovering what I am, or have Eolus suspecting me."

I tried to hide my disappointment, tugging a corner of the cloak flat. "How will you get into the city? You and Nisien, I mean. He can't disappear into the wind."

"I've lived long enough to know my way in and out of Apharnum," Estavius said. "Once we're in, I'll visit my adopted father—my former High Priest—under the pretense that I've been captive in the far north this last decade and finally escaped with the help of my Soulderni companion. I'll learn all I can about the Ascension, whether Bresius's claim to the throne could hold, and what it means for the North."

"Could hold?" I repeated. "Surely Thvynder doesn't want me to truly crown Bresius."

"For now, proceed with the intention of doing what's best for the North," Estavius replied. "Whatever that will be. Once we know more, that route will become clear."

That was not the answer I wanted, far too uncertain and out of my control.

"Well, if something goes wrong," I said. "If you're out of reach, and Imnir and I are left to act alone… I'm putting Bresius down."

Estavius hesitated. "Do as you think is best. But someone will have to wield that power eventually, for many reasons. Rule will stabilize the Penumbra and protect the Arpa people from themselves… The Blood of Eiohe *is* the Empire, in a way. The essence of the land and the people. The core of what they are."

I took this quietly. It wasn't as though I was fond of the Arpa, but when I thought of the tainted Penumbra, crumbling Mircea, and the young woman I'd let flee into the fog last summer, a wailing child at her breast—I didn't wish total destruction on them, either.

My friend continued, "And we cannot predict what the future holds, what other troubles may arise—Larun proves that. But I've learned that the blood can only be wielded by one person at a time, until their death or abdication—so if someone we trust holds it, the North will be truly secure."

"Thvynder can't just destroy it?" I asked.

"They cannot." He shook his head. "Nor use it themselves. Even when they wear the faces of Omaskat and Vistic, they're not… like us, not mortal enough, not physical enough."

"But you are, and the Arpa are your people," I remarked, watching his face. Cool fingers crept up my spine. "Avi… would you do it? Take the blood, if Thvynder allowed it? Souldern would certainly be freed then, and we'd never have to fear—"

"No." Estavius's voice was flat and hard, but as soon as he spoke, he regained control of himself. His throat flexed in the firelight. "It would mean… It would mean too many things that I do not want."

His sentiment fell between us like a weight, heavy and ominous. I cleared my throat, tugging my sword belt around to make it more comfortable for sleeping.

"Then let's pray another option presents itself," I said, forcing a smile. "Perhaps Bresius will be a willing ally. Not all Arpa are despicable, after all."

I meant the last as a joke, but Estavius didn't smile. "We'll see."

I took the hint, offering him a resigned smile and settling down on the cloak. I didn't truly believe Bresius would be a trustworthy ally, but our other options were either too vague or too close—there in the pain around my friend's eyes.

"I'm exhausted," I said. "You'll wake me when the others arrive?"

He crossed his arms but his posture eased again, and he smiled, warm and handsome, in his pale Arpa way. "I'm sure Nui will do that for me."

TWENTY-SIX

I n the dream, I stood on a wasteland of gray rock. The sky billowed with stars and the moon set herself low on the northern horizon, spilling pale light across swaths of lichen and distant pockets of waving marsh grasses. Silhouettes of gnarled pines scented the air with sap, and to the south, east, and west I could see the other quadrants of the Eangen High Halls' sky.

A clacking began, distant and soft. My head spun, trying to comprehend where I was and how I'd gotten here, but my disorientation was momentary. I was dreaming, but there was more to this than a simple dream. And I knew enough of the Gods and the Miri to suspect what was happening now.

The clacking became more distinct, backed now by a swish, a rustle, and numerous, softer taps. A loom.

There was only one Weaver in the High Halls, and that was Fate herself—sister-god of Thvynder and Eiohe.

"Weaver of Time," I called, my voice low and steady. "I am listening."

Two more figures appeared in the wasteland around me, then another, and another. They came and went, as if time sorted through her memories. None of these newcomers appeared conscious of me and I didn't know most of them, but I recognized Omaskat several times, and Estavius. I saw Imnir on his knees with his head pulled down, face buried in his thighs as he prayed. My eyes snagged on him, but the memories, fragments of history and future, flickered on.

Next, I saw Eang, my former goddess, black-haired and flint-eyed.

She was younger than when I'd known her, her gut-wrenching beauty softened with youth, and her body clothed in armor of brassy mail and decorative leather. Galger and Gammler were visible at her shoulders and her belly arched with the presence of a child—Ogam, Thray's father.

Next to her stood a younger woman, sweet-faced and clad in a red gown, like the petals of the poppies. This woman was pretty to Eang's devastating, but it was obvious what they were. Sisters. I was looking at Eang and Frir, before the birth of Ogam, before Frir had taken the mantle of Lady of Death.

"Weaver of Time." Eang's voice echoed mine across the stone, rich and strident—the same voice that had brought armies to heel and bound lesser gods beneath the earth. The voice that had once demanded every drop of my devotion, my blood, and my life. Even now it clutched at my ribs like claws.

"I would speak with you," Eang continued, even as the memories moved on and she and Frir began to fade. "I carry a life inside of me, the child of Winter himself. I would ask what that child will become..."

More voices rose up then, and for an instant, I heard the entreaties of a thousand supplicants at once; those who had dared to seek the council of Fate.

"Weaver of Time, must I become like them?"

"Weaver of Time, what lies beyond the tree in the East?"

"Weaver, Weaver, when will I die?"

The voices abruptly hushed, leaving me with the clack of the loom. The moon lifted her face a little higher, casting light across me and making me squint.

"Weaver, why have you brought me here?" I asked.

For the space of five or six heartbeats, I received no reply. Then a vision came, sweeping over me like a wave. I saw a hall with high, smoke-darkened beams. I smelled sage and sweat and birth-blood, earthy and raw and dark. I saw a man in the shadows—reluctant, yearning. There were others with us—I felt them but could not see them, and I heard the crackling squalls of not one, but two new lives.

For an instant that man in the shadows was my first husband, Eidr, with tears in his eyes and his red hair disheveled from anxiety, hope, and shared suffering. Then he became Imnir.

More visions came and went. I saw us sharing one home, one bed—a future where there was peace between us, where his and my lives were interwoven. They came in a thousand fragmentary images, each so fleeting they were little more than impressions—laughter and pain, changes and upheavals, the mundane and the extraordinary. But they were, all of them, rife with purpose and life; purpose yet to be fulfilled, and life unlived.

The visions ended and my stomach dropped. The Loom of Fate whooshed and clicked. The moon still watched me curiously. But I stumbled back, reeling with all that I'd seen. Frir and Eang, seeking Fate's council. Imnir and I, at peace? Having a family?

Why had I seen this now, of all times? Why would Fate draw me to herself tonight?

Did she know what Frir had done with Imnir's son? Of course she did. Fate knew all things, wove all things, and it was in trying to decipher her motives that mortals met their end.

Still, I'd seen this for a reason. I couldn't determine why I'd seen what I had of Frir and Eang, not yet, but instinct told me why Fate had showed me Imnir.

I had a future, he and I, and whatever happened next, I needed to know that.

We needed to be united.

Nui nosed me awake, shortly after dawn. By the time I'd ruffled her ears and kissed her head, Nisien had dismounted and pulled me up into an embrace. He stank of horse and sweat and smoke as I buried my face in his chest.

"Here," he said, pointing to the saddle of his horse, where Galger and Gammler were hooded and strapped. "I thought you'd want those back."

I grinned in thanks. Sillo came next as Ifling and Lida crowded in, all of them questioning me while Nui licked Uspa into wakefulness with a great sloppy tongue to the face.

While I told my friends and Vynder what had happened, I watched Imnir crouch beside Uspa. I was not the only one. Sillo glanced at the girl more than once, but he did not interrupt her reunion with her guardian.

Uspa fought Nui down, holding the dog under one arm until she rested her head in the girl's lap. She and Imnir spoke, low and quiet, while the Algatt Vynder circled the clearing, eyeing Eolus, who was struggling into wakefulness.

Imnir ruffled Uspa's hair and she flushed under his attention with a brave crook of a smile. I saw the softness and concern at the corners of his eyes as he looked over her injuries, and thought of Frir cradling his son in the Penumbra.

Your father will be with us soon.

Fear for Imnir flickered through me, compounded by the warmth of the visions Fate had sent. Did my husband know what Frir was doing? If he did, what did that mean for me and our journey?

And what if he did not?

Imnir looked at me. The concern he'd shown Uspa still clung around his eyes, but there was more hesitation when he looked at me, as if he feared how I'd respond.

I smiled. It was a warm thing, a true thing, and relief rushed into his face. He gave a half-salute, and returned his attention to Uspa.

Castor and Mrandr arrived last. The legionary passed his reins to the Iskiri, who gave a deep, welcoming nod. His beard was freshly woven into two braids, gathered under the chin in a tuft, and his hair was windblown.

Castor pulled off his helmet. The scar in his hair looked especially white as he grinned, smug and fox-like. The would-be emperor was now fully awake and on his feet, gauging my milling friends.

Eolus's narrowed eyes rounded as he saw Castor in his plate armor, clearly a countryman. Tension laced up his legs and back, and his feet strayed towards the forest.

"He's going to run," I said to Nisien wearily and nodded to the prisoner. "Can you?"

The Soulderni made for Eolus and the rest of my Vynder turned. Around the campsite, half-hidden in the shadows, the Algatt Vynder solidified a perimeter. Imnir helped Uspa up, and they stood shoulder to shoulder with Nui to heel.

Estavius, still seated under the tree, eased himself to his feet and slipped back into the darkness. As he had said, if Eolus recognized him and told Bresius, he and Nisien would be in jeopardy.

Eolus didn't notice him anyway. All his focus was on Castor.

"You," the would-be emperor shot at our guide. He skittered sideways as Nisien stationed himself close by, and glared indignantly at the Soulderni before he continued to his countryman, "Who are you and how do I know you?"

Castor gave a mocking bow. "Eolus, sir, we met once at a parley. If you recall, I stood beside your esteemed cousin, Bresius, who is my lord."

Eolus's eyes snapped to me, but even as he asked his next question, I could see he already knew the answer. "Woman?" he asked, raking panicked eyes from Castor to me. "What is the meaning of this?"

"I've already been bought." I offered him a fatalistic smile, little more than a twist at the corners of my mouth. I didn't relish this situation, but there was no point in caring. "Bresius saw the value of an alliance long before you did."

"No." Eolus backed up a step, hemmed in on every side. "Listen to me. Whatever Bresius has offered you, all of you, I will triple it. I will give you honor and glory and recognition! My cousin is a fool, he hasn't the strength to take Apharnum from Cassius. I was there, I know! I lived like a dog in the sewers until I managed to escape that damned city. Lay your sword at *my* feet and I shall…"

He trailed off, his eyes flicking from face to face, searching for interest or recognition. Only Castor, Nisien, Imnir, and I had understood him, and none of us had moved. Estavius still wasn't in sight, though dawn had lightened the shadows beneath the trees.

"Make your demands, I bid you." Eolus's voice cracked. His eyes had lost a little of their roundness now, his cheeks slackening as he realized just how heavily the odds were stacked against him.

"Kneel," Castor said lightly.

Eolus's throat worked, but after a minute he forced himself down, the movement awkward with his bound hands.

Firelight played over Castor's face. His eyes were alight as he ordered, "On your face."

Eolus began to crook forward, haltingly. He fought himself all the way, but under Castor's gaze he finally rested his face in his bound hands.

Castor crouched and scratched at the would-be emperor's head, as if he were a dog. I watched our guide's expression, noting how he relished his power over the bound prisoner.

"Good man," Castor said, his voice rumbling with false warmth. Now he tucked his fingers into Eolus's hair with a lover's gentleness, just above his ear, and tilted his face up. "Now, be heartened. You'll be with family soon."

Eolus stared at him, all color drained from his face. "H-how? Who?"

"Bresius."

"Bresius? Where is he?"

"Waiting for you," I said, drawing all eyes to me. "At the siege of Apharnum."

We resumed our journey south to the Apharni border with Estavius and Nisien in tow. We rode towards a crossroads where we intended to camp together for the first night, Estavius hidden from Eolus's red-rimmed eyes by a bag, which Mrandr had gruffly thrown over his head.

Nisien and I rode side by side, and though I was still bone-weary from my ordeal, it felt good to be with my friend again. Imnir and I still hadn't had a private moment to talk, but I watched him as I rode.

"Can I confide in you?" I asked Nisien after some time. We'd fallen back, letting the length of a few horses open between us and the rearmost riders.

"I'd hope so," Nisien returned. His helmet hung from his saddle and his black hair, cropped close, hazed against a sky of billowing gray cloud and bursts of sunbeams. The wind was fresh, autumnal, and some quiet part of my mind wondered if the Laru's curse wasn't altering Nivarium irreparably. But that wasn't what I wanted to speak to Nisien about.

"It's Imnir," I admitted, dropping my voice lower. "And…"

"What of him?"

"I…" I wrinkled my nose, trying to form my suspicions into logical, simple words. "Ah… I don't know how to put it."

"Tell me you're not pregnant."

I looked at Nisien sharply, that aspect of Fate's vision rushing at me again. "No. And if I was?"

The Soulderni looked over his shoulder, a routine scan of the road behind us. It stretched on, empty and girded by fallow, dead farm fields to the horizon.

"Then I'd congratulate you," he said in a tone that made me suspect he wanted to say something quite different.

"Things are better than they used to be," I said. "He's changed, recently."

"Would he die for you?" Nisien asked coolly. "Does he care about your happiness? No? Then he doesn't deserve you."

"That's not the way it is, between us," I protested. "But that doesn't mean it might not be, one day."

Nisien snorted, and I regretted trying to confide in him. I tucked Fate's vision close and closed my mouth.

Nisien, realizing he'd derailed my revelation, sighed. "I'm sorry. Tell me what's wrong."

I hesitated, trying to find something less inflammatory to share. I noted Uspa riding with Imnir, and Mrandr riding next to Castor, close behind.

"The Iskiri," I said, snagging on the sight of Mrandr's back. "I gave him to Imnir as an aide, but he came to me first. He introduced himself while I was bathing, saying he knew Eidr and that he wanted to come with me to Apharnum. He was very... forward."

Nisien eyed Mrandr's back too. "He's handsome." The words were barely out of his mouth before he twisted in the saddle to stare at me. "Wait, bathing? No. Hessa, you're not bedding—"

"I'm not bedding *anyone*," I snapped, exasperated and slightly flustered. "I'm as celibate as a stone and I've the temper to prove it. Mention that again and I'll push you in the ditch."

Nisien's irritation evaporated. He angled his face away and I had to lean forward in the saddle, craning to see his face before I realized he was trying desperately not to laugh.

"Stop it!" I protested, my cheeks burning. I would have struck him, but he rode on the side of my bad hand. "Nisien!"

He was laughing openly now, and a traitorous grin stole its way onto my own cheeks. Still, I was flushed and tried to scowl.

"Uspa knows Mrandr from back home," I said with forced temperance, though Nisien's eyes were still dancing. "He shares his living brother's wife. He's been after Uspa, too, and pays Ifling too much attention. And now he spends a great deal of time with Castor, which I cannot imagine being a good thing."

Nisien schooled his expression into seriousness. "I see. So send him home, unless you've decided to make use of him."

"What about your 'Will he die for you' philosophy?"

"Well, would he?"

"Nisien."

"Sorry."

We rode for another moment while I mused. "It's not like I haven't thought of it," I admitted.

"Making use of him?"

I managed to keep from blushing this time. "Sending him home, you bastard. But it would be a death sentence, traveling north alone.

Besides, he hasn't actually done anything wrong *here*. And Uspa said the bit about his brother's wife was just hearsay—well-known hearsay, but not enough to banish him on."

Nisien seemed to take this seriously, and we rode in silence for a minute.

Then he asked, "Mrandr is Iskiri, isn't he?"

I nodded.

"Didn't one of them try to kill you last year?"

I knew where Nisien was going, and I did not like it. "A follower of the old ways, yes. A Devoted, trying to avenge Eang. But the Iskiri have been cooperating since then."

"Still." Nisien shook his head, all his earlier teasing forgotten. "Why would an Iskiri warrior—I assume of some repute, from his clothes and the quality of that sword—pledge himself to you?"

Up ahead the road turned and our party spread out before me, riding in pairs or single file through sunshine and into a patch of cloud-cast shadow. A gap in the clouds passed overhead, the sun flashed into my eyes, and I squinted away.

"I'd like to say it's out of devotion, a sign that the Iskiri are finally accepting me," I said carefully. "Even attraction would be… acceptable, and isn't… entirely ruled out. But in truth, he thinks being by my side will make him rich."

"I see."

Warm sunlight slipped from my eyes and shade fell around us again. Nisien settled in his saddle and surveyed the patchwork sky above us, deep in thought.

"That might be his only motivation," the man acknowledged. "But all the same, I'd keep him at arm's length."

The crook of a smile settled in the corner of my mouth. "You want me to keep every man at arm's length."

"I have little trust in men," Nisien returned. "Little trust in anyone."

I took this quietly. I knew his past, and where his distrust came from. When he was young, he'd loved his former captain, Telios, and that had ended in abuse and bloodshed. Even his own mother had deceived him in the end, and I'd been central to that betrayal. She'd thrown me to the wolves rather than risk me dragging her son back into a life of violence, long ago when we still called the Miri gods. He'd never forgiven her.

"Little trust in anyone except Estavius," I pointed out.

Nisien's gaze softened, but there was melancholy there. He and Estavius were as close as two people could be without sharing inborn familial bonds. But I'd long suspected that Nisien would have welcomed more from their relationship, if it had been offered.

"Of course," he said. "And you. And Sixnit."

Up ahead, the rest of the party stopped to wait for us. The road had divided, one heading south-east while the other headed west, along a dike and the Nivari River, broad and black under the sun.

Estavius, the glint of his armor hidden by his cloak, turned to watch our approach. He'd removed his helmet, and I could see in his face that it was time for him and Nisien to go. It was an expression I'd seen a hundred times over the last decade, and always dreaded.

I gave Nisien a warm, slightly heart-sick smile. "I truly wish we could travel together to Apharnum."

"I do too," Nisien said. His eyes had found Estavius too. "But I'd rather make sure you'll be safe when you get there."

I nodded, though his admission almost made my longing worse. "I understand."

"Besides, I trust you," he reaffirmed. "And in that trust is expectation. Watch your back with Castor, and that Iskiri. And when I see you next, be in one piece."

"I will."

Soon we sighted the delta of the Nivari River, and with it, the border of the province of Apharni. This was where the end of our journey would begin, and we would meet Bresius—the man I would, supposedly, crown Emperor of the Arpa Empire.

The land opened, the languid expanse of the river broadening into a long lake. A series of rock islands decorated the far south, crowned with the ruins of a settlement. Spires and crumbling domes looked down upon the waterway as it split into channels—the beginning of the Delta—and passed out of sight beyond the city. At least some of this diaspora ended in waterfalls; mist rose beyond the ruined structures, capturing the sun and casting each tower, each roofline and peak into ethereal silhouette.

As the afternoon waned, we traversed farmland and forest along one the side of the lake. The forests rumpled in the occasional shallow ravine, while the fields draped the land in every other direction.

We stopped to make camp in one of the valleys. As we dismounted and saw to the horses, Castor sat Eolus against a tree and surveyed the company.

"Tomorrow we'll cross the border," he said. "Be ready to move at the first light of dawn. We won't stop again until we're with Bresius."

His words sat heavy in my chest. The greatest leg of our journey was nearly over. By tomorrow night, I would stand by Bresius's side in the heart of an Arpa army and I'd be one step closer to the decision, the action, that would shape the future of our world. Would I put a knife in his back? Forge an alliance?

Our party dispersed to their separate tasks. I began to clear a space for a firepit while Uspa gathered wood and Nui settled in the shade, alternately panting and shaking off flies.

Mrandr heaved Imnir's saddlebags from horseback and set them down with an oddly emphatic *thump*. When I met his gaze, he offered a tight, half-smile.

"Thought I'd be richer by now," he quipped, but there was something insincere about his eyes. Unsated greed? "It's been a long journey."

"There's months to come yet," I reminded him, sweeping deadfall aside with a boot. "I'm sure Bresius will compensate us well."

Mrandr gave a half-shrug and turned back to his work.

"Who's fetching water?" Silgi called from a pile of packs, where she'd dug out a pot and iron stand. She pushed stray bits of hair from her face with the back of one hand, drawing my eye to the dark blue Algatt paint smudged into her hairline.

"I will." Uspa, who'd just begun to brush down one of the horses, tossed her brush to Mrandr without looking and made for a bucket. "I'll be right back."

She headed in the direction of a creek we'd noted before we stopped for the night, and Mrandr scowled at the brush.

I finished clearing a space for the fire and stood to stretch my back, watching while Castor, speaking in quiet Arpa, bound Eolus to a tree. A bag was still over the captive's head, damp with moisture from a day of breath and sweat.

The would-be ruler coughed as Castor finally pulled it off. "Water," Eolus rasped. "Please."

Castor glanced across the camp and asked in Northman, "Where's that water?"

"The girl's gone for it," Silgi replied. "But I need to get that boiling now if we've any hope of eating before dark. Your pet will have to wait for the next bucket."

Eolus coughed again.

Castor, looking unimpressed by Silgi, flicked a hand at Mrandr. The Iskiri immediately abandoned his task with the horses, grabbing a flask and vanishing through the pale poplars in the direction of the creek— the same direction as Uspa.

And from the way he glanced over his shoulder, checking if anyone followed, perhaps he was thinking of Uspa's solitude too.

Recalling Nisien's and my conversation on the road, I grabbed another bucket and started after the Iskiri.

I trailed him through the cool shade of the afternoon forest. Squirrels chattered in the distance and birds sang, varied calls echoing one another. My steps were soft and Mrandr was far enough ahead not to notice me. But I watched the shape of him move, ascending a short incline in two long strides and vanishing over the other side.

I could hear the creek now, the rush of water mingling with the constant sounds of the forest.

I remembered Nisien's comment about how odd it was that an Iskiri, of all of the tribes, had volunteered to accompany me. I remembered Imnir's insistence that if he did not bring Uspa with him, she'd have been killed in retribution for the man—the Iskiri—she had shot. Even when I'd suggested he send her back north, he'd said that she would be in just as much danger then—that there were those among my people who would see her dead on the road.

I started up the rise with greater urgency. And hadn't Mrandr only offered to come as my aide *after* he'd found out Uspa was to accompany Imnir?

My foot skidded on loose leaves and soil. The night Uspa fell from her horse, charging through the Arpa village—hadn't Mrandr appeared there, too, in the smoke and flames? I grabbed a sapling, heart thundering with the realization that, perhaps, the Iskiri's presence here had nothing to do with me at all.

Perhaps it was all coincidence. Perhaps I was simply paranoid. Still, I came over the rise with a huntress's stalking gate, straightening behind a thick tree and looking towards the creek from the concealment of its shadow.

Uspa stood on the shore, her boots braced between the roots of a huge, leaning cedar and a rock in the center of the creek. Clear water rushed under her legs and she had a full bucket braced beside one boot as she caught her breath, staring up the line of the creek with one hand on her hip and the other on her forehead.

She was alone.

A hand seized my hair and a foot struck the back of my knee.

My shins hit the ground with bone-cracking force. I grabbed the hand in my hair and twisted, lashing back with my elbow in a quick, sharp jab to the gut. My attacker buckled but didn't go down, bracing their legs behind me and putting a knife to my throat. The other hand locked over my mouth, pinning my jaw closed so I couldn't even bite, let alone shout for help.

Above me, the leaves of the forest canopy spun and blurred into a glimpse of Mrandr's looming face. Blood thudded through my ears. Fear screamed through me, every nerve and every muscle livid with it. But beneath that torrent, other emotions burst.

Helplessness. Loneliness. Uspa might have been nearby, but she could not hear, and she was not the husband who should have stood at my side, or the friend to guard my back. Here I was, at the mercy of one of my own people—who I'd bled and killed and sacrificed for every day of my life—with no one to intercede. I'd die, far from home. Far from Thray and Vistic, Sixnit. Separated from Nisien and Estavius, Sillo and… Imnir. He was there, too, a flicker of a face and a feeling as my head spun.

All at once I was a girl again, alone and broken and facing the end of my world. I fought that feeling, ground my teeth, and screamed against the hand locked over my jaw, but it was useless.

"I'd almost decided not to do this," Mrandr panted, clenching my head tighter.

Never turn your back on an Iskiri. The words howled through my skull with the blood and the fear and the rage.

"The right moment never seemed to come," he said. "But once we reach Bresius—it never will, will it? Die, Eangi, in the name of the goddess you betrayed."

TWENTY-SEVEN

The knife moved. I jerked sideways, shoving myself into his legs as the blade slashed.

He staggered. He didn't let go, but the slice of the knife went wide. Amber-tinted blood spilled down the side of my neck, down onto my shoulder, but I felt no pain. Blind with instinct, I dug my nails into the soft undersides of his wrists and wrenched.

We fell, rolling down the hill I'd just climbed. The knife clattered away. Rocks and roots slammed into my body and underbrush cracked beneath us. I shouted—a winded, muffled thing—and was cut off as his forearm smashed down over my mouth.

I bucked and bit. Blood welled around my teeth, filling my mouth with the taste of hot iron. We flipped. More blood ran over my collarbones and soaked into the collar of my tunic. My head felt light—blood loss? Shock?—but my left hand found his throat. My right knocked the sword, still sheathed, at his belt.

His fist struck my face. He grabbed my head in a barrel-hold, trying to snap my neck. I was strong, but his grip was iron. I let my body roll with the movement, hitting the earth and kicking at his stomach as my vision cracked, my lips burst on my own teeth, and blood roared through my skull.

His grip loosened. My elbow hit his mouth. He shouted, reeled back, and cracked his head off a rock.

His disorientation was momentary, but that was all I needed. I climbed up him, using all my weight to thrust his bigger frame into the forest floor. Then I turned, driving my knee into his throat and jerking his sword from its sheath.

His hands scrabbled at my leg, my clothing, his head locked back and eyes bulging. His face was going red, but he barely slowed. His hands clawed at my arm and braids.

My head was light and the blood—I had to stop bleeding before it was all gone and I died here, at the hands of one of my own people, in the dirt and deadfall of a forest a world away from home. From Albor. From Thray.

"Hessa!" I heard Uspa screaming, but she might as well have been back in Eangen.

I stabbed the sword straight down into Mrandr's gut. I twisted off him at the same time, jerking free from his hands and throwing all my weight into the hilt of the sword like a lever.

I felt stone and dirt grind under my battered knees, felt Mrandr's body heave itself up into one last, roaring attack.

Somewhere beneath his flesh, the blade met bone. I levered the sword a second time and kicked Mrandr back down.

His stillness was immediate, so sharp and quiet that my mind struggled to catch up. The desperate rake of my breath filled my senses as I sunk back onto my haunches and blinked, shaking with adrenaline.

The blade had wedged firmly in the Iskiri's spine. The only sign of life was pumping blood, the flutter of his belly and the skittering of dirt from his gaping, open mouth. The latter dusted into the pool of our blood, mingling on the forest floor.

"Hessa!" Uspa was right beside me now, stumbling one last step down the hill.

I couldn't speak. My mouth was full of blood. I licked my teeth weakly and spat, but most of it just stuck to my chin.

"Hessa!" Uspa knelt, grabbing my arms, my face. She was still talking, asking me questions, but her voice skewed in my ears.

Mrandr stared at us with the same blank, unyielding stare as Siris had. Death. Always death, so close and so vivid. Was Frir already here, stalking towards us? Or would she send the child? Imnir's child.

Uspa's voice again: "High Priestess. Hessa!"

I realized my hands were on my own throat, clasping, hot, and slick. The wound—I felt the sides of it with disconnected fingers—was over muscle, close to my shoulder. Perhaps it would not be deadly. Perhaps it had missed the vein. Perhaps...

Uspa's hands replaced mine at my throat, fumbling, trying to find grip and not choke me at the same time.

"Thvynder," Uspa began to pray, her voice rattling, "Thvynder, don't let this be. Thvynder!"

Warmth spread from her hands. My pain retreated, and I wondered if this was what death felt like—this slow sinking, this spread of consolation into blood and breath and bone, swift and inexorable.

No, more than inexorable. Eager. Eager in a way that tasted of the Penumbra's insidious magic.

My hand closed on Uspa's wrist. I pushed her back, ignoring her grief-stricken protests, and felt at the wound.

It had closed—not completely, but enough for the blood to stop gushing. Uspa noticed this at the same time, confusion rushing into her eyes.

"It's not... but there's so much blood." She glanced from me to her scarlet hands. I followed her gaze.

I was not surprised at what I saw. Magic hazed about her fingers, gold, but not in the amber way of the High Halls. This magic had come from the Penumbra, and it was nearly white.

My head still spun with the shock of Mrandr's attack, but now it was my turn to grab Uspa. I forced her to look at me, forced my own head to stop spinning. I was alive, and it didn't appear I'd die any time soon. So now I needed to ensure Uspa didn't condemn us all before I figured out what to do.

"Tell no one what you just did," I said, holding her gaze. Her eyes flicked over my face and I knew I had to look horrific, split-lipped and dirty, but there was no time. Surely, someone back at camp would have heard the commotion, or they'd come to investigate why we were taking so long at the creek. "No one but Imnir, understood? We'll talk to him tonight."

She nodded dazedly. "I don't understand what I did."

"I'll explain later." I brushed her question aside. "But no one can know. *Especially* the Arpa."

She nodded again, this time with more strength. "Yes, yes. All right."

I stood on shaking legs. Whatever healing Uspa had wrought, it hadn't replaced the blood I'd lost. It soaked my clothes. At least I could claim that most of it was Mrandr's, and if I was fortunate Castor wouldn't question why I was so much weaker than my wounds suggested.

Uspa's arm slipped under mine, steadying me as we made our way back through the forest. By the time we sighted camp I walked on my own, but Silgi, still tending the fire, dropped a ladle at the sight of me. Everyone else was gone, except Eolus, bound to his tree.

"Priestess!" Silgi shouted, sprinting towards us.

I looked past her to Eolus, gaping at us with eyes round as coins.

If Uspa had brought back this much power from the Penumbra, he had too. I'd been a fool to ignore that so long, too distracted with Imnir and Estavius and Nisien and the end of my journey. Not only was the possibility of our prisoner wielding unknown magic dangerous, but if he realized where it had come from? If Castor did, or Bresius?

Iskiri traitors and Larun would be the least of my concerns.

We didn't hold a funeral for Mrandr, nor did we release his spirit—Imnir refused to do it, the other Vynder did, too, and I'd no inclination. So Sillo and Mynin dug a shallow grave and rolled him in as the sun went down, and covered him with just enough earth and rock to ensure scavengers wouldn't be attracted overnight. Then the beasts and the beetles could take him.

I sat by the fire with Nui on one side and Uspa on the other. The girl hadn't left me since the attack, though I'd a sense that it was only half out of concern for me. She fidgeted with her hands and her shoulders were laced tighter than a bowstring. This wasn't an odd reaction to happening across an unexpected murder. But I knew she was waiting, waiting for everyone else to set the shock of the day aside and sleep, so I could explain what was happening to her.

As darkness settled in and the churr of insects began, Castor stopped beside me.

"I didn't see that in Mrandr," the Arpa said, meeting my gaze with a grim twist to his mouth. "I'm sorry, and I'm glad you survived. Is there anything you need?"

I glanced at him, too tired to decide whether I believed him. "Not at the moment, no."

Sillo took the first watch. My cousin, nearly as on edge as Uspa since he'd learned of the attack, paced the periphery of the camp as Imnir settled down near the girl and I. Nui lay with her spine along my thigh, twitching in her sleep.

"Now tell me," Imnir said after the breaths of our companions lengthened into sleep and gentle snores. "What really happened?"

Uspa turned her hands over in her lap, palms up, and looked to me for explanation.

I took a settling breath. "While we were in the Penumbra, it rained."

Imnir's lips tightened.

Uspa's fingers contracted inwards. "What does that have to do with…"

I held up a hand, letting golden power swell under my skin. Her eyes fixed on it, Sighted now as she was. "You know that no living being is permitted to eat and drink in the High Halls. The same goes for the Penumbra. Because if you do, Uspa, you absorb the magic of those higher realms. You're changed. This is where much of the Miri's power was sourced. They were not born with it, not so much, anyway. The High Halls are where the Vynder's power comes from, by Thvynder's consent. None but Imnir and I know this—and you must not speak of it to anyone, even Sillo."

Uspa's lips froze, parted between a host of questions. "But… I didn't… I didn't drink anything. I didn't even sit down."

"The rain," Imnir repeated. He brushed one hand across the back of the other and sat straighter, looking at me. "I'm surprised it changed her so easily, though."

"The Penumbra is wild." I shook my head. "The rules are different there, and its magic is aggressive. More aggressive than I realized."

Uspa processed this information for a silent moment. "What does it mean? You say the power is aggressive but... it healed you." As she spoke her voice tightened, edged with awe, disbelief, and unease.

I nodded. "The power of the High Halls manifests differently with every Vynder. I assume the power of the Penumbra does too."

"Has it affected you?" Uspa asked.

Imnir looked at me, too, and I shrugged. "Not that I've noticed. I've been taking in the magic of the High Halls for a decade; it may not be able to infect me so easily."

Uspa took this with a nod, already distracted. Her eyes moved towards Eolus. "And him?"

I let out a long breath. "We don't know yet."

Imnir frowned. "I don't think we can wait to find out."

"You mean..." Uspa's gaze flicked between us and the captive. "You mean to kill him?"

I shook my head wearily and Imnir grunted in affirmation. "I suppose so."

"Maybe it will wear off," Uspa protested, sounding both hopeful and uncertain. Her hands now worried at the hem of her tunic, picking at the even stitches that held its decorative edging in place. "You need to hand Eolus over to Bresius."

"The magic of the High Halls doesn't wear off—we can assume the Penumbra's won't either. But Castor won't let us kill him. Eolus must die on the road, accidentally." I pushed tangled hair from my eyes. It snagged on my fingers, reminding me how disheveled I was, and I began to absently work my hair out of its leather and matted braids. It helped me keep my mind off the fact that this very sentiment—Eolus conveniently dying on the journey south—seemed to be exactly what Mrandr had planned for me.

"Uspa, will you?" I asked.

She blinked at me, momentarily uncertain of what I wanted, then she noticed my hair. She shifted without question, grabbing a comb from her nearby pack and beginning to work.

As I'd hoped, the task gave her something to focus on, and the next time she spoke her voice was more level. The consolation went two ways—I found my shoulders beginning to relax, easing into the familiar feeling of comb and fingers in my hair.

"What about Castor?" Uspa asked quietly from behind my shoulder. "You said he won't let you do it."

Imnir watched the legionary's small tent. Beyond it, Sillo moved through the night, an eye on us as he maintained his pacing vigil.

"I'll take care of Eolus," Imnir said. "I can do it quietly. Tonight."

Something unspoken passed between him and I. The soothing passage of Uspa's comb paused.

A dark kind of resignation haunted Imnir's eyes. I saw his son in the shape of them, in the hollow backdrop of sadness to Algatt-green irises and pale lashes.

I still hadn't talked to him, not about that. We'd spoken of everything else to do with my venture into the Penumbra, but I hadn't had the courage to bring up his son and Fate's subsequent vision.

I decided then and there that I had to, tonight. After.

He rose to his feet. "I think it's for the best. Try to get some sleep, both of you. By morning the problem will be solved."

I didn't speak again, but offered him a sad, knowing twist of a smile. It hid the trepidation in my own heart, both for Imnir's sake and for Uspa's. The girl didn't need to know the truth of her guardian's power. I knew enough to fear it. But more than that, I knew how reluctant Imnir was to work this particular kind of magic.

A few minutes later, my hair was bound in a simple braid. I would have tended to Uspa's, but both of us were too aware of Imnir sitting on his bedroll, repairing a tear in his tunic while he waited for us to go to sleep. He didn't want us to see this.

We laid down. We'd pitched no tent but lay under the clear sky, close to the fire. Nui tried to curl up on my bedroll with me, but I pushed her off towards Uspa. The dog looked at me pitifully before settling down against Uspa's back, lending her a canine bulwark against the night and all its uncertainties.

Uspa's breathing took half an hour to steady. I pretended to sleep, my mind drifting from Imnir to his son, to Thray, and to the vision Fate had given me, not so long ago. I wondered how the future she'd described, the unity I'd glimpsed between Imnir and I, the children we would have—how that could possibly come to be in a world so uncertain, so full of death and betrayal?

When I heard Imnir set his work aside, I cracked open one eye.

I could just see the two of them from where I lay; the dozing would-be emperor, bound to a tree with a bag over his head, and my husband, cross-legged on his bedroll. Imnir had unbound his hair. It fell about his face, casting it into shadow as he closed his eyes and settled his shoulders back.

I saw his power creep across the earth. It passed over dirt and leaves, around roots and our sleeping companions like golden, spectral fingers. To me, it smelled of Frir, but this power was his own—necromantic, and scented with the salt of the sea.

Eolus seized as his soul severed from his body. It was a brief thing—his fingers twitched and his body spasmed for the space of two over-loud heartbeats. Then he was still. I might have thought him asleep, had his trousers not darkened and his head not fallen just so.

My stomach turned. I closed my eyes and counted my breaths. I'd seen death a thousand times. I'd dealt it myself, not a few hours earlier. But this magic, the ease of its conjuring and the fact that it came from my husband—that made my gut roil and my nerves twist. Furthermore, I remembered the attack on the fort, meeting Frir over the body of a dead woman, and the feeling of her trying to rend my own soul from my flesh.

Sometime later, I felt movement as Imnir dropped his bedroll down beside me. Our eyes met in silent question, then affirmation, and I lay back down as he settled in.

He sat behind me. He was close, but not overly so, leaving a breath between the warmth of his side and my back.

I rested my head back onto the extra tunic I'd rolled into a pillow and closed my eyes. My heart beat too fast, and I was so aware of his presence I was sure I wouldn't sleep.

After a time I rolled over, facing him in the darkness.

"I know you didn't want to do that," I said lowly.

There was quiet, filled by the soft pop of the low-burning fire.

"Let's not speak of it," Imnir murmured back. "Are you sure you're all right? After Mrandr…"

"I'm all right," I assured him gently. I still needed to speak to him about Frir, but the day had already been hard for both of us. Dared I do it now?

I had to, though. We'd be with Bresius tomorrow. Imnir and I needed to be united, and I needed to know where my husband stood.

"I know she has your son," I whispered, laying soft fingers on his thigh.

Imnir stilled. "What?"

"I saw Frir with him, in the Penumbra. And she said… she said you'd join them, soon."

Imnir cursed, his voice thick with emotion.

When he didn't explain though, I finally pulled back my hand and asked, "Did you know?"

"I knew she had him. But…" He cleared his throat, obviously trying to recover himself. "But join them? Hessa, no. I don't even know what that means."

"Death?" I offered the obvious answer, soft and low.

Another stretch of quiet. The fire popped and the wind rushed through the treetops.

"I'll confront her," Imnir said at length. "I'll send an owl. I'll sort this out."

I nodded, unsure, and rested my hand on the blanket between us. Did I believe that he didn't know what Frir meant? I wasn't sure. But I wanted to believe him, and that left me in a cloud of flickering, half-formed feelings.

After a moment, he reached out and put his cold hand over my warm one.

"You changed, this time," he pointed out. "What happened?"

I thought of Fate's vision, but its images still felt too frail, too close, and too vulnerable to voice. And, for all that they *had* changed the way I looked at Imnir, uncertainty wormed in my stomach. Fate's visions could not be taken at face-value.

But this, he and I, our hands touching? This was progress, and I'd take that.

"I don't want to be alone forever," I told him simply, and it was true.

His smile was small, almost hidden in the dark. Then he squeezed my hand and released it, patting the blanket in front of him.

I rolled over, putting my back to his side once more. I doubted I'd be able to fall asleep, not after the events of the evening and all that we'd said. But my eyes burned, and the moment my muscles settled into my bedroll, fatigue washed over me. My last conscious thought, between slow, half-waking breaths, was of the coals burning down, their flames growing shallower and shallower.

Eventually, Imnir's watch ended, he lay down, and the gap between us closed. The warmth of his breath seeped into my hair on the pillow, and I felt some of the tension leave his body, replaced with a halfway belonging that made my heart ache in passing.

And then, we slept.

TWENTY-EIGHT

The next day I nudged my mount beside Castor's as we traversed the eastern side of the lake. Fields of tufting wheat and barley spread down the rocky shoreline, though most farmhouses lay abandoned. Those that were not shuttered their windows as word of our approach spread, carried down the road by unseen messengers.

To our surprise, the locals left hasty baskets at the end of their paths or lanes; fish and grain, round bread and berries and vegetables. Other than these offerings, made all the more valuable with Nivarium's current state, trails of hearth smoke and the lowing of hidden cattle were the only things to betray the remaining lake dwellers.

"Do they think this would sate a proper horde?" Sillo asked from down the line. His hips rolled easily in the saddle, reins tucked under a knee as he tore a loaf of bread in half and tossed part of it up to me.

"It's southern tradition to leave these for any warriors on the road, foreign or otherwise," Castor answered stiffly, as I sniffed at the bread. It was heavy, studded with toasted grains and seeds. I held the piece up, offering Castor some, but his face was a stormy mask, and the waxed leather bag, bulging with its contents, hung from his saddlebags.

The discovery of Eolus's death had not gone over well. But with no marks on the body and no obvious signs of poisoning or unnatural intervention, Castor had been forced to conclude that the captive's heart had simply given out in the night. Whether or not that excluded magic was yet to be seen, but there was no one obvious to blame and no reason for anyone in the group to kill Eolus. Thus our Arpa guide had simply taken an axe and tucked proof of Eolus's death into the leather bag.

Our gruesome gift would keep until the end of the day.

We passed over the Nivari-Apharni border without incident. Arpa scouts met us on the other side and Castor rode ahead to parley while the rest of us held back, watching as cool wind off the lake brushed hair into our eyes and chased great, towering banks of clouds across the sky.

The scouts took us to a fort on the Delta, and there we bid a temporary goodbye to our horses—Castor arranged for them to be kept and fed at the fort until our return—and boarded a boat. The following evening, we disembarked in Apharnum.

We clattered onto a dock in sight of the city, backed by mountains layered in shades of violet and dusk. The city filled my eyes, dragging me back to a vision I'd seen when I was young, at the hands of an Arpa priest.

Apharnum was, by far, the largest settlement I'd ever encountered. Elevated canals stretched into the city from the surrounding mountains like the spokes of a wheel, bringing water to its very heart. The smoke from innumerable cookfires hazed the waning daylight, shrouding domed rooves of silver, gold, and tarnished copper. Even this far away, the wind smelled of woodsmoke, cooking food, and stinking humanity.

Situated around the city, as far as I could see, was an army. Temporary walls and battlements had been constructed, while thousands of tents clustered around strategic points in the defenses.

"Only two of the aqueducts remain in Apharni control, the ones to the south, which are still within the city limits," Castor told me as we stood on the docks, waiting for the rest of our party to join us. He had Eolus's head, still in its bag, hanging from one hand. Slaves ferried our packs around him.

"How much longer can the city hold?" I asked, eyeing the elevated waterways with grudging awe.

Castor gazed over the city with obvious contentment. "Not long."

The camp opened to us, soldiers and slaves lining the ways to watch the barbarians pass. Whispers rippled through the crowd, but Castor's face was well-known. No one shouted or accosted us.

At a large, scarlet tent, Castor signaled a halt. Our escort of soldiers withdrew, forming two lines with shields and spears displayed, and I stood close to Imnir's shoulder.

Castor's eyes glinted with satisfaction. "Here he comes."

Soldiers stepped out from the door of the big tent and fanned out to either side, preceding the would-be emperor of the Arpa Empire.

Bresius was older than I'd anticipated, at least fifteen years Eolus's senior. He was dark-haired for an Arpa, clad in a tunic of pure white and a knee-length robe of summer's blue. He had the bearing of a warrior, his muscles dense and his movement easy, and the sword at his hip was practical instead of elaborate, with an eagle-head pommel.

Evening sunlight filled his hair as he strode out into the open air. He nodded in welcome and clasped one wrist over his stomach. "Welcome, travelers."

"My lord." Castor smoothly fell to one knee. "I present to you Hessa, High Priestess of Thvynder among the Eangen, Queen in the North, and her husband, Imnir, King and High Priest of Thvynder among the Algatt."

"My lord," I echoed Castor, but did not kneel. If the Arpa insisted upon calling me a queen, I would suffer the title to its fullest extent. "Castor, our gift."

Castor gave me the barest glance, irritated that I'd stolen his grand reveal, but lifted the leather bag from his feet and held it out with a second bow of his head. "The head of Eolus, my lord."

Bresius closed the space between them and took the bag with curiosity. Castor rose back to his feet, exchanging an affirming glance with his master as the elder man opened the bag and surveyed his prize.

"Cousin," Bresius intoned in greeting to the severed head. A grin twitched across his lips, broadening as he looked up at Imnir, myself, and Castor. Suddenly he laughed, wrapping Castor in a wrestling hug and kissing him on the top of the head.

Castor bore his lord's affection with his own grin.

"Come!" Bresius declared, releasing Castor and tossing the bag to a soldier, who caught it and turned rather green. "This calls for celebration!

And a tale, but I will not have that without wine in my belly."

Around us, the soldiers—all by now realizing what was in the bag, and just what it meant—began to murmur.

"You, too, my faithful brothers. Tonight, we feast!" Bresius called, raising his voice and turning to survey the gathered. They cheered. Catching my eye, the would-be emperor beckoned and proffered an arm. "And you, my Sword from the North, will sit by my side."

Torches lit the great scarlet tent and the air filled with the smell of meat, bread, sauces, roasted vegetables, and wine. Bresius's commanders and loyal aristocrats sat at two long tables, facing one another, while Bresius sat with Castor, Imnir, and myself. Ours looked down the length of the other two, giving me a nearly unobstructed view of everyone present.

And so, while the men ate, I looked for Frir's spy.

There were gray-haired commanders, swords at their hips. There were pretty young men, laughing and boasting and currying favor. There were civilians in draped robes, belted at the waist and open at the chest to reveal the finely embroidered, straight necklines of the long tunics they wore beneath. All were beardless. All were Arpa in tongue and mannerisms, though the colors of their skin varied dramatically, particularly among the young men—Bresius's supporters, gathered from all corners of the Empire. And all were as human, as magicless as one would expect in a nation whose gods were dead. None of them appeared to be more than Bresius's loyal followers.

"What is it you see, Hessa of the Eangen?"

I sat back and surveyed Bresius, who in turn studied me. His cheeks were a little red with wine and good humor, but his eyes were keen and sober.

"Arpa," I replied, too tired to come up with a more elaborate answer. I'd already sat through two hours of conversation earlier that night, as Castor informed Bresius of our journey and the capture of Eolus. By now I was growing so tired of the language that I struggled to put words together.

On my other side, Imnir's sleeve brushed mine as he reached for his wine. Though he could certainly hear our conversation, his focus remained on the crowd and potential threats.

His vigilance soothed me.

Bresius leaned on the arm of his chair, closer to me. "And what strikes you about them? What do they look like to your eyes?"

The question was presented lightly, but I knew my answer had to be calculated. "I see strangers. Threats."

Bresius made a begrudging, affirmative noise and glanced back out over the guests. I did, too, and we sat together for a moment, side by side, before he admitted, "I feel the same about your people. We all do. That's part of why I hired you—it makes a statement. See how my men watch you? Those small glances?"

"I do," I returned. I picked up my cup of wine, which I'd barely touched—its dark, tart flavor was not to my liking—and took a small sip to give myself time to string more Arpa words together. "I'm used to being watched. And judged."

He seemed to think about this for a time, and when he spoke it was with a casual solidarity. "That is leadership, is it not?"

I was well aware that I was the only woman seated at the tables, and I knew that Arpa women did not hold the same stations as their men. But there was no amusement in Bresius's voice, no jest or condescension. He was, to all appearances, stretching a sympathetic hand between us.

The thought that I might put a knife in this man's back in the near future crossed my mind, and I wasn't quite sure what to do with it. He was certainly nothing like Eolus had been. But one conversation, one instance of supposed solidarity, did not mean he would be a fitting ally.

I turned in my chair to consider him straight on. He did likewise, interest playing through his eyes. His gaze certainly had an edge to it, a constant guardedness that I was familiar with, but there was an openness, too, a regard that took me by surprise.

"You're not what I expected," I informed him.

"You're not what I expected," he returned. "You're quieter, more level. And you truly look like a woman, which most of my council declared you would not. Femininity stands in direct opposition to the militaristic, after all. That is the predominant Arpa wisdom, among the great minds."

"Then perhaps your great minds should reassess," I suggested.

"Perhaps they should. It is a new age, after all," he said with a nod, and took a drink of his wine. He added, "I also expected you to wear a great deal more fur."

I looked at him askance, perplexed. "It's… summer? Why would I wear fur in summer?"

Bresius chuckled at that and gave a half-shrug. "Fair enough. It's the image, you see. It's expected."

I refrained from making a comment as to my own image of the Arpa and their ignorance of the North. Instead, I took another sip of my wine.

"Are all Northern women like you?" Bresius asked, watching my expression over the brim of my cup.

I shrugged. "Northerners are whatever their inclinations and capabilities allow—women and men, both. It's a matter of practicality."

"What of your children? What of them while their mothers roam Nivarium, burning and raiding?"

"You mean while their parents roam?" I said. "Anyone with small children, regardless of gender, is not *expected* to fight. Death is so close in this world, and the arrival of young life is considered a time of reprieve for parents."

Bresius made a considering noise. "Well, I've no wife or children, but I can appreciate that sentiment."

We spoke for a little longer, of lighter things, before Bresius settled back in his chair, hands on the armrests, and nodded out to the company again. "So, Castor has explained to you about the door to the Penumbra? In the temple?"

"He has."

"And what will take place on the other side? Has he told you that?"

I shook my head, trying not to look as interested as I was.

Bresius waved a slave over and they cleared his empty plate, the carcass of a small fowl sucked clean and even the scraps of vegetables consumed. Bresius, I noted, was not wasteful.

"Well, then I will tell you," he said. "Though my information is not as detailed as I would prefer—these secrets were held closely by the elite of Lathian's priesthood, you understand, and much of that wisdom has been lost. Or intentionally destroyed. But what I have uncovered is this; beyond the doorway, there is a pool, and I must drink from it to take my rightful throne."

The liquid would be the Blood of Eiohe. Though the Arpa now knew of the Four Pillars, it seemed they had yet to make the connection between them and the origin of the blood that blessed their rulers.

"However, as I understand, the liquid is resistant to touch," Bresius added. "It must be fetched by a priest—or priestess—and taken into a very specific vessel. Then I can take that vessel, and drink."

I frowned at this. "Do you have that vessel?"

Bresius nodded. "I do. A number of them were found hidden in the temple, before the Laru seized control of it."

"Good." I glanced back out over the company, touching my Sight again and searching for anything out of the ordinary. There was nothing.

My thoughts were divided, half pondering the ritual of Ascension, and half searching for Frir's spy. Bresius was distracted as one of his aristocrats approached the head table with a bow, and they began a rapid conversation.

By the time all the plates were cleared, more wine fetched, and the conversation settled into intimate knots, I sat at ease in my chair. Bresius left the table, moving to confer with his men, and the formality of the meal eased.

Pulling one foot up onto the chair, I leaned my knee against the armrest and looked at Imnir. He'd barely spoken so far, immersed in his own thoughts, observations, and, no doubt, eavesdropping.

"So?" I prompted, picking a piece of roasted fowl off his third plate of food—which he'd refused to let the slaves take away, much to their chagrin. "What do you think of all this, husband? Bresius is an interesting man."

"He's still Arpa." Imnir batted my hand away and leaned forward over his dinner, elbows on the table as he squinted out across the room. "I think that the fact that I have yet to identify Frir's spy is disconcerting. Why aren't they more evident? And what are they doing here?"

A little of my ease retreated. If Imnir knew more about the situation than he let on, he was doing a good job of hiding it. And, rather than console me about my husband's loyalties, it simply made the whole situation more unsettling.

"I was hoping you'd be the one to figure that out," I said. "You said you'd speak to Frir?"

He looked down at his plate, half seeing it, then sat back and pushed it across the table. A slave immediately swooped to take it away, and my husband stood up. Standing there in his Algatt clothing and tattoos, his beard and hair full of torchlight, he looked utterly out of place. He seemed to know it, too, and scowled. "I'm going to find my tent. If you want to talk, let's do it there, where I haven't a hundred Arpa eyes gouging into me."

The Arpa were staring at me more than Imnir, but pointing this out seemed unhelpful. I unfolded from my own chair and we made for the door. The Arpa parted, though it seemed that they did so more to stare from a proper distance than out of deference. I met a few eyes, looking again for any flicker of Frir's magic or influence, but there was nothing more than appraisal.

We ducked out of the tent flap and into the night.

TWENTY-NINE

The food, wine, and warmth of the tent was replaced by the dank scents of the river, mud, and amassed humanity, interspersed with woodsmoke, hot iron, and horseflesh.

Castor stood outside in the company of another Arpa who'd been seated at the head table. He was brown-haired, with hooded eyes and skin darkened by the sun. His accent matched Castor's, and he surveyed us critically as we came in sight.

"Our gear was taken away," Imnir said to Castor in prompting, ignoring the other Arpa.

Castor bid his companion goodnight, then nodded to the pair of us. "I'll show you to your tent."

We set off through the settlement, weaving through several rows of tents before we came to an open space. Two tents stood here, marked as ours by the fact that no Arpa banners flew from their central poles, and Hete lounged outside the larger dwelling, a pipe between her teeth and smoke eddying into the overcast sky.

Nui, leashed to a horse's hitching post nearby, barked animatedly at the sight of us. I went to unbind her, rubbing her ears as Castor pointed towards the smaller of the two tents. "That's for the two of you."

Imnir glanced at him. "Only us?"

"You're married," Castor said, though he knew very well we rarely slept in close proximity. "I managed to convince Bresius that the rest of your company would share a single tent—they tried to separate the women, but I think that's a rather bad idea in the middle of the army. For everyone's sake."

"Agreed," I said. Nui, unsatisfied with the sincerity of my greeting, leapt up on me, bracing her forepaws on my shoulders and licking my face. I fought to push her back down. "Thank you for that."

Castor nodded. "Of course. Goodnight."

"Goodnight."

Imnir went into our tent first, casting Hete a distracted greeting, to which she raised her pipe. I followed him and Nui darted past the both of us, enthusiastically sniffing around the inside of the dwelling.

It was surprisingly comfortable. The reed mats on the ground smelled clean and sweet. A bed, just big enough for two, was built of raw wood. Our saddlebags hung from the central pole and all our weapons were on a side table, where a single oil lamp sat next to a pitcher of water and two cups illuminated the chamber.

Imnir promptly unwound his legwraps and pulled off his boots and socks, leaving the latter two beside the door and draping the former across the back of a chair. Barefoot, he strode over to the bed and sat. The ropes that supported the mattress—straw-stuffed, and recently, from the scent—creaked.

Imnir raised his eyebrows at me. "Loud, but not uncomfortable."

I realized I was still lingering in the doorway. I unfastened my own legwraps and took them off. My boots and socks came next, and I added my belt to the growing pile on the back of the chair.

Nui nosed up to the side of the bed as Imnir sat cross-legged on the wool blankets. "*You* will sleep on the floor, mongrel."

"And I won't?" I prompted.

"Don't be coy, it doesn't suit you," Imnir quipped, but didn't look at me, scratching Nui's ears. He seemed more relaxed now that we had some privacy.

I sat down at the end of the bed, on the other side and looked at him, promptingly. "Frir?"

The silence stretched long enough to grow uncomfortable. He

gathered himself, sitting up against the head of the bed and staring past me.

"Why did you wait so long to tell me?" he asked. "About what you'd seen? Frir, and my son, and what she said about us?"

I tugged at the bottom of my tunic, straightening it across my knees with a thumb. "I wasn't sure what it meant. I was afraid of the answer. I was afraid that you and she had… I don't know. Maybe you cared for her, too, and had an agreement to go to her after this journey ends."

Imnir was overcome with shock. "I… Hessa."

I smoothed the hem of my tunic again, permitting myself another second to find some composure, then met his eyes. "Was I wrong?"

He scowled in frustration. "No. And I haven't made it easy for us to… discuss anything. You haven't helped, but that's beside the point."

"So you don't know what she's doing?"

"That Frir is making a home for me and my son in the Penumbra so we could become some kind of twisted family? No. No, I did not know. I *did* know that she was sending the boy to any deaths around you. I thought it was her way of driving a wedge between us—and I allowed her to do it, and for that I'm sorry. But if what you say is true…"

He trailed off. I gave him a few moments to pick up his thoughts again, but he didn't say anymore.

"How does she intend for you to join them? And when?"

"She said she won't kill me," Imnir said immediately, and though I'd had the same thought, hearing him speak it aloud filled me with relief. "Frir isn't dead. She wants a normal life. She's always wanted that."

I looked at him quizzically.

"It's because of Eang's son." Imnir pulled his knees up and locked his forearms around them. "When Eang was pregnant with Ogam, she went to visit Fate to ask what her child would be. But she only went because of Frir's encouragement."

I stayed quiet, recalling my vision of Eang and Frir in the High Halls, under the starry sky where the Loom of Fate whisked and tapped. Goosebumps prickled up my arms.

"Fate told Eang that the son she bore would bring her death. So Eang had him cut out of her belly and left him to die, an infant, in the cold."

"On top of a mountain, for a hundred days and nights," I added. The story was a familiar one nowadays, as was its motif—the mortal, acting upon Fate's word, and causing their own destruction.

I swallowed. I wasn't doing that right now, was I? By allowing myself closer to Imnir? No, I was not proceeding blindly. My eyes were wide open.

Imnir nodded. "But of course, he did not die—he was immortal. Eang thought that was the only reason for his survival, and it was. What she did not know was that every night, Frir came and held the child and sang to him through the darkest hours and the worst storms, trying to atone for the part she'd had in his suffering."

My mouth felt dry and tasted of sour Arpa wine. Swallowing, I slipped from the bed and went to the side table, where I poured two cups of water.

"You know the part Ogam played in the Upheaval and the death of his mother," Imnir said as I sat back down and offered him a cup, which he took. "Now Frir blames herself for all of it."

"She blames me too," I pointed out, between two long swallows.

"You wielded the axe." Imnir shrugged in agreement. "But she was the pawn of Fate that brought it all about."

I considered this for a quiet moment and drained my cup. "What does this have to do with you and your son?"

"Frir never had children of her own, for fear of what those children would become. Instead she took the children of others, the unborn, under the excuse of needing servants to fetch the souls of the dead. And yes, she took my son too.

"She fell in love with me, when I was her priest. I was already married so I had an excuse not to lie with her, and she was patient, assuming I'd grow tired of my wife and succumb to her one day." His voice hardened. "I did not. Her anger grew. My wife died and Frir came to me in the mountains. She took me... I don't know where. For all I know it could have been that very cave in the Penumbra, the one you saw. I was her prisoner, and I feared that I no longer had a choice—

that Frir would kill me for my soul and my supposed love, or keep me chained until I 'willingly' lay with her."

He stopped again, staring at the blankets between us with a vaulted, unfathomable expression.

Out of sight on Imnir's side of the bed, Nui let out a huff and resettled into the mats.

"But then Thvynder came." Imnir's voice was nearly emotionless now, locked away. "Frir was not there, at the final battle, because she was hidden away with me. Word did not reach her in time. And she raged.

"She couldn't hide from Thvynder once they arose, though. She had to bow, and Thvynder offered me the priesthood. I took it, and found shelter from her. When it came time to marry, I didn't want to, but I thought having a wife again would protect me. I never meant to bring her wrath down on you."

"I did that to myself," I said. "The axe that killed Eang, remember?"

Imnir gave a half-hearted shrug. "Well… What matters is that Frir has my son, and ideas about us still making a life together. And she has a spy in Bresius's midst, not to mention this other servant, the one you saw in the flames. She evaded all my questions, Hessa, when I spoke to her. All of them."

That was troubling. Deeply.

"What interest would she have in Bresius?" I asked, my thoughts drifting down murky paths. "Does she intend to betray Thvynder somehow? Might she have sided with Larun?"

Imnir shook his head. "Frir sides with no one, and betraying Thvynder is the most assured form of suicide. She hasn't a fragment of the power needed to withstand them. She's up to her own devices, and there are two explanations."

"Oh?"

"The first is to kill you."

This was no real shock. "Thvynder wouldn't allow it."

"If Thvynder knew."

"I want to know the second option."

"To ensure our success." Imnir sat forward now, and a little earnestness entered his face. "To protect me, in her own twisted way. To keep me indebted to her, and use it as leverage. Or to endear herself to me, though I think she's likely given up on that by now."

I cradled my cup between my hands, deep in thought. "I'd like to believe that. It's better than thinking she's arranging me a convenient death. I've had enough of that already."

At the mention of Mrandr's attack, Imnir shifted closer. The ropes of the bed creaked and my mind flicked between half a dozen rapid observations—the way the muscles of his arms stood out against his sleeves, our proximity, the growing quiet of the camp, and so on— before his fingers brushed my wrist, and my mind staggered to an ungainly halt.

"I'll keep her at bay," Imnir promised, simply. "I can do that. I can guard you from that threat, at least."

"All the other threats are still up to me?" I quipped, because I had to say something.

"If that's what you want. I'll never be more than you ask me to be, never take more than you want to give—and I ask the same of you. But the offer stands... as does the one I made last winter, back in the High Halls."

He was no longer speaking just of Frir. He spoke of family, of trying again to be a proper couple. I wondered if the wine had gone to my head, if I was mistaking the way he looked at me now, the vow in his level gaze, and the simple way his touch occupied all my senses. I still bucked against that feeling, the demands it made of me, the way it pulled me toward him despite all the uncertainties and history between us.

If I accepted his offer, I'd be inviting Frir's wrath down on my head anew. But he seemed confident he could withstand that tide, and I'd never known Imnir to lie—even when the truth hurt me. He meant what he'd said. He meant all of it.

And I meant what I'd said, before the ambush on Eolus. I didn't want to be at odds anymore. I wanted to be his ally, and I wanted to let the rest go.

Imnir's hand left my wrist and he pulled back, giving a pragmatic sigh to mask a flash of—was that hurt, in his eyes? It could have been regret, even guilt. Whatever it was, it was outside his usual stunted array of emotions, and it disconcerted me.

"I've said my piece." He shook his head. "I'll lay my bedroll on the floor, tonight."

I started to nod, started to form a sentence, before something inside me broke.

I closed the space between us and kissed him. There was an aggression to that kiss, a challenge, a willing blindness and forced disregard—because if I thought too deeply, if I second-guessed this moment, it would be gone. Our relationship would return to tension and halfway belonging, and I did not want that.

No. I wanted to trust Imnir, to stand beside him, to belong to him and him to me, fully and unequivocally. I wanted Fate's visions to hold true. He was not the husband I wished I had, nor I the wife he'd once loved. But we were all we had.

And maybe, when the morning came, we would no longer feel so alone.

THIRTY

A week passed. I'd expected to spend my days shadowing Bresius, dragged through one council and patrol after the next, but the would-be emperor had been inhabiting this camp without Vynder guards for months.

"Rest," he told Imnir and I when we arrived at his tent the first morning to find him sitting before a spread of breads, fine meats and cheeses, and an ornate pot of tea. "The Laru are in the city. I'll need you at my side for the push, but until then you're of most use healing. If I need you, you'll know."

So that was what we did, as battle loomed and the future of our world hung on the edge of a blade—though in the privacy of Imnir's and my tent, there was more to be done than sleep, mend clothes and tend our weapons. Imnir and I had made a kind of peace with one another, and neither was about to let the advantages of that reprieve pass by.

That peace spread. Our Vynder hadn't been as segregated as the rest of our armies but in the evenings on the road, they had still gravitated to their own—Algatt with Algatt, Eangen with Eangen. But somewhere over the course of that week, that habit slipped our minds.

Hete taught Ifling and Lida to smoke her pipe. Mynin and Sillo sparred together, and Silgi brought me tea in the mornings. Imnir and I sat together at the fireside in the evening, watching it happen, and there were moments then that I truly believed he and I could change the North. It gave me hope for the future—not only for our people, but for us. If we survived the battle to come.

· When Imnir and I were not preoccupied with one another or Vynder matters, we separated. I took to wandering the camp with Uspa and Sillo and Nui, searching for any hint of Frir's spy or other signs of supernatural unrest. I found a spot on a hill next to the river, above a stretch of beach where dozens of boats lay like sunning seals, and from there I'd survey the besieged city. It was a haze of smoke and glistening towers, and beyond them the mountains loomed.

It was at one of these moments, while the sun rose from the mountains to the east and Nui sat patiently at my heel, that I saw the death. It had come overnight—though between the fall of the dew, the darkness, and the trampled condition of all greenery in the camp, I hadn't noticed until then.

Now the land around the camp was dead, colorless, and dry. The city seemed to be the axis of this destruction, though it was hard to tell. It spread over what remained of Apharnum's fields, and even on to the distant mountains. They had lost their luster in the dawn-glow, turned dull and blunt.

The Laru were in Apharnum, as Siris had told me long ago, and Bresius had affirmed. From the size of the land they'd just harvested, they would be more powerful than ever. But what did they need the power for, and why this morning? They were still trapped in a city under siege.

Something of an answer came as a flutter of wings drew my gaze north, and an owl alighted on my hand. Its news was simple, a message rather than a vision, told in Estavius's accented Northman.

The city is ready to fall. Tell Bresius the third and sixth gates will be opened, the night after next.

I took the news to Bresius myself, the owl at my shoulder and Nui at my heel. The occupants of the camp had barely grown used to my presence without an owl glowering at them, and by the time I reached Bresius's tent, the guards had noticed the commotion and were ready for my arrival.

I was admitted, noting more than a few moths clinging to the outer canvas of the tent.

Nui, not one to be left behind, darted through before a guard could stop her. I followed into the scarlet shade.

"Where did this information come from?" Bresius asked, blinking once in surprise at my owl, who blinked back and let out an ear-bending screech. Nui flinched where she nosed about one side of the huge tent.

"A friend, sent ahead into the city," I replied.

"What friend? One of your Vynder?" Even as Bresius asked the question, his eyes cleared. "Or the Arpa allies Castor spoke to me of? The two legionaries, the Soulderni and the priest's son."

I paused. I didn't want to admit to Estavius's and Nisien's roles, but there seemed no way around it. "Yes. They're converts to our god, and trustworthy men."

Bresius rounded the table where he'd been sitting with a stack of scrolls and faced me across an open space of elevated, mat-covered floor. "An Arpa converted to your religion? The Soulderni's conversion I can swallow but the other? Estavius?"

I narrowed my eyes a fraction and on my shoulder the owl shifted, feathers brushing my ear. "Yes, they both did, and they're in the city now, offering you a way in."

"I should have been informed of this. Does Castor know?"

"Castor has met them, yes, but he didn't know their purpose." I gave a small shrug. "I understand why you chose Castor for the task of fetching us, but you must understand that I'm reluctant to trust him. Given our history."

Bresius nodded in consideration, though his eyes were narrowed too. "I understood your previous relationship to have been amiable. Relatively."

"Castor forgot a great deal," I said.

Bresius took this with a thoughtful purse of the lips. "I see. I knew there were holes in the man's memory, but his story was verified by Onamus. I am glad that the two of you have made the alliance work, despite the past."

"Who?"

"Onamus, one of my advisors. He returned from the North with Castor." Bresius returned to his table and sat down, closing one scroll with a smooth, dry rasp and opening another to scan it. "They've both proven invaluable to me. How did your friend get into the city?"

When Castor had spoken of his journey south, back in the Temple of Mircea, he had mentioned that another soldier survived, but I hadn't thought anything of it at the time. But now wasn't the time to dwell on it, either.

"My friend told me he knew a way in," I answered.

"I see." Bresius turned his gaze to Nui, who trotted up to my side and sat, curling her tail around her legs. "Well, I've sent spies into the city myself, but getting word out is the challenge. I'll send a man in tonight to verify your claim. Can the bird…?"

"I'll instruct her to bring his response," I finished. "All the messenger needs do is speak to her, and she will bring the message directly to you."

"This is very strange magic." Bresius leaned closer, dropping his head slightly to stare into the owl's face. The owl stared back, unblinking. "But useful. Fine. Do it."

The next day, I awoke to a scratch at the tent flap and Castor's voice. "Imnir. Hessa."

Nui barked and, from behind my head, I heard Imnir softly curse.

"I'll see what he wants," I reassured him, hefting his arm off my chest. "Move."

Imnir rolled over and started to sit up, pushing hair out of his eyes as I pulled on my overtunic and went to the flap.

Outside, the air was cool and scented with dew. As soon as the flap lifted, an owl swooped in with a thunder of wings and soared towards the bed, where it landed on the post beside Imnir's head.

Imnir flinched and cursed again, still stupefied with sleep.

I bit back a laugh and looked out to where Castor stood in the pink and gray of dawn, backed by a few fluttering moths—which, by now, had thoroughly invaded the camp. Castor wore no armor or cloak or helmet, and his expression seemed lit from within. I saw the same glinting determination I'd seen when he looked into Eolus's face, but more—he glowed like a man who had run a stretch on a winter morning, healthful and alive and a little breathless.

"Your bird returned," he said, nodding into the tent. "Bresius is mobilizing, quietly. Tonight, after midnight, we take Apharnum."

The camp maintained a façade of normality as dusk fell. Carts bearing fresh goods trundled in, while others bearing manure and empty casks trundled out. Soldiers, servants, and slaves went about their routines, watches changed, and cookfires provided pockets of warmth and light as the sun slipped lower in the western sky.

But in the shelter of tents and behind the hills, Bresius's men made ready for war.

The assault would begin small, with several hundred soldiers sneaking through the gates Estavius had promised to open, clearing the way—silencing watchmen and bells and occupying watchtowers—before the greater numbers followed in the darkest hours of the night.

The Vynder, Bresius, and I would be with the first group, as would a small force of flint-eyed legionaries in light armor, intended to hunt down Bresius's last contender for the throne, Cassius.

Anticipation left my stomach raw. I knew this feeling, and my people had their ways of embracing it. The Vynder gathered in our little corner of the camp. Snatches of incense drifted to me on the breeze as the Arpa prayed to idols of dead gods. But though we Northerners prayed, under our breaths or in the quiet of our minds, our focus was on one another.

I sat beside the fire in my gear as Imnir pulled his fingers through my hair and began to braid. I wore mail and a padded leather vest, cinched at the waist with two belts and crossed at the chest with Galger and Gammler's brace, though the axes still waited in our tent.

Across the fire, Hete gathered Mynin's hair in a dozen smaller braids and bound them into a leather-wrapped tail. The others were at a similar stage of preparation, though Lida and Ifling already sat together, hair mirroring one another's in tight, twin crowns, studded with their traditional Addack pins of ivory.

It was Ifling, eventually, who began to sing. She started low, with a few lonely lines, before Lida joined in. They'd been singing together since they were small children and their voices perfectly intertwined, falling into minors that echoed one another until Sillo joined in, too.

He sat patiently while Uspa brushed his hair out, taking much longer than was strictly necessary. The girl was nervous—I saw it in the tightness of her breaths and the way she kept glancing at the darkening sky—but her expression was set, and hard. She was ready.

Imnir tied off my braid with my habitual beaded leather and I stood, giving him a small smile in the firelight as we traded places. He smiled back, but the expression was a distracted thing, and he looked overburdened.

"What is it?" I asked as he sat down and I pulled my fingers through his pale hair, separating out his angular fringe and beginning to wind a few, small braids.

He didn't answer for a few moments. His back buffeted my knees as he tried to relax, the songs of our people rising around us. The others had joined in now and my stomach warmed at the familiar melody.

"Imnir?" I prompted, nudging him with my knee.

"Uspa shouldn't come," he said quietly, though his admission felt placating. There was more on his mind. "She should stay here, with the dog."

"Alone with the Arpa?" I clarified.

"It's safer here. Most of the soldiers will be gone."

"Safe is a relative term." I wound the end of one tiny braid together between my fingers and began another. "I'd prefer she stayed behind, too, but she's old enough to decide herself."

"She's seventeen."

"Old enough to have children, a home of her own, and four seasons of raiding scars," I pointed out, though if I was entirely honest I wasn't sure Uspa should be coming with us either. Neither Imnir nor I would have attention to spare for her tonight. "Sillo can watch her back."

He made a dissatisfied grunt. "He already watches her back. Constantly, and with his eyes too low."

I leaned around to peer into his face. Silgi had started a new song, an Algatt one. I knew some of the lyrics, but this particular song was sung in Algatt dialect.

"You're being a grumpy old father," I accused.

He stopped glaring at Sillo, looking abashed. "She's not really my daughter."

"No, but does that matter?" I tied off his hair in a knot of leather at the back of his head and sat down beside him.

"Maybe not. Not exactly, anyway," he granted, but I saw memory linger around his eyes, and a burden I'd come to know well. His gaze strayed back to me, heavy and hesitant. "I don't want to lose another family. A daughter… or a wife."

I wasn't sure what to say. Did he mean he *was* beginning to consider Uspa and I family? Or was he explaining why he still maintained a measure of distance between us?

My silence prompted him to go on.

"I wish the both of you would stay behind," he admitted, morose. "Anywhere will be safer than that city tonight. Even an Arpa camp. We still don't even know exactly what we'll do."

"Estavius will know. If he didn't have a plan, he wouldn't have arranged to open the gate," I replied, but I'd stiffened. My instinct was to rankle at the suggestion that I stay behind, but I tempered myself. Fear of losing loved ones was something I understood, even if his way of expressing it was impractical and selfish.

"I'm not staying here," I stated, clearly but gently.

Imnir shrugged. "I know. But I can wish for it."

I didn't have anything helpful to say, so I rested my hand on his thigh as the Vynder's song carried on. He let it sit there for a moment, warm and gentle, before he squeezed it with his own and set it aside.

The movement was simple, not gruff or irritated, but there was something about it that felt final, like closing shutters against the winds of an early winter, or the first bite of a grave-digger's shovel. When I looked at him again, I sensed that there was more in Imnir's eyes than thoughts of Uspa and myself, and even his long-lost family.

There was no room for me in that gaze. Again, something had changed, and this time it wasn't for the better. But I knew that pushing him right now, on the edge of battle, would do neither of us good.

I suppressed a rush of embarrassment and leaned back on both palms in what I hoped was a nonchalant pose. But Imnir's response had dragged my own nerves and tension to the surface, and I fought now to keep myself composed.

Soon after, the song ended and Hete fetched the paints. I stood and approached the fire. The sounds of the rest of the camp swelled through the break in our singing—a low, steady murmuration of men preparing to fight for their lives, and perhaps to lose them; men driven by the knowledge that tonight they would put an emperor on the throne, and the Arpa Empire would enter a new age.

The owl, returned to me after bearing Estavius's message to Bresius, fluttered onto my hand. I began to pray.

The owl watched me as I spoke. I slipped into the Eangi's old tongue—an instinct from my childhood and reawakened on this momentous night. The owl's eyes sunk into my own, taking every word. Aside from the Miri, the owls and I were the only ones in the world who remembered this language, and that was a heavy thought.

The prayer was not long and my requests were simple: for protection and most of all, for guidance. Once the city was in Bresius's hands, the time for Imnir and I to act would come. But Thvynder's verdict still had not been given. Would they bless the crowning of a new Arpa emperor, or would I be putting a knife in his back?

Uncertainty sat in my stomach like spoiled meat.

That, however, was a worry for tomorrow. As I finished, the owl took flight. We watched it wheel north, over the glow of a thousand fires and the fluttering banners of the Arpa.

Imnir came to me with a small pot of kohl and a supple brush, and I stood quietly as he painted my face. He darkened my eyes and the bottom of my jaw in a nearly solid swath, creeping upon my bottom lip with thick lines. When he was finished I painted him, pulling out the existing darkness under his eyes and turning it into weeping spearheads of black.

I could sense the Arpa watching us, discreetly beyond the reach of our firelight, but I paid them no mind. This moment was for Northerners, and Northerners alone.

Hete began to sing again, a Vynder song that had come into being in the last few years. It spoke of the White Lake and the forest at its edges, the temple we'd reconstructed there, and the way the wind came through the high mountain valleys. It was repetitive, a call-and-response song that soon pulled everyone into its rhythms, increasing in tempo and fervor until my heart swelled in my chest and my uncertainties almost slipped away.

At the end, we howled. We roared and the Algatt yipped and Uspa laughed. Nui barked and joined in, loosing a true canine howl to the sky.

Tonight, we would enter the Temple of No God.

After that, we dispersed to pass the remaining hour as we desired. Imnir went walking with Uspa, likely to convince her to remain behind, while the rest sat together at the fireside—Algatt and Eangen, sitting close in the deepening night.

I walked back to the riverside with Nui, assuming my spot on the hill with a view of the besieged city. Someone had left a bucket here, and I flipped it over to sit down and wrestle my nerves into line. Nui trotted off, a canine-shaped hulk of shadow with a boar-bristle spine, snapping at moths and sniffing tufts of dead grass.

Soon after I settled in, the wind came. A lone moth that had been fluttering towards my outstretched hand was buffeted away by the breeze. Down the hill, Nui raised her head and gave a deep-chested huff as Estavius materialized in the shadows.

Nui darted to the newcomer. He appeared as the perfect Arpa legionary, armed and armored, his pale eyes obscured in the night. His helmet was under one arm and his hair windblown from the journey.

"Is all well?" I asked, careful to speak low. We were alone, all voices from the camp distant, but I couldn't help fearing we'd be overheard.

He took in my prepared state, my hair, and the paint on my cheeks with one glance. "Yes, though… Hessa, I have news."

He crouched across from me and I leaned forward. "Is it Nisien?"

"No." Estavius still held my gaze, but there was reluctance there now—the look of a man bearing ill news, all concern and grimness and bracing.

"Someone must be crowned, to harness and lock down that power, prevent it from future abuse, and settle the Penumbra," he said. "Thvynder has decided this. But it must be someone who can bring stability to the Empire, be an ally to the North, and keep that power in the temple from falling into the hands of anyone else—especially the Laru. For that, I'm sure, was their ultimate goal in allying with Eolus. I doubt they ever intended to let him ascend."

Cold trickled into my gut, and I knew the answer to my question before I asked it. "I understand. Who must I crown?"

Estavius's expression tightened. "Me."

THIRTY-ONE

E stavius looked as pale and uncomfortable as I felt as he stared at the distant boats, still nestled next to one another like seals on the shoreline below our hill.

"I thought you didn't want this," I reminded him, trying not to sound accusatory. He'd told me, there in the firelight after Uspa and I escaped the Penumbra, that Eiohe's power was not something he sought.

Estavius shook his head. "No."

"Then…" I wanted to ask why it had to be done, but he'd already answered. Someone trustworthy needed to control Eiohe's power, so that no one else could. That was the only way to safeguard the North with any kind of surety, and settle the Penumbra.

"You won't be coming back home," I stated.

He shook his head a second time.

"What about Nisien?"

Estavius dragged his hair back from the sides of his face with both hands. "I can't ask him to stay. He's a Northman."

"He'd stay with you in a heartbeat," I said, though the thought of losing my friend pained me more than I could say. "You wouldn't even have to ask."

The Miri let out a long breath, fingers still dug into his hair and head bowed. "Nisien loves me, and I care greatly for him. But there is a reason I have never taken lovers, never married nor sired children nor formed a bond I could not bear to lose. I will not be like the other

Miri, either leaving broken-hearted humans in their wake or spending eternity next to the grave of a love I could not keep. We were made for more than that, to govern and keep beyond the lives of those we protect—and we must honor our purpose. Nisien will go back north with you. Perhaps not immediately, but eventually."

Estavius rose without letting me reply, his abruptness the only real betrayal of how deeply our conversation had affected him. "Do you understand what you need to do?"

I nodded, blinking through a head full of Estavius and Nisien and impending heartbreak. "Yes. I will crown you."

"Good." Estavius had already turned back towards the hillside, where the darkness would hide his leaving. "Make your way to the temple as quickly as possible. I'll see you soon, Hessa."

His name came onto my lips in return, but I chose not to speak it. Instead I spoke another title, his old one, the name of the god he'd once masqueraded as over the Arpa people. Perhaps there was a little warning in my choice, even a little rebuke on Nisien's behalf. But there was a farewell too.

"Aliastros," I said.

Standing in the shadow of the hill, he turned to me. I instinctively touched my Sight. Pale golden power shone in his eyes, and his skin seemed to shift with the subtlety of summer clouds.

Then the wind came, tugging at my clothes and cooling my cheeks. The Miri fragmented between one blink and the next, vanishing into the night like smoke from an extinguished candle.

"Aliastros."

For an instant, I thought the wind had repeated his name to me. But that voice was not Estavius's, nor Imnir's, or Sillo's.

It was Castor's. He stepped out of the night like a breath of wind himself, so close that I stifled a gasp and lurched to my feet.

My thoughts raced. How much had he heard? How had he gotten so close? Not even Nui had heard him.

Nui. I looked around sharply, but the dog was nowhere in sight.

"I knew something was not right about that man," Castor said, looking from me to the place where Estavius had vanished. He tapped his head and asked me, "Did I ever know? It was so hard to pick up my memories after my rebirth."

He was speaking too calmly, too levelly. A moth landed on his tunic, wings fluttering softly, but he did not brush it away.

"He's an ally, and a useful one," I told the Arpa, matching his calmness. I couldn't tear my eyes from that moth, and a sickly, vague unease turned in my guts. "It wasn't my place to tell you what he was."

"He may be an ally to you, but not to me or to Bresius. That seems very clear after what I just heard." Castor began to circle me, coming between me and the camp so that my back was to the emptiness of the hill and riverside. "Did you ever intend to keep your word to my lord?"

My whirling thoughts settled into one clear impulse. Kill. Castor had heard our conversation, and there would be no keeping him silent. I would have to silence him—somehow, here, in the middle of the camp, where anyone might see and overhear and—

Dust gusted off Castor's clothes. The moth took flight, swirling and fluttering.

I recoiled, momentarily shocked from my murderous thoughts. The dust thickened rapidly, gusting towards me in swirls and eddies—like so many birds upon the wing. The moth remained in the center of it, merging with the pattern of the dust.

I finally realized what the Laru magic was. It was not dust at all. It was moths, indescribably small, barely distinguishable as they formed into a cautious swirl around me.

Laru magic. Coming from Castor.

I barely had time to comprehend what I was seeing, but I pulled up my own power in a swelling tide. The moths' swirling cloud stretched outward, fighting me, pressing back—and winning. The space I'd gained spasmed, cinching tighter again.

Castor flicked a hand. The moths vanished, turning to true dust that settled among the dead grasses and drifted away on the breeze.

"Traitor, meet my brother Onamus," Castor said, holding out an arm towards the night.

A second man appeared, striding up from the riverside. The man I'd seen him speaking to at our welcome feast. Onamus, who Bresius had told me had come south with Castor after the Upheaval.

And Castor just called him… brother.

There was no time to hesitate, despite these revelations. I couldn't see magic about Onamus, but I lashed out at the both of them, hurtling amber power into both their chests.

Neither moved, but a ripple passed through the air. The grass at our feet, already dead, seemed to curl upon itself even more. The nearest fires, glistening in the camp, went out with a *whump* of vacated air, and I understood.

The death I'd seen yesterday morning, the harvesting of Laru magic that had killed the grass beneath my feet. Had that been one of them? Both of them?

My brother.

The word jarred through my skull as miniature moths exploded into the night again, rushing at me from both sides. I threw out my magic, screaming in shock and revulsion. For a moment my power held, locking me into an orb of invisible glass. Thousands of wings fluttered and battered, tiny eyes boring into me and tiny legs flailing for a place to land.

My barrier shattered. Moths rushed into my nose, my mouth, my ears. I collapsed, gasping and choking as the life ebbed from my limbs. Siris had been strong but this—this was overwhelming, fresh and stark and brutal.

"What are you?" I choked.

Castor smiled, gesturing to his brother. "On our own? Favored men. Together? Larun."

I heard Nui barking, and I stared into a night suddenly full of running soldiers. They didn't see the dust, and not just because their human eyes couldn't register it. It was already gone, and Castor and Onamus were mere men once more, grabbing my arms and hauling me to my feet.

"What is this?" Imnir's voice broke the night as he and Uspa sprinted into sight. "Castor!"

Castor jerked me forward, past my husband and Uspa. Nui darted up, barking and snarling, but he kicked her back.

The dog yelped, and anger momentarily blinded me. I pulled my magic, driving it out through my veins in a cleansing blast, but I was still weak, still helpless.

Helpless. I raged against the word, managing to jerk my arm from Onamus before Castor dug his fingers into my hair and forced my head down, driving me away over the hill.

Uspa grabbed Nui to her chest, eyes wide with shock and fury.

"You'll be crowning the emperor tonight," Onamus told Imnir without explanation. "I'll escort you into the city."

Castor gave him a sharp look, but I was a woman imprisoned in her own body, as my eyes dragged closed and the hum of my magic retreated to a distant, ineffectual blur.

No. Imnir hadn't heard Estavius's message. He didn't know what to expect, nor did he know about Castor and his unforeseen "brother." The brother who we'd found at Bresius's side, who wielded Laru magic just like he did, and called themselves Larun.

Frir's spy? Larun's identity. I tried to scream at Imnir as we passed, tried to warn him even though I barely understood it all myself. But I choked on my deadened tongue.

Imnir, for his part, laid a hand on the axe at his belt. There was rage and concern in his eyes, but undergirding that, I saw a kind of resigned relief. He didn't draw his axe, didn't move forward to intervene or threaten Castor. Finally, as the Arpa thrust me along, my husband withdrew his fingers from the weapon altogether.

The sight gouged me. Imnir had confessed he didn't want me to come to the temple tonight, but surely this wasn't what he'd had in mind. Was he truly about to stand by and let this happen, or was he biding his time?

"What are you doing with her?" Uspa shouted after us, her ire more than making up for Imnir's strange passivity.

"Your High Priestess is a traitor," Castor called back, though his gaze was still locked on Onamus in... was that a challenge? "Don't worry, she won't be harmed. Just get ready to move out without her. *All* of you."

I was bound and gagged and stripped of my knife. A bag was pulled over my head and hands rolled me over the edge of a freshly dug latrine pit. Or—what had been a freshly dug latrine pit as of yesterday. I hit the ground with a moist squelch and lost all the air in my lungs. I tried to keep my head raised but within moments the stink and damp crept through the bag and the fabric of my clothes, armor and all.

The refuse of thousands of nerve-ridden men assaulted me, bile and piss and shit alike.

I managed to sit up against the side of the pit eventually. I strained to hear through the bag and the blood pounding in my ears, listening to the hushed departure of the first group of invaders—presumably including my Vynder, and Imnir, and Uspa.

Loneliness struck me like an arrow from the darkened sky. Imnir had left me behind. I didn't want to believe it, but that look in his face, that resignation, gnawed at me. That wasn't the face of a man plotting a rescue. It was the face of a man doing what he thought needed to be done.

Options raced through my mind, each one bitter and burning. Maybe Imnir had tried. Maybe in the chaos of leaving, Bresius wouldn't hear any requests for leniency, or had simply refused. Maybe my husband had accepted the turn of events as fate. Maybe he truly thought leaving me as a captive of the Arpa was the safer option.

Still, what about Sillo? Ifling and Lida? The Algatt would follow Imnir without question but my Eangen... Would the trust they'd built with Imnir be enough for them to follow his lead, even if it meant leaving me behind temporarily? Had Bresius bullied them into submission, or had they trusted that I could take care of myself?

Helplessness. Castor. Brother. Spy. Frir. Larun. The words rattled through my head. I tried to breathe evenly, but the bag and the stink and the damp choked my lungs. I wriggled, grinding my head back against the side of the pit until it snagged on a root.

I pulled down. My hair pulled, the bag lifted, and the stink became worse, but the trade of unobstructed air was worth it.

I moved until the bag was completely off, then took a second to rest, breathing hard and squinting up through matted hair and stinking dirt.

The pit was about six feet deep. I could see no guards around the rim, but that didn't mean they weren't there. And I was still bound and gagged.

I closed my eyes, snatching at my haphazard thoughts and forcing them into order.

Castor and Onamus were Larun, that fact seemed inescapable—between their claim and the strength of their magics, newly fed by the dead land around Apharnum. Brothers of circumstance, one of whom had been at Bresius's side, just like Frir's spy.

But Imnir had insisted that Frir would not ally with anyone. She wouldn't dare risk Thvynder's wrath—she hadn't the power to withstand my god. But what if she'd found other power, darker, stranger power—power of death and life-magic and given it to Larun? Temporary power, unsustainable power, yes. But enough to put a plan into action.

I thought of what Estavius had asked me to do—to crown him with the power of the Arpa emperors. He himself had said the Laru's endgame had likely never involved Eolus. They intended to crown Larun with the Blood of Eiohe.

But what if Larun's goal was not their own Ascension—or one of theirs—but Frir's? With the power of Eiohe in her veins, one of the Four Pillars, would she be able to rebel and withstand Thvynder's wrath?

I didn't have a flawless answer, but perhaps that didn't matter. If Frir thought Ascension would protect her, would give her power enough to weather the storm, that was all that mattered.

I was almost certain now that Castor and Onamus were her puppets. That meant Bresius was not long for this world—and if Frir took the power of Eiohe's blood for herself, neither was I.

Did Imnir know any of this? My stomach, already in my throat thanks to the stink of my prison, surged into my mouth. I coughed against the gag and closed my eyes, pushing my bile back down.

Was the truth of Frir's involvement the reason he'd been content to leave me behind, and been so fixated on Uspa not coming into the city? The Miri had his son, toted him as her own, and she needed a priest to crown her. He must have known. Not everything—he'd worried over the spy and he'd shown no sign of knowing what Castor was. But he knew more than he'd told me, and Frir *was* coercing him.

Betrayal and a shock of loss shot through me, but I hardened myself against it. Until Imnir proved otherwise, I would believe he was a victim, forced and mislead—not an enemy.

And if I was wrong? I couldn't answer that now.

Time slipped by. I scratched runes on the pit wall to summon an owl, praying they were legible. I prayed that Uspa had been left behind, Nui with her, and that they'd come rescue me. I sifted the refuse of the pit, but it hadn't been in use long enough to boast the shards of shattered pottery or fallen daily items that I hoped for. I did find a sharp rock though, and set about trying to cut my bindings.

I worked at it as bells and horns shattered the dawn. I labored as the rest of the army moved out and the tramp of boots and hooves merged with a distant roar—that of fire, and screaming, and a city under attack. I cut until my hands cramped beyond use and the rock dropped, and under a noonday sun I sunk back against the wall and screamed my rage into my gag.

The afternoon came and went. I felt sick, hunger and thirst merging with the fumes of my prison and making my stomach burn. Dizziness assaulted me, but I staggered upright, scratching the runes for an owl again. Where were they? Were they all too distant, or already occupied?

I ground my forehead into the side of the pit.

Thvynder, Thvynder. You must see this. You must—

The end of a ladder squelched down into the pit beside me. I looked up, blinking eyes thick with tears from sickness and stench, and saw someone descending.

It was Castor. I reared back, throwing magic at him in an instinctual, vengeful burst.

The Arpa wavered, scowled, and held up a knife. "I'm cutting you free, woman."

I growled with all the bitterness and loathing the gag would allow.

Castor contemplated me. "Why would I do that, you're asking? Because my brother has left me behind, and it seems I require a new ally. So—come with me into Apharnum, do as I bid, and you and yours will live."

Growing impatient, he sheathed his knife and reached out, grabbing my gag and turning my head so that he could untie it. I let him.

"It seems I, too, am not to be trusted at Bresius's side," he said. He pulled the spit-sodden fabric away and dropped it into the refuse around us. "You've contaminated me."

So *that* had been the look between the two men at my capture.

"And what do you want from me now, Larun?" I asked, spitting the foul taste from my mouth.

He didn't flinch at the name or my spit, which landed on his boots. "Exactly as I said." He tapped the sheathed knife at his hip pointedly. "Come with me, do my bidding, and I will see you rewarded."

I narrowed my eyes. "I knew you when you were a younger man, Castor. You traveled north with no one you called brother and you were not... you were not this *creature*."

He smiled. "Onamus and I were brothers of rebirth, Hessa. A lot happened in the mountains after the White Lake. But now is not the time for stories—you know all you need to. Will you come with me, or should I fish that gag out of this muck and shove it back in your mouth?"

"You threw me in a pit for betraying Bresius," I said with forced dignity. "Why would you trust me?"

"Trust is irrelevant," Castor returned flatly. "Aliastros has been dealt with. You have one way forward and one alone."

My throat tightened. "What do you mean?"

"He will not interfere."

Anger was hot and close, as was fear for my friends. I stepped forward, glaring at the man. "That's not an answer."

He leaned forward, closing the gap between us without any care for how much I stank. "Come up into the light. Clean and arm yourself and remain part of the game. Or stay in this and rot until several thousand victorious soldiers return to this camp looking for sport."

I ran a tongue over my teeth and spat. I knew I didn't have a choice—the thought of getting out of this pit alone was enough to make me agree—but I felt sicker than ever.

"Where's my dog?" I finally demanded. "You kicked her. Don't think I've forgotten that."

Castor only smiled, produced the knife again, and held it promptingly. I turned and let him cut my bonds. I almost threw myself at him then, but when I glanced upward I saw the silhouettes of Arpa soldiers against a sky hazed with smoke and distant flames—orange swelling from the south, sunset pink from the west.

I rubbed my cramped hands and looked back at Castor.

I made allies of my enemies, I reminded myself, or put them in the ground.

Now it was time for the former.

THIRTY-TWO

I was delivered straight to my tent, where I hastily washed and changed. I did not look at the bed as I raked out the braids Imnir had woven into my hair and scrubbed my head briskly with soap. I washed my face, too, removing filth and kohl until my skin was flushed and clean.

I dressed in fresh clothes. My mail was caked with muck so I left it behind, donning a simple padded tunic of forest green and cinching it tight at my waist.

Galger and Gammler were gone, as were any other weapons, but as I stepped back out into the twilight Castor handed me a long knife. He didn't warn me not to try to use it on him, but the look in his eyes spoke clearly.

"Where's my dog?" I asked again.

"She's safe. One of Bresius's men keeps hounds. You should be grateful, Onamus would have killed the beast otherwise."

My hackles rose. "I want her back."

"After this is over. Odd, that you only ask about a dog and not your people."

I didn't reply, unfastening one of my belts to slip the new knife on. "They did what they had to."

"And nearly killed themselves in the process." Castor fitted his helmet on his head, amusement in his eyes. "That cousin of yours is a beast."

Ice trickled into my belly, even as my heart swelled. So my Vynder hadn't simply complied. "Are they all right?"

"Save a few bruises, yes," the Arpa reassured me, closing his cheek plates and resting a hand on the hilt of his sword. "Your husband brought them into line."

That both comforted me and left me feeling hollow. "I see. Let's get this over with."

We mounted up in a company of what, at first glance, seemed to be a dozen Arpa soldiers. But when I touched my Sight, each bled dust, and they made no effort to hide it from me. They were all Laru priests, but the way they rode and wore their armor told me they were militant ones.

We splashed across the river at a ford and headed up a road into the mountains at a gallop, crossing dead plains in the bizarre illumination of the burning city.

For Apharnum was, truly and properly, burning. Orange firelight swelled across the belly of low clouds, turning the river into a snake of liquid metal and the plains into a deathscape of parched plants and rolling smoke.

I kept low to the saddle as we rode, but the desolation drove deep into my soul. Eangen lore spoke of the inevitable end of the current age, when all creation would succumb to smoke and ash, and be born anew into the next era.

This, I thought, was what such an apocalypse would look like. But tonight would not be the night the world fell, or even began to crumble. I was still alive, the power of Ascension was in *my* hands, and all I needed to do was ensure the crown rested on the right head, before Imnir could—unwillingly or not—put it on someone else's.

I didn't have a chance to ask Castor where we were going until we were high in the mountains west of the city, and by then it was clear. We rode to where a high, natural lake ended in one of the Arpa's great aqueducts. The aqueduct had been dammed, however—a great door of wood and iron held back all but a trickle of water. The lake had overflowed its banks, bursting into a dozen streams that tumbled off down the dead mountainside and into the smoke. The miasma hazed our view even here, and the city was an obscure blanket of smoky light.

We abandoned the horses as four Laru legionaries, two to each side of the aqueduct, threw their weight against a pair of levers. The dam opened with a groaning squeal and water began to flow into the aqueduct again, just enough to be knee-deep.

I watched the glistening tide of water cascade along the great bridge as Castor said, "Let's go."

Thus, we entered Apharnum from above. We followed the aqueduct straight into the heart of the city, passing over and through the burning capital on our liquid pathway.

The closer we came, the more heat buffeted me. I splashed my hair and clothes against the temperature and dancing sparks, but soon the water, too, began to heat. Below us the supports of the aqueduct, level upon level of archways, groaned. That sound merged with the roar of the fire until it was all I could hear.

The Laru legionaries pulled up scarves around their necks, dampened them and covered their mouths. One passed me an extra scarf and I took it without thanks, stopping to drench it before I tied it loosely over the bottom half of my face.

The aqueduct ended in a great, roofed tower of a cistern. We crawled up onto the edge of the structure and around, blinded now with smoke. It was nearly a relief to climb a ladder down to street level, but the heat proved to be an ill-trade.

The city was an oven. Collapsed buildings smoldered around us: piles of blackened stone and the remains of hundreds of thousands of lives. The worst of the flames had died here, all that could burn already being reduced to embers and ash. Sweat trickled down my spine and caked my lips beneath my face covering.

There were few living people in these streets. Those that I did glimpse fled at the sight of us, looted collapsed homes, or dragged away limp, charred bodies. A dozen fountains, built into the walls of the cistern behind us, steamed in the heat.

"This way," Castor said, scanning the murk.

We began to jog through the destruction. My nerves jarred, my focus leaping between the immediate danger and less practical thoughts: Estavius, Nisien, Imnir, and Uspa—and even Thray, so far away.

I wanted nothing more, in the heat and the flames of that burning city, than to stand on the ice with Thray again, under a sharp winter sun.

Strange legionaries moved through the miasma, a group of twenty—bloodied, charred, and battle-worn. At the sight of us they paused, shields shifting in front of their bodies and spears lowering. Their shields bore a symbol I'd never seen before, that of two wolves chasing one another's tails around an eight-pointed star.

One of them called by way of greeting and warning, "For Cassius!"

Had Bresius's forces not captured the last contender for the throne yet? How much control of the city had he actually managed to gain?

Were Bresius, Imnir, and my people even still alive?

"Cassius! Long may he reign!" Castor declared, no falsehood in his booming voice. He flicked his sword in acknowledgement.

The legionaries resumed their course, and we ours.

Another street filled with smoke. Another grand forum, its pillars charred, its statues defaced, and its fountains boiled dry. Another pile of rubble to ascend and another roasted body to step around.

Over and over these events played out, until I glimpsed a great dome through the smoke.

I recognized the dome of the Temple of Lathian from a vision I'd once had, under the direction of one of Lathian's priests. But I also recognized it on a deeper level. Power saturated the stones beneath my boots as we slowed to a careful walk. This power was not gold to my Sight, but rather a bloody kind of copper, hedged with white-gold. It crept like lichen up walls and pillars and doorways, across the paving stones and through the soles of my feet, tugging at my own magic and… welcoming me.

A building collapsed in the distance with a cracking, thunderous crash. Billows of displaced smoke, ash, and dust gusted into our path, and Castor diverted down a side street.

I blinked sweat and grit from my eyes, almost grateful for my lack of weapons and armor as we climbed another pile of debris and skittered down the other side, eyeing the fractured walls around us with apprehension. At least I could move more quickly than the legionaries, with their armor and shields and spears.

The urge to bolt overtook me. I glanced down an alley and back at the legionaries, still clambering down over the charred pile of stones and beams. Only Castor and two others were ahead of me.

But the city was still rife with warring factions and the temple likely still under control of more Laru. And, from the determination in Castor's step, he knew how we would reach our goal. Perhaps it was best to stick with him until I was in the temple. That, after all, was where I needed to be. Then I could only pray that Estavius escaped whatever trap he'd fallen into, and would show up before the Ascension.

Thvynder, I called in the quiet of my soul, reaching out for the magic saturating the stones around me and trying to pull at it, using it to amplify my prayers across the distance between Apharnum and the North. This power was the Blood of Eiohe, sibling-god to my own. Perhaps, just perhaps, it might work.

Thvynder, I need more power. I need more strength.

I heard no voice and received no vision, but I felt the magic around me stir.

Castor noticed it too. He turned back to me, watching me over the cloth covering his nose and mouth, as moth-dust began to flake from his eyes and hands with renewed urgency. But he did not attack. There was almost pleasure in his eyes, and a touch of hunger too.

"We'll be there soon, Hessa," he said in warning, and temperance. "Control yourself."

I tugged at the covering on my own face, gave a short nod, and continued walking.

As we went, more and more moths flaked from Castor's skin. They seeped through his clothing, and those of the Laru legionaries around us. Finally moths surrounded our company completely, thickening and thickening as we approached the end of the street.

Beyond, I saw more strange legionaries run down a broad thoroughfare. Streaked with soot and blood, they shouted and cursed, shields forward, swords and spears braced. We stepped out into the open but they didn't see us. Instead, they separated like water around rocks.

We came to stand in the center of the thoroughfare. Three times wider than any I'd seen so far, it was lined with the most exquisite architecture the Arpa had to offer. Pillars and arches spread before us to either side, charred and crumbling now. Livid flames burned in the direction from which the blinded legionaries had come.

A narrow canal flowed down the center, lined with the stumps of trees, long felled during the siege. The canal was now full of rubble and bodies and toppled statues, but it pulled my eyes down its length, through the smoke and over the heads of the soldiers, to the temple.

It looked more of a fortress than a holy place, only its octagonal structure nodding to the usual composition of Arpa temples. Its central section was the largest, boasting the dome that had guided us here, while four smaller octagonal bastions clung to it at each point of the compass. Once gardens filled with trees and statues spread between these bastions, but now they were dead and obscured by smoke.

In the center of it all, beyond where the canal ended in a steaming pool, lay the main doors. They were the height of a tall Eangen pine and painted a charcoal gray, studded with brass. The gates were closed, guarded by two figures in billowing yellow robes.

The charging legionaries, still oblivious to our presence in their midst, threw themselves towards the temple gate.

"Bresius!" one bellowed, then another and another. "Bresius! Bresius!"

They made it no further than the dead gardens around the temple. There they turned on one another, hacking and screaming as if they faced the Laru themselves. The two priests by the gate remained where they were, yellow robes shifting in the wind and smoke.

The soldiers slaughtered one another, their own comrades and brothers, in moments. As the last few fled down side streets and into houses—running as if Eang herself was on their heels—a hush descended on the great thoroughfare. Only the keen of dying men and the roar of distant flames came to us now.

I realized I wasn't breathing. I pulled down my face covering, staring at the fresh piles of twitching, choking bodies.

"Where are my people?" I asked Castor. My voice sounded dead to my own ears, distant and impassive. "If those were Bresius's men, where is he?"

Castor pointed back up the street. I couldn't see anyone, let alone Imnir and Sillo and the would-be emperor, but Castor didn't wait. He led the way towards the temple.

A dying legionary stared up at me from a pool of blood as I stepped over him. His helmet was gone and his green eyes were wide, confused in a coal-streaked face. Another reached for my ankle, but I quickly sidestepped his shaking fingers.

I'd seen such things a hundred times, but never companions cutting one another down in an ensorcelled frenzy. I was suddenly grateful I hadn't eaten anything since the day before, as my stomach turned in revulsion.

The smoke parted as we circled the pool and approached the main doors. One of the Laru guarding them opened a smaller door in the larger barrier and nodded us inside.

We stepped into the Temple of No God.

THIRTY-THREE

The temple swallowed me like the jaws of a great whale. I stepped into the quiet, taking in my surroundings as Castor and his Laru legionaries gathered inside the threshold.

We were in a circular chamber, half a dozen paces wide and curving out of sight around the temple's main body. Alcove after alcove lined the interior wall, statues of fallen Arpa gods formless and faceless beneath sheets of undyed linen.

The closest of these coverings rippled in the breeze as two fresh Laru guards took up station outside and their predecessors, their power spent, moved off down the hallway to the left.

The outer door closed. The very last sounds of the burning city, the smoke and the night and dying men, cut off in a weighty thud.

"Come." Castor's voice echoed up to the high ceiling, where narrow windows with murky panes of glass let in the city's half-light. "This way."

He began to walk, heading away up the curve of the outer chamber. Several of his Laru legionaries split away, going in the other direction after the spent priests. That left him and me with an escort of six, moth-dust curling in their wakes.

I resisted the urge to finger the knife at my belt. I could smell little beyond smoke—it was in the air, in my hair and clothes—but as we continued past statue after statue draped in cloth, I caught the tell-tale musk of incense. My skin crawled.

Thvynder, Thvynder.

Castor led us to a huge door in the inner wall, inlaid with golden

Arpa runes from top to bottom, one side to the other without border.

"'Devoted ground of Lathian,'" Castor read for me, gesturing to the topmost line. "'Let my sons kneel, let my daughters bow. Speak my name, and you shall have my ear. Lay your blood on my altar, and you shall partake in my power. Obey me unto the death, and you shall have my love.'"

"Fine words," I returned. "Pity that his power was nothing compared to Thvynder's."

"It wasn't, in the end," Castor acknowledged, surveying the doors for another, critical moment. "Though if he had reached this temple and drank of the blood that lay beneath... how different our history would be."

"And now you seek to follow in his footsteps," I said. "Or are you doing this for Frir?"

Castor gestured several of the legionaries forward to open the door for us. He didn't reply to me, but gave me a self-satisfied glance.

The doors swung open. Castor led the way, and I, lowering my chin, followed.

We entered the inner sanctum. My gaze instinctively lifted toward the great domed ceiling, where more small, patterned windows were obscured by settling ash. Still, some of their myriad colors shone down at me, jeweled tones parched by the smoky, firelit sky beyond.

The power in this place was as thick and penetrating as the stink of incense. It saturated everything; air, mortar, iron, and stone. And it congealed around the feet of the great statue in the center of the room, situated across an expanse of empty, echoing floor.

Lathian: fallen Arpa God of Gods, and instigator of the Upheaval.

The monument was enormous, as tall as the outer doors. Clad in robes with a broad, flat belt, he looked down at the chamber floor in an expression of grave, gentle condescension.

I blinked as my Sight flared, and I realized that the light illuminating the fallen god's features did not come from the muffled windows. It seeped through the huge tiles of the floor beneath Lathian's feet, hedging out each worn, ancient stone. Like bloody copper sunlight, these rays struck the ceiling in a pattern that perfectly aligned with the ash-laden windows.

Power. This light was power, pure and unadulterated and yearning to break free. The power of Eiohe.

Only one shaft of light did not end at its corresponding window. Instead, it reflected off a smooth, glistening silver circle and back down, directly into one of twenty alcoves. This one lay on the opposite side of the room, distant enough that I could only just make out a Penumbra rift shimmering in the shadows.

The song of a bird came to me from somewhere high, high in the dome of the ceiling. Three mournful, descending notes.

Before I could process this, before I could so much as blink, there was a disturbance in the hallway outside. I heard the outer door open and close, elevated voices erupt into shouts and screams and—an Algatt battle cry. Imnir.

A thunder of footsteps filled the corridor. Castor snapped a hand at his legionaries and they rushed to the doors. The huge, thick barriers began to swing closed.

The footsteps grew closer.

"Castor!" a voice bellowed.

The doors slammed shut just as Onamus skidded into view, bloody and helmetless, hair caked with ash and sweat. He charged, followed by a blur of what I thought might be Bresius, Imnir, Silgi, and Ifling. Instinctively, I flinched towards them.

Castor's legionaries threw a huge bolt, then lowered a bar of wood so thick that the impact of Onamus's body barely shook it.

A puff of fine dust rained from the doorframe as I turned on Castor.

"Explain this," I demanded. Onamus and Castor being Larun and somehow allies of Frir—that I could somehow rationalize, in an inescapable, mad kind of way. But this? This division between them? "Now. You said you'd lost Bresius's trust because of me. But what is *this*?"

Something slammed into the door with a resounding crack.

"Sir, we haven't much time," one of the Laru legionaries said.

Castor grabbed my arm as he passed, heading across the room in the direction of the rift.

I jerked away. He turned on me, Laru magic billowing like wings at his back. My magic surged in response, flooding my mouth and eyes.

"The door will hold long enough for an explanation," I said, my voice like ice.

Axes assaulted the barrier and more dust rained. The temple echoed with the rhythm and crack of it, Lathian watching over it all with unseeing eyes.

"Frir found Onamus and I in the mountains after the Upheaval, at the moment of our deaths." Castor spoke swiftly. "She offered us life and power, in return for service. She healed our bodies with herbs stolen from Aita, and our souls were returned. We were reborn."

I glanced at the scar marring his hair. I'd known such healing was possible, but bringing a human back from the dead, or even the edge of death, never resulted in a true restoration.

"You forgot your former life," I concluded, flicking my gaze to the scar ending on his cheek.

Castor nodded. "Much of it. Onamus"—he stabbed a finger towards the door—"serves Frir still. He would see her crowned. I, it seems, must serve myself."

More and more pieces shifted into place. I had to know: "Does Imnir know any of this?"

Castor's lips turned in a scornful pity. "Would it make it easier for you if I said he did not?"

The thudding against the door dulled in my ears. Castor gestured me towards the Penumbra rift. "You comply, I answer more questions. Move. Now."

Skin prickling, I vacillated between him, the quaking door, and the rift. Everything in me burned to make a stand now—to throw all my magic into Castor, to steal a legionary's sword and put every man in this room on the floor. Or, at least, try—there were still seven of them, and Castor's magic had subdued me before.

But his power was a temporary thing. It could be used up and needed to be replaced—the same as every Laru here. And where could they take it, in a city charred and abandoned? There was no life left to harvest—aside from the blood of one another. And me.

The thought chilled me, but I felt a rush of resolve too. My power needed no such replenishing. When they were mere men once more, I would still be the woman who had slain Eang.

For a second, I imagined the battle. I imagined my people breaking through the door and we, together, making our stand against the Laru. We would take the temple for Thvynder and crown Estavius once the Laru were spent.

But Frir and my husband were so entangled I couldn't find the ends of their knot. I couldn't trust him, even if he was being coerced—especially if he was being coerced. I needed to move *before* that door came down, before Frir could force Imnir to do whatever she'd planned. I had to finish this... alone.

Alone. The word tasted like regret, like old pain, but just as it settled inside me, I felt the wind. It slipped through the Penumbra rift, making the fine white-gold crack shiver, and brushed across my fingers with a surreptitious tug.

Estavius. Castor had said he would be preoccupied, but this wind—could it be him, or was it just the Penumbra luring me in? Were Estavius and Nisien on the other side of that rift waiting for me?

I started across the chamber, my footsteps echoing up to the distant ceiling. Castor looked suspicious at my sudden change of heart but fell in without complaint. His legionaries, too, moved into position, flanking us as we passed Lathian's feet.

I stopped at the rift. It bloated and glinted, ready to allow me to pass through, but I wanted one more answer first. "How did you hide yourself, all this time?"

"I harvested no power until we arrived," Castor said simply, his eyes on the rift full of the same hunger I'd seen back in the Temple of Mircea. "I knew you'd see through me otherwise."

I reached out to the rift. The golden line snapped open at my touch, slicing up toward the ceiling and out into the shape of a small, but proper gateway. Visible to me alone, white-gold light poured around us, casting our shadows across the smooth floor towards Lathian's inept, hulking form, and the shivering main door.

The draw of the Penumbra tickled over my skin.

A resounding crack echoed through the room. An axe-head flashed into the darkness of the chamber, then retreated through shattered wood with a second, snapping jerk.

"No more questions." Castor grabbed my arms and hustled me through the rift. Just before we passed through, he nodded toward the shattering door and commanded his men: "Hold them back."

Castor and I appeared, alone, on the other side. The gate closed behind us with a hushed, almost intimate sigh as Castor released me and turned full circle, looking with ravenous eyes at the world we found ourselves in.

The rift glowed against the backdrop of the cavernous, empty temple. On the Penumbra's side the statues were no longer shrouded, the faces and stony gazes of lost Arpa gods staring back at us. Everything was covered by a layer of dust.

I looked away, into what had been an alcove back in the Waking World. Now it housed a staircase, illuminated by the light of the rift. Broad, straight steps stretched down into the darkness, the dust on the first few steps visibly disturbed. By Estavius and Nisien?

As the toes of my boots touched the edge of the first step, a line of lanterns lit with soft *whumps* of flame, evenly spaced in small recesses down the passageway.

Castor started off immediately, glancing back at me only once he'd descended half a dozen steps. "Well?"

"You want me to crown you, not Frir," I said, coming down the steps and passing him, forcing him to catch up to me instead. I spoke loudly, not loud enough to alert Castor to my suspicions, but loud enough for my voice to echo down the stairs—to where I hoped Estavius and Nisien waited, at the end of a trail of subtle, dusty footprints.

Behind us, the rift remained subdued and sealed. If Imnir and his companions had broken through the sanctuary door, they'd yet to cut their way through the Laru we'd left behind.

We had time, but not much. I picked up my pace as the stairs stretched on.

"Before, when faced with a goddess who could not stand the tide, you betrayed her for the sake of your people," Castor reminded me. "But I'm not asking you to betray your god now. I'm asking you to be a worthy ally in my coming reign."

"I can't trust you," I said, exasperated. Could Castor truly be this delusional?

"As I said before, trust has nothing to do with it," Castor said. The stairway was ending, leveling out into a long corridor towards a squat doorway. That was open a crack, and the lanterns nearest to it rustled in a draft. "Both Onamus and your husband are intent on crowning Frir. That will not go well for either of us—you, or I, Hessa. Frir cares nothing for the Empire. I know now that she'd let it be stripped into a desert, if it served her. She cares nothing for my people. But I... once I have the blood, I'll have no need to harvest power anymore. I will restore my home and find a way to give my servants a purer magic."

I didn't reply. His desire to protect his homeland was honorable, but Castor himself was not an honorable man. And I knew how easily power corrupted.

He looked at me over his shoulder. "What will she do to you, wife of her beloved? Once Thvynder's wrath cannot touch her?"

Doubt assailed me. *Was* Imnir truly intent on crowning his former goddess? Would he do it, when the moment came? All his talk of protecting me from her, our hard-won peace—would that come to nothing?

We stopped at the doorway by unspoken agreement. The draft brushed across my skin, cool and smelling of summer breezes.

Castor reached to his belt and produced a small stone bowl, fine and artful. It fit perfectly into my palms as he nodded to the door. "All you must do is fill this with the blood and give it to me. I'll drink it, and this will be over. There was more to the ritual once, but this is the core of it."

I eyed the vessel, running a thumb across its smooth rim. "Where did you get this?"

Castor smiled. "Bresius's collection. I may be something of a thief."

"So Onamus will have one too?"

"Yes, but that will be irrelevant if you do what you need to do quickly."

I put a hand on the door's single brass ring. "One last question."

He growled in frustration and made to shove me bodily through the door, but I pushed it open of my own accord and stepped inside.

"How was it that you held back Estavius?"

THIRTY-FOUR

Any reply Castor intended to give faded as he stared through the archway.

Instead of a passage, a cave, or some other subterranean chamber, the door led outside—not into the city, but somewhere else entirely. A moist, forest wind buffeted our faces, rustling the hem of my tunic and the sweat-thick curls around Castor's face.

With the wind came the sound of rustling leaves and, for an instant, I thought I heard the same patter of rain that had greeted me last time I was in the Penumbra. Trepidation curled in my stomach.

I could smell petrichor on the thick air, and the lush, rich flavor of moist deadfall. But there was no rain; it was only a trick of the wind, swaying the treetops against a clear, star-speckled night sky. Beneath the bows, darkness lay among ferns, moss-cloaked tree trunks, and tangles of vines.

There was a path, though. It took me a moment to spy it, searching as I was for any sign of Estavius or Nisien or even Frir. The narrow, overgrown trail swam into sight as my eyes adjusted, and I couldn't decide whether it had been there all along, or whether it was forming as I watched.

"Stay behind me," I told Castor, pulling my knife, and for once he didn't question me.

"There should be a pool," he murmured at my shoulder.

"I know. Hush."

I stepped off the doorway's indented stone ledge. My boot sunk into the thick, wet deadfall covering the path and I took my next step with care, listening for any change in the forest around us. There was only the wind in the trees, the canter of my own heart, and Castor's shallow, measured breaths behind my shoulder.

One step turned into two, and I picked up my pace. The night forest loomed over me, like the presence of a stranger behind a closed door, but as I moved the pressure became… clearer.

It separated into two entities. One was the forest, the Penumbra itself—corrupted and whispering, promising me power and satiety. The second was underneath it, pervading it. It was the same sense I'd had in the city above, of coppery power weaving through the stones of the street. The power of Eiohe. It was part of the Penumbra here, lacing through both worlds, and it knew the magic in my blood.

The leaves of the trees and the snaking tendrils of vines pulled back as I passed, but I heard Castor pushing aside branches and undergrowth. I glanced back at him as a vine snagged his wrist with almost intelligent control, and he cursed.

He lifted his eyes to mine. Anger flicked across his jawline as he saw the leaves around me—or rather, the absence of them. "What is happening? Is this forest… alive?"

I started walking again, turning away and settling a deep lungful of air in my chest. "It is. And it knows you don't belong."

That silenced him for an instant. "And you do?"

"I'm a High Priestess," I reminded him. "That's why you need me, isn't it?"

He slapped another reaching branch from his path with a frustrated grunt, but didn't speak again.

The path began to wind. I started moving, faster now, but I kept part of my focus on the wind, trying to find that wisp of Estavius I'd sensed earlier.

I still hadn't found it when the gloom began to lighten. The pull of Eiohe increased, and by the time we stumbled out into an open space, we were jogging.

Liquid sat among the roots of a handful of massive, mossy trees—more a series of small, stagnant creeks than a pond, settled between roots and the occasional crumpled, rotting trunk. It did not look deep, but it was opaque—a thick, bloody copper with a white-gold sheen, just like the power that seeped through the stones of the temple in the Waking World.

The presence of Eiohe's blood resonated through me like a drumbeat, and the scent—that of the Penumbra's sweet, sodden forest—filled my lungs in a forceful rush. It acknowledged it, and perhaps, just a little, feared it.

I skulked around the edge of the clearing, knife in one hand, the warm stone vessel Castor had given me in the other. There was a proper path of recognizable Arpa stones, and as my eyes drank in the shadows, I realized that some of what I'd mistaken for standing trees were actually overgrown pillars. So were many of the trunks on the ground, pale stone discolored under layers of moss and ridges of thin, black arrowhead mushrooms.

There had been a structure here, long ago, perhaps even another temple. But this place had been inaccessible for a decade, and time in the Higher Realms didn't always flow as it did in the Waking World.

Castor did not follow me right away. He lingered briefly at the edge of the thicker forest, staring about us like a wary hound.

"Estavius," I murmured under my breath. "Where are you?"

Then I saw Nisien. In a blinding, instinctual burst, I leapt an arm of the bloody pool to a long, snaking island, staggering on mounds of roots and falling to my knees beside Nisien's prone form. Lying beneath the reaching, gnarled branches of one of the trees, he was dressed as he'd been on our last meeting, his fine cloak crumpled around his large frame. There was no blood on him, no wounds for my desperate hands to find. Just cold skin. Closed eyes.

Somewhere in the trees, a bird called out. It was a mournful sound, three descending notes. But at the last note, another bird joined, then another and another, until the whole of the forest around me reverberated with their doleful, lilting song.

I lifted my head to the trees with stunned, grief-stricken eyes, but I couldn't focus on the birds, not now. I was in danger. Nisien was... I didn't know. Everything about this moment was wrong, and the weeping of the birds only magnified my agony.

Shaking, I bent an ear to Nisien's mouth. A breath on my cheek, and a shallow rasp. He wasn't dead, but he wasn't precisely alive either, contorted and bent by the roots under his body.

A child materialized before me, crouched between Nisien and I and the trunk of the nearest mossy tree. His eyes were green and melancholy, and I saw his father in them more than ever.

"She comes," the child warned, so softly that it might have been the wind.

Before I could retreat, before I could grab Nisien's arm and try to haul him to safety, Frir stepped out of the shadows near Castor.

All at once, the birds stopped singing. The world returned to its wind-rustling hush and my insides clawed up my throat.

Backed by a towering fan of fine, dark ferns, Frir's ebony hair reflected the copper light of the pool and fell past her waist in two half-braided cascades. The skin of her chest was pale around her strip of tattoos, between the deep V of her now solidly black, wrap gown.

Her eyes cut over to me.

"The Horseman's soul is suspended," she told me without introduction, without inflection. Gracefully, she advanced on the paralyzed Castor.

From the way the Arpa's eyes flashed wide, he hadn't expected to see her here. Not yet, anyway. He glanced from Eiohe's blood to the vessel still in my hand, then fixed on Frir's face.

"Unless I bind him back to his body tonight, he will die," Frir called to me over her shoulder. Her attention was fully fastened on Castor, and I saw her head crook slightly to the side as she studied him. "Aliastros knows this, and that is why he has left, and will not come back. It is also why you will not interfere, now. You will do as you are told, Hessa. And Castor, need I remind you of the same? Why are you so nervous, my pet?"

I couldn't speak. Roots dug into my knees as I wedged the stone bowl between them, then found Nisien's hand and clasped it. Every fiber of me burned with the urge to pick him up, to carry him away and separate him from this—but I didn't have the strength, and instinct told me that I could not risk him touching the pool of blood. He was no high priest.

"Nis," I croaked, leaning over him, my eyes darting to Frir every few seconds. She advanced on Castor another step, speaking in a low voice, and I took that moment to push magic through my friend's veins.

What I found made my skin feel cold and my stomach leaden. This was no curse I could break in a burst of cleansing fire. What ensnared him was a knot, of dark, sea-salt magic, tangled and wound through every part of him. I couldn't unravel it, not in the sparse moments I had.

"Nis, wake up, please."

Frir and Castor came face-to-face, Frir asking a question and he answering in a low, indecipherable tone. If she realized his reason for bringing me here, without Onamus, she gave no sign of it. Perhaps Castor could talk his way out of this.

But Onamus and Imnir were not far behind. I'd no idea how the Penumbra would react to their presence, but Frir knew this place better than any of us. If she wanted them to come, they would find their way.

Imnir's son reached out to poke my hand. I looked at him, still bleary with shock and grief.

"Can you help?" he whispered.

Goosebumps rushed over my skin. "W-who? Nisien? I... I don't know."

"No." He shook his head. "My mother and my sister."

My heart, already tearing at the sight of Nisien, rent a little more. "They're at the Hidden Hearth, waiting for you."

His eyes creased with a child's fresh, untempered anguish. "They're not. They're in her cave, and they won't wake up. I can't wake them up."

My world tilted, the rustle of the forest and the distant murmur of Frir's and Castor's voices skewing in my ears. His mother, his sister—Imnir's wife and daughter—were in Frir's cave? The cave I'd seen in the Penumbra not long ago? But they were dead. Long dead. Dead and buried in the Algatt Mountains.

In graves that, as Uspa had confided, had no bones in them. Frir wasn't using Imnir's son against him—she was using his whole family.

"That's not possible." My voice emerged as a croak. "What do you mean?"

Onamus's voice roared through the trees, just as it had in the temple above: "Castor!"

Castor whirled. Frir cocked her head and turned at the same time, watching with flinty eyes as Onamus, Imnir, Bresius, the Vynder, and half a dozen legionaries poured onto the shore of the pool.

Castor bolted for the forest, but Onamus was already upon him. Laru magic erupted through the clearing, thundering like the wings of a caged eagle as Onamus took Castor to the ground in a blur of moth-dust.

Everyone else halted at the edge of the thicker trees as they fought, Vynder and Arpa alike. Bresius stood at the center of them, behind the shoulders of two gaping legionaries. His eyes found me as I slowly straightened over Nisien's body, then he looked to Frir. His lips parted and his hand raised, the beginning of an order or a demand.

Sillo broke the line, sprinting towards me around the side of the clearing, and more Vynder came behind—Ifling, Lida, Hete. Imnir remained where he was though, looking at Frir with the flat, empty eyes of a prisoner facing a long-awaited execution.

Frir let it all play out for one chaotic minute. Then the fabric of the Penumbra seemed to ripple around her. She raised her empty palms, and said in a voice far too loud for her calm expression, "Enough."

Bresius and the legionaries fell to the earth with sudden, shocking limpness. The Vynder—except Imnir—collapsed, breath leaving their bodies in wordless sighs before they crashed to the earth. Castor and Onamus rolled apart, the former nearly coming to his feet before the cloud of magic around him shattered and he, too, went down. Only Onamus staggered upright again, wiping blood from his eyes.

Frir's command hit me last, seizing my soul and pulling. This was what I'd felt at the border fort, but more insistent, more hateful. My head spun and my knees cracked back down beside Nisien's body and Imnir's son.

I fought back with every scrap of honeyed magic in my bones, nails digging into bark and dirt and moss as my vision blurred and my consciousness flickered. I glimpsed Imnir, still standing at the side of the clearing, stricken and unmoving. I saw Uspa lying on the moss,

Galger and Gammler beside her. She and the others, from Sillo to Bresius, were as limp as Nisien. Frir had pulled the soul from each of them, leaving them as suspended. Holding them hostage.

That realization ignited inside of me, burning through my veins with amber magic, and I rose back up. Frir's power receded as I found my feet on the uneven ground and tilted my head back, dragging a ragged breath into aching lungs. It snaked back toward her, leaving the clearing deathly silent in its wake. In that hush Imnir's eyes dragged to Uspa, then to the ghostly child at my back. I saw him tremble, conflict saturating every line of him. The sight made my heart ache, despite pangs of betrayal, fear, and uncertainty.

His son. His wife. His daughter. And now Uspa, her soul suspended. If Frir had held Eidr in her grasp, what would I do in his place?

"You may bring the girl's soul back when this is over, if that is what you wish." Frir's soft voice drifted to Imnir, then sharpened as it encompassed Onamus and myself. "But now that we're alone, let us begin."

THIRTY-FIVE

"Hessa, bring that vessel." Frir's demand sent a spike of anger through me, her hand outstretched and her eyes fixed on mine. Then a thought appeared to cross her mind, and her face broke into a predatory smile, all teeth and sweet malice. "Better yet, fill it with the blood, and bring it to your husband. Or the Soulderni and your priests will die."

The moment stretched, blood and fury roaring through my ears. I looked from her to Imnir, to Nisien. My friend was still limp, still helpless. And my husband? His expression was closing again, locking away as he strode past Frir to meet me. He stepped over the motionless bodies of Bresius, our Vynder, Castor, and even Uspa, not letting his eyes fall on any of them.

Trembling, I picked up the stone vessel Castor had given me from between the roots. I moved slowly, and not just because I felt as though I'd be sick, or scream, or fracture at any moment. I couldn't see a way forward. Nisien's life was in my hands, Estavius was nowhere to be found, and the Vynder... Sillo. Uspa.

I blinked a fluttering, hard blink and forced myself to breathe. Standing on the bank of the blood with the bowl clutched in my hands, I called to Frir: "You'll give them back to me, if I obey? All of them?"

"If you obey," she intoned, cool and somehow still sweet. "I may have mercy."

May have mercy. What was that possibility worth, and what did her mercy look like? Even if she gave her word and I believed it, could I allow this to happen for the sake of a few, precious lives?

But if I didn't take up the blood, Imnir would, and I didn't want to force him into whatever violence that would necessitate. The sliver of control I still retained with the stone vessel in my hands would be gone.

Imnir stopped on the other bank of the pool, its opalescent light illuminating his face from beneath and casting his eyes into shadow. I saw him glance at his son, crouched at Nisien's side.

Imnir met my gaze again across the blood. "You should have stayed at the camp."

I stared back at him, betrayal turning in my stomach. "That's why you wanted me to stay behind. Not to protect me—to keep me from interfering."

"Both," he corrected. There was no satisfaction in his eyes, but there was regret, sore and bitter. He dropped his voice even lower. "To protect you from her."

"You should have just told me what was happening," I shot back, but in the corner of my vision I saw Frir shift an impatient step closer. I didn't think she could hear our words, but time was short.

"I didn't know. Not about Larun, not everything," Imnir insisted, but he knew our time was running out too. He flicked his gaze to Nisien again. "I'll do what I can, Hessa. I'll make sure she doesn't let him die, or the rest of them. You… I don't know what she'll do."

My throat felt thick, a hundred frustrations and rebukes lodged on my tongue. But the thought of Nisien and the others living through this? That gave me hope, and pushed my focus beyond Imnir's betrayal.

Imnir continued, "We can't fight her. Please, believe me. I've tried… I can't find another way. She controls our *souls*, Hessa. Theirs."

That truth rang sickly and wrong in my ears, far too reminiscent of the days when Eang had ruled the North, and priestesses like myself bled and died for her. Frir had no right to our souls. She was a Miri, not a god, no matter what we'd once called her.

I crouched on the shore to hide my face from his pleading eyes. The stone vessel in one hand, I stared down at the blood, wrestling down a wave of betrayal and remorse. The blood's coppery light filled my eyes and power thrummed off the surface, curious and searching.

"I know what she has, or seems to have," I told Imnir, and I hoped he understood all that I meant. My anger and remorse cracked then, memories of the peace we'd found back in the Arpa camp clashing with thoughts of his son, his wife's empty grave, and paralyzed bodies of our people. "But it's not right. Your family is gone, Imnir, and they have been for a long time. She can't bring them back, not as they were."

"With Eiohe's power, she can."

I didn't know if that was true, but it gave me reason to pause. Still, I urged, the words feeling raw: "You have a new family, Imnir. A new life. Don't abandon us for the word of Frir. Please."

That silenced him. For a few, ragged beats of my heart, his pleading cracked into tormented indecision.

I took the chance to deliver one final appeal. "Don't let her do this. Don't let her become something we can't stop."

Imnir's face slipped from torn to iron-clad. "Do as she says, Hessa."

Something new curled inside me at that. It wasn't fear. It wasn't determination or bloodlust or enmity. It was weariness, and a single, grim thread of hope. It came with the wind, warm and fresh and softening the pain of Imnir's decision. It came with the scent of a summer breeze. Estavius.

He was coming.

Placing my feet carefully between the roots, I leaned out and pressed the edge of the bowl beneath the surface of the pool. Frir drew closer at the same time as Imnir, and, breathing a sigh of relief, stepped back.

My body went rigid. I felt momentary resistance, a presence that pushed against me, rushed in, and searched me. It was an ungainly thing, half-awake—an impression of the intelligence that had once shed this blood, once fought the Miri over this very place.

You are not of Lathian. You are not of my tormentor.

I heard no voice, but understood nonetheless.

Nor are you Miri.

That intelligence found the magic in my blood, but that did not sate it—it rushed past, more impatient now, until warmth spread through my mind itself.

Thvynder.

The pressure abated. There was a tremulousness to its retreat, like a prisoner shedding shackles. With that came relief, a rush of knowledge, and revelation.

I returned to the shore in one step, bowl in hand, and paused beside Imnir. Droplets of Eiohe's blood trickled over my fingers, impossibly warm after so long on the forest floor, but they did not harm me.

"I'll give it to her myself," I said to him, the maelstrom of my emotions clarifying into tired, hard conviction. Estavius had asked for time, and there was only one way I could see to secure it now. Frir needed a distraction. A lengthy, violent distraction. "For Nisien and our Vynder."

That gallows look was back in his cool eyes, chased by a thread of suspicion, but he didn't stop me.

I approached Frir. Behind her, still skulking around the edge of the trees, Onamus observed us.

"Oh, I enjoy this," Frir decided, smiling between Imnir and I as I stopped a few paces away from her. Her fingers laced over her stomach, sleeve brushing at her odd, bone-hilted knife. "Yes, Eangi, this is atonement, isn't it? You slew my sister and betrayed her for another god, yet now you hand me the power to truly avenge her. Thank you."

Blood dripped from my fingers onto the moss.

"What will your vengeance be?" I asked, my own voice sounding distant to my ears. Cool. Level. So like the dead goddess of whom we spoke. "Will you kill me? Torture me?"

Frir drifted forward a step, shortening the space between us. "That's far too simple. You swung the axe, yes. But Thvynder put me under their heel. Gadr betrayed me. All the Miri betrayed me. So I will rule them. I will take your husband, *my* priest, and I will do with you as I please. And the North, the Empire, the Higher Realms—they will all come to me. I—"

There, in the middle of her tirade, as vows of vengeance dripped from her lips, I drank the Blood of Eiohe. I held her gaze as I did, watching her mouth freeze around her next word. Her eyes widened in growing, revelatory horror.

I didn't know what the blood would do to me. I didn't know if there would be any coming back from this act and the changes it wrought. But Estavius had said only one person could hold the blood at a time— until their death, or abdication. And if I did not do this, if I didn't take this upon myself and buy enough time for Estavius to come, everything Frir said would come true.

The bowl dropped from my hands, hitting the earth between my feet with a fateful thud. I'd intended to run, but my legs wouldn't obey. I lowered my chin instead, blinking as the world skewed. Power spread through my chest like the first drink of water on a hot day, wheedling into my veins.

Frir jerked her bone-handled knife from her belt. As she did it shifted, lengthening and curving like a sickle moon—a sword that I'd once seen in a carving, back on the doors of the Temple of Mircea.

Imnir stepped between us. "Frir, she doesn't have to die—"

"Out of my way! I will bleed you, Eangi," Frir hissed around him, her voice cracking like a whip in the sudden silence. "You may be Ascended, but you will still die. I will bleed you and strip your soul from your body. I will chain it to the gates of my realm until the Unmaking of the World. You will live every moment of it, alone, abandoned, and in agony. You will never, ever rest beside the ones you love."

Her words sounded distant, oddly flat. I coughed. The pool drew my eyes and, in a corner of my mind not overwhelmed by the blood and the threats, I saw the surface begin to solidify. Ice crept out from the shore, connecting and interlocking.

Frir hadn't noticed yet. She shouldered past Imnir, drawing that sickle sword back to strike. I took a step away but my limbs were languid, slow to respond.

Imnir stepped between us again. "Frir, please—"

The last threads of the Miri's control snapped. "Move!" she bellowed in a voice that could have shattered mountains.

I retreated, battling to stay upright and face my enemy. Maybe this had been a mistake. Maybe Frir would dispatch me here and now, before Estavius arrived, before that ice finished creeping across the surface of the pool. Once I was dead she'd have full access to the blood. Imnir would give it to her, and the world would…

Another step backward, two. Imnir stood his ground between Frir and I, speaking words I didn't catch. But the emotion of his intercession, all that it might mean, was something I couldn't take the time to acknowledge.

To our right the Blood of Eiohe solidified even more, locking down under a sheet of iridescent ice.

All at once its brightness dimmed and the clearing fell into deep, ominous twilight. The blood had a new bearer, and it slept once more. Relief made my knees weak, but the reprieve was momentary.

"No!" Frir screamed in rage. If her bellow could shatter mountains, this cry ruptured souls. Birds erupted from the darkened forest all around in a shrieking, fluttering cacophony. "Kill her!"

Imnir spun and I braced. Some of my control was returning, muscles strengthening and heart rate steadying, but it still wasn't enough to run.

"Imnir," I started, mind stuttering, hardly unable to believe what I saw. His hand fell to the axe at his belt and the look in his face—would he truly do this? Hadn't he just interceded for me? "Imnir!"

He lunged towards me—no, around me, reaching for something other than myself.

A sword rammed through my back and out my stomach.

I staggered, breathless and mute as Onamus freed his weapon from my gut with a jerk and circled me, watching my face through the twilight.

Imnir tried to hold me up, shouting something at Onamus that I didn't hear, but I pushed him away. There was no pain but my ears rang as I fumbled at the wound. Blood pumped, black and amber in the dim light.

The wound healed under my searching fingers, leaking soft copper light as it did. The Arpa emperors' long life. It wasn't immortality, but it was healing me now.

Before I fully understood, I moved. I bolted as Onamus lunged at me again, sword swinging for a more conclusive blow. I leapt over Castor and Silgi and stooped beside Uspa, just long enough to snatch Galger from the girl's side before I threw myself into the trees.

Trees and branches slapped closed around me. Guided by the barest light from the Penumbra's sky I thundered across the loam, dodging branches and leaping over tangles of roots. A crumbled wall, overgrown with ivy, blocked my path. I vaulted it, Galger in one white-knuckled hand, stomach wound healed and muscles singing with ferocious, indominable life.

A branch cracked. I rolled to the side just as Onamus's sword flashed out of the shadows, trailing Laru dust in its wake. He threw himself after me with a roar, cutting for my head.

I smashed the weapon aside, came up against a tree, and scrambled to my feet. The tip of his blade slammed into the trunk and I twisted, slashing Galger into his extended arm. He shrieked and toppled forward. A knee to the gut, a crack across the back with Galger's haft, and he was on the ground.

Laru magic burst into my face. A thousand tiny moths assaulted me, crawling into my nose, my ears, my eyes and mouth.

I went down, crying out in horror and disgust. Galger slipped—not from my hands, but into a useless grip. My own magic lashed back, winning me a panting, sputtering breath of reprieve.

Onamus started to climb to his feet. Before he could find his balance, I lunged onto one knee and spun my axe. The blow was clumsy but it struck, Galger's armor-punching back biting into his neck. He screamed, magic billowing and snapping.

I pulled Galger free, turned the weapon, and finished the task with a clean, single cut. The moths disintegrated. I coughed and choked and spat, lurching backward as Onamus twitched on the forest floor.

Silence fell. The Penumbra's trees seemed to hold their breath as I wiped dust and spittle from my lips and searched for any sign of Frir.

"There will be no mercy now." Her words drifted to me through the night, soft and full of wrath. "None at all."

I took Galger in a two-handed grip. I felt for the wind of Estavius's arrival, but it didn't come. Tension rattled through me and my breaths came heavy.

"Hessa." Frir's voice curled out of the darkness, coming from my left. "Stop fighting, child. Stop running."

"Very well," I agreed, shoving every scrap of fear and tension into a vault inside me. They wouldn't serve me here.

I faced her voice and started to stalk in a wide circle, holding Galger low. But it was so dark beneath the trees—I couldn't make her out. I needed more light.

As if in response to my thoughts, the forest began to whisper. Leaves rustled, branches swayed, and the sky above the bows turned from bruised twilight to a blossoming sunrise. The Penumbra was responding. To me.

Frir emerged from the shadows as they retreated, her back straight, her sickle sword at one side. She glanced up at the lightening sky overhead, then settled her gaze back on me. An expression touched her face then, not a smile or a frown, but a twitch of acknowledgement. And warning.

Frir raised her sickle in front of her chest and clasped the sharp inner edge with her free hand. She squeezed, ichor welling up from around her fingers and trickling down the arc of the blade.

The forest around her died. Fluttering leaves rained from the branches overhead. Bows cracked and trunks creaked. Undergrowth shriveled and moths emerged from all sides, separating from bark and leaves, from wind and air, and from Frir's own black robes.

The death spread between us like an arrowhead, widening around Frir and cutting off through the forest. But it stopped before my boots, the line between life and death eerily clean.

Dread washed over me.

"My vengeance has been long in coming," Frir told me, backed by falling, parched leaves. "I uncovered many secrets during that time, forgotten ways and rituals of the Old World." She gestured to Onamus's corpse, still visible behind me. "I taught them to my servants. But I am their master."

The world before my eyes blurred for an instant, then Imnir was there. He stood behind Frir's shoulder with a satisfied smile on his lips, his posture possessive, commanding. Frir reached up a hand to sink her fingers into his beard, stroking his chin affectionately before he vanished into thin air. An illusion.

Nisien came next, kneeling on the ground, battered and bruised, clutching at a gaping slit across his throat. I saw the Vynder, too, each of them dying, each of them helpless.

I knew it wasn't real, but I couldn't look away, couldn't stop the rise of panic. I wanted to clench my eyes shut, but that meant losing sight of Frir.

The image of Sillo started keening, looking down as his hands now filled with gore from a split belly. No, I didn't have to see this. I let out a cry of frustration and anger, sending magic with it.

The illusions vanished. So did Frir.

A sickle hooked around my neck. Before I could move it bit in, slicing to bone and hauling me forward. Frir grabbed my hair on the way and threw me to the forest floor. I screamed, the pain of the wound momentarily blinding. Paralyzing. Then it was gone and Frir came at me again.

Her sword met my axe with a force that made my jaw crack. I grabbed her wrist with one hand and pulled, jerking her onto the ground with me.

She vanished before she hit the crumbling moss. I rolled to my feet, instinctively putting a hand to the back of my neck as I turned, panting. Blood remained, and dirt and dry flakes of moss, but no wound.

I threw out another wave of magic and the Miri flickered into view two paces away, her sickle sword transitioning into a throwing knife in the space of a second.

I barely moved in time. The blade sliced across my temple, just beside my eye, and disappeared into the trees.

A second later it was back in her hand. The sword reformed, longer this time, lengthening into a poleaxe with a sickle blade and a long spear's tip—akin to the one I'd seen Siris wield on our first meeting.

Wind brushed across my sweating, bloody face. I raked it into my lungs and, demanding my magic hold, I sprinted for Frir.

Her longer weapon slashed, catching Galger as I swung. I flipped the weapon at the last second, letting the sickle blade hook around Galger's haft. I twisted. Frir nearly lost her grip and stabbed her weapon forward. The spearhead drove into my shoulder.

All my instincts screamed to pull back, to retreat. But I released Galger instead, letting it swing into one hand, out of the sickle's grasp, and back into play.

I tore free of the spearhead, goring myself further in the process. As it healed I lunged into Frir's guard, batting the poleaxe aside and bringing Galger back into a two-handed grip. My left arm was weak, and my blow hit the trunk of dead tree behind her.

Frir slipped aside, fluid as water, and darted into a clutch of tall, shriveling ferns. I tried to jerk Galger free but my left arm was still healing, and it took two more tugs for the weapon to come loose in a spattering of desiccated bark and dust. By that time Frir was nearly out of sight. I sprinted after her.

We burst back out onto the shores of the Blood of Eiohe. The death Frir had wrought on the forest hadn't reached here and sky still lightened overhead, golden light cutting through the Penumbra's lush, ancient trees.

Frir spun, sweeping the area with a sharp, rapid gaze. I did the same, eyes instinctively going to Nisien and the Vynder. Sillo still lay among the trees, as did the other Vynder, legionaries, and Castor, but Uspa was nowhere to be seen.

My heart lodged in my chest. Imnir now stood in the center of the overgrown temple with his son in his arms and Gammler resting against the tree behind him. The child buried his head in his father's chest and Imnir looked at me over his arc of fine blond hair, suspended between two lives. The anguish of it, the rage and the turmoil, burned in his eyes.

I felt no anger toward him then, no blaze of betrayal or blinding drive for revenge. I just saw a child, and a father with an impossible choice.

And Uspa—she was gone. Frir had said that Imnir could restore her when this was over, and now the girl wasn't here. Gammler, which had lain at her side, was at my husband's feet. But what did that mean? Just because he protected Uspa didn't mean he would disobey Frir when it came to the blood. Or me.

The Miri kept one eye on me, but she saw the change too. "Imnir?" she demanded. "Where is the girl?"

"I took her to safety." He shifted his son in his arms and I noticed that he held the stone bowl, still stained with the Blood of Eiohe. His eyes went to me, then the trees behind us.

Estavius stepped out, his head helmetless and his hair windblown. His short Arpa sword was in one hand and his pale eyes set upon Frir.

Imnir set his son down among the ferns at the edge of the thicker trees, picked up Gammler, and approached his mistress. His child darted after him a step, but Imnir didn't turn back. He drew up beside Frir, expression indecipherable.

I couldn't tell what was in his face, but Frir seemed to think she did. She smiled at him, warm and possessive, flashed a snarl at Estavius, and set the butt of her weapon on the dirt beside her feet.

"So, Aliastros," she asked, using Estavius's former title. She gestured towards Nisien, still motionless on the island. "You've chosen to kill him?"

Estavius's face was pale, but there was no weakness to it. "I've made my choice."

Frir looked at Imnir, who slipped the stone vessel into a pouch at his waist and hefted Gammler in both hands. "See to your wife," she instructed, hefting her weapon, which transitioned back into a sickle sword. She turned her attention to Estavius. "I'll finish the Arpa."

She stepped away, turning her back on Imnir, and he looked at me. Fatigue slipped into his eyes as the Penumbra's growing light ran down Gammler's blade, mirroring Galger in my own hands. Then he smiled, a small, nearly invisible thing, and I saw *him* again. The man I'd ridden south with. The man who watched over Uspa. The man who'd slept beside me in the quiet of the night, and given me hope for a better future.

"It's fitting, isn't it?" I sensed that Imnir spoke the words to Frir, but his eyes remained on me. "That she die by Eang's blade?"

Imnir turned and swung Gammler at Frir in a sudden, roaring burst of strength. The axe sunk deep into her back and the former Goddess of Death, sister of Eang, staggered.

The forest went silent as Frir fell, save for the crack of Imnir tugging Gammler free. Kneeling, the Miri braced her palms on the earth and sunk, sideways, onto one hip. Her strength left her in a stream of amber ichor as she stared at Imnir in a baffled kind of rage.

Imnir dropped Gammler and took up Frir's own curved sword. He held it out toward me, long fingers extended, his expression quiet and grim. An offer.

"I'm sorry," he said, and there was so much more to his words than simple apology. There was years of division and conflict, there was rejection and betrayal. And there was finality. Because this moment was the end of one life. The beginning of another.

"Imnir," Frir rasped, though I'd no clue how she could speak anymore. "You know the price. Your wife, your daughter."

"I lost them a long time ago." Imnir looked only at me. "Go on, Hessa."

I took one last look at Frir's wide, shocked eyes, stacked both hands on the sword's hilt, and swung.

THIRTY-SIX

I mnir woke the Vynder, one by one, as Estavius approached me. Uspa emerged from the forest, falling in at his side as our companions came, coughing and trembling, to life. They ignored Bresius and the legionaries, leaving them until we could decide what to do with them. But Castor we left to his final, eternal sleep.

I pulled my eyes from Castor's quiet face as Estavius stopped beside the pool. Imnir had given him the stone vessel and he held it absently, taking in Frir's corpse. I disentangled her braids from the bone-handled sword and let her severed head fall to the ground with a *thump*, then set the weapon aside on a moss-covered pillar.

"How does an Arpa emperor abdicate?" I asked, offering him an exhausted, fragmented smile.

"I understand it's a matter of will." Estavius's attention dragged to Nisien, lying on the island of roots. Throughout it all the Soulderni had remained unmoving, but Imnir approached him now and crouched down at his side. Estavius watched, eyes edged with strain.

"Imnir is healing him," I reminded my friend. The relief of those words threatened to break me, but there was still work to be done.

"I know," Estavius returned, drawing a deep, steadying breath. The wind rushed around us, smelling of sweet summer evenings and the clarity after a storm. He held the stone bowl toward me. "But this will change… many things."

I took the vessel and moved to the edge of the pool. Its ice-locked surface was still quiet, shedding the faintest light into the Penumbra's dawn.

I glanced at Nisien again as I crouched by the blood. Imnir helped him upright, old enmity cast aside, and happiness broke through my fatigue as the Soulderni steadied himself and looked from me, to Estavius. He was haggard, but alive.

I forced my attention back to the pool and laid my palm on the ice. It was warm instead of cold, like rock under the sun, and tingled pleasantly against my skin. I let my will seep out.

The hard surface gave way, and light burst up into the treetops as the Blood of Eiohe reawakened. Quickly, reverently, I filled the bowl a second time and returned to Estavius.

Imnir drew up with his son wrapped in his arms, the child's head held beneath his beard with one strong, gentle hand. Uspa came to his shoulder and the Vynder clustered in, forming a silent, vigilant ring. They were battered and bloodied, and Silgi leaned against Hete for support, but they were all here.

Nisien came too. Steady on his feet now, he stepped across the blood and drew up to Estavius's side. Estavius smiled at him, a smile that looked a lot like a farewell. Nisien didn't manage to smile back, but he nodded.

Estavius closed his eyes and drank the full, brimming bowl. When the vessel was empty, he passed it back to me, and I unceremoniously threw it into the pool. It sunk from sight with a single, silvered, gulp. The others like it would need to be tracked down and destroyed, but that was a task for another day.

Estavius opened his eyes as the vessel vanished. His face was paler than I'd ever seen before, and his eyes began to change. Their former blue had darkened to a bloody copper, one that thickened with every passing second.

"We made the right choices," Estavius said, his voice cracking, his composure lost. He looked at Nisien, the sadness in his eyes clouding with each passing breath. "The honorable choices. Didn't we?"

Nisien managed to smile then, a sad twist of the mouth. "We did."

At the same time, I felt Eiohe's blessing leave me. Exhaustion hit me like a wave, but Imnir's hand was already there, on my back, steadying me. I leaned into him, letting myself draw strength from the warmth of his side, and his encircling arm. His son, still cradled to his chest, blinked at me shyly and buried his face in Imnir's neck.

Estavius's expression drew taught, a vein standing out on his temple. His eyes were still darkening, white-gold light cracking around his irises, and as that light strengthened, his grief seemed to retreat.

At the same time, he raised his hand. The pool of blood responded, losing its light a second time. The surface hardened from liquid to ice to dim, opalescent stone.

Overhead, the dawn I'd called to the Penumbra broke into a fresh, vivid day. Light and warmth flooded through the forest and a bird trilled, but this time, its three-noted song continued, rippling off into a higher, merrier call.

A scrap of awe tugged at me. What sway I'd held over this place as a human was nothing compared to Estavius's. But that was not the only difference. As the last droplet of blood solidified, Estavius's emotions, his awareness, withered from his face. He was... changed.

I wondered if that was part of his sacrifice, and if he'd known it would come. And I wondered what that change did to Nisien, watching wordlessly at Estavius's side.

The evening came, clean and cool. I stood beside Imnir in the shadow of the temple in Apharnum as Estavius presented himself before the remaining legions and occupants of the city, those who had not fled or had returned when the fires died down.

Unnatural wind had brought rain from the north over the course of the day. Now the sky above Apharnum brimmed with post-storm banks of cloud. Sunlight burst through at intervals, illuminating the last drifts of smoke and steam over the haggard, blackened city.

Estavius spoke to the masses in eloquent Arpa. He still wore the armor of a legionary, soot-streaked and bloodied, but no one could doubt what he was. The wind held its breath, letting his voice drift out over the heads of thousands. His words sparked magic in my Sight, and there was no dissention among the crowd, no disquiet.

The Arpa had not forgotten what it was to look upon an emperor. The face before them was not the one they had expected to bow to—all three contenders were dead—but that was irrelevant. He held the Blood of Eiohe, the blood that saturated this land and all that was in it. Now, they answered to him.

Nisien stood at my side. He looked worse for wear but stood straight, watching his blood-brother with a wistful kind of pride.

"You know you can stay with him," I reminded him, softly.

Nisien nodded, but I knew from the look on his face that he would not. "I belong in the North, now more than ever. Estavius told me this… change, might happen. I was ready."

"How long?" I asked, and he looked at me with heavy eyes. "How long ago did you know he might have to do this?"

"We knew from the beginning," Nisien admitted. He blinked hard out to the crowd, his shoulders square. "We've said our goodbyes. It's worth the cost—for the North. For Souldern. For the Arpa. For all our peoples."

On my other side, Imnir shifted. He looked as weary as I felt, his face gaunt. His son was still there at his side, visible only to the Sighted, but we both knew that arrangement could not last forever.

Estavius gave a pronouncement that made the crowd roar. The sound battered me, setting my nerves on edge even though I knew Estavius to be an ally, and this situation the will of our god. But these people were not my own, this city was not mine, and the sound reminded me of that.

"I'm ready to go home," I said to both Imnir and Nisien as the roar died down.

"There's something I need to do first," Imnir said. "In the Penumbra."

He had yet to explain himself to me, but that was a conversation for quiet and privacy, none of which we'd had. "Are you leaving?"

Imnir shook his head and, at our sides, his hand slipped into mine. His grip was weak, but I squeezed it tightly.

"No," he said. "I'm asking you to come with me."

EPILOGUE

I cautiously follow Imnir into Frir's cave. Uspa is my shadow, Imnir's ghostly son held in her arms, and Nui trots at my heel.

Rock closes in around us, and the smell of herbs drifts to my nose. There, on an altar at the back of the cave lies a woman with a round belly, and a small girl at her side. I had expected to find bones—the bones that Frir stole from their grave, long ago. But these corpses are whole and real, from the lightness of the woman's eyelashes against her pale skin to the gentle curl of the little girl's fingers. Bowls of herbs lie around them, smoldering with an ever-burning flame. The scent is sickly-sweet— lavender and cedar, sage and blood—and it turns my stomach.

Imnir slows as he sees the bodies, and all the strength leaves his frame.

"She remade them, not with true flesh but…" His voice is distant, his expression hidden from me. "She told me she'd done it, back in the marsh, on that first night in Nivarium. She lied to me, too, telling me she'd held their souls back from the Hidden Hearth, and that they could live again. I knew the stories. I knew how jealous she was. But I wanted to believe so badly, Hessa. And when I doubted her, when you and I started to become something and I began to let go of them… She threatened to separate us forever."

He approaches the altar, the tears in his eyes thick and bright, and I fear that he might buckle.

"I saw this moment, once," he tells me, quietly. "At the feet of Fate."

I recall when I, too, stood under Fate's starry sky and saw Imnir, kneeling on the stone, wracked with pain.

Imnir touches his dead wife's face, his daughter's hair, and the belly that his son never left—now whole and unblemished.

Dust comes away on his fingers, and he considers it dully. "They're fading."

We knew this would be the case. Through an owl, Omaskat has explained to the both of us what these bodies are—constructs, like the owls themselves, but without the life to animate them. They are nothing more than weapons that Frir wielded against Imnir, promises that she could never keep.

His wife's and daughter's souls are truly gone, passed ahead to the Hidden Hearth long before Frir's plan for power came into being. There is no coming back from that depth of death.

Only the little boy remains now, lingering with Uspa by the entrance.

Imnir doesn't look up as he asks, "Will you help me carry them?"

I take the body of the little girl as he lays her in my arms. He picks up his first wife, cradling her head to his shoulder, and we leave the cave.

The Penumbra is less wild, now, brighter and calmer. Estavius's rule has settled it, and a sketch of runes from Uspa's hand—I've wasted no time in teaching her to use her new power—manipulates the fabric of this High Realm. Soon, we pass the border into the Eangen High Halls and reach the Algatt Mountains. There, we leave the Halls through a forgotten rift, and Imnir leads us to a secluded house in the Waking World.

He digs a new grave behind it in a copse of trees—high-mountain ash and pine, sheltering the small, steep-rooved house, built into the mountainside. Uspa calls this place home, and as Imnir and I labor she opens the doors and shutters, and treks down a short stair to a fast-flowing creek to fetch us water. Imnir's ghostly son follows her every step of the way.

She stokes the fire and makes us grains, which we eat without tasting.

When the bodies are laid to rest, Imnir kneels beside the freshly turned earth. I stand at a distance, just close enough for him to take strength from my presence, if he chooses.

The ghostly son goes to his father, and Imnir holds him close.

"Would you hate me," Imnir asks after a long moment of silence, his eyes closed, his face buried in the child's hair, "if I went to be with them?"

Afternoon light drifts through the trees, and the wind holds an autumnal chill. Thvynder has offered Imnir the position of Shepherd of the Dead, now that Frir is gone, but I sense that's not what he means.

"I wouldn't hate you," I say. My own emotions swell behind my tongue—uncertainty, memory, grief, reluctance. I force them back. "I would understand."

He stands, hefting his son up with him. He wipes the back of one dirty hand across his forehead and tries to gather himself as the child rests his head on Imnir's chest, unspeaking. Understanding, even in his unnatural youth.

"But?" Imnir prompts.

"But there's still life to be lived," I remind him, and I hear the truth in my own words. "And I'd gladly live it with you, if you give this world another chance."

Imnir looks to where smoke rises from the chimney of the little house. Nui lays on the overgrown stoop and Uspa can just be seen through the windows, tidying uselessly with tears in her eyes, pointedly not looking outside.

"You're free of Frir," I remind him, coming a step closer. I reach out and snag the fingers of one hand in mine; equally dirty, equally scarred. "Your son can be free now, and go to his mother and sister. But there is so very much left to be done here."

Imnir's fingers tighten slightly on mine. Finally, he brushes his cheek across his son's hair, and looks back to me.

"Well, if there is life left to be lived," he says. His fingers tighten a fraction more. "I've no desire to do it alone."

"You won't," I promise, and in that promise is an offer, one that still makes me feel raw and vulnerable.

His free hand reaches up to cup the back of my head. He kisses my forehead, just once, then releases me. He turns back to the graves and crouches to set his son on his feet. They speak then, exchanging soft words that aren't mine to share. And though there are tears, the boy smiles and offers Imnir one last, child's kiss in his rough beard.

I can see from the shaking of his hands that it takes all Imnir's strength to draw three runes in the dirt—runes for closure and finality, for rest and peace.

Imnir presses his open palm into the earth and looks into the child's quiet eyes. He whispers something and the boy smiles, sad and happy and everything in between. Then Imnir lets his magic flow.

Spring comes to Albor. Winter once again pulls the hem of his cloak from the forests and fields, hills and valleys. Beyond the doors of the hall, Uspa trains Thray with spear and shield in the muck, laughing and hurling mud into one another's faces as old warriors pass around a pitcher of hot mead, lay bets on who will slip next, and offer the combatants dubious advice.

Nui has whelped. I stare in disapproval at the writhing mass of puppies around her on a blanket in the corner of the hall, already despairing of how I'll find homes for them all. Nui just blinks back at me in pride, tail thumping on the wooden floor, white-gold magic gusting up with each slap. None of us saw her drinking from the puddles outside Frir's cave, but my hound, it seems, is no longer quite normal.

Imnir stops beside me and crosses his arms over his chest. "Maybe we can give the pups to wedding guests?"

I furrow my nose in a frown. "Or give them all to Sillo? A dowry of half-Arpa, Penumbra-blessed puppies?"

Imnir nods thoughtfully. "I approve."

Outside, Uspa hooks the butt of her spear under Thray's ankle. The younger girl topples onto her back and the crowd roars, half in approval and half in disapproval, according to their bets. Several losers are shoved off down a side street to fetch more food and drink.

Uspa grins and helps Thray back to her feet. I spy Sillo on the sidelines, cheeks flushed with pride and drink as he watches Uspa move. Nisien sits with him, one of Nui's puppies sleeping between his chest and a big, protective hand. He looks tired, even after all these months at home, but he says something sly to Sillo and my cousin breaks into laughter.

At the laugh, Imnir starts for the door. The sight of him, partially silhouetted against the light, with Thray, Uspa, and my people beyond, drives into me, and I remember what it was to stand before Fate on that great stone plain.

I know the rest of my days will not be easy. Estavius's rule has solidified, but there is still unrest among the Iskiri, and threats to both Uspa and myself. With my husband now bearing the mantle of the Shepherd of Souls, I am often without him. But I no longer feel alone: alone under the eyes of my people, alone with the responsibility of their guidance and protection. With Imnir's and my growing bond, the North unites, and our family, in Uspa and Sillo, has already grown.

I give Nui one last disapproving glance—to which her tail wags— then I follow Imnir outside. He looks down at me in surprise, and welcome, as I take his hand in the light of a spring day.

And then, we live.

THE END

GLOSSARY OF NAMES

A

Addack—The Eangen province on the western coast.

Aegr (*Ahy-ger*)—An eternally wounded bear of Eangen mythology.

Aita (*Ahy-tah*)—A Miri who serves under Thvynder. The Great Healer.

Alathea (*Alla-thee-ah*)—A fallen Arpa Miri of the lowlands, reeds, and marsh.

Albor—The town in which the Hall of Smoke once stood, now the home of the Morning Hall.

Algatt—The land, and the people, of Gadr, the God of the Mountain. Raiders, they reside in the mountains north of Eangen.

Aliastros (*Al-ee-ah-stros*)—Estavius, a Miri and former member of the Arpa Pantheon. A Miri of wind.

Amdur—The people of Dur, a subordinate god to Eang. A central Eangen people.

Apharnum—The capital of the Arpa Empire, where the Temple of Lathian and its hidden well of power resides.

Arpa—The land and people of the great Arpa Empire, who control much of the known world.

Athiliu (*A-thil-ee-oo*)—Commander of the Ilia Gates, 1st General of the Outer Territories of the Arpa Empire.

Ayo (*Ey-oh*)—Omaskat's dog.

B–C

Binding tree—A tree in which an unnatural beast, being, or a god is imprisoned.

Bresius (*Bress-ee-us*)—An Arpa noble and contender for the Arpa throne. Cousin of Eolus.

Briel (*B-reel*)—Vynder war chief and Hessa's friend.

Cassius—An Arpa noble and contender for the Arpa throne.

Castor—An Arpa legionary, son of a senator.

D–E

Eang (*Eeng*)—A God of the New World who rose to be the strongest and most influential of the New Gods. Goddess of War and patron of the Eangen people.

Eangen (*Een-gehn*)—The people and land devoted to Eang.

Eangi (*Een-gee*)—The order of warrior-priests who serve Eang and protect the Eangen people.

Eangi Fire—The power that Eang blessed an Eangi priest or priestess with via a shard of her own life-force, tied to the blood of the Eangen people.

East Meade—A town on the western foot of Mount Thyr. The birthplace of Hessa.

Eidr (*Ee-der*)—Hessa's first husband, an Eangi warrior-priest.

Eiohe (*Eye-oh-heh*)—An ancient, forgotten deity. One of the Four Pillars of the World.

Eolus (*Ay-o-luss*)—An Arpa noble with a claim on the Arpa throne. Cousin to Bresius.

Esach (*Ee-sak*)—Goddess of Storms and Harvest.

Estavius—An Arpa legionary and Miri called Aliastros. Adopted son of the High Priest of Aliastros.

F–G

Fate—Also called the Weaver, Fate was once a deity and now exists in a non-corporeal state, weaving the patterns of time and destiny for all.

Frir (*Fr-eer*)—A Miri, former Goddess of Death, sister of Eang. Aunt to Ogam, great-aunt to Thray.

Gadr (*Gad-derr*)—God of the Mountain, god of the Algatt people and land. A God of the New World, peer to Eang.

Galger—One of Eang's set of legendary axes, Galger and Gammler.

Gammler—One of Eang's set of legendary axes, Galger and Gammler.

Geda (*Gee-dah*)—A sister of Eang, executed for a grave betrayal. Her final breaths were used to give life to Eang's owl messengers.

H–I

Hall of Smoke—The former hall of the Eangi priesthood, located in Albor in the south of Eangen.

Hessa—Former Eangi warrior-priestess, born in East Meade, raised in the Hall of Smoke in Albor, current High Priestess of Thvynder. Wife to the Eangi Eidr, then Imnir of the Algatt.

Hete—A Vynder priestess, Algatt. Adopted mother of Mynin.

High Halls, the—The upper realms in which the Miri, the rivermen, the woodmaidens, and various other beings dwell or once dwelled. In death, humans travel to the High Halls to tell of their living days and await the passing of loved ones. Then, they may lie down together for the Long Sleep in Frir's Realm of Death.

Ifling—Sister of Lida, of the Addack people.

Ilia Gates—Lying south of Urgi, these gates form the northernmost outpost of the Arpa Empire. Commanded by Athiliu.

Imnir—An Algatt, High Priest of Thvynder, and Hessa's second husband. Former priest of Frir.

Iskir (*Isk-eer*)—A town and region in north-eastern Eangen.

Iskiri (*Iss-keer-ee*)—The people of Iskir. An Eangen clan.

J–L

Laru (*Lar-oo*)—Priests of Larun.

Larun (*Lar-oon*)—A mysterious, powerful creature masquerading as a god in Nivarium.

Lathian—The Arpa Empire's fallen God of Gods.

Lida—Sister of Ifling, of the Addack people.

Lysta (*Lee-stah*)—Former Arpa Goddess of Death.

M–N

Mircea (*Meer-see-ah*)—A fallen Arpa Miri of the highlands and waterfalls. Also the city where her main temple lies.

Miri—The fallen Gods of the New and Old Worlds.

Mrandr (*Mh-rand-er*)—An Iskiri warrior.

Mynin (*My-nin*)—An Algatt Vynder, adopted son of Hete.

Nisien (*Niss-ee-en*)—A Soulderni horseman, former member of the mounted Arpa auxiliary.

Nivarium, Nivari—The Arpa territory south-east of Eangen, held by Eolus, a contender for the Arpa throne.

Nui (*Noo-ee*)—Descendant of Ayo. A most noble canine companion.

O–P

Ogam (*Oh-gam*)—Immortal son of Eang and the elemental being Winter.

Omaskat (*Oh-ma-skat*)—The Face of Thvynder.

Onamus—An Arpa legionary.

Orthskar (*Or-th-skar*)—A region, people, and large settlement in northern Eangen.

Oulden (*Old-en*)—A Miri, former God of the Soulderni people.

Pasidon—The great river that flows from the Headwaters, down through Eangen and into the Arpa Empire.

Penumbra—The Arpa's High Halls of the Dead and realm of the Miri, corrupted after the fall of the former gods.

Polinus (*Poe-lie-nus*)—An Arpa commander.

Q–R

Quentis—An Arpa priest of Lathian who once traveled with Hessa, Nisien, and Castor.

Ridings, the—The northern half of Soulderni, occupied by extensive grasslands and pastures.

Riok (*Ree-oak*)—Woodmaiden goddess of the Rioki people. One of Eang's court.

Rioki (*Ree-oak-kee*)—The central-most province and people of Eangen.

Rivermen—A subclass of male, river-dwelling demi-gods begotten by the Gods of the Old World (Miri).

S

Serka—Hessa's horse.

Silgi (*Sill-gee*)—A Vynder priestess, Algatt. A common Algatt name, this is also the name of Nisien's mother.

Sillo—A Vynder priest, Hessa's cousin and stepbrother.

Siris—The Laru High Priest. An Arpa.

Sixnit—An Eangi woman of Albor, mother of Thray and Vistic.

Souldern (*Sol-dern*)—The land of the Soulderni people, occupied by the Arpa Empire.

Soulderni—The people of Souldern, devoted to the God of the New World called Oulden. Occupied by the Arpa Empire.

Spines, the—A natural border of rock formations between Eangen and Arpa-occupied Souldern.

T

Telios—One of Nisien's superiors during his days in the Arpa legions.

Thray—Daughter of Sixnit and Ogam.

Thvynder (*Th-vin-der*)—An ancient deity, one of the Four Pillars of the World.

Thyr, Mount—A mountain in south Eangen that looks over Albor and East Meade.

U–V

Unmaking of the World—The end of an era, when all that exists is unmade and the next era begins from smoke and ashes.

Uspa—An Algatt-Eangen huntress. Imnir's ward.

Vist—An Eangi man, husband of Sixnit.

Vistic—Son of Sixnit and Vist.

W–Z

Waking World—The material world in which human beings live and die.

Winter—A reclusive, elemental god, father of Ogam and lover of Eang.

Woodmaidens—A subclass of female, forest-dwelling demi-goddesses begotten by the Gods of the Old World (Miri).

Yske (*Yih-skah*)—Hessa's cousin and stepsister, sister of Sillo. An Eangi.

ACKNOWLEDGEMENTS

One of the things I love most about the publishing journey is that it takes what can be a very lonely enterprise and transforms it into a team effort. When it came to *Temple of No God*, which I wrote during the chaos of the Covid pandemic and personal upheaval, that team became all the more important to me.

To my beta readers, critique partners, and cheerleaders—I know for a fact I wouldn't have finished this book without you! Cheryl Bowman, my dear friend, mapmaker, question-asker, worldbuilding and linguistic genius, all my books would be a shadow of what they are without our brainstorming sessions. Stephanie Rinaldi, who alpha-read this manuscript chapter-by-chapter, encouraged me every step of the way, and kept me focused. Jenny Anderson, Loie Dunn, and Jean Malone for your ever faithful beta reading and invaluable feedback. And a huge, huge thanks to Kritika H. Rao, who swept in with a last-minute read that saved the day—and my sanity. I'm so grateful for each and every one of you talented, wonderful humans.

Thank you so much to my intrepid agent Naomi Davis, for your tireless work, your perseverance and optimism. To my brilliant editor, George Sandison, I can't thank you enough for your insight into and enthusiasm for the Hall of Smoke world. Joanna Harwood, for your thoughtful notes, questions, and all your hard work perfecting Temple and getting it where it needs to be. Julia Lloyd, for Temple's beautiful cover. Louise Pearce, for superb copyediting. My publicity team, Lydia Gittins, Katharine Carroll, Polly Grice, Sarah Mather, and Julia Bradley, for all that you do both behind the scenes and on stage for myself, *Hall of Smoke*, and *Temple of No God*. To everyone else at Titan Books who has left their mark on this book, no matter how small, thank you.

Thank you to my incredible network of author friends, for celebrating every win, for your invaluable advice and guidance, your honesty and continued support. My agent siblings—I'm honored to be part of such a talented group, and I'm so grateful for your support! Thank you to my 2021 Debut buddies Genevieve Gornichec, Mallory Kuhn, and all the talented authors who've been with me through the debut trenches with encouragement, sympathy, and so many Book Birthdays. To my writing support group—Stephanie Rinaldi, S. D. Vitale, Melissa Sloan, and Rachelle Tremblay. I appreciate each and every one of you so very much.

As to my family, it's hard to know what to say. You've supported my love of writing and stories since I was a child, given me the opportunities and stability I needed to pursue the dream, and consoled me through all the challenges along the way. I would never have picked up a pen—or picked one back up, a hundred times—without you.

Last but certainly not least, the category I never thought I'd have—my readers and fans. You. Some of us have connected on social media, some in real life, and some I've simply come to know through your kind words in reviews, but I'm beyond grateful for your love for the Hall of Smoke world. I'm thrilled that you've connected with Hessa, and I thank you for every review, every share or mention or recommendation, the book club picks, the list features, and the Instagram posts with one of my books. I do see them, and I cherish them.

It takes a huge team to get a book into print, but readers are the ones that carry it across the world and enable me to keep doing what I do. Thank you.

ABOUT THE AUTHOR

H. M. Long is a Canadian fantasy writer, author of *Hall of Smoke* and *Temple of No God*, who loves history, hiking, and exploring the world. She lives in Ontario, but can often be spotted snooping about European museums or wandering the Alps with her German husband.

For more fantastic fiction, author events,
exclusive excerpts, competitions, limited editions and more

VISIT OUR WEBSITE
titanbooks.com

LIKE US ON FACEBOOK
facebook.com/titanbooks

FOLLOW US ON TWITTER AND INSTAGRAM
@TitanBooks

EMAIL US
readerfeedback@titanemail.com